A
Yellow Room

Alby Stone

The Heisenberg Picture first appeared on the Vainglorious Lunacy website on 13th November 2012. © 2012, 2015 Alby Stone.

The Enemy Within first appeared on the Vainglorious Lunacy website on 26th November 2012. © 2012, 2015 Alby Stone.

The Confabulists Club first appeared on the Vainglorious Lunacy website on 1st February 2013. © 2013, 2015 Alby Stone.

The Wild Man of Bournemouth first appeared on the Vainglorious Lunacy website on 8th April 2013. © 2013, 2015 Alby Stone.

The Actress and the Bishop first appeared on the Vainglorious Lunacy website on 15th August 2014. © 2014, 2015 Alby Stone.

The Beautiful Beast first appeared on the Vainglorious Lunacy website on 17th August 2014. © 2014, 2015 Alby Stone.

The Rocket Man first appeared on the Vainglorious Lunacy website on 20th September 2014. © 2014, 2015 Alby Stone.

Copyright © 2015 Alby Stone.

All rights reserved.

ISBN-10: 1508911541
ISBN-13: 978-1508911548

Contents

Introduction i
The Heisenberg Picture 1
The Enemy Within 42
The Confabulists Club 93
The Wild Man of Bournemouth 134
The Actress and the Bishop......................................176
The Beautiful Beast..226
The Rocket Man 267

Introduction

What part did the occult play in the Second World War? It has often been suggested that witches and occultists were recruited by the British government to wage war on Hitler's (inevitably black) magicians; or that they took it upon themselves to do their patriotic duty by waging war on the astral plane and by casting spells.

The occult certainly had a major role in the rise of Nazism and the perpetuation of Nazi ideology after the war had ended. Whatever Adolf Hitler's personal beliefs might have been – and those who dismiss the part played by occultism invariably focus on Hitler and lose sight of the cultural milieu in which he was propelled to power – Germanic (or 'Aryan') occultism was a major factor in establishing the *Völkisch* movement that gave rise to much of the symbolism and imagery of Nazism.

I don't know if there is any truth at all in the idea that the authorities in Great Britain utilised witches, magicians and psychics to fight the war on a spiritual level. People like Gerald Gardner and Dion Fortune claimed it was so; but they were practising occultists and not entirely reliable historians of their own lives. Ian Fleming, creator of James Bond and a member of Naval Intelligence, wanted to influence Nazi decisions with fake horoscopes; and Dennis Wheatley, employed as a propagandist by the British government, imagined an occult aspect to the war in his 1941 novel *Strange Conflict*. There's also some evidence that the British made use of Aleister Crowley as a secret agent and influencer of Nazi occult opinion, but it's mostly circumstantial.

Winston Churchill was a champion of the laterally-thinking boffins and maverick innovators responsible for key military projects, but as far as I am aware he never considered using psychics or witches to beef up the nation's defences. That doesn't mean it never happened, of course – absence of evidence is not evidence of absence. But if it did I would have thought that after seventy years, declassification of secret documents and the Freedom of Information Act, *something* would have emerged from official sources. Yet it's a fact that the US military tried to make use of supposed paranormal abilities to gain an edge in the Cold War, and it's just as true that the Soviet Union did the same. Why not Great Britain, and why not in the war against the Nazis?

I have no opinion one way or the other, though I have always assumed that patriotic believers in the magical arts would naturally have made their own small contributions to the war effort, just as Christians prayed for victory. But this isn't a history book. My sole interest has been to use the idea to create the Yellow Room, which features in my *Havensea* and *Wonderland Investigations* novels, stories set in a world that is very much like our own but is not quite the one we inhabit. I wanted a semi-autonomous, quasi-governmental organisation with a moral compass, a counterpoint to the pragmatist nature of politics and the dehumanising authoritarianism that arises in a militarised environment. For me that meant locating the Yellow Room's origins in an authentic fight against a destructive ideology, and giving it a continuity of conscience and purpose beyond any party politics or national policy.

The Yellow Room adventures are about my imaginary organisation's origins and formative years. There are no spoilers for the books, though they do intertwine and if you put them all together, the novels and the short pieces collected here tell one bigger story. Anyone reading these short pieces first and my novels later may look back and say 'Aha!' once or twice, which is never a bad thing.

Although these stories adventures are built around a skeleton of real historical events and real people, they are fiction. I stretch facts, take liberties, make connections that would make a reputable historian reach for the smelling salts, and generally let my imagination run riot. These tales are basically me having a lot of fun mixing real history with weird fiction – but I try to make a few serious points along the way.

The Yellow Room stories were first published on the Vainglorious Lunacy website between November 2012 and September 2014, and have been lightly revised for this collection.

Alby Stone
London, March 2015

The Heisenberg Picture

Wind was the observer's greatest problem. Even the weakest breeze changed the angle of vision so that he saw things in a new light. Stronger gusts changed everything. One moment he would be looking across the courtyard at the building opposite and hearing the voices of the men and women going about their business; the next he would be staring at a wall that only encrusted filth saved from blankness, with all sound carried away. Then he might find himself staring into that yawning black space that every now and then spewed forth those frightful creatures that tormented him. Eventually they would work out how to reach him. And when they did, it would all be over. It probably wouldn't be a pleasant end.

'Well, that was a bloody queer dream,' said Violet Pugh when she opened her eyes and found she was sitting up in bed, wide awake. 'I've never been somebody else before.'

She couldn't tell if it was light outside yet, thanks to the blackout curtains. The clock was nowhere to be seen, though she could hear it ticking. Her husband must have knocked it off the table again as he was getting into bed, the clumsy old sod.

Beside her, Bert stirred and shifted. 'Get back to sleep, you silly mare,' he mumbled.

Violet wasn't listening to her grumpy spouse. She knew the dream was important, like the others she'd had in the three months since she had been recruited by Mr Crane. She was much more focused now, thanks to his encouragement and from listening carefully to the others. Learning her craft, she liked to tell herself. She was surprised she'd learned so much, so quickly.

She was due to be in Whitehall at ten sharp for the daily briefing and allocation of tasks. She would tell the Old Man then. Old Man? That was a laugh. He was at least fifteen years younger than her, younger than any of them except Mr Bartley and the dancer, that tart Ethel Bingham. But that's what they all called him and he did have a certain air of wear and tear, as if he'd been around a lot longer than any of them. It must be all that responsibility.

No, that wasn't fair. Ethel wasn't a prostitute or anything unsavoury like that. She was just a young woman who lived in a world very different to that of Violet's youth. The nation's moral compass had shifted. Things were acceptable today that would have made Violet's mother faint with shock, bless her.

Every morning at nine o'clock Violet Pugh gladly abandoned her work in the Three Hussars to convene with her Yellow Room colleagues. Her husband Bert was welcome to the sweeping and scrubbing. She was thoroughly browned off with life as a publican's wife – expected to forever be cordial, polite and hard-working even when the customers behaved like hooligans and her arthritis was playing up. And she was fed up with Camden. She longed for the day Bert decided to pack it in and they could retire to a nice little bungalow by the sea – Clacton, perhaps, or Southend. She liked Southend. It had a bit more life about it than Clacton. But that seemed a long way off. Until then she had her spirits to console her, and now the Yellow Room to give her life purpose.

Poor Mr Crane – so young but so tired and old-looking, not like Mr Bartley, a twenty-nine year old who looked much younger than his age and was always bouncing around and talking animatedly, so full of energy you'd think he was plugged into the mains. He was alright but she didn't like his son. He was a nasty piece of work, not like Mr Crane's little boy.

Violet realised that she was drifting. She wanted to go back to sleep. The clock didn't matter. Bert always woke at half past six on the dot, his own internal alarm rousing him so that he could get himself and the Three Hussars ready for the day's business. He'd make sure she was up and about in good time, if only so that she could help with the cleaning. Anyway, it wouldn't do any harm to shut her eyes again for just five minutes.

Wheatley wasn't at all impressed. 'That wallpaper is truly ghastly,' he observed, reluctantly sipping the dark brown tea, his little finger extended because the bone china teacup's handle was too small for his hands.

Tony Crane followed Wheatley's gaze. The wallpaper in question was the colour of daffodils and the paintwork was mustard. The floorboards were varnished a yellowy-brown and the rug was ochre, the heavy curtains lemon.

Even the ceiling was saffron-hued; Crane suspected that was down to decades of tobacco smoke rather than design, but in view of the rest of the room he wouldn't have been at all surprised to learn that it was deliberate. The room had evidently been decorated by someone with a bit of an obsession, and he had added the finishing touches. He knew it wasn't to everyone's taste but he rather liked it. He certainly liked it a damned sight more than he liked Wheatley.

'You get used to it after a while,' he smiled, smugly inserting all four fingers of his left hand into the handle of his outsized enamel mug. If he'd had six fingers there would still have been plenty of room. 'Besides, it's given us a name, you know. We call ourselves the Yellow Room now. Rather easier on the tongue than the Irregular Strategies and Investigations Section. Try saying that after a few gins. I suppose calling ourselves ISIS for short would be apposite but frankly it sounds a bit too grand. You have to remember that all my people are civilians and I like them to feel comfortable, and 'Yellow Room' does have a homely ring to it. That colour is a bit much on all four walls and the ceiling, but it makes Fleming feel physically ill, which is quite entertaining. He does turn an alarming shade of green. It goes nicely with the decor. Anyway, I'm sure you haven't come here to chat about the wallpaper, Wheatley. What can we do for you?'

Wheatley placed the cup and saucer carefully on Crane's enormous mahogany desk, and leaned forward. 'This is on a need to know basis only, old chap. Your crystal ball gazers and table-turners don't need to know all the details – though I expect the beggars will have their own ways of finding out anyway, so I don't really know why I'm bothering to tell you that – but we've had word from one of our chaps in Berlin that Jerry is up to something on Heligoland, something that has *streng geheimen* written all over it in very large Teutonic lettering. Our man can't get more than a bloody sniff. All he knows is that it's something called *Unternehmen Uhrwerk* – Operation Clockwork. Someone or something was taken out to Heligoland by U-boat a month or so ago with a detachment of Waffen-SS to watch over it. Heligoland is impossible to penetrate by regular means and after December's bloody fiasco we can't exactly go swanning in to bomb the buggers, can we? I was wondering if you'd be able to deploy your – er – specialists to find out what's going on there.'

Crane rubbed his forehead. He'd had a late night and was up early, so he wasn't in the best of moods. His people were already stretched thinly. Still, this was just the sort of thing the Yellow Room had been created to undertake. Not that they'd had any successes as yet. Without a definite target or anything more than vague geographical parameters this task too would probably end in failure. Crane had an uneasy feeling that his unit was deliberately being set up to fail. Hore-Belisha, the previous Secretary of State for War, had been keen to explore every avenue when it came to fighting the Nazis. As a Jew with German connections Hore-Belisha was only too aware of what the Nazis could and probably would do to Europe if Great Britain was defeated. No method was too outlandish to be ignored without being tested. But, undermined by Chamberlain, soured relations with the leaders of the British Expeditionary Force and – with bitter irony – anti-Semitism among his fellow Members of Parliament, the colourful and unconventional Hore-Belisha had been ousted. His successor, Oliver Stanley, appeared to be wholly uninterested in the Yellow Room. Crane was convinced that senior War Office and military figures were conspiring to sideline the team, perhaps believing that the funding would be diverted to their own pet projects.

Crane ruefully smiled to himself. Except for him, the Yellow Room's personnel consisted entirely of carefully-vetted civilians who worked for nothing, knowing they would be unlikely to receive any financial reward or public recognition. The only costs relating to the Yellow Room were for cleaning and maintenance of the room itself and a few pence each week for tea and biscuits – and Crane's salary, of course, though the gathering vultures would find that the meat from that wouldn't stretch far.

'Of course,' he told Wheatley. 'I'll get my people onto it straight away. I'll let you know how we get on. More tea?'

The last downward blast of air had shifted his viewpoint again. The worried-looking German was out again, slouching moodily around the courtyard with his hands thrust deep into his greatcoat pockets, a scarf wound tightly about his neck. The black-uniformed bodyguard, each man tall and blond and blue-eyed, followed him at a discreet but somehow not respectful distance. Their charge – or was he their prisoner? – muttered distractedly to himself, a frowning Pied Piper with the soldiers following him like a small pack of big black rats. The troubled German walked out of the observer's sight and beyond the range of his hearing. The wind blew hard again from above and suddenly the black opening loomed once more. In the deeper darkness beyond, something moved.

'That's not much to go on,' complained William Simmons, shifting uneasily in his seat so that the brace didn't chafe his legs quite so much. 'It's something called Operation Clockwork and it's happening somewhere on Heligoland. I say, isn't that where we lost all those bombers in December? That was a bad do.'

Thirty-two years old, Simmons was a clerk at the Ministry of Food. Simmons was thought stoical by his colleagues but he raged internally at the polio that had crippled him as a child and appeared to have prevented him from doing his bit against the Hun. When approached by Crane, who had somehow heard of Simmons' reputation for uncannily accurate intuitive leaps, he had figuratively jumped at the chance to join the Yellow Room.

Ethel Bingham, a glamorous platinum blonde in her mid-twenties who spent most nights on the chorus line at the Windmill Theatre, stubbed out her Lucky Strike in the glass ashtray Simmons had so eagerly and painfully fetched her. He was smitten with the dancer, hardly able to remove his gaze from those long legs and the Promised Land of her chest. Simmons twitched seismically when she winked at him. It was meant kindly. She seemed happily oblivious of the effect she had on the man.

'Shall I read the cards?' Without waiting for a response she opened her bag and took out a deck of tarot cards, the sort designed by the occultist A.E. Waite and the illustrator Pamela Colman Smith, manufactured by William Rider and Son. She had inherited the cards from her late mother, who had purchased them in 1913. Then she closed her eyes and composed herself for a minute or so before shuffling the pack, cutting the cards into three smaller packs and moving the ones in the middle to the top. She dealt three cards from the top.

Crane was fascinated. Miss Bingham seemed to become a completely different person when she exercised her talent. She was transformed – gone was the coquettish, sarcastic girl and in her place was a serene and still woman who could have been twenty or thirty years older. He'd always been inclined to scoff at such homely methods of divination, but the young woman's reputation as a cartomancer had been fully borne out during the tests she had undergone prior to her recruitment.

Ethel Bingham stared at the cards for a few seconds and frowned. 'None of this makes any sense, yet I feel it is full of meaning. For some reason I keep seeing a boot in my mind's eye. The first card is the eight of Pentacles, a man working at his craft – but I think it means a factory or some other kind of workplace. The next card is the six of Swords, a man ferrying a woman and a child across a body of water with the swords upright in their boat. That speaks for itself – a dangerous journey across water. The final card is the Hanged Man. I have a strong impression of someone watching and waiting.'

Mrs Pugh eagerly added her two penn'orth. 'That's a bit like the dream I had last night,' she said. 'I dreamed of boots and someone hiking. In my dream I was someone else – a man, I think. I felt alone and unseen even though I could see people kept coming and going, though sometimes I couldn't. I remember there was a doorway or a hole in a wall, and it was all dark and very frightening.'

Crane was intrigued. 'You say you saw people – do

you know who they were? What kinds of people? How many were there?'

'There were quite a few,' Mrs Pugh replied. 'I saw a group of young men; and another group, all young ladies this time. All of them had fair hair. They were laughing and joking. They seemed excited about something. There was a man who seemed worried and was always talking to himself. Then there was a big fellow with a scarred face, wearing a black uniform. He wasn't excited at all – he just seemed fed up. And there were other soldiers, like guards, watching the others. There were two other men, older than all the rest. One had glasses and a little Hitler moustache, and a black uniform like the scarred man. He was very self-important but didn't look very well. The other one – well, I don't like to say this but he was always, you know, in a state of undress. As nature intended, you might say.'

'As nature intended? You mean he was naked?'

Mrs Pugh reddened. 'Yes, that's right. He wore shoes and socks but not a stitch otherwise. But he seemed perfectly happy, even though he must have been cold. He certainly looked cold, if you understand me.'

All the men in the room suddenly pretended interest in the yellow wallpaper. Mrs Pugh was a married woman, so she probably knew about such things. But none of them were sure about Miss Bingham's level of experience with the frailties of masculinity and were reluctant to embarrass the young woman. They needn't have worried.

'A bit shrivelled was he?' Miss Bingham laughed. 'Oh, don't mind me,' she added when she saw Crane's mortified expression. 'I've got three younger brothers and we lived in a small house with a tin bath. You can't help but notice, can you?'

Crane decided to take a break so that he could think carefully about how to approach this mission. When the others had gone down to the canteen for lunch, he sat at his desk with a pot of very strong tea. He lit a Black Cat, hoping the combination of caffeine and nicotine would stimulate his brain and help him make sense of those strange messages. Crowley had recommended a mixture of cocaine and opium as an excellent means of sparking the imagination, but Crane had politely declined the Great Beast's offer of a guided tour of the narcotic Otherworld. His wits, he firmly believed, were best kept about him.

He had gathered those three members of the Yellow Room together that morning and asked them if they had lately encountered or felt anything that resonated with Heligoland and an intensification of Nazi interest in the place. And what had he got? Boots and hiking, a journey across water, a mysterious waiting man, and an assortment of strange characters including, it seemed, a naturist, a gaggle of blondes and some SS troops. He would, he thought, have been better off looking for information among the clues to the *Times* crossword puzzle.

The first thing he needed to do was to show Mrs Pugh the Black Book – a photograph album with pictures of as many high-ranking Nazi politicians, SS and Wehrmacht officers, scientists and other important Third Reich figures as they had been able to gather. Indeed, the Black Book now ran to two bulky volumes and a third was in preparation. Hopefully she would be able to identify some of the people she had dreamed about, and that might give them a clue as to what Operation Clockwork was all about. Then he would call together the remaining Yellow Room specialists. He had found that the more of them there were in one place, the more focused their abilities became. Some of them – notably the women – even seemed to synchronise. One day, when the war was only a distant memory, he might write a paper on the subject for the SPR.

Crane had been chosen to head the Yellow room for three reasons. Firstly, in his professional life he was an excellent organiser with a reputation for innovation and cutting through red tape to get things done. Secondly, he had read anthropology at Cambridge and specialised in so-called primitive belief systems and magic. Lastly, and most importantly from his point of view, he was a member of the Society for Psychical Research and had been personally involved in the investigation of mediums, mind-readers and fortune-tellers of all stripes. He knew which ones were fraudulent and had personal acquaintance with the few who had satisfied his own criteria for successful demonstration of psychic ability.

Indeed, the Yellow Room had been his idea. Hore-Belisha had been sceptical when Crane approached the Secretary of State with the suggestion of setting up a section that might be able to obtain intelligence and foreknowledge of enemy action by the most unconventional means imaginable, but Crane's testimony had been both eloquent and passionate. He'd been given his room at the Ministry of War, *carte blanche* to recruit whosoever he deemed both reliable and effective, and a small allowance for refreshments. He'd also been given one very specific instruction.

'And make sure you keep this little venture completely under wraps,' Hore-Belisha had instructed him. 'If word of this mumbo-jumbo ever gets out, justifying the expenditure and arguing its effectiveness will be the least of our worries. This isn't exactly routine military or Civil Service business, is it? Let's face it, Crane - we'll both look very silly indeed. I for one will be a public laughing-stock, and if I'm forced to resign over it I'll make sure that you're in the bloody dole-queue ahead of me.'

There were six men and the same number of women. They were all aged between twenty-one and twenty-seven, all in excellent health – and each of them was a splendid example of the Aryan race, fair-haired, blue-eyed, tall and well-built. They were led by a charismatic man even taller than any of them, a man with a beaky nose and cauliflower ears, whose perpetual sardonic grin was marred by a *schmiss* – a duelling scar – that curved from his left ear almost to the point of his chin, narrowly skirting the corner of his mouth. He wore a black uniform with insignia that marked him as a member of the *Leibstandarte SS Adolf Hitler*, the SS division that was the *Führer*'s personal bodyguard. He'd been on the U-boat with the rest of them and had seemed in his element – a man on a mission, even if he didn't then know what that mission entailed. But here he looked and acted like a fish out of water. He was restless and bored, clearly a man of action who wasn't pleased to be playing nursemaid to young men who should be out fighting, young women who should be back in the Fatherland making babies and homes, and old men who should be doing anything else in the whole damned world but wasting his time.

He threw his half-smoked cigarette to the earth and ground it out with his heel when he heard someone call him. Turning, he saw the scientist, who was accompanied by a prim-looking man with a toothbrush moustache and wire-rimmed spectacles – Heinrich Himmler, *Reichsführer* of the SS and head of the Gestapo. He looked like a shopkeeper. The uniform did little to disguise the fact that Himmler was a man with no physical presence. The uniform did not strengthen the weak chin, nor did it make up for the small grimaces that crossed the *Reichsführer*'s face as he rubbed absently at his constantly ailing belly. The scientist seemed as perturbed as ever. This project was making him less comfortable by the hour.

Dutifully, the soldier snapped his together and raised his arm in the expected salute. 'Heil Hitler,' he cried.

Himmler half-heartedly returned the salute and readjusted his features into a false jovial smile. 'So, Skorzeny – how are our boys and girls this morning? No unfortunate liaisons in the night, I hope? Herr Doktor Schertel was most insistent on that point – no sexual activity for any of the participants for at least one lunar month before the operation, especially the young men.'

'They have been closely guarded, *Reichsführer*. The men in particular have been under scrutiny at all times. Not even relief of the individual kind, as you instructed.'

'Splendid. These are the flower of Aryan youth, you know. They were carefully selected for their health and high intelligence. It is crucial that they are capable of understanding what Schertel and Werner here are teaching them. It would be most unfortunate if we wasted Werner's time. As it is we are keeping him from his important work with the Uranium Club, eh?'

Skorzeny had no idea what Himmler was talking about – was this something to do with astrology? Well, he'd heard rumours that various members of the Nazi upper echelons were obsessed with horoscopes. That didn't concern him. All he cared about was getting this nonsense over with and getting back into the real war.

'Of course, *Reichsführer*. I can assure you there has been no untoward behaviour. The young ladies are untouched and we made the men sleep with their hands above the bedclothes, so they are doubly untouched.'

Himmler smiled thinly at Skorzeny's little joke. The scientist merely looked heavenward. Skorzeny did his best to pretend he hadn't noticed that. *Otto*, he told himself, *try not to punch that stuck-up prick on the nose. You'd get even less action in a bloody labour camp.*

The scarred man again, and the insignificant one who thought he was so grand. At least the naked old man had been absent, for which the observer was dimly thankful. He wondered who these people were. He knew they were German – he could hear them clearly, when the wind was in the right direction and they were within range – so he couldn't understand what they were saying. But he knew it was of great importance. Something terrible was about to take place here. He wished he could move of his own volition, so that he could perhaps escape and take the information home to people who would know what to do about it. But he was unable to move anywhere but where the wind took him.

Crane surveyed the assembled Yellow Room specialists. In addition to Simmons, Miss Bingham and Mrs Pugh, there were Gerald Tompkins, a retired teacher from Hastings; Calum Archibald, a fifty year old accountant from Dartford; and Edward Vance, an actor in his late forties, presently 'resting' in a boarding-house near Vauxhall Cross. The three newcomers each had military training and experience, having fought and been wounded in the Great War, where they had experienced the worst horrors of trench warfare. The eager Simmons was always asking for their war stories. Unsurprisingly, their tales of adventure and heroism had so far not been forthcoming.

Tompkins was a Spiritualist, a medium. Crane still wasn't entirely sure that the man could actually receive messages from beyond the grave, but he had been present when Tompkins produced some remarkable results, including one memorable test in which Crane had provided a subject, chosen from among his friends, with an elaborate and convincing false biography, including fictitious deceased parents and loved ones. Tompkins had cut through the deception with ease, accurately described the man's real mother, who had died only the previous year, and passed on some detailed information about something Crane's friend could not have known but which turned out to be true.

Archibald was an expert on Norse mythology, magic and runes, but also claimed to possess second sight, by virtue of his mixed Highland and Viking ancestry. His mother had been a 'spae-wife' who could foretell the future. He had made several uncannily correct predictions, most notably telling Crane he was to be a father two days before Mrs Crane had joyfully announced the news. Archibald's family had moved to Dartford when he was still a baby, so he spoke with no trace of a Scottish accent, but he was fiercely proud to be a Scot.

As for Vance – that was a little more complicated. He was a gifted clairvoyant and psychometrist. Given a physical or visual connection with a subject, he could provide a picture of what they were doing and clues as to their location. Vance had volunteered to fight and served with distinction in the Great War, and had been decorated for valour before losing his left leg at the Somme in 1916. He once confessed to Crane that he had been terrified throughout his military service but had forced himself to face whatever might be coming. He'd always known there was a German bullet or shell with his name on it and that he would be injured, but somehow knew he would live through the conflict. His 'gift' had only manifested fully while he was in hospital recovering from the amputation of his limb. Vance had also confided that he was homosexual. Crane didn't care about that. The candid admission only reinforced his view that although Vance wasn't fearless he was braver in what Crane thought was a far better way.

Crane had a list of other potential recruits. They were being discreetly but thoroughly checked for reliability, talkativeness and loyalty. If they passed those superficial tests they would be approached and subjected to the final part of the vetting procedure Crane had devised – they would meet Dakessian. That would be frustrating because Dakessian came and went seemingly at random so it would have to wait until the next time he showed his face. And it would be nerve-wracking for the recruits.

He'd known Mikaiel Dakessian for seven years. The Turkish-born Armenian had been present at a SPR meeting

Crane had attended, and had made several interesting observations, claiming that many supposedly psychic talents were nothing of the sort but could be explained by an unconscious reading of the minutiae of facial expression, posture and tone of voice, as well as slips of the tongue and where people looked as they spoke. 'The language of the body is the language of the heart and of the mind,' he'd said. 'They tell the truth more surely than the language that is spoken.' When Crane collared Dakessian over the post-meeting refreshments, he had been disconcerted by the way Dakessian's gaze seemed to both roving and intensely focused, as if he was making sure that every visual clue was observed and thoroughly interrogated. When Crane spoke, Dakessian was attentive to the point of rudeness. But they had become good friends. Dakessian clearly trusted Crane on some level beyond the trust that people usually place in each other. Crane made it a point never to lie to the little man, even by omission, because Dakessian would know immediately. On the other hand, it was crystal clear to Crane that Dakessian himself was neither wholly frank nor completely honest.

There was one other member of the Yellow Room to come and, as Crane surveyed his team, the man appeared. Charles Bartley entered the room, cheerfully greeted everyone, and as he usually did flicked his hat across the room. And as usual it landed with uncanny accuracy on the one empty place on the hat stand.

'I say,' he said, 'is that tea fresh or is it Crane's usual over-stewed horror?'

Bartley's attendance at the Yellow Room was haphazard. He was a businessman, an industrialist specialising in furnishings and farm equipment, and he was presently engaged in turning his factories over to munitions and weapons production. Although he had a reputation for sharp business practice and shady financial dealings, Bartley was a patriot. He'd been too young to sign up for the Great War and had failed the medical for service in the present show, but he was keen to do his bit for the war effort. He had become involved in the Yellow Room at Hore-Belisha's recommendation, having once drunkenly confessed to the politician at a fund-raising dinner for the Conservative party that he owed his business success to an uncanny foresight. He had no real understanding of finance or even of the business world. Yet he always seemed to know exactly what he should do – what to invest in, how much money to put in, who to hire and fire, where to set up a factory, what lines of goods to produce. Hore-Belisha had told Crane that Bartley might well have some kind of genuine psychic ability – and more to the point, if Bartley was involved he would probably help fund the Yellow Room if it needed development. To Crane's relief, he and Bartley got on well. In fact, he rather liked the businessman, whose infectious sense of fun often broke the tension when things weren't going well. He was a likeable rogue. And he had indeed paid for the scientific equipment Crane had requested, which was currently housed in a cottage in the grounds of Bartley's mansion in Surrey. The equipment hadn't yet been used but Crane had plans for that – just as soon as Dakessian returned from wherever he'd gone and could finish the screening of new recruits.

'So what's going on, old man?' Bartley flung himself into an armchair and lit a cigarette, nodding thoughtfully as

Crane filled him in.

Mrs Pugh was leafing through the Black Book. At last she gave a triumphant cry. 'He was there,' she told them, pointing at a photograph. Bartley stood and looked over her shoulder.

'Good God, it's bloody Himmler,' he announced. 'Sorry ladies, that was most uncouth of me. Please accept my apologies. But still — bloody hell, if he's personally involved it must be something very big indeed.'

Crane couldn't disagree. The news had sparked a buzz in the room. Mrs Pugh finished examining the first volume of the Black Book and moved on to the second. It wasn't long before she found another familiar face.

'Here, this is the other man. I almost didn't recognise him with his clothes on.'

Bartley, who had not been apprised of the man's nudity, raised an eyebrow questioningly. Miss Bingham snorted with laughter, her chest heaving as she strove to compose herself. Simmons looked as if he was going to pass out at the sight. Crane took a look at the picture, made a note of the name and made a telephone call to the clerk responsible for the files on the Black Book's rogues' gallery. Ten minutes later a young woman brought him a bulging manila folder. Crane leafed through it, absorbing as much as he could and making notes in a jotter.

'Well, this is a strange one,' he told his team ten minutes later. 'Ernst Schertel is a controversial chap. He's an expert on magic and dance, of all things, and — um — erotica. He's written a lot about the relationship between religious ecstasy, dance and eroticism; and he's got a bit of a bee in his bonnet about sado-masochism, flagellation and all that. Pardon me, Miss Bingham, Mrs Pugh, but we shouldn't ignore or overlook anything and this could be important.'

The naked man was back, happily strutting around in only his shoes and socks as usual, goose-pimpled and in genital retreat from the cold. It was not a pleasant sight, yet the observer didn't find it as repellent or absurd as he would once have done. All he felt was vague anxiety and a curious detachment. He was, after all, an observer, not a participant. The wind blew and once again he was facing the blank wall, then the dark space. Then he was seeing the naked man again, though now the nudist had been joined by the worried-looking man. They were talking animatedly. The younger man – the one wrapped up against the elements – appeared to be disagreeing vehemently with what the older man was saying. The naked man merely smiled complacently and said something that seemed intended as reassurance. The younger man retorted sharply, his expression scornful. The observer wished once again that he understood German. Then there was another gust and he was facing that black space again. He heard the scrabbling of claws and saw those eyes reflecting light. If he could have moved, he would have shuddered.

'This one, he was there too. This is the worried-looking man who was talking to himself.' Mrs Pugh jabbed her right index finger at the Black Book. Crane was shocked when he saw the photograph she was pointing at.

'Werner Heisenberg? But he's a scientist, a theoretical physicist. He won the Nobel Prize back in – when was it, '32? What's he doing on Heligoland with a man like Schertel? Himmler I can understand. The files say he's interested in occultism and science. But as well as being like chalk and cheese Heisenberg and Schertel are considered ideologically suspect by the Nazis. There is a movement in Germany called *deutsche Physik* which accused Heisenberg of promoting what they call 'Jewish science' because of his use of the theories of Einstein and other Jewish theorists; and Schertel was condemned by the Nazi party for propagating perversion and obscenity. And all those young men and women – what in the world is going on?'

'Beats me, old man,' said Bartley with a grin. 'I think perhaps it's time we called in some experts. Don't you?'

Crane agreed. And he knew exactly who to consult. When he had made two telephone calls he turned his thoughts to matters of strategy. He had an idea. He would hypnotise Mrs Pugh and ask her to dream. The other Yellow Room specialists would be placed in a lighter trance and instructed to tune in to her dreams if they could. When he was up at Cambridge Crane had been shown how to hypnotise people by an alcoholic former stage magician named Cecil Devere who owned a small bookshop. He didn't understand how it worked and had only practised hypnosis a few times but he was confident that he could do it. But he kept his fingers crossed anyway.

When Mrs Pugh was in a deep trance and the others were in a light hypnotic state, Crane refilled his enamel mug and lit a Black Cat, then perched on a stool by Mrs Pugh's armchair.

'You can begin dreaming now, Mrs Pugh. But I want you tell me what you are dreaming about as you dream it. Please don't leave anything out.'

Mrs Pugh stirred in her chair and mumbled incomprehensibly. Crane asked to speak more loudly and clearly.

'I can see boots,' she said in a calm monotone. 'Lots of boots but they're all up in the air. There's a man wearing boots and he's striding across water but over it, not on it. Now he's me and I'm waiting. I can see and hear but I can't move. There's a dirty wall, then I'm looking at the people outside. Then I can only see that dark space. There's something in it that I'm afraid of.'

'That's excellent, Mrs Pugh. Now look more closely and try to observe without feeling afraid. Tell me everything you can about where you are, everything you can hear.'

'I can hear wind. It's over my head. It comes in gusts and makes a sort of booming noise, as if it's blowing down a chimney. There's a smell – no it's two things I can smell. One is ash and coal; the other is foul, the stink of rotten meat. I can hear voices but they are speaking in German and I don't understand what they're saying. The people outside are talking too fast for me to remember any of it.'

'The people are outside? So you're in a building of some kind?'

'Yes, I can make it out now. It's like an old kiln or a brickworks, one of those big buildings where they fire the bricks. This one's partly ruined and I can see out through a hole in the wall which overlooks a courtyard. There's a big empty space above me where the wind blows down. Whenever it blows I move. That's because – oh, I'm hanging from something. That's the only way I can move at all because my arms and legs don't work. None of me works anymore. That's because I'm – oh no, that can't be true, surely?'

Across the room, Miss Bingham stifled a sob. The

men were groaning and seemed to be trying to rouse themselves. Mrs Pugh began to weep silently. Her limbs feebly writhing as she attempted to move that body she had dreamed herself into. Crane's hair was standing on end. This was most unexpected. But he wasn't going to waste time exploring the matter. It was time to move on.

'Mrs Pugh – Violet, I would like you to separate yourself from this poor soul, if you can. I would like you to try to move out of the building and have a look at that courtyard. Can you do that for me?'

Mrs Pugh was silent for a long minute, becoming gradually still. The others quietened too and Crane relaxed.

'I can see the building now, from the outside. Yes, it is like a brickworks or a ruined factory. There's the stump of a big chimney and broken walls. Opposite the ruin is another building. This one's in good condition. I think it's a school. There are some soldiers outside, talking and smoking. That big scarred man is with them, telling jokes. I'm going to try – yes, I can move through the walls. It's quite easy, really. Inside there are several rooms. One has been set up like a dormitory. It's where the soldiers are billeted. There are some soldiers sleeping there now. This must be a school because across the corridor is a small classroom. There's a blackboard but there's nothing written on it.'

'Can you go anywhere else, Violet?'

'Yes. I'm going down the corridor. There are two doors facing each other. There are soldiers guarding them. They can't see me so I'm going in. Oh, this one is another dormitory but much smaller. There are six young men in there. They're playing cards or reading. One is listening to a radio. Nothing much is happening so I'll try that other door. This room is another small dormitory, only there are six young women. They're doing much the same as the young men. Shall I look somewhere else?'

'Yes please, Violet. See if you can find the other men.'

'Yes, I can. They're in the next room along the corridor. Himmler and the other two men – Schertel and Heisenberg? – are talking. Schertel hasn't got any clothes on. Heisenberg is complaining about something but Himmler is telling him something. Heisenberg looks surprised, shocked. He stops talking. Schertel is saying something now. Heisenberg stands and starts to walk toward the door. But Himmler says something and Heisenberg sits down again. He's suddenly gone very pale. Schertel is getting angry. He's looking around the room, as if he's suspicious. Now he stands up and starts drawing on the wall with a stick of charcoal. It's some sort of symbol like those runes Mr Archibald told me about but they were all straight lines and this one has curves. It's very complicated.'

'Can you describe it, Violet?'

Mrs Pugh didn't reply. Crane tried again. 'Violet, can you describe the symbol?'

There was no response. Crane tried several more times but she didn't say a word. When he looked around the room to check on the other specialists, he realised that they were no longer merely under hypnosis. They were all soundly asleep.

'Well, I'll be buggered,' he swore.

The specialists were still fast asleep when the two men Crane had called in as consultants arrived. Aleister Crowley, the self-styled Great Beast, described by sections of the press as the Wickedest Man in the World – they obviously hadn't heard of Adolf Hitler – looked amused at the sight of the seven sleepers, though he spared a professionally lascivious grin for the inert Miss Bingham, who was snoring in a strangely attractive manner that would probably have given Simmons a heart attack. Crowley settled his bulk into one of the extra armchairs Crane had requested from the next room. It was fortunate that the Yellow Room was spacious even by Whitehall standards.

The other consultant was as eminent in his field as Crowley was in the area of magic and occultism. Paul Dirac was a theoretical physicist. In 1930 he had published a book titled *Principles of Quantum Mechanics*, which had been hailed as a classic scientific text. Like Heisenberg, he was a Nobel Prize-winner, sharing the 1933 physics award with Erwin Schrödinger. Crane, who liked to keep abreast of the latest scientific ideas, even though he barely understood many of them, knew that Dirac was familiar with Heisenberg's work. Indeed, Dirac and Heisenberg had built upon each other's ideas.

Dirac looked askance at Crowley, who merely smiled beatifically. When Crane had supplied them with tea – holding back on pouring his own until the brew reached his favoured treacly consistency – he explained that the War Office had discovered that Schertel and Heisenberg were apparently working together on some project. He told them about the other people they were aware of, but omitted to mention either Himmler or Heligoland. Dirac required a separate summary of who Schertel was and what his interests were. When Crane asked his guests if they had any idea what the two Germans could possibly be cooking up together, Dirac laughed heartily.

'Werner Heisenberg – working with a perverted magician? Sorry, Crane – I think you've been had. I honestly can't see what Heisenberg and this Schertel character could possibly be working on together. Look here, you intelligence chaps are a valuable weapon against Hitler. This is a trick, a diversion to tie up your resources while they do something else on the sly.'

Crowley stared innocently at the physicist. 'Schertel may be a perverted magician but allow me to set your mind at rest – I am without doubt the most perverted and best magician you are ever likely to meet. Tell me, Dirac – what is Heisenberg known for?'

Dirac drank more tea and wiped droplets from his moustache. Crane judged that it was time to fill his own mug.

'Well, I suppose Heisenberg is mainly known for three things. Matrix mechanics, which sees the properties of particles as matrices that evolve over time; the famous Uncertainty Principle, the idea that mathematical inequalities limit the precision with which pairs of physical properties of a particle can be known at the same time; and what is known as the Heisenberg Picture. The Heisenberg Picture is a model of quantum mechanics in which the functions incorporate a dependency on time, but the state vectors – the variables that describe a system – are time-independent. I'm sorry if this seems complicated. I know quantum mechanics can sound like utter nonsense to the layman but I'm trying to simplify it.'

Crane was already completely lost. Crowley, however,

simply nodded. 'I see. What it boils down to is this. We can never know the world with utter precision because it is constantly changing around us, and that is partly because we are responsible for those changes. Something can be two things at once until we start paying attention to it, and when we do it mysteriously becomes a single thing and the other aspect vanishes. This can affect those things in the past and the future, as well as in the present. Time isn't quite what we think it is. Correct?'

Dirac was astonished. 'I suppose those are the fundamental implications of Heisenberg's ideas, yes. I wouldn't put it so crudely, though, and I'd be inclined not to speculate above the subatomic level. This branch of science is in its infancy and we still have much to learn and understand.'

'It's not too different from magickal theory,' said Crowley airily. 'Magick is the art of causing change by an act of will. The will is the observer, if you like, and reality is equivalent to the function or operator in quantum mechanics. In my terms, the Heisenberg Picture is another way of saying that a magickal act in the present can affect both past and future. I know this from personal experience.'

Dirac became thoughtful. 'That's an interesting point of view. I don't know whether Heisenberg would agree though. He's always thinking and his ideas are constantly evolving. Quantum mechanics has come a long way since Heligoland and that's largely down to him.'

'Hang on a second,' said Crane excitedly. 'Did you just mention Heligoland?'

'Yes,' replied Dirac. 'Heisenberg stayed there in the

'Twenties. That's where he formulated the theory of matrix mechanics.'

'Well, well,' said Crane. 'Heligoland, eh?'

'I'm not at all surprised that Heisenberg is talking to Schertel,' Crowley put in. 'I read Schertel's book *Magie: Geschichte, Theorie, Praxis* shortly after it was published in 1923. He has a good understanding of the philosophy behind magickal thinking. And I am familiar with his work on erotica, naturally. Like me, Schertel understood that sex can be harnessed for magickal purposes. I recall that in *Magie* he writes "He who does not have the demonic seed within himself will never give birth to a magical world." It would be easy to misunderstand that, as some sour-faced puritans have. By "demonic seed" Schertel refers to the imagination, of course – specifically the imagination aroused and inflamed with the act of love in one or other of its many forms. It would be fair to say that is what *Magie* is all about – much like my own books, in fact, though I must modestly propose that my books are rather more entertaining.'

Crowley produced a pipe and filled it with an especially malodorous brand of tobacco. 'Anyway,' he said when the pipe was lit. 'I think I can tell you something of what they are trying to do. First of all, I need to know one thing. I know you haven't been able to tell me every detail, Crane. Walls have ears, need to know and all that, eh? Don't look so crestfallen, old chap – I've done cloak and dagger work myself, so I know the rules. But I'm willing to wager a few pounds that there's a certain high-ranking Nazi on Heligoland with Schertel and Heisenberg – a fellow with a silly little moustache like Adolf's and spectacles that make him look like a schoolteacher or a grocer.'

Crane stared at him open-mouthed. Crowley grinned broadly. 'It's alright, Crane. None of your people have been indiscreet. You gave the game away by asking about Heligoland when Dirac mentioned it. As for Heinrich Himmler – well, I make it my business to know at least a little about a lot of things. For one thing, I know that Himmler's mother and Heisenberg's knew each other, and that it was Himmler's personal intervention that put an end to that 'White Jew' slander the *deutsche Physik* idiots were propagating. If it wasn't for Himmler, Werner Heisenberg would probably be digging ditches or sweeping factory floors for a living. I also happen to know for a fact that a certain Adolf Hitler was very impressed with Schertel's book on magic. Schertel told me so himself. You probably don't know this but Schertel was in bad trouble with the Nazis a few years ago for publishing so-called obscene material. He was even sent to prison for a few months. Yet somehow he was accepted back into the German academic fold at a time when anyone who didn't follow the new morality to the letter was excluded. If you ask me, that was Hitler's doing. And knowing as I do that Himmler has a very serious interest in both science and occultism, it wasn't hard to hazard a guess that he would be there on Heligoland. I could rule out Hitler because he's running a war. Himmler's running a very different sort of game.'

Crane couldn't fault Crowley's reasoning. 'But what are they up to? And why Heligoland?'

'Schertel developed a means of inducing magickal states of consciousness through dance and eroticism. This involved gymnastics and the use of incense, lights and music; and drugs and sex, of course. The sex could be heterosexual, homosexual or sado-masochistic – or a combination of all three. I suspect that the object of this particular exercise is to hold an orgy to magickally imbue someone or something with some sort of power. As Heisenberg is present I would guess that it is to provide a human subject with the ability to mould reality to suit himself, to move through time and space as he so wills it. In their place I would choose a soldier, a man of action, someone resourceful and fearless. I deduce this from the fact that there are twelve young people we know are participants – and in magickal workings such as this, where there are twelve there is always a thirteenth. In this case, that would be the person who would benefit from the rite. Think what a weapon such a man could be. No general or politician would be safe from assassination. No factory or military installation could be safeguarded against sabotage. And if they do it once, they could do it again and again. Can you imagine trying to fight an army of such men? As for Heligoland, that is where Heisenberg formulated his first major theory. Like all the Nazis Himmler has a mystical notion of the power of place upon the human psyche. I would guess that he is hoping for resonance – a repeat performance.'

He'd had enough of this. Always watching, always waiting – and for what? Observing those Germans was dashed tedious and when that old man wandered around in the raw – well, that was just too bloody much. The observer was yearning for home and for sleep. At least he wasn't cold or hungry or thirsty. He couldn't have been in this place all that long. Yet he had counted the days and was sure he'd been there for about two months. That was impossible. He must be sick, perhaps delirious. Abruptly, he was facing the dark space again, hearing the movements and seeing daylight reflected in those eyes. He wanted to go home. When could he go home?

Otto Skorzeny couldn't believe his ears. Schertel had told him twice but he still found it impossible to process what he was hearing. He tried to clarify matters.

'You're telling me that I have to sit in the middle of a room, stark naked, surrounded by those young people while they dance and take drugs and screw themselves into a state of insanity? And that I mustn't join in? Alright, I can accept that – I have no desire to either whip or be whipped, and I most certainly have no wish to either penetrate or be penetrated by another man. I am broad-minded but there are limits. Naturally I would happily offer my services to the young ladies, but I expect they will all be rather busy anyway. But you are asking me to believe that it will turn me into some kind of – I don't know – a superhuman, able to move wherever I want through space and time at a click of my fingers? Pardon me, *Reichsführer*, gentlemen – but that sounds to me like the kind of shit one reads in American science fiction magazines. Do I look like a bloody idiot?'

Himmler pursed his lips and Heisenberg hastily raised a hand to his face to cover a smirk. Schertel gazed serenely at Skorzeny.

'No, you do not look like an idiot. You look to me like a big, brave soldier who would rather be out shooting someone than being stuck here with us. And that is precisely why you were selected for this experiment. The idea is that these intelligent young people have been prepared by being taught Heisenberg's theories of space and time, and have now learned the movements and actions that are required to pass that knowledge to you and awaken your innate ability to make use of it, that ability I believe lies within every human mind. Of course it may not work. It is, after all, an experiment. But if it succeeds, then you will be the first of a new kind of man, one who can go when and where he chooses. Yes, you will be superhuman. You will become the perfect soldier.'

Himmler nodded furiously. 'Yes, that's right. You will be the first Aryan Superman – an unstoppable soldier, a relentless weapon that will never be defeated. You will be the first, the foundation upon which the Thousand Year Reich shall be built. '

Skorzeny could see why Himmler was so keen on the idea. But he wasn't at all happy about it. What they were proposing would take all the risk and excitement out of soldiering. Making war would be just like any other job – take the order, perform the task like a machine, come back for the next order. It wouldn't be *fun* anymore. He may as well quit now and go to work in a factory. But he had to consider his duty to the Fatherland, to the Third Reich and to the *Führer*. It was unthinkable to go against those. He was trapped.

'And when does this ritual take place?' he asked, resigned to his fate.

'Tomorrow night,' Schertel told him. 'And that means that tonight it's your turn to keep your hands above the bedclothes, young man.'

By eight o'clock that evening the Yellow Room specialists

were all awake. Crowley and Dirac had long since left – Crowley had mentioned something about buying the physicist a drink – and left Crane alone to consider what he had heard that day. He arranged tea and sandwiches for them and while they were eating told them what Crowley had suggested – though he left out certain details, for the ladies' sake.

Crane had his doubts about Crowley. Dakessian – who in Crane's view knew far too much about far too many things – had once told him that Crowley was the genuine article, a magician of real power and perception. Consequently, the Great Beast had been at the top of his list when the Yellow Room was set up. Yet Dakessian had told him that there was something not quite right with Crowley. He could be trusted to keep his mouth shut about the Yellow Room but Crane couldn't risk recruiting him. Crowley had become somehow diminished, Dakessian said. The Crowley of 1940 was not the same man Dakessian had known in the early 1920s. It wasn't down to Crowley's advancing years, either. The magician had lost some vital part of himself. As an operative he would be a liability, though he would still be able to offer useful information and advice. In this matter, Crane's intuition told him, Crowley was right. And he knew with utter certainty who would be the first German superman: the big SS officer with the scar.

The others were talking excitedly among themselves. Archibald was telling them that the symbol Schertel had drawn upon the wall was a charm of concealment dating from the Middle Ages – he recognized it from an Old Icelandic book of spells known as *Galdrabók*. It was that which had broken Mrs Pugh's link to Heligoland and left them all temporarily comatose. There was, Archibald said, a counter-spell they could employ next time.

Then there was a sudden silence. Crane looked up from his notes and saw them all looking at William Simmons. The man's face was blank and his eyes gazed into a distance only he could see. Crane leaned forward expectantly. He'd seen this before. Simmons was making connections.

'Got it,' Simmons said at last. 'I understand it now. The boots in the air are bombers – Wellingtons, the ones our boys flew at the battle of the Heligoland Bight last December. The hiker is the pilot – his name is Walker. That's the dangerous journey across water that Ethel – I mean, Miss Bingham – saw in the cards. His plane was shot down and he parachuted to what he thought was safety, down on Heligoland. But he came down inside that broken chimney and died. He was probably injured when he baled out or he may have hurt himself coming through the chimney. His parachute was caught up inside. He's still in that ruined building, hanging from the parachute webbing. Whenever the wind blows down the chimney his body is turned round and his viewpoint changes. That's the Hanged Man in the cards. The other card simply meant he was in a workplace, as Miss Bingham suggested.'

Archibald broke in excitedly. 'You know what it means, don't you? It means we have a man there.'

Vance raised a finger tentatively. 'Archibald, I don't mean to dampen your enthusiasm but this chap's just a touch on the dead side.'

'Vance is right,' said Crane. 'Walker, or whatever his

name is, won't be much use to us except as a conduit. Mrs Pugh would be able to make contact with his body or spirit or whatever, and she'd be able to see what happens. But we won't be able to do a damned thing about it.'

'That's where you're wrong, Mr Crane,' Archibald replied. 'He may be dead but we can still use him.'

Bartley, who had been listening carefully, jumped to his feet. 'Of course! Don't you see, Crane? Archibald is right. Walker may not be able to actually do anything himself, being two months dead and all, but we can do something *with* him. If we could do something to redirect that magic Crowley was talking about, away from the SS man and into Walker's corpse, the Germans would think the procedure had failed. They probably wouldn't try it again. And I wouldn't want to be in Schertel's shoes – I have a good idea that Himmler doesn't take failure too well.'

'I see what you're getting at. But how do we do it?'

'You remember that woman you were going to recruit until Dakessian warned you off? Firth or Fortune? She's a witch. I remember reading about something called a 'cone of power' that can deflect magical energies. If we can get her coven to do something like that, but raise it around the soldier they've chosen...'

Crane finally grasped what they were saying 'Then we can prevent it from affecting him and it would either flow to the nearest suitable candidate – the late Mr Walker – or rebound destructively on the other participants. It's what Crowley calls the law of magical returns. Walker would surely be the nearest vessel for that energy. Crowley said the ritual would be so delicate that Schertel would have to ensure no one else was close by in case their own emanations disrupted the procedure. And Mrs Pugh can use our connection with Walker to make sure the cone of power is in the right place at the right time. By George, I think you're onto something.'

'We'd better get ready quickly,' Bartley pointed out. 'We don't know when this ritual is going to take place but we have to work on the assumption that it will be very soon. We shall just have to keep watch every night for as long as we have to. The fate of the British Empire – perhaps the fate of the whole world – lies in our hands. We must not fail.'

Bartley's patriotism was inclined to shade into jingoism, but Crane understood that on this occasion the man was absolutely right. Failure was unthinkable.

'Failure is unthinkable,' had been Himmler's last words before the ritual began and he and the guards had retreated to a safe distance. He had hammered that point home by slamming his right fist into his left palm. From the glint in the *Reichsführer*'s deceptively mild eyes, Otto Skorzeny had a shrewd idea that Schertel might pay a very high price if the unthinkable happened. Thankfully, he was merely a tool in this enterprise and as such he would probably be spared whatever retribution Himmler might see fit to visit upon the occultist. Heisenberg too would be spared Himmler's wrath. He had made it abundantly clear that he thought the enterprise was a fool's errand and had told Himmler that in no uncertain terms. Besides, he was the son of Himmler's mother's friend. Even the *Reichsführer* would surely not be so foolish as to offend his mother.

A Yellow Room

The room was hot and strangely lit, smoky with incense. Skorzeny, suitably prepared with a substance called 3,4-methylenedioxy-*N*-methylamphetamine – otherwise known as MDMA and obtained from the Merck pharmaceutical laboratories in Darmstadt – was smiling happily. Schertel had chosen that particular drug for him because it was known to induce feelings of empathy and openness that would facilitate the transfer of knowledge and energy from the dancers to Skorzeny

The strange dancing had stopped some time ago and now he was surrounded by young men and women enthusiastically engaged in various sexual activities and in a variety of combinations. The couplings – not to mention the triplings and at least one eye-watering quadrupling – seemed deliberate and precise, as carefully choreographed as the preceding dance, as calculated as the dosage of drugs administered to the participants. He dimly recognised the music, Wagner's *Tristan und Isolde*. The ambience, the drug and the music were filling Skorzeny's head, expanding his mind toward horizons he'd never before dreamed of. Now that the flagellation had stopped, he was a bit more relaxed about the sex that was taking place, though he averted his eyes when the young men got busy with each other. That was fine as far as he was concerned. Those boys could get on with it. There was a good deal of naked female flesh elsewhere in the room for Skorzeny to feast his eyes upon. He grudgingly admitted that he was becoming aroused in spite of himself. It was such a shame that he wasn't allowed to join in. This assignment was no bloody fun at all – though his thoughts were definitely becoming more interesting.

He still thought Schertel's idea was rubbish. Giving those young people an intensive course on quantum mechanics so that their ritual could magically transfer an understanding of the nature of reality, time and space to him – and so enable him to transcend all three? It was horseshit. Still, what about that pretty young woman with the nice smile and the large breasts who was doing *that* with another girl? He sighed wistfully.

The Yellow Room's carpet was rolled up and put to one side. The armchairs were fully occupied by men and women in differing depths of hypnotic trance. Mrs Pugh was in very deep, awaiting Crane's command to dream. Three woman chanted within a circle they'd chalked on the floor, preparing to raise their cone of power. Miss Firth had refused to be there in person, seemingly still in a sulk over being refused admission to the Yellow Room, but she had sent these friends to perform the ritual. They appeared to know what they were doing.

When they were ready one of the three witches raised a hand and nodded. Crane was tense but ready. He gave Mrs Pugh her instructions.

Skorzeny felt it – a sudden dramatic change in the atmosphere, like the time he had watched a demonstration of static electricity when he was a child, sparks arcing between two steel spheres. This time his hair didn't rise and his skin didn't prickle but otherwise it felt exactly the same. The men and women cavorting around him suddenly became absolutely still, and those that were standing, kneeling or crouching fell to the floor, seemingly drained of both consciousness and energy. Skorzeny closed his eyes and awaited apotheosis.

It was dark. When it was this dark it didn't matter if the wind blew because wherever he faced it was the same – impenetrable blackness – unless he was facing the courtyard, in which case he could see lights through windows that made him think only of home, and that only increased his yearning. Something was going on behind those windows tonight – he could hear music, moans of passion, yelps of pain. He was curiously unable to distinguish between them. It didn't really matter because now the rats had found the parachute webbing and were beginning their descent, nervously at first but getting braver. One had already bitten his ear. It would soon be over. And he would never go home again. That made him as sad as he was afraid.

Then something unexpected occurred.

Mrs Pugh could no longer see anything. She had been – with great reluctance – watching those dreadful goings-on with those German youngsters and then she was back in the darkness, back inside poor Walker. She hadn't done that of her own volition. Something was wrong. She began to panic. Then there was a mighty jolt and she was opening her eyes.

Crane looked down at her anxiously, his face white. 'Violet, thank God you're back. Did we do it? Did it work?'

Mrs Pugh stared back at him, confused and disorientated. For a moment Crane thought she had been damaged in some way, and his heart went out to her. Elderly ladies should not be waging psychic warfare on behalf of the nation. It was a very bad show. Was this what the world had come to?

But Mrs Pugh's face cleared and she smiled mischievously as her senses returned.

'Well I never. Now that's something you don't see every day, dear!'

Daniel Walker felt it entering him, a charge like electricity making his limbs jerk and his nerves tingle. He seemed to know so much more than he had only seconds ago. He knew that time and space are artifacts of the human mind. He knew that reality is what we make it. And he knew how to get home. That was all he wanted. And that's what he did. He went home.

A solitary rat fell twenty feet to the rubble-strewn floor, squealing with outrage.

The young people were stirring now, waking from their brief spell of unconsciousness. Skorzeny closed his eyes. He didn't feel any different. Perhaps the change was in his subconscious? Well, there was only one way to find out. He willed himself to be back in his barracks on the mainland, back in his bed, with his comrades, awaiting his marching orders. Awaiting action.

When he opened his eyes he was still in that bloody room in the school building they'd requisitioned on Heligoland. *That went well*, he thought bitterly. *All that boredom and irritation, for nothing. A whole month of my bloody life wasted on this shit.*

The pretty girl with the nice smile and the large breasts caught his eye. He returned her smile and she began to walk unsteadily toward him. *Oh well*, he said to himself. *I'm sure Schertel and the* Reichsführer *won't mind if I have a little fun now.*

A Yellow Room

Gladys Walker sat alone in her parlour and listened to the wireless. The music was happy but she was not. It had been almost two months since she had received the letter from the War Office regretting to inform her that her son Danny had failed to return from a mission. He was missing presumed dead. That was all they'd told her. She hadn't known what to do about it. How do you arrange a funeral for someone when you don't have a body? Now she was waiting in hope and trepidation. At some point she would have to accept that Danny was gone and would never come home again. The thought of that drove her to the edge of heartbreak so she retreated from the brink, just as she did every time.

He's not dead, she told herself. *I don't want him to be dead. I won't let him be dead. One day he'll come home, just like he always does, with a present for his old mum, chocolates or flowers. He'll come home.*

And as she had done every night since that letter had arrived, Mrs Walker switched off the wireless, made sure the fire was down and turned the light out. She went into the kitchen and washed up her cup, saucer and spoon. Then she took the teapot outside and emptied the cold wet leaves onto the garden, went back inside and rinsed the pot, and bolted the back door.

She walked wearily upstairs. Before going to bed she stopped at her son's bedroom door, just as she had every night for the last two months. She opened the door, praying as usual that she would find him lying in his bed.

And this time, she wished to God that he wasn't.

The Enemy Within

Most hunters prefer darkness and this one was no different. It was his friend, allowing him the privacy he needed to carefully arrange his creations for maximum effect. This night was especially dark – not only were the surrounding windows blackened and the street lights turned off, but it as a moonless, cloudy night. Occasionally a car crawled by, headlamps dulled and blinkered. It was two o'clock in the morning when he finally stepped out of the vehicle, the signal for the driver to unlatch the trunk then disembark to join his employer in the street. He gestured toward the dark maw of a nearby alley – for a moment he wondered if the driver could see even his own hand in the darkness, but the driver seemed to know what was required of him and opened the trunk. Between them they manhandled the heavy bundle out of the cavity and carried it into the alley. The driver went back to the car to close the trunk and wait. The man removed the blanket that had held his work together, and placed the parts in the desired order. It was both a demonstration of his prowess and a territorial marker: I am here.

Satisfied, he smiled to himself, folded the blanket into a square and rejoined his assistant. The man gazed at the empty streets as they drove back to his home. Working at home was all very well but he was tired of the inevitable cleaning up and the annoyance of conveying his work to where it would be put on display. But he was still familiarising himself with his new territory and had to be careful. The darkness helped but he looked forward to a time when it would be even darker, and when chaos would distract even those who might wish to monitor the darkened streets. Then he would begin hunting in earnest, just as he had back home.

Anthony Crane was feeling rather pleased with himself. He'd just managed to spin out what should have been a routine ten-minute meeting with Fleming to nearly an hour. The Yellow Room's colour scheme always made Fleming feel unwell and it was gratifying to witness the man's rising discomfort.

Crane wasn't usually vindictive but Fleming had been even more arrogant and demanding than usual, which was saying a lot. Naval Intelligence had got wind of a mole passing information to a Nazi agent. So far it was fairly low-level stuff, by Fleming's own admission – trivia concerning the quality of uniforms, NAAFI food, morale and what have you – but it was an embarrassment to Fleming's immediate masters. Naturally, the man had declined to tell Crane how they knew someone had been passing the information to Jerry, but he had been at pains to stress that although the leak was minor at present, it had the potential to be much more damaging. When Crane pointed out that the Yellow Room would need something more to go on – a person or location as a target for his people to focus on – Fleming had first brushed those concerns aside then made a veiled threat that failure to accept this task would feature prominently in his next report on the Yellow Room's effectiveness to Hore-Belisha. Crane had reluctantly capitulated; they certainly couldn't afford to incur Ministerial opprobrium so early in their existence. But he had retaliated by keeping Fleming in that overwhelming room for as long as possible.

Crane loathed bullies and – what was that marvellous American expression he'd heard in *The Thin Man*? Oh yes, *stool pigeons*. Fleming certainly deserved the first epithet and Crane knew full well that the picture of the Yellow Room that was being drawn for the Secretary of State for War was not exactly favourable. Crane wondered if Fleming might be after his job. Crane had heard rumours that the fellow was fascinated by the supernatural. Well, Fleming might eventually wear down Hore-Belisha – who had enough on his plate with the war and the constant sniping of his own colleagues – but Crane wasn't going to go down without a fight. If that meant playing childish games to unsettle the enemy within, as he privately styled Fleming, then so be it.

Crane was disillusioned with Hore-Belisha. The politician had sworn him to absolute secrecy when they'd set up the Yellow Room, yet the first thing the man had done was appoint Fleming and Wheatley to be his liaisons with Naval Intelligence and the Secret Intelligence Service – and to keep him apprised of what the Yellow Room people were up to. Wheatley, who fancied himself an expert on the kinds of technique used by the Yellow Room specialists, was only loosely connected with the SIS. However, at least he seemed not to have designs on Crane's position. Wheatley had been earmarked for some other role, as yet unclear. He might even have been likeable if he wasn't so obsessed with social class and obsequiously royalist. Crane didn't care much for the upper classes, loathed the Royal Family and didn't trust politicians. How could he feel otherwise when they were the very people responsible for the bloody awful mess the world was in? As for the intelligence services – well, he saw precious little intelligence in those quarters. Look at the Venlo incident – the SIS had been played for fools by the Germans and two agents had been taken. And as for spies – how could you trust someone whose whole life was a lie?

To make matters worse, the streets outside his office were increasingly unsafe at night. There had been another bad murder in Soho, the third since Christmas. Another prostitute had been tortured to death and mutilated under cover of the blackout. The police were tight-lipped but the rumour was that they were all victims of the same killer. Serious crime – sexual assault, rape and murder – had soared. The police were focused on foiling fifth columnists and making sure no stray beams of light escaped from chinks in curtains. Meanwhile, predators ruled the unlit parks, streets and alleys. Their victims were those whose trade was traditionally plied at night. One senior Scotland Yard man had recently confided to Crane that it was no longer possible to even pretend to guarantee the safety of barmaids, dancers and other women returning home after finishing work late at night. Prostitutes, in his view, were all at serious risk and it would be impossible to protect them. The Government, of course, thought the murders would be bad for public morale and had hushed them up.

'It'll get even worse when the bombing starts,' his friend had gloomily predicted. 'We'll have so many bodies we'll be unable to tell murder victims from the casualties of war. All the fighting's going on at sea or in Norway at the moment, but sooner or later Jerry will make a move in France or Belgium and the war will really begin. When that happens the Luftwaffe will be regular visitors to London and they'll cause so much confusion that we'll be unable to cope. There will be more burglaries and robberies, and we can expect looting. People will literally be able to get away with murder.'

The pessimistic prediction troubled Crane. He hoped that if the worst happened and London was subjected to prolonged bombing, the city's residents would find it within them to work together, look after one another and act decently. He'd heard several senior civil servants talk about 'pulling together' and 'team spirit'. And he knew how well the playing fields of Eton had prepared their sort for the Somme and Ypres. Too many of them had remained forever in Flanders for such words to ring true, and the public school ethos had done little to prevent their Old Boys sending good men out to die for little more than empty patriotic gestures. Crane's uncle, a geography teacher who had volunteered after hearing the stories of violated nuns and bayoneted babies, lay somewhere in a foreign field, beneath a blanket of soil and grass, and poppies in the summer. His father, who had joined up at the same time and served in the same detachment, saw his older brother blown to pieces as they fought to capture a small copse that was blasted to splinters before they'd advanced two yards from their trench. Dad told him that team spirit and comradeship had been an early casualty of his war. He couldn't trust his officers and couldn't bear to make friends among replacement troops because he had already lost so many. The only bonds they had were those of duty, and facing common enemies – the Hun and their own commanding officers. All ties were stretched thin and in many cases they snapped completely as the strain told. And they were trained soldiers. How would civilians react when the carnage began?

Crane stood at the window and looked down at the street below. It was a lovely spring morning. From the Yellow Room the city – or that part of it he could see – looked busy but quiet and peaceful. Men and women smiled at one another as they went about their business. He wondered uneasily how many of those men would become monsters and how many of the women their prey when night fell and the city became a hunting-ground.

His first efforts had been inspired by a fellow hunter preying on the homeless and derelict of Cleveland and other towns and cities on the shore of Lake Erie. The Cleveland Torso murders, they'd been called. Most of the women had been his; the other hunter had been responsible for all the men, which led him to believe that a third person was responsible for some – definitely the black woman, maybe that first white woman in '36 and the one in '34. That would have been a year before he joined in the fun. He remembered the first time, a night in February 1937. A dirt-poor woman, drunk and dirty but not unattractive, had offered him sex for the price of a quart of gin. Well, why not? It had been his birthday, after all. He'd driven her down to Euclid Beach, where he first screwed her then gave her the money. He considered himself an honourable man. Honour satisfied, he'd taken a knife from the automobile and set about the real work. He'd known exactly what to do. He'd been imagining it and planning it for years.

That was also the night he discovered the Name – when he got home, sated and giddy with what he had done, he fixed himself a drink and settled down with a book, Louis Ginzberg's Legends of the Jews, *and in it was the Name. After that he'd had to go away but he returned to do two more in '38, before having to leave the area again. But he kept his hand in wherever he went.*

'Let's get this straight,' said Bartley, chewing on a pencil. 'Fleming wants us to find and identify the source of this leak. But he doesn't have a clue as to where that person might work or in what capacity. All he knows is that it's possibly a serviceman. I emphasise the word "possibly". Furthermore, he has only a vague notion as to what's been passed on to the Germans and what he does know is the sort of information that could be picked up by anyone. How on earth does he expect us to find someone when we don't know where to look or what to look for? We may be psychic but we're not magicians.'

'I'm not even psychic,' Crane pointed out. 'I'm only the supervisor. I have the occasional idea and make sure we have enough tea but it's the rest of you that do all the actual work. But you're right. We've been dealt a bad hand here. I have an uneasy feeling that we've been set up to fail.'

'Did Fleming give you anything at all that we might use?' asked Edward Vance, rubbing at his left lower limb, which was actually made of wood, though that appeared not to prevent it suffering arthritic pain and cramp. He often joked that he was the only clairvoyant he knew who was haunted by his own leg.

Crane waved a manila folder at him. The folder was very thin. 'This is all he could or would give me. It's just a list of things that Jerry seems to know rather too much about — a depressing litany of ill-fitting tunics, chafed crotches, sour milk and bacon on the turn. Oh yes, and stale bread. We mustn't forget that. Presumably, the tide of war could turn on an unsatisfactory slice of toast. But I suppose Fleming's right — this is a leak and it must be plugged before it gets any worse.'

Ethel Bingham laughed chirpily. 'I can't imagine square-bashing being much fun with all that chafing.'

This drew a blush from William Simmons, who was much taken with Miss Bingham. 'Chafing's no laughing matter,' he said feelingly. He had a similar problem with his leg-brace, which tended to rub unpleasantly in the groin, especially when he was sweating — as indeed he was now, thanks to Miss Bingham's merrily heaving bosom. 'May I see it?' he requested. 'I might be able to narrow it down a bit.'

He took the folder from Crane and while the others chatted among themselves he spent a few minutes poring over the two foolscap pages he found within.

'All this is from the RAF and the Royal Navy. No information about land forces at all. From the way it's written I'd say that Fleming's people picked it up from an overheard transmission. It's almost like a trial run — as if whoever was passing it on was just doing it as a test. And here's something interesting — the informant uses the word "cookies". That's an American expression.'

'Very good, Simmons,' said Crane. 'We can suppose that Fleming is correct in assuming that this is a potentially dangerous source. We can further suppose that the culprit might be from the United States; and that he is connected to the Navy or RAF. I couldn't say if Fleming and his chaps have come to similar conclusions, but at least we know slightly more now than we did five minutes ago. Perhaps you could all take a look at this material and see if you notice anything else. I'm open to suggestions.'

The folder was circulated in silence. Mrs Pugh was the first person to break it. 'He's not a Royal Navy man,' she announced. 'It says here that our sailors still receive a tot of rum every day to "splice the mainbrace". Well, my Bert joined the Navy during the Great War and stayed on for years. He told me that splicing the mainbrace is only ordered on special occasions. Only a member of the Royal Family or the Admiralty can give the order. It certainly doesn't happen every day. The last time it happened was in 1932 – Bert was still in the service then. A Navy man would never use that expression for an ordinary drink. And there's one other thing – a lot of these complaints refer to the NAAFI. Well, Bert said commissioned officers aren't supposed to use the NAAFI. So you'd be looking for a junior rank, NCO downwards.'

'Excellent,' Crane smiled. 'Now we're getting somewhere. Thank you very much, Mrs Pugh. Does anyone else have anything?'

'I have an idea,' offered Bartley, his pencil now reduced almost to a mash of damp splinters. 'I'd say that whoever is supplying our man with this information is the kind to kick up a fuss and make a lot of complaints, and to encourage others to do the same. To us, they seem like trivia – but to a serviceman who has to endure it day-in and day-out, it must eventually become intolerable. There's probably someone in Whitehall who keeps track of complaints in the services – I honestly can't conceive of any bureaucracy that would miss an opportunity to collect masses of data about things as crucially important to the nation as stale bread and sour milk. The densest concentration of complaints might give us somewhere to start looking.'

Two days later, Crane had the information Bartley had suggested he should obtain. The Naval complaints were distributed fairly uniformly around bases and vessels. No location stood out. The RAF figures were a different matter. Over the past two months there had been a spike in the number of complaints about supplies and catering in a small area including the RAF bases at Bentley Priory, Hendon, Heston, West Drayton and the new airfield at Stanmore Park. All were in Middlesex and were close neighbours. At last the Yellow Room had somewhere to look.

Crane's colleagues were as relieved as they were excited. They were bored with scratching around for things to keep them occupied, and were eager for something to challenge their abilities. Crane reflected that it really was about time he organised the team properly. He would need to plan activities and find a way to utilise their talents more productively. They couldn't carry on reacting, waiting for someone to drop a mission in their lap. They would have to make the running, become an assault weapon as much as a defence. The Heligoland business had shown him something of what he believed his team was capable of. He had an idea that by measuring and monitoring what happened to his specialists while they were working, they could work out how to make them perform more effectively, perhaps even develop new techniques and skills. It seemed logical that a psychic faculty could be adapted for multiple purposes. If only he could recruit people to use all that scientific equipment presently gathering dust in Bartley's big house in Surrey, they might be able to make a start.

But for now they had to make the best use of what they had. He drew up a rough plan: divination by Miss Bingham first, building on that with some predictive activity from Bartley, Simmons and Archibald, then using Vance and Mrs Pugh to home in on anything they turned up.

Miss Bingham was using her old deck of tarot cards. As usual for a Yellow Room operation, she dealt a spread of three cards. The first one from the top was the High Priestess. 'This is all about secrets and hidden things. The next card is Death. Usually that means a significant change. The third and final card is the Devil, which usually signifies carnal pleasures and materialism. We normally look below the surface appearance for these cards' meaning but the Priestess suggests that the hidden meaning is that these cards should be taken at face value – death and the Devil.'

Bartley, Archibald and Simmons were sitting together. They looked at each other, fidgeted and lit cigarettes, unable to relax. Eventually Archibald spoke. 'Sorry, Crane – nothing's happening. I still don't have enough to make a connection.' Bartley and Simmons sheepishly indicated that they too had nothing to offer. Crane sighed and turned to Mrs Pugh, but she had already fallen asleep.

The following day Crane organised an outing. He and

A Yellow Room

Bartley packed the entire Yellow Room team into their cars and drove them to the Middlesex RAF bases which had seen those unusual surges of complaints. They received no impressions or ideas whatsoever. At the last on the list – RAF Stanmore – Simmons made a suggestion.

'I say, why don't we just ask the commanding officer if he knows who's been making all the complaints?'

Crane could have kicked himself. Of course – it was blindingly obvious. And naturally it simply hadn't occurred to him. He'd been so focused on making use of the Yellow Room's talents that he'd overlooked what would probably have been the first thing that occurred to a policeman: ask someone.

Group Captain Whittaker, the Station Commander, was a dashing fellow with a David Niven moustache. When Crane asked him about the complaints, Whittaker sighed and turned his eyes to the heavens. 'Ah yes, that would be Leading Aircraftman Talbot. A good fellow, very competent, always does an excellent job. But just lately he's been a damned nuisance, always moaning about something. Yesterday he made a formal complaint that his socks were too big. I told him to take his boots off so I could see for myself. They looked alright to me, and I told him so. He said he respectfully disagreed. He was very polite, but in a damned insolent way, if you get my meaning. I honestly don't know what's got into the man. Do you want to speak to him about it?'

Crane found Talbot at a table in the NAAFI canteen, drinking tea and reading Eric Ambler's *The Mask of Dimitrios*, which Crane had read when it was published by Hodder and Stoughton late in the previous year. 'Not a bad yarn, that,' he said.

Talbot raised an eyebrow. 'I'm only about halfway through it but it's a decent enough yarn. Is there anything I can do for you?'

'Yes,' agreed Crane. 'As a matter of fact there is. Leading Aircraftman Talbot, isn't it? It's about all those complaints you've been making.'

Talbot sighed and placed the open book on the table. 'Oh, bugger – I should have known it was all too bloody easy. You're from the Ministry, aren't you?'

'I am indeed, and I think it would be a very good idea if you told me all about it. Would you like a cigarette?'

'Don't mind if I do, thanks. Well, as you must have guessed they weren't really about anything. It began a couple of months ago when I was approached by this American chap – Adam Eugene, he said his name was. He said he was playing a practical joke on a friend of his who works in the Ministry of War. He said he'd pay me a hundred pounds if I made a lot of formal complaints about the NAAFI food and the uniforms. He said it wouldn't hurt anyone but it would be a bit of a headache for his chum. I had my doubts but it wasn't anything that could get anyone hurt. And a hundred quid is a lot of money. He also gave me another twenty-five pounds to recruit some people from other bases to do the same thing. And that's just what I did – paid five people a fiver each to make a few complaints. The easiest money any of us will ever make, I'd wager.'

'Could you describe him for me?'

'About the same height as me, five ten or so, a bit scrawny; ordinary-looking, dark grey suit with a blue tie. Seemed a bit – you know, theatrical. He approached me in a pub in Stanmore. I'd seen him in there before. This time he was talking to quite a few RAF chaps. I expect one of them must have told him I was a bit skint and that's why he thought I'd do it. I'm terribly sorry – I didn't imagine it would cause any trouble.'

Crane obtained the name of the pub and sent the others home crammed into Bartley's car while he paid the place a visit. He didn't want to waste their time and besides, he was the only one of the Yellow Room who actually got paid so he might as well do the work.

The pub was called the Duke of York. It was packed with off-duty RAF men and WAAFs, and a few men in civvies, probably locals. He asked the barman if he knew a man named Adam Eugene.

'The Yank? Oh yes,' the man replied in an Irish brogue. 'He's been in here a lot lately. Always seems to have plenty of money to spend. Actually, he's here now – see that man sitting in the corner reading the *Daily Mirror*? That's him. Mind you, I'd watch my step if I were you. He's involved in some funny religion. He's always going on about ghosts and magic and the supernatural. It gives me the shudders sometimes. Nice enough bloke, though. Theatre type, I think.'

Crane thought furiously. If Eugene was an occultist then the best way to approach him would be to pretend that he too was a member of that fraternity. That wasn't so far from the truth. He thought he'd picked up enough of the terminology from Crowley to be able to elicit an opening. He bought himself a pint of bitter and strolled confidently across the bar to where the man sat.

'Adam Eugene, I believe. Greetings, brother,' he said.

'We have heard of you. I thought it was time we made contact.'

Eugene regarded him with evident suspicion. 'Kindly identify yourself,' he pompously demanded. 'How do you know about me? Who do you represent? Why do you want to contact me?'

Crane was momentarily stumped. Occultists tended to like grand-sounding magical names and titles, and they didn't like to admit ignorance of rival adepts and organisations. What was that bloody star Crowley was always harping on about, the one that was so important to his personal symbolism? He dredged up what he could recall from his conversations with Aleister Crowley concerning the naming conventions of magical orders. It was all Classical mythology and codswallop as far as he could make out. 'I am known as Frater – ah – Chiron. I am here on behalf of the Brotherhood of Sirius. You will have heard of us, I'm sure.'

Eugene's eyes narrowed. 'Frater Acheron? What kind of name is that? It sounds bloody German to me. And what's the Brotherhood of Sirius when it's at home? Is it a jazz band?' The generic American accent had slipped into fluent East End.

'Er – no, actually it's Latin and Greek. We're – um – an order of adepts.'

Eugene regarded him blankly. 'Adept at what?'

Crane ignored the question and tried to resurrect the moment. 'I'd like to talk to you about your payments to Leading Aircraftman Talbot and the complaints you paid him to make,' he said.

The other man pretended to be baffled at first, but

then laughed. 'Oh dear, you've caught me out. Alright, I admit it. My name isn't Adam Eugene and it wasn't my idea. My name is really Duncan Mayhew. No, it was someone else's scheme, I'm afraid. Adam Eugene approached me a couple of months ago and offered to pay me twenty-five pounds a week if I'd come here for a couple of months, pretend to be him and get someone to make a lot of trivial complaints – he said it was a joke on a friend of his at the Ministry of War. I didn't think twice. I needed the money – I normally work on the scenery at the Adelphi Theatre but we've had nothing on since *The Dancing Years* closed in September, and I was running low on cash. Why, have I done something wrong? I know it was a bit of a strange thing to do but I don't want to get into any trouble. And what was that "Frater Acheron" nonsense?'

'With regard to the complaints, no action will be taken against you. But don't do it again or we'll be down on you like a ton of bricks. I'm sorry about the mix-up. I was led to believe you belonged to an occult order.'

Mayhew laughed. 'Well, I go to a Spiritualist church once a week, if that's what you mean. I'm not all that religious but I like to catch up with my mum.'

Crane had no interest in that. 'Can you describe Adam Eugene? Is there anything about him that stood out or made you think?'

'He was a few inches taller than me, maybe six foot one; muscular, dark brown hair, brown eyes – very attractive, though I don't suppose he'd be your type. He had a genuine American accent, well-dressed and friendly. I think he might be a military man – very upright bearing, air of authority bordering on arrogance. Likeable but not quite likeable, if that makes any sense. He never smiled with his eyes. But it's odd that you should mention the occult. That's how Eugene engaged me in conversation. Someone here told him I was interested in the supernatural – it was probably that bloody fool of a new barman – and he asked me some questions about my beliefs, whether I was a Freemason, that sort of thing. He seemed genuinely interested, even asked me if I knew of any esoteric groups in the area. I told him that apart from the Spiritualist Church I didn't, unless you count the White Eagle Lodge, and I'd stopped going to that because I couldn't afford to get there. It was when I told him that I was an out-of-work stagehand that he asked me if I'd do him that little favour. Then he gave me a lot of money – two hundred for myself and another two hundred to pay someone to make the complaints.'

'Did he say anything about his own beliefs?'

'Well, he said that the Spiritualists didn't really know what they were doing or what they were communicating with. He rather sneered at us. But then he offered me the money so I let it go.'

'Do you still have any of the money he gave you?'

'Yes,' said Mayhew reluctantly. 'Forty-five pounds. Why, do you have to confiscate it?'

'No, you can keep it. But tell me, why did you go along with it? Why not just take the money and run? Why did he trust you?'

'Well,' Mayhew replied. 'Between you and me, I found him a bit unsettling. I reckoned it would not be a good idea to scarper with the cash. And he knew it. That was all the trust he needed.'

A Yellow Room

Wartime London was a hunter's paradise – a big jungle teeming with prey, dark enough to conceal the predator and tempt the victims out into the open to forage. He looked forward to chaos erupting alongside the bombing. Indeed, he was taking steps to ensure that it did. The next transmission to his German friends would be far more consequential than the test messages he had so far delivered to ensure that their system was working. They had been mere gestures of a good faith that was wholly calculated and selfish. When the bombing started he would be in his element. He needed the true hunt, the excitement of selecting and stalking his prey then dispatching and preparing it out in the open. The three he'd taken so far had been little more than gifts, purchased from a pimp who was himself wanted for murdering a woman. The man protested that it had been an accident – but he knew a jury would send him for the drop. But it wouldn't be long now until he could dispense with the man's services. When the time came he would instruct one of his associates to get rid of the parasite on a permanent basis. Until then he would just have to be patient. Hunters learn to be patient. The Name was the most patient of all.

The tea was brewed to what Crane considered perfection – the colour of tar and the consistency of treacle. He added a drop of milk and took a grateful sip, then lit a cigarette and gazed at the five-pound note on his desk. The fiver was weighted down with a half-crown. With any luck the banknote would be enough of a physical link to enable Vance to make psychometric contact with their quarry.

They had some firm information about their suspect. Adam Eugene was almost certainly not his real name. But they did know that he was American, aged around thirty. They had a vague physical description, and a possible military connection. Furthermore, the man was evidently interested in occultism and his disparaging remark about the Spiritualists suggested that he might have some sort of experience with such groups.

The knowledge placed him in a quandary. By rights he should pass what little information he had to the Secret Intelligence Service and let them deal with it. But he didn't trust them to place any store in any information the Yellow Room acquired – he didn't trust them in any way you could name, full stop. As for their competence – well, he shuddered at the thought of what those idiots might do. If he took what he had to Hore-Belisha the Secretary of State would only tell him to pass it to the SIS. Scotland Yard would do the same. Besides, Crane was sure there was something else going on. The United States had its Nazi sympathisers, as did Great Britain; and the Nazis' interest in occultism was pretty much common knowledge. The thought of fascist-leaning occultists in Britain and her allies, and in neutral countries, joining up to form a subversive network that could potentially destabilise the whole world – that was something that hadn't occurred to him until now.

Fleming had been in again. His people had picked up a further radio transmission from the same source, in a simple substitution code. This time the message included details of troop deployments in and around London, with suggestions as to which locations would be best for the Luftwaffe or German agents to target for maximum impact on Londoners' transport and morale – the main railway stations and road junctions at the busiest times of day. Once again, this was information that could have been amassed by anyone with good eyesight and a bicycle. But the sender had also suggested using chlorine or mustard gas in the tube stations at night if they were used as shelters when the bombers came. As if war wasn't enough, they now faced a campaign of terrorism and mass murder. It was chilling.

The depressing train of thought was interrupted by Vance, who entered without knocking. Yellow Room personnel didn't stand on ceremony – it was their workplace and they were entitled to be there, after all – but everyone else had to observe the usual formalities. Crane insisted on that. The military and his fellow civil servants looked down on his people and he wanted a bit of respect to be shown. Vance, Mrs Pugh, Miss Bingham and the others were as much combatants in their way as any uniformed soldier – and a damned sight more so than any of the self-important mandarins and puffed-up generals who sneered at them.

Vance was doubtful. 'Look here, Crane – this fiver has probably been handled by dozens of people, perhaps hundreds. How do you expect me to sort out the right man?'

Crane handed him a sheet of foolscap that bore a list of everything they knew about the putative spy. 'This might help. I know it isn't much but it could narrow the field a bit. We need to do something fast – our man has upped the ante with a plan to attack civilian targets.'

'Well, I'll do what I can. But don't get your hopes up too high, old man. Can you draw the curtains? It might help me concentrate.' Vance sat and closed his eyes while Crane darkened the room. Crane liked to observe his specialists at work. Vance breathed deeply and evenly, relaxing one part of his body at a time, from the toes upward. It was similar to one of the hypnotism techniques Crane had been taught. As he watched, Vance became utterly still. He remained so for several minutes, then he became agitated, his fingers twisting the sheet of paper.

'Got him – Crane, I think I've got him. Yes, this is our man. Good Lord, this is bad. There's blood on his hands, a lot of blood. I can't see the details – there's a sort of fog around him. He's not like you and I – there's something wrong with him, a sort of cold emptiness I've never encountered before. Whoever he is, I believe he is an extremely dangerous man. But I've made contact now. We can find him whenever we want. My goodness, that was most unpleasant.'

In Crane's desk drawer there was a bottle of brandy that he kept for emergencies. This wasn't exactly an emergency but he thought Vance had earned a snifter.

When the rest of the Yellow Room personnel had arrived, Crane and Vance briefed them on what they had discovered.

'And that's it,' Crane concluded. 'We can't trust the intelligence boys to take us seriously – or to do anything useful about it if they did. We can't go to the police without something more solid. Just to ice the cake, we don't even know who we're dealing with. Yet we can't sit here twiddling our thumbs while this fellow gets up to mischief. We need to find some way of tracking him down. Vance has been able to give us a few hints but he won't be able to give us a name and address. Anyone have any ideas?'

Charles Bartley, the industrialist, stuck a finger in the air. 'Yes, old boy – as a matter of fact, I think I know precisely what we should do. I'm surprised it hasn't occurred to you already. You need to hypnotise us all, use Vance's psychic link to this chap to establish a connection, then set Mrs Pugh dreaming about the man. Having us all there will amplify the results. Simple really – it's almost exactly the same as we did during the Heligoland affair.'

In fact, Crane had already thought of that. But the procedure had been profoundly unsettling. At one point the entire complement of Yellow Room staff, excluding only Crane, had been placed in a deep sleep when one of their targets had taken counter-measures. Worse still, making contact with a very dead RAF man had upset all of them, especially Miss Bingham. And Mrs Pugh had witnessed something she still refused to discuss.

But Bartley was right. In the absence of any concrete leads, they had no choice but to create their own. Reluctantly, he agreed. As he had done before, Crane hypnotised each of his specialists. This time, both Vance and Mrs Pugh were placed in deep trances. When they were ready, Crane placed the manuscript in Vance's hands and instructed him to make the connection but not to speak. Then he took a jotter and pencil from his desk, and told Mrs Pugh to dream about whatever Vance was receiving.

Violet Pugh was silent for a few minutes. She spoke just as Crane was beginning to think the procedure had failed. 'I can see a man – he's thinking about darkness and hunting, chaos and ruin. There is blood – blood running over his hands. But it isn't real blood. He's remembering, and looking forward.'

'That's very good, Violet,' said Crane when she trailed off. 'Now I want you to dream about what he's doing at this very moment. Tell me if you see or hear anything that might tell us who he is or where he lives. Describe your dream to me.'

'He's quite tall, very handsome, American. He's with two men – one is young, wearing a blue or grey uniform. Light brown hair and blue eyes, a good-looking man. The American calls him Gordon. The other man is named John. He's older than either of them – bald, serious-looking, spectacles. They're talking about someone called – Samuel? It's someone very important to them. The American is telling them that when they're with Samuel they must use different names – Lacerato and Praefoco? He's talking about a ritual, an initiation. I don't understand any of this. The young man in uniform, Gordon, calls Samuel their master. The American tells him Samuel is just a metaphor, but he doesn't say what that means. He expects the other two to know. The one called Gordon is nodding but he's only doing that to please the American. He doesn't know what a metaphor is.'

Mrs Pugh stopped talking for a short while, then suddenly resumed talking. 'The American is showing them his passport, telling them he's untouchable. I can see his name quite clearly. John Marshall Lloyd Worthington. He's laughing, telling them to call him Jack. He says Samuel knows him as Frater Eviscero. He thinks that's really funny, but he's not laughing with his eyes. He doesn't have a sense of humour. He knows what's funny, but not why. There's a big hole inside him, empty and dark. All that's in there are nightmares. The others are just the same. Can I wake up now, Mr Crane? Please?'

A Yellow Room

United States Naval Aviator John Marshall Lloyd Worthington, known familiarly as Jack, lived in a large rented house in Surbiton, a far cry from his home town of Philadelphia. Independently wealthy, thanks to inheriting a large share of the Worthington Locomotive Company, he had shown no interest in industry, preferring a military career. He worked at the United States Embassy in Grosvenor Square as a Defense Attaché, but divided his time between the Embassy and the nearby United States Navy's European headquarters. At twenty-nine years old he had limited combat experience but was known as a capable officer and strategist, and was held in high esteem by his colleagues. But although he was valued as a military thinker, he wasn't a popular man. 'A cold fish, by all accounts,' Fleming had said. 'You know what the Yanks are like – they love a good time. Worthington's a bit too serious, doesn't socialise much, bit of a wet blanket. Not a ladies' man but no suggestion that he's a poof, either. He doesn't even drink, for God's sake.'

Asking for Fleming's help had been risky, but he was the only person Crane knew who could obtain the information the Yellow Room needed. He'd given Fleming a cock and bull story about meeting Worthington at a dinner party and promising to look him up but losing the man's address. Indeed, he'd lied, after a few drinks too many he could barely remember a thing about the man but didn't want to appear rude. Fleming had such a low opinion of Crane's competence that he hadn't even stopped to consider whether the request might be something to do with the Yellow Room's activities. The success of the falsehood had been worth the naked contempt in Fleming's eyes.

Now he and Bartley were waiting by Worthington's house. They had been there for two hours. Bartley was whistling cheerfully. Crane was tired and depressed. It was raining and the sky was the colour of his mood. They had smoked and occasionally chatted to pass the time. Bartley was still indefatigably upbeat but Crane had just about had enough.

The sight of Worthington, dressed in civvies and accompanied by a moustached man of about his own age in a chauffeur's livery, striding from his garden gate to the parked Bentley roused Crane from his growing torpor, while the alert Bartley started the motor. When the chauffeur drove off with Worthington in the back seat they followed at a discreet distance. At just after noon their quarry pulled into the kerb outside a pub called the White Hart on the Bath Road, near Hounslow. Worthington left the car and entered the pub. The chauffeur stayed in the vehicle. They gave Worthington ten minutes to get settled; then Crane drew a deep breath and went in after him.

Worthington was sitting at a table with a young man in a RAF uniform and an older, priggish-looking bald man wearing spectacles and a tired-looking suit. They were all drinking pints of bitter. Crane went to the bar, ordered a pint of the same, and casually walked over to their table with it. He'd deduced from the way Worthington had referred to himself as 'Frater Eviscero', and that the others had similar pseudonyms, that they were members of an occult group. He decided that he might as well continue with the deception he had begun with Duncan Mayhew in the Duke of York. There was a fourth chair at the men's table. Without asking, he sat in it and placed his glass on a beer-mat.

'Good afternoon, gentlemen. I'm sure you won't mind if I join you.'

Worthington glared at him. 'Do you mind? This is a private conversation.'

'Oh, I don't mind at all, old boy,' Crane replied with a smile. 'Frater Eviscero, Frater Lacerato and Frater Praefoco, I believe. Or would you prefer to be called Jack, Gordon and John?' He nodded at each of them in turn as he named them.

The young RAF man looked panicked. For a moment Crane thought he was going to bolt, but the bespectacled man put a steadying hand on his friend's shoulder. Worthington's face was impassive but Crane saw surprise in his eyes.

'Who the hell are you?'

'You can call me Frater Acheron. I represent an order called the Brotherhood of Sirius. I believe we have interests in common.'

'And what might those interests be?'

'Let's just say that they involve taking measures that might be interpreted as – how should I put this? Measures advantageous to those engaged in certain nocturnal activities. Actions that would benefit those whom some might perceive as an enemy. Metaphorically speaking, following a strategy that would please the one who is your master and mine.'

'You are a follower of Sammael?' The young man blurted the question before Worthington's withering gaze had a chance to fasten upon him. The American's look was enough to silence him but it was too late. He had given Crane another piece of the jigsaw.

Not Samuel but Sammael. The name Lucifer had before he was cast out of Heaven; the rebel angel, Satan himself – the Devil. Mrs Pugh had made an innocent mistake. How many people would have known what Sammael was? These men didn't belong to any old magical order – they were Diabolists. He would have to tread carefully.

In answer to the youth's question, Crane merely smiled and inclined his head. Worthington's angry gaze intensified. He seemed on the verge of exploding with fury. And the man appeared to be enjoying the feeling. He began to grin.

'That's mighty impressive, Frater – Acheron, did you say? How did you find all that out?'

'I am an adept of the dark arts, Frater Eviscero. I have my ways – unconventional ways – as I'm sure you do. As I said, we share certain aims and interests. I would like to propose an alliance.'

'An alliance? Well, that sounds fine and I admit that I'm impressed that you seem to know so much about us. But before we talk about that I'd like to know more about you and this Brotherhood you represent. I need to know if we really do have the same objectives – and if you can be trusted.'

'The Brotherhood of Sirius was founded twelve years ago,' Crane extemporised. 'Our founders belonged to Crowley's A∴A∴ but they left that order because they believed him to be weak and dissipated – the women and drugs, all that notoriety. I was approached six years ago and asked to join. We wish to inspire a new order of the world, one based on sound scientific and – um – philosophical principles. I think you understand me. We want to restore balance and put our nation back on the path of sanity. Undesirable elements must be put in their place or removed. We must reassert masculine dominion. Women should know their place, and miscegenation must be prevented. The strong must reaffirm their relationship to the weak. We must become a nation of warriors and hunters, like primordial man.'

By that point Crane didn't have the faintest idea of what he was talking about. It was a regurgitation of scraps he'd heard from Crowley, and half-baked ideas he had heard from Oswald Moseley, the Nazis, eugenicists and other people he considered dangerous lunatics of the sort that would probably meet with Worthington's approval.

'Well, Frater Acheron,' Worthington replied, 'The Sons of Sammael don't follow a political ideology as such. We don't follow any particular religious path, either. Our 'master' Sammael is a metaphor for something that exists within us – our inner beast, if you like. It's a spiritual concept, sure. But it's really a symbolic system designed to help us understand our true natures. As an adept you will understand what I mean by that. We don't follow any political leader and we don't worship any so-called higher powers.'

'Nor we,' Crane quickly interjected, 'except insofar as it suits our – ah – purposes, to obtain the Knowledge and Conversation of our Holy guardian Angels. "Do what thou wilt shall be the whole of the law", eh? Crowley was right about that if nothing else.'

He was sweating heavily when he emerged from the pub, the business concluded. He wasn't quite sure how he'd managed it, but he'd wangled an invitation to the Sons' May Eve celebration, which was to take place the following Tuesday night at the American's house in Surbiton. Worthington had promised him 'something special'.

'I'm not quite sure what their game is,' he told the others when he was back in Bartley's Austin. 'I went at it from the political angle and tried to draw them out about their ritual activities. Worthington claimed they were non-political and practically sneered at the whole idea of worshipping the Devil. My guess is that Worthington is running the show and the others are dupes he's sucked in with all that nonsense about Sammael being a symbolic system to help them understand themselves. But the Sons of Sammael are obviously a front for something even more sinister. One of them – the man called Gordon, "Frater Lacerato" – is RAF. He'd be in a position to give Worthington sensitive information over and beyond that which he already enjoys. The other chap, John, looks like a clerk. I was unable to find out anything else about those two. The frustrating thing is that Worthington simply wouldn't be drawn on anything that might relate to Nazi sympathies or espionage. He could be in it for the money, of course – what with the house, the Bentley and a chauffeur it's clear that he likes the good life, and that means spending in a way that he really shouldn't be able to afford on US Navy pay. But we know he has substantial independent means. We simply don't have enough. We need more before we can be in a position to turn this over to SIS.'

Archibald was puzzled. 'So you think Worthington is just playing at being a Satanist and the others are just in it to make their lives a bit more interesting. Worthington could be using them as camouflage. But you never know. Groups like that would be an ideal cover – all that secrecy, the passwords and funny handshakes. And they form a kind of network – many occultists belong to more than one order. These chaps may all be Nazi agents. They'd hardly discuss it in public, would they?'

'So what do we do next?' asked Bartley, lighting another cigarette. The non-smoker Archibald wound down a window to let some of the smoke out.

'There's not much we can do until next Tuesday. I'll go along to their May Eve celebration and you chaps can wait outside in case there's any funny business. Archibald, make sure to bring your revolver. Bartley, can you drop me off at home? I've had enough for one day. All that subterfuge has given me a rotten headache.'

This man – this intruder – knew the Name but he did not know what the Name meant, not beyond its religious connotations. He would be shown how it bound men like the hunter to one another, how it signified that crimson-handed demon that lived in the hearts of all such men. He would show how men like him truly became alive, when the Name rose in their hearts and coursed through their minds and hands and loins like red fire, making them whole and purposeful, giving meaning to their existence. The Name was death and pain and the act of magic that created them – the magic he had finally awoken at Euclid Beach after years of searching fruitlessly in the dusty corners and hidden rooms of human knowledge. The Name would delight in the chaos to come and all hunters of his kind would revel in the knowledge that they were all one and the same, that they were all soldiers of the Name, feeling nothing until the Name rose within them.

The May Eve celebration was a bit of a let-down so far. Crane had arrived at eight, as instructed, and been patted down by a large man who looked like a boxer with one or two fights too many under his belt. Inside, the house was as ordinary as it seemed from the outside – a fairly roomy detached residence with few distinguishing features. The drawing room had a large bay window that would have shown the leafy avenue outside had the blackout curtains not been drawn, and a smaller oriel that offered a view of a small garden that was screened by high walls and discreetly lit by downward-pointing lamps that bathed the plants and terrace with a dull glow. Worthington aside, Crane counted only five others – as well as Frater Lacerato and Frater Praefoco there were the pug-nosed doorman, Worthington's driver, and an uneasy young man with a spiv moustache and a striped suit with wide lapels. Those three were not introduced and made no effort to engage Crane in conversation. Worthington produced a tray with glasses, a jug of ice, bottles of whisky and gin, and soda and tonic water. Crane accepted a small whisky with ice and soda, and made small talk with Lacerato and Praefoco while Worthington hovered at his shoulder, not joining in the conversation but listening intently to every word Crane uttered. About fifteen minutes after Crane arrived Worthington had a brief conversation with the spiv, counting out a hundred pounds in fivers. The spiv casually saluted Worthington and was shown out by the pug.

Lacerato and Praefoco were disappointingly non-political, Crane thought. It was not at all what he was expecting from a meeting of German spies or Nazi sympathisers. Indeed, Lacerato in particular seemed both patriotic and keen to engage with the enemy. Praefoco, who spoke in a curiously low voice that he barely raised above a whisper, seemed to have no opinions on anything whatsoever, though he did express an interest in police work and briefly speculated as to the kinds of criminal activity that would proliferate if the Luftwaffe bombed London.

And that was about as interesting as it got until eleven o'clock, when Worthington suddenly announced that they would begin the celebration. As the others filed out of the drawing room to make their preparations, the American took Crane aside.

'I hope you don't mind, Frater Acheron – this is for the Sons of Sammael only. You may observe but I'm afraid you won't be able to join in.'

Crane was relieved. He wouldn't have known what to do – and he suspected the celebration might prove a little rich for his stomach. He took further comfort in the knowledge that Bartley and Archibald were waiting outside in Bartley's Austin Seven, and that Archibald was armed with the Webley that had been his constant companion during the Great War. 'That's quite alright,' he said easily. 'I was expecting nothing more than that.'

'That's good,' Worthington returned. 'You can watch through that window.' He indicated the one that looked into the hidden garden. 'My boys here will be right outside the door if you need anything. We start in ten minutes.'

Whatever it was, it wasn't a ritual. This was no

religious celebration or magical working. It was something else entirely, a kind of performance. First Lacerato and Praefoco had entered the garden from a door Crane was unable to see from the oriel. They were dressed in black. The pair took up positions on either side of the terrace. Then Worthington appeared. He was naked – and he wasn't alone. A young woman, also nude, was with him. She was giggling and swaying slightly, either drunk or drugged, probably a prostitute Worthington had hired for the occasion. The young spiv must have been her pimp. Crane recalled that May festivities were usually fertility rites. He had an uncomfortable feeling that he was going to witness something that might severely test his moral sensibilities. Ordinarily he would have averted his eyes, but he was worried that Worthington's people might be keeping an eye on him. He couldn't give the game away now, so he simply had to brazen it out. *I'm a married man*, he told himself. *If I can do it without embarrassment then surely I can watch other people doing it without getting too upset. It's perfectly natural, after all. And it's not as if they're asking me to join in, is it?*

If it had been sex as he knew it, Crane might have been able to maintain a stiff upper lip. But the woman willingly submitted to being tied up, gagged and briefly flagellated before being taken rather brutally by Worthington while Lacerato and Praefoco watched avidly. Crane didn't find any of it at all arousing – in fact, he found it repellent. He supposed the woman must have been paid well for her services. Indeed, she even seemed to be enjoying it. But he supposed it wasn't so bad, really. Yes, it was distasteful and rather disturbing, and he would much rather have been at home with his wife, listening to the wireless with their little boys safely tucked up in bed, but no real harm had been done and everyone in the garden seemed happy with the performance.

Then Frater Lacerato handed Worthington a knife.

Crane looked on, frozen with disbelief and powerless to intervene, as the horror unfolded.

He must have fainted with the shock. He'd certainly vomited on the carpet. The room stank of sour whisky and gastric juices. The three Sons of Sammael were standing there, all in their robes now. Worthington regarded him with amusement.

'So "Frater Acheron",' he asked sarcastically, 'what did you think of that?'

Crane was mute with dread. He wanted to be sick again but there was nothing left in his stomach. He had wanted to help the woman but the drawing room door had been locked and even if he'd smashed the glass, the oriel was too small for him to crawl through. With five of them to contend with it would have been a pointless gesture anyway. If he'd had his wits about him he could have broken through the main window, called his colleagues and drawn the neighbours' attention by pouring illegal light into the darkened street. But he'd been in a blind panic and transfixed by the sight of Worthington carving up his victim. He dimly remembered weeping but all the rest was a jumble of red, raw ruin. At the end, Frater Eviscero had fully lived up to his name. That was when Crane had passed out.

'What's the matter – cat got your tongue, Crane? Yes, I know who you really are. I had my driver Haigh follow you and your friends that afternoon when you left the White Hart. Once he had your address it was easy to find out your name. *Kelly's Directory*, Crane. I made some enquiries and found out that you work in the Ministry of War. But you're not a regular pen-pusher, are you? That means you're probably SIS. I'd guess you've got people waiting outside, huh?'

Crane nodded and finally found his voice. 'I suppose you're going to kill me now,' he murmured. After what he'd just witnessed, it might the best thing for him. He knew that terrible scene was going to haunt him for the rest of his life. But he had his family to think of.

'Why would I do that?' Worthington was amused. 'You're not my type. You can go whenever you want. Go on, go out and call the cops – hell, you can use my phone. Be my guest. Do that and you'll find out just who you're dealing with, Crane. I think you'll find that not only do I have diplomatic immunity but this house is the sovereign territory of the United States of America. I can't be arrested and my house can't be searched. Sure, you can accuse me of whatever you like and try to have me expelled – but do you think your government is going to kick up a stink about me when they're trying their damnedest to get the US on Britain's side against Hitler? Not a chance.'

'But what you did to that poor woman – that was unspeakable. What kind of man are you? Why let me see it?'

Worthington sat in an armchair and made himself comfortable with a cigarette. 'I'm a Son of Sammael,' he replied. 'There are others – Lacerato and Praefoco here, some friends of mine in the States, a few in Germany and France that I know of. I'm sure there are many more. You must have heard of Jack the Ripper. Well, he wasn't the first and he wasn't the last. How about H.H. Holmes or Joseph Vacher? Peter Kürten? Albert Fish? Yeah, I see you recognise a couple of those names. We're the children of the Devil, Crane. And he doesn't care if we believe in him or not – he's just happy that we do his work. If Satan exists, then he's the beast inside us. We don't care about governments or politics. We don't care who rules who and what they do to each other, just so long as we get to have our fun. I haven't been passing information to Germany because I love the Nazis, though I do admit those guys have potential. Those suckers think they recruited me but the truth is that I recruited them. It's to our advantage to increase chaos, confusion and fear. It keeps the cops occupied and the streets dark. And when the bombing starts we can take our little pleasures and those of us who want to can hide the evidence in the rubble. If it's any consolation, we've got people doing exactly the same thing in Berlin. When the time comes we'll be doing it in Washington and New York, Los Angeles and Chicago.'

Crane couldn't think of anything to say. His head was empty of all but horror.

Worthington shrugged. 'You probably think I'm crazy. I don't think so. Years ago, when I first started to get my little cravings, I had myself assessed by a psychologist. He told me I was completely sane, as far as anyone can be. But he said I lacked something called empathy – the ability to feel what other people are feeling. He said it like it was some kind of big deal, like I should be sorry not to have it. Why should I be sorry about that? I really don't give a damn what other people are feeling. All I know is that what I do makes me feel pretty good. The only times I ever enjoyed sex was when I knew was going to kill the girl at the end of it. And as you saw for yourself, the messier it gets and the longer they last, the better I like it.'

The Yellow Room came to a virtual standstill while Crane struggled to come to terms with the appalling murder he had witnessed. He couldn't focus on the work and he seemed unable to make decisions. All he could think of was what had happened – *what had been done* – to that poor young woman.

It had taken two days and half a bottle of brandy before he was able to tell Bartley what he had seen in that house in Surbiton. Even then he glossed over it. He had to tell someone, even if he didn't want to talk about it. He supposed it didn't really make any odds. It wasn't as though he could forget it. The girl's death was seared into his mind. Bartley had been predictably shocked but seemed as concerned for Crane's state of mind as he was for the victim. It was obvious to him that Crane's nerves were shot and he was going to pieces.

Bartley reluctantly concluded that Crane was in no fit state to be in command the Yellow Room. In any other circumstances Bartley would have gone to Hore-Belisha and suggested that Crane be given a leave of absence to recover his composure. But the rumour was that Hore-Belisha's days as Secretary of State for War were numbered, and in any case Bartley didn't really fancy the idea of a rotter like Fleming or a clown like Wheatley being put in charge of the Yellow Room. That would be disastrous. Besides, he had come to think of Anthony Crane as a friend. No, he couldn't do that. He would have to take charge himself, on an unofficial basis, until Crane's nerve returned.

The first thing Bartley did the morning after Crane's drunken outpouring was type a detailed report of the situation, stuffing Crane's battered Remington with extra foolscap and carbon paper so that he could send the top copy to Hore-Belisha and a carbon to Fleming. It was time to bring in the big guns.

'This is a very delicate situation,' said Fleming. 'It will need to be handled very carefully. Are you sure about all this?'

'Are you calling us liars, old chap?' Bartley made it sound like good-natured banter but his smile was dangerous and Fleming recognised it for what it was.

'No, of course not,' Fleming hastily replied. 'But we can't afford to make false accusations – or make claims that cannot be substantiated. You have no evidence other than psychic impressions, hearsay and supposition. We need the Americans on our side if the war escalates. If we accuse one of their diplomatic staff of something like this and we can't prove it, then we're sunk. God knows the situation will be bad enough if we *can* prove it.'

'You've read Crane's report,' snapped Bartley. 'Whatever the government or the Yanks may think, this Worthington man cannot be allowed to go around slaughtering women. For God's sake, man – he sliced that poor girl up for an hour and then cut her open and started removing her internal organs one by one until she died. He's a bloody monster and he must be stopped.'

Fleming sighed. 'Yes, it does sound rather horrible. But it's not as if she was anyone important, is it? She was only a common prostitute, like the others. Women on the game are asking for trouble and sometimes they get more than they bargain for.'

The assembled Yellow Room people were outraged. Ethel Bingham stood and pointed an accusing finger at Fleming. 'Listen, you might think Worthington was doing the world a favour by doing away with a few tarts, but if you ever say anything like that in my presence again you'll be going home without your knackers, do you hear me?'

'You tell him, Ethel,' said Mrs Pugh. 'Mr Fleming, if you really think that, then you're a dirty rotten bastard just like him. Pardon my language.'

'Ladies, gentlemen,' Fleming was placatory, especially as he had noticed that both Bartley and Vance seemed poised to punch his lights out. 'I'm merely pointing out how it might be seen by respectable people. Anyway, where is Crane today?'

'He's at home,' Bartley replied. 'He's suffering from a migraine or something. He sounded rather unwell when he phoned me earlier, poor fellow. Not his usual self at all. Not at all *respectable*.'

'Oh. Well, if he calls again please convey my best wishes. Look here, I can't promise anything but I will see that this gets looked into. Leave it with me.'

As Fleming was leaving, a courier arrived with a reply from Hore-Belisha. It was addressed to Crane and marked 'private' but Bartley opened it anyway. Inside the envelope was a folded sheet of foolscap with only seven words scrawled on it.

Are you out of your bloody mind?

Several weeks passed. The British Expeditionary Force and its Belgian and French allies were routed by the Wehrmacht, their fate merely delayed by the bad weather that had grounded the Luftwaffe at the beginning of May. The crushing defeat culminated in the rescue of more than three hundred thousand British and French troops from the Belgian port of Dunkirk by a ramshackle flotilla of vessels.

On the fourth day of June, Anthony Crane was at home, listening to Winston Churchill on the wireless. He was now pretending to be recovering from bronchitis – but really he was simply depressed and ashamed of his inability to prevent a gruesome murder. Churchill's speech made him sit up and think. He wasn't particularly enamoured of Churchill – he had always regarded the politician as a jingoistic opportunist – but something in that broadcast resonated with both what had just taken place in the English Channel and with what he had failed to prevent in Surbiton. It was, he admitted, a stirring piece of oratory, but Churchill's direct reference to 'all the odious apparatus of Nazi rule' made him understand that Worthington and the Nazis – or least the true believers among them – were cut from the same cloth. They delighted in tormenting those less powerful than themselves. They tortured and killed simply because they could; and because they enjoyed it. The Nazis had turned their entire nation into a Jack Worthington. When Churchill said 'we shall fight in the fields and in the streets, we shall fight in the hills; we shall never surrender', the words spoke directly to Crane. The Nazis were rampaging through Europe, the physical expression of a madman's lust for war – and they were the same as Jack Worthington.

Crane knew what he had to do. He had to go back to work. He would do it not for his own sake, but for the dead girl and all those others who would suffer if decent people stood by and did nothing.

The Yellow Room looked as if a bomb had gone off. Sheets, blankets and clothing were strewn across every piece of furniture and here and there were piles of dirty dishes and crockery, stacks of newspapers and magazines, books and bottles. Every ashtray was overflowing.

Archibald was stretched out on the rug, snoring. Vance and Mrs Pugh occupied two armchairs, also seemingly asleep. Bartley was perched on a stool next to Mrs Pugh. He was unshaven, his hair was uncombed and there were bags under his eyes. He looked worse than Crane felt.

Crane couldn't believe the state of the place. 'What on earth is going on?'

'Welcome back, Crane,' replied Bartley, too tired to offer his customary smile. 'We've been keeping an eye on Worthington, round the clock, taking it in shifts. Vance and Mrs Pugh are in contact at this very moment. I think Archibald's just asleep. I certainly didn't put him under. At least I don't think I did. Sorry about the mess – haven't had time to do any tidying and we can't let the cleaners in while we're working.'

Crane felt humbled. While he had capitulated to horror and taken to his bed, his colleagues had not only carried on without him but appeared to have worked themselves to the point of exhaustion. Their dedication fed his resolve.

'Where's Worthington now?'

'According to Mrs Pugh, about ten minutes ago he was at home, settling down to a game of poker with his chauffeur and that chap you described, the one who looks like a boxer.'

'Any news from Fleming or Hore-Belisha?'

'Not a word, though Hore-Belisha did question your sanity when I wrote to him about what we'd found out. I'd taken the liberty of forging your signature – sorry about that. But I understood from his response that we couldn't expect anything from him, and Fleming has been silent. I think we've been hung out to dry.'

Crane nodded, wandering idly around the room, picking things up and putting them down again. *He's still restless*, Bartley thought sadly. *The poor bugger really is having a rough time over this. I can't say as I blame him. I'm just glad I didn't have to see what he did.* 'How are you feeling, old man?' he asked.

'Oh, much better thanks,' Crane replied. 'Listen, I'm going round to see Hore-Belisha. I'll try to make him see sense over this. See you later.'

When Crane had gone, Bartley checked on Worthington's status with Mrs Pugh.

'He's just won ten bob,' she advised him from her dream. 'But he's been cheating, palming aces. The others know but they're too scared of him to do anything about it. I really don't like that driver bloke. He's got staring eyes, like a mad dog.'

Shortly after that, Archibald awoke, yawned and stretched. He groggily helped himself to stewed tea from the nearly-cold pot. As he was sipping the brew, he looked down at where he had been sleeping and became still.

'My Webley's gone,' he said.

He knocked on the door and took one step backward to keep some fighting room between him and whoever might open it. Faced with a choice between trying to break into Worthington's house at night and making a more direct daylight approach, he had opted not to risk breaking a leg trying to climb over the garden wall in the pitch darkness. The Webley was tucked into the waistband of his trousers, fitting snugly into the small of his back.

The door opened to reveal Worthington and his broken-nosed bodyguard. The American grinned. 'Why, Mr Crane – this is an unexpected pleasure. I thought you'd probably be back to see me but I must say I was expecting you to be a bit more sneaky about it. Please, come in.'

When Crane entered the drawing room he was dismayed to see Fleming sitting there, nursing a glass of whisky. Fleming was not at all pleased to see him.

'Bloody hell, Crane – this is too much. What are you doing here?'

'I might ask you the same thing. Christ, Fleming, you know what this man is and yet here you are drinking his bloody whisky. What's going on?'

Worthington laughed. 'Allow me to explain, Crane. In his capacity as liaison with US Naval Intelligence Mr Fleming has come to deliver a letter from the United States Ambassador informing me that at the request of His Majesty's Government I have been recalled to the USA for redeployment. The reasons appear to be a little hazy but the gist is that my talents would be better employed in combat if need arises. I don't mind that. I've achieved what I set out to do here, and I've had a good old time of it. And I must say that the ladies of London have made my stay here very pleasant indeed. I've really enjoyed their company.'

Crane couldn't believe his ears. No arrest, no charges – not even one plain accusation. If the politicians had their way Worthington was going to get away with it. But he wouldn't get off scot-free if Crane could do anything about it. He reached behind his back and retrieved Archibald's Webley.

Fleming jumped to his feet. 'Crane! Have you taken leave of your senses?'

'No,' Crane replied, pointing the revolver at Worthington and cocking the hammer. 'I think my senses are with me all the way on this, Fleming.'

'But this could cause an international incident. We've got enough on our plate with the Germans – we can't afford to offend the Americans. We're counting on their support, man. They've already gone along with removing Worthington from the country even though your accusations are baseless. If you kill him it could ruin everything.'

'I'm sorry if this mucks up Churchill's plans, but I cannot let this man leave this room alive.'

'Then think of yourself, Crane. Think of your wife and child. You'll end up on the gallows. Is that any way for your family to remember you?'

Crane was calm. 'Bartley will tell them the truth of it. They'll remember the man who rid the world of a beast. I suggest you leave now, Fleming. This is going to be unpleasant.'

But Fleming stayed where he was. Crane shrugged and

aimed the weapon at Worthington's head. The American laughed. 'Oh, this is good. Come on, Crane. Pull the trigger, if you've got the balls for it.'

Just as Crane began to squeeze the trigger, Fleming sprang from his armchair and slammed into him. The gun went off and the oriel window shattered. Worthington didn't even flinch. Crane staggered sideways and clubbed at Fleming with the Webley. Worthington laughed even louder.

'I don't believe it. I've got two guys fighting over me. Now I know how the dames feel at a Saturday night bar-room brawl.'

Seeing that Fleming was dazed, Crane punched him hard on the chin. His opponent went down like a sack of potatoes. But that wasn't the end of Crane's problems. He heard a footstep behind him and whirled round just in time to avoid the haymaker Worthington's bodyguard had launched at him. Crane stepped back and shot the man in the chest. The pug fell to the floor beside Fleming. Crane looked up to see Worthington's driver staring at him. As he raised the Webley again, the man ran for it. The front door slammed behind him.

Worthington was no longer laughing but he didn't seem particularly concerned about his imminent death. 'Looks like it's just you and me then, Tony. Go on, shoot. It's your funeral. Well, not just yours.'

Crane wavered. 'What do you mean?'

'Well, you seem willing to face the hangman for putting me down. But I took out a little insurance. You see, when I found out where you live – well, I couldn't really keep that to myself now, could I? Frater Lacerato and

Frater Praefoco know too. And they have instructions. If anything happens to me while I'm in Britain – anything of a fatal nature – they will pay your home a little visit. It won't be straight away. They'll wait until you drop your guard. But they'll do it, make no mistake about that. They're faithful and dedicated Sons of Sammael, Crane. Frater Praefoco, he likes to have a little fun with the ladies before he finishes them off. So does Lacerato, but in a very different way. Your wife won't be a pretty sight by the time they're done with her. You can imagine what they'll put her through. It'd be such a shame. Irene is such a pretty little thing, isn't she?'

Crane was immobile once more. Half of him badly wanted to pull the trigger and blast Worthington back into whatever hell had spawned him. The other half flatly refused, concerned only for the well-being of his family. He aimed the gun at Worthington, lowered it, and raised it once more. Conscience *versus* love – whatever he did would be a crushing defeat. He knew what he wanted – to keep his family from harm and to rid the world of the bloodthirsty creature that was Jack Worthington. But he couldn't do both. He couldn't risk Irene and his sons being murdered, and he couldn't abide the thought of them living in a world where Worthington was free to commit mayhem. And he couldn't possibly make a deal with the man. He was paralysed by indecision.

He was saved from having to make that impossible choice when something hard and metallic was pressed against his temple. Fleming had regained consciousness and was holding a gun to his head. At last Crane relaxed. He even smiled when Fleming prised the Webley from his unresisting fingers.

He was still smiling when two SIS men drove him back to Whitehall.

Wheatley knocked on the door of the Yellow Room less than fifteen minutes after Crane arrived for work the next morning. The room had been tidied and cleaned, thankfully, and Crane's stock of tea, sugar, milk and biscuits had been replenished. The first brew of his working day was stewing nicely when Wheatley turned up.

'I've been speaking to Hore-Belisha,' Wheatley told him. 'He put me in the picture about what happened yesterday. He wanted to carpet you but it seems he would prefer to cover it up in case your actions reflected badly on him. Luckily that fellow you shot is going to be alright – the bullet missed his vital organs. If he'd died I think Hore-Belisha would have had no choice but to disown you. Between you and me, I think you tried to do the right thing. I know you think I'm a bit of an ass but if you've read any of my books you'll know I have no time for people like Worthington, none at all. The world would be better off without him. Hore-Belisha told me you had the chance but didn't shoot him. Why on earth didn't you do it?'

Crane shrugged. 'He gave me an impossible choice. Let him go or see my wife and child killed. As it turned out, Fleming made the choice for me.'

'But I don't understand. You seem quite calm about it – almost cheerful.'

'Oh, I'm not at all cheerful, Wheatley. I don't think anything but time will repair the scars this business has left on my spirit. But I do feel strangely calm and at ease with myself. That's because Worthington made me realise that

I'm not the kind of man who could make a choice like that. And you know what? It made me think better of myself. I may not be a hero like those brave souls who put to sea bound for Dunkirk but I've found out that I'm a man who will stand up to do the right thing – and is unable to do the right thing when two rights make a wrong.'

Wheatley shook his head in bewilderment. Crane really was becoming impossibly cryptic lately. It was spending so much time in this ghastly yellow room that was doing it, surely. Being in the company of all those psychics probably didn't help.

Portsmouth on a June morning wasn't much better than Portsmouth at any other time of year, so Crane thought. The last time he'd been there was in 1935 when he and Irene passed through the town in the old Morris, having opted to take the scenic route to their honeymoon in Cornwall. It was very different now, seething with soldiers and sailors, and festooned with barrage balloons.

Wheatley had surprised Crane by telling him when and where Worthington was going to take ship for the United States. 'I thought you might want to see him off, old chap – you know, make sure he's really left the country.' Crane was touched. Wheatley may have been a fool but he had shown that his heart was in the right place. He was almost beginning to like the man. Time and further idiocy would probably cure him of that.

Now he stood by the gangway as Worthington approached. The American grinned when he saw who had come to see him off.

'My, you do look miserable. Don't feel too bad about

it, Tony. Even if you had any proof I wouldn't be punished. Washington wants to keep this under wraps as much as Whitehall does. I'll go wherever Uncle Sam sends me and when the USA enters the war I'll be shooting down German boys instead of taking my pleasure with the ladies. When the war ends, I'll take up where I left off. There's a neighbour back in Philly who shares my taste in women, if you get my meaning. Sam's promised me his daughter, says I can do whatever I like with her. I haven't decided yet – I might do to her what I did to the others; or I might do something else, maybe start a family. There's plenty of time to figure that out. Little Louise is just sweet sixteen and I don't know when I'll be around to show her what I've decided. I know how to wait, though. I'm a hunter, Crane – and the first thing a hunter learns is patience. When I'm done with her I think I might move to California. The weather's better there.'

Crane was puzzled. 'You want children?' Somehow he couldn't imagine that Worthington had a paternal bone in his body.

'Shit, no,' Worthington laughed. 'I want a dynasty, Crane, a little friendly competition to spice things up. I don't really know how I came to be the way I am, but I have this theory that if you raise a kid the right way he has a good chance of turning out just like me. I've read Freud and Kraft-Ebbing, and I've studied the lives of those who came before me. It's a question of realising potential. I've already helped Lacerato and Praefoco on their way. You'll be reading about them in the newspapers one day, Crane. You'll hear about them and many more of their kind. One day you'll hear the Name again and know what it means.'

Worthington snapped into a military salute, turned smartly on his heel and strode toward the waiting vessel. Crane watched him board, momentarily wishing he still had Archibald's Webley. One bullet might save a lot of suffering. One bullet would avenge the suffering that had already been visited upon the women Worthington had murdered. But that bullet would also endanger his family. He turned away, feeling as helpless as he had on that dreadful night in Surbiton.

Suddenly, his mood began to change. The American and British governments both knew what Worthington was, yet they were refusing to act for the sake of diplomacy, the war effort and public morale. Didn't the fools realise that turning a blind eye to brutal murder for the sake of political expedience made them as bad as the Nazis? Didn't they understand that they couldn't claim the moral high ground when they too acted immorally? Were they unable to comprehend that cynical lies and cowardly deceit made them calculated propagandists in the same vein as the despicable Joseph Goebbels? Did they feel nothing for those poor women and their families?

He was raging inwardly by the time he reached the car. That was good – the heat of anger was better than the guilt and horror he had been feeling for the past few weeks. And he had made a decision. Yes, the Yellow Room would continue to fulfil its function as an unacknowledged part of the nation's defences and an arm in the fight against the Nazis. Other German agents remained at large, as did the men known as Frater Lacerato and Frater Praefoco, and Worthington's driver. The Yellow Room would be on the look-out for them. But Crane would ensure that they also watched their own political and military masters very closely indeed. They could not be allowed to fall into the habit of despotism.

There was more than one enemy within.

The Confabulists Club

Edward Vance sipped his pint of bitter and took a bite from his cheese and onion sandwich. He chewed slowly, savouring the taste, making the most of every mouthful. The bread was slightly stale and he'd used an entire week's cheese ration to make it but it was nice to eat something that was both tasty and filling. Ham and bacon were scarce and it was likely that cheese would soon follow. There probably wouldn't be too many more thickly-filled sandwiches for the likes of him in the near future.

He wasn't a materialistic man – all he really wanted to do was work at his trade, to act and scratch out a living – but the war had brought home to him one simple truth: money could buy safety, comfort and a reasonably full belly. The docks and aerodromes were no longer teeming with the well-tailored, bejewelled and fur-coated, all eager to do their patriotic duty *in absentia*, but that was only because they'd all gone to safe havens in New York, Rio de Janeiro and Lisbon. At least the King and his family had made it clear that they were staying put, not that Vance gave a tinker's damn one way or the other. When it came to the aristocracy, Vance sometimes thought the Bolsheviks had the right idea – put the buggers up against a wall and give them a practical demonstration of popular feeling. The idea that someone was special, better than other people just because of their ancestry, seemed to him to encapsulate all that was wrong with his species – idolising people because of their lineage or their bank balance; or because their carefully made-up faces flickered prettily on a silver screen. But the alternatives history had so far provided were just as bad. Robespierre and the Terror that had followed the French Revolution; what Cromwell did in the aftermath of the Civil War in England; Lenin's brutal suppression of dissent in post-revolutionary Russia. And now the Soviet Union had Stalin and the Nazis were busily rewriting the book on the evil that can be created by one charismatic man in the right circumstances. He shook his head sadly and drained the last few drops from his glass.

He stood awkwardly and limped to the bar for another pint. His leg was playing up again. That was doubly annoying because it was the leg he'd left on the Somme many years before. How the hell can you get cramp in toes that aren't there? How can a vanished knee become arthritic? Oh well, at least there was beer, at least until that too became a refuge only the rich could afford.

As he turned away from the bar with his freshly filled glass his attention was caught by a small poster on the wall by the hearth. Something called the Confabulists Club was holding events once a month in a pub called the Boar's Head in Soho. According to the poster the Confabulists Club was in need of short stories. Aspiring writers could submit their masterpieces to the Club secretary who would select the best and arrange to have them read aloud by professional actors. The successful authors would also be given a free drink on the night. It was, thought Vance, a foolproof money-spinner. In the weeks or months ahead – perhaps years, if the last European conflict was any yardstick – people would need all the entertainment they could get. There were hundreds of would-be authors out there who would be deliriously happy to see their stories have a public airing. The pub would do well out of it. The Confabulists Club would surely turn a nice profit. Money made, egos flattered and a good night out for all – it couldn't go wrong. The real prize, as far as Vance was concerned, was that they needed actors to read the stories and would pay five shillings a session. That would nicely augment the meagre interest from his capital and his war pension, his sole income other than occasional small payments for minor parts in stage productions or as a film extra. There wasn't much demand for one-legged leading men of his age but he could stand around looking aimless in crowd scenes with the best of them. The Confabulists Club wanted references, naturally, but would hold auditions anyway. And the next audition was that very afternoon. He looked at the pub's clock – it was two hours away yet so he had plenty of time for another pint and to retrieve those references from his lodgings. This was an opportunity he wasn't going to miss.

Vance had heard of the Boar's Head, a regular haunt of London's bohemian set. It had a small function room for music and dancing, two large bars and several smaller rooms that could be hired by the hour for meetings. Vance presumed there were other rooms set aside for other, less licit purposes. It was Soho, after all.

Matthew Sanders, co-founder and secretary of the Confabulists Club, was seated at a small table with a very large gin and tonic, polishing thick-lensed spectacles with a napkin. He was tall and thin, around thirty years old, and seemed exceedingly bored. He was also quite handsome, in a world-weary, dissipated way. The pencil moustache made him look like a lanky Errol Flynn after an epic night on the tiles. His face lit up when he saw Vance.

'Are you here for the audition? Bona – do come in.'

Vance immediately recognised a fellow member of the necessarily twilight world of his own sexual persuasion. Sanders' gestures and mode of speech were by no means camp, yet he had that indefinable air which enabled people like them to recognise one another. It was clear from the man's greeting and knowing smile that the recognition was mutual. Vance rather fancied him but there were formalities to be observed, safeguards that had to be met unless one wanted to risk imprisonment and a prurient paragraph or two in the *News of the World*. More than one of Vance's friends had been had up on charges of gross indecency and the experience had been far from pleasant. Besides, this was business. Anything else could wait.

'You must be the only omi in the Smoke to varda one of those bloody posters. I've had nanti takers so far. Plant your dish in that chair and let's have a polari. First off, if you've never heard of us, the Confabulists Club has been going for about a year now. The idea was to give aspiring writers an outlet for their stories and at the same time turn it into a bit of entertainment. We select three stories each month from the ones we receive. Luckily, it's our chairman and treasurer, Bill Murdoch and Margaret Decker, who read the entries and pick the winners. Between you and me, most of the stories we get are terrible. I'd probably end up bloody shooting myself if I had to read them all. The three that get through are read out in the function room and we print the best five each quarter in our magazine, *The Confabulist*. We charge a tanner to get in, and a fifth of the dinari goes to the landlord. On a good night we can get a hundred people, sometimes more – all the winners bring their friends and family, and we get a decent number of people who just want a bit of fun. We even get some magazine editors and publishers on the varda for new talent. They'll be bloody lucky. Right, that's enough about us. Tell me about yourself.'

'Nanti to say, really,' Vance replied, deciding that he rather fancied Sanders. 'I lost a lally at the Somme, which meant my original ambition to be a hoofer or a serious actor went down the khazi. Over the past few years I've done a bit of theatre and film work, mostly as an extra. If it wasn't for that and a small inheritance I'd be on the national handbag. I've got my references here.'

'Fantabulosa. Don't bother with the refs, sweetheart. You've got bona diction, a dolly eek and a bit of butch presence. Better than the last old fruit we had – she put the palone in omi-palone, know what I mean? Mincing around the stage like a tart on the troll. The missing stimp won't make any difference. Flat feet and naff ogles kept me out of uniform. Lucky for me and the army both, I reckon. Is five bob a night alright? And I'll park you a buckshee buvare.'

'I could use the metzas and I never say nishta to a free schlumph. When's the next event?'

'Two weeks from now, the thirtieth of April. Seven o'clock on the onk – I hope you can make it or we're charvered. We've already had to cancel one night and if we had to do it again the regulars would give up on us and go to another bungery. It would be bona nochy to the Confabulists Club.'

The turn-out was impressive. There must have been fifty or sixty people crammed into that function room and they were all drinking like fish. Sanders was flitting about from one group of people to the next, leaving Vance to read through the selected stories and familiarise himself with their pace and mood. Luckily there was no requirement to learn the texts by heart. All he had to do was get up on stage, read and add a spot of character. It would be easy money. He was a good sight-reader and didn't suffer from stage-fright. When you've endured bullets, shells and gas – not to mention lying for nearly twenty-four hours with a shattered leg in a trench stinking of excrement, urine and dead comrades – it takes more than a few dozen noisy drunks to worry you.

Vance had cleared his new job with Anthony Crane, who agreed that the Yellow Room could probably manage without Vance's talents for one Wednesday evening a month. Indeed, Crane had seemed positively eager for Vance to take the job. Presumably that was his way of expressing his gratitude to Vance, who had played a significant part in each of the Yellow Room's major tasks to date – the Heligoland Affair, the Worthington Case and the

Doorless Room Mystery, the last of which had caused poor Tompkins' breakdown.

Now, as he read through the stories he became aware that someone was watching him. Most people have that additional sense that tells them they are being observed, at least to a degree. In Vance, because of his psychometric talents, the faculty was well-developed. He looked up to see a familiar figure, the Yellow Room's very own consulting magician.

Aleister Crowley looked terrible. He had lost a lot of weight and looked much older than his sixty-five years. Vance knew Crowley was a long-term heroin addict, but even so the change was shocking. The last time he had seen Crowley, over a year previously, the Great Beast had been composed, confident and still fat. Now he seemed frail, uncertain and gaunt. Perhaps it was down to rationing and the declining quality of what food was available; or maybe he had increased his intake of heroin. Perhaps it was both. Crowley was staring hard at him, perhaps trying to decide whether to make an approach. To Vance's surprise, Crowley's face relaxed. He smiled and waved at Vance, then made his way unsteadily between the knots of drinkers.

'Vance, just the fellow I wanted to see,' said Crowley. 'Crane told me you were reading the stories here now. One of them is mine, you know.'

Puzzled, Vance leafed through the sheets of paper in his hand. As far as he could see the three stories were by Alfred Horn, Tony Bales and Caitlin Weinberg.

'Sorry, Crowley,' replied Vance. 'I don't see your story here.'

Crowley produced a conspiratorial grin from his facial

repertoire. 'I'm Caitlin Weinberg,' he whispered. 'It wouldn't really be good form to provide a secret document under my own name, would it?'

'Secret document? What in the world are you talking about?'

'Crane has had me working on a ritual to influence a senior Nazi to defect. No names, no pack-drill – but we're attempting to influence one of his top advisers on occultism to persuade the man to try to make peace. The story is a disguised incantation. Take a good look around you, man. All your Yellow Room colleagues are here. Crane is trying something new. The idea is that the incantation will help you make contact with this chap we're targeting, and that will be amplified by the other Yellow Room specialists. They in turn will try to use the latent psychic abilities of tonight's crowd to further increase the signal strength. Crane didn't want you to know until the last minute – something about not wanting to cause you any stress. I will be upstairs in a room directly above your little podium performing an act of magick to kick the whole thing off. I've acquired the services of a big, strapping member of the Household Cavalry for the occasion. I'm rather looking forward to it. It might take my mind off my troubles.'

'You have troubles? I'm sorry to hear that, Crowley. What's the matter?'

'Oh, it's nothing of concern, merely the usual things that plague men of my age: the feebleness of that which was once strong; the disappearance of fortune and fame; and the waning of one's powers of attraction. Time was when I would never have had to pay a soldier for this kind of assistance. I'm also somewhat embarrassed to admit that I asked Crane for funds for my part in this venture. But Soror Morphinum is a harsh and demanding mistress.'

Vance took a closer look at Crowley's story. It barely made sense. The sentence structure was odd and the prose changed bewilderingly from short, staccato utterances to gentle, rhythmic passages and back again, seemingly at random. The characters had unusual, polysyllabic names. Their dialogue was incomprehensible and some, Vance was sure, unpronounceable.

'What's this word? "Ohooohaatan"? What on earth does it mean?'

'It's pronounced OHOOOHAATAN,' Crowley loftily corrected him. 'It's the Enochian name of the Great Elemental King of Fire, who this rite is designed to invoke. He shall be the key to ensuring that our target is gifted with the inspirational wherewithal to influence the Nazi in question. While you read the story I shall utter a subsidiary invocation, once my soldier-boy has suitably prepared me.'

Vance knew what Crowley's magickal technique involved: the attainment of sexual ecstasy. In the mid-1930s he had met Victor Neuberg, who had been the Great Beast's magickal partner for some time. According to Neuberg, the infamous magician preferred to take his magical preparation *in ano*. Each man to his own, thought Vance, whose personal opinion was that it was better to give than to receive. He wondered if Sanders was of a like mind – that might be a problem, though by no means an insurmountable one.

As he mounted the podium, Vance spotted Anthony Crane leaning on the bar with a pint of bitter in one hand and a cigarette smouldering in the other. Crane pretended to ignore him. Then, at a nearby table, he saw Miss Bingham, Mrs Pugh, Charles Bartley and William Simmons. They all had drinks in front of them but seemed to be in too dreamy a state to consume their tipples. He assumed Crane had hypnotised his colleagues. He wondered for a moment where Calum Archibald was, then remembered that he had been in Brighton looking after his elderly mother, who was in a bad way after suffering a fall and breaking several bones.

The first story, a sentimental boy-meets-girl romance, wasn't badly received. There were some catcalls and a few would-be amusing comments from Alfred Horn's friends, but otherwise it met with polite applause. When he had finished, Vance went to the bar for a quick half of light ale to wet his whistle. Crane was nowhere to be seen.

While he was reading Mr Bales' story, an inane comedy revolving around a calamitous attempt to buy black market bananas, he saw Crane leading Calum Archibald to the table where the other Yellow Room people were sitting. Vance was surprised to see him – presumably the Scot's mother had either improved or died, as there was no way he would have been in London if the poor old girl had still been poorly. Archibald sat and stared straight ahead, not acknowledging his colleagues. He too had been hypnotised. Crane glanced up at Vance and nodded.

Another bottle of light ale later, Vance stood on the podium and began to read the bizarre story submitted by 'Miss Caitlin Weinberg'. Fortunately, Crowley had given him a quick lesson in the pronunciation of Enochian, supposedly the language of angels, so the strange words and names sounded solemn and impressive rather than weirdly comical. As he read, silence fell. Except for the entranced Yellow Room people, who were staring into space, everyone in the function room was looking at him, spellbound by the meandering, meaningless story. Halfway through, he felt a crackle of electricity and his hair stood on end. By then people had even stopped moving. The whole room seemed frozen. Vance could smell roses and ozone, and he could feel a presence, something gigantic yet intangible hovering around him. Then the temperature rose rapidly and he began to sweat. By the time he finished the story he was gasping for air and would cheerfully have killed for a cool breeze or a sip of iced water. He had a sudden flash of vision, a momentary glimpse of a man with a greying moustache, dressed in old-fashioned clothing, and an intense-looking, thickly-browed younger man. Did he know the latter? He couldn't remember.

The impression flickered out and the strange atmosphere abruptly collapsed. The audience seemed to sag collectively, and the temperature returned to normal, leaving him dripping wet. From somewhere there came a short cry of pain and fear. The Yellow Room people awoke. Archibald put his head in his hands and began to weep, joined almost immediately by Miss Bingham and Mrs Pugh. The men were ashen. Vance could feel it, too. Something was wrong.

A burly man in a hastily-buttoned khaki uniform pushed through the bemused punters and spoke urgently to Crane, who caught Vance's eye and beckoned to him.

Crowley was sitting naked in the middle of the room. It

wasn't a pretty sight. The soldier had vanished, preferring to melt quietly into the night than stand around hoping to receive his payment for the services he had rendered the Great Beast – presumably he'd thought there was a good chance the police would be summoned. Crane seemed unconcerned by the man's disappearance. He was focused on Crowley, whose face was a picture of anguish.

'Crowley, what's wrong? Did that fellow hurt you?'

The magician strove to compose himself. 'No, Crane – that part was most satisfactory. But the rest...' He trailed off, shaking his head.

'What happened?' Vance demanded.

'It was the elemental, OHOOOHAATAN. It required a fee, a payment. They all do. Like a fool, I agreed without a second thought. I assumed it would be the usual sort of thing – a piece of wood or coal, a box of matches, perhaps some petroleum. Elementals rarely ask for more than a token, usually something small they can consume. But tonight is May Eve, one of the times when the walls between worlds are at their thinnest. It was more powerful than I could have imagined. I tried to argue but those things are beyond reason, especially when they're hungry. For a moment I thought it was going to get very bad, like the night I invoked Pan – or worse still, that other time when I – no, I don't even want to think about that. Whatever opinion you may have of me, I'm not an evil man, Crane; and I never intended that. I did what I could but those poor people...'

Crane had found a flask of brandy somewhere among Crowley's clothing. The magician took a long drink from it.

'I couldn't control OHOOOHAATAN at all. It made

me agree to give it whatever it wanted. If I had known I would have let it burn my flesh to ashes. But I had no idea, I swear to you – no idea at all.'

Suddenly, Vance felt sick. He knew he was about to hear something truly appalling. He could smell singed hair, roasting meat, charred wood and plaster, seared mortar. He imagined a droning sound, high overheard, then another and another until they merged into cacophony. He felt sudden waves of intense pressure, shockwaves pulverising his body – then anxiety, terror, pain and grief, the emotions of strangers. He knew what Crowley was going to say next.

'I'd already agreed. There was nothing I could do once the bargain had been made,' Crowley whispered, his eyes wide with horror. Tears ran down his cheeks and the Great Beast sobbed. 'It wants a city.'

At a quarter past ten the following evening, the first bomb landed on Merseyside. It was the first of 2,434 bombs, including incendiary devices, to be dropped on the area by the *Luftwaffe* in the first seven days of May, 1941. Ships, cargo berths and homes were destroyed or damaged, and there were many casualties. It wasn't the first aerial assault on the Liverpool area and it wouldn't be the last, but it was the most protracted and intense. By the morning of the eighth day, Crowley was inconsolable.

'I know you all think I'm a bit of a cad,' he told Vance, who had volunteered to stay with Crowley to make sure the man didn't do anything foolish with a hypodermic needle and a too-large dose of heroin. 'And heaven knows I don't often see eye to eye with either our government or the public. But this is still my country, Vance. More than that, I don't like to see people hurt through no fault of their own. Oh, I couldn't care less if an idiot reaps the harvest of his own stupidity, but the innocent should always be protected from the folly of others. People have died because of my arrogance, my carelessness – my folly. Children have died, children.'

Crowley was a big man, but to Vance he now seemed smaller, shrunken in some way beyond the physical decline Vance had remarked a week earlier. He'd heard that Crowley was devoid of sentimentality except where children were concerned. The man had several of his own and by all accounts loved them dearly. But this seemed something deeper than even grief. He remembered what Mikaiel Dakessian had told Crane the previous summer. The Great Beast had lost something, or it had been taken away – perhaps one botched magickal working too many. He could be relied upon as a consultant but not as a specialist or operative. Despite Dakessian's assessment Crowley had remained outwardly lively and confident. But the decline had been steep and swift. Was this the same man who had them all in stitches not twelve months earlier with his hilarious imitations of Winston Churchill? Was this the man who had worked for the intelligence services during the Great War and had done so ever since in one way or another?

'Look, you weren't to know,' Vance replied. 'As you said, elementals are normally satisfied with only small payments.'

Crowley wasn't having it. 'Vance, I should have at least considered the possibility. It was my arrogance, my vanity. An ordinary elemental would have done just as well – but no, I had to summon their damned king because I wanted to talk to the organ-grinder, not the bloody monkey. You know, I'm seriously thinking of packing it all in – retiring to the seaside, some dreadful place like Hastings where I can paint and write in peace. Do you know, yesterday afternoon I actually went into a church and came within a whisker of praying for forgiveness? Me: the Great Beast, Perdurabo, the Wickedest Man in the World – praying to a metaphor!'

The magician seemed as horrified by that as he had been by the destruction and loss of life on Merseyside. That flash of conceit reassured Vance just a little. 'Do you think it's over? Will the Luftwaffe return to Liverpool tonight?'

Crowley shrugged. 'It's probably finished now. Seven has a mystical significance, and I suspect the cycle has now been completed. That bastard creature OHOOOHAATAN has had its city. I sincerely hope he it hasn't developed a taste for it. The greater elementals rarely seek out humans to make a pact but it has been known. Can you imagine what the Nazis would do with a few pet elementals at their disposal? The weather would always be on their side and they could raise the intensity of incendiary attacks without even having to puff on them. Oh, I have no doubt that the Luftwaffe will bomb Liverpool again but it surely won't be as bad.'

'At least it's only an elemental,' Vance tried to lighten the mood. 'Think what Adolf could do with a couple of regiments of vampires! It's a good job those buggers don't exist.'

Crowley looked at him strangely. He seemed about to say something serious but instead forced a thin smile. 'Yes, the Orlok, Dracula and Varney regiments. Or perhaps they will take a leaf out of Victor Frankenstein's book and reassemble all their dead troops to make new ones. Boris Karloff and Bela Lugosi would look quite dapper in SS uniforms, don't you think?'

He turned away to gaze out of the window. 'I was convinced that it was a better idea than Fleming's half-baked scheme. For crying out loud – fake horoscopes? Did the bloody fool really think the Germans would fall for that? They've got their own damned astrologers, for heaven's sake!'

'Liverpool and the rogue elemental aside, do you think the procedure worked?'

'I don't know. I've tried for years to make magick more scientific but the truth is that outcomes are still unpredictable. I got into a bit of a state and completely lost my thread after OHOOOHAATAN sprang that little surprise on me. Frankly, I have no idea.'

Two days later, just after eleven in the evening, a Messerschmitt Bf 110D crashed in Scotland. The pilot parachuted to safety, landing near the village of Eaglesham, where he was confronted by a ploughman. His name, he told the farm-worker, was *Hauptmann* Alfred Horn. Horn told the ploughman he had a message for the Duke of Hamilton. The ploughman called the Home Guard, who took the German into custody.

Two days after that, Anthony Crane received a telephone call from Winston Churchill himself, instructing him to report to the aerodrome at Stanmore, where he was to board an aircraft for Scotland. He was to take one of his best operatives, but it would need to be someone who could be trusted to keep their mouth shut. And they would still require special vetting by SIS.

'I can trust all my people to be discreet,' said Crane reprovingly. 'There will be no need to pry into their private affairs.' He didn't care that Churchill was Prime Minister; no one was going to delve too deeply into the Yellow Room people's lives if he could help it.

Churchill chuckled. 'I wish I could say the same for my people. Very well, Crane. If you trust them to that extent, I'll trust your judgement. You're one of the few people I actually do trust to do a proper job. If SIS and the War Office think you're a crackpot that practically proves you're trustworthy. Bloody idiots – most of them don't know their arse from their elbow but here they are, running the country in wartime. You must come to Downing Street for dinner one evening. We can broach a bottle of brandy and you can enlighten me as to exactly what the Yellow Room does. Your reports are fascinating but I'm sure the Yellow Room can't be as – ah, *unconventional* as they suggest.'

Crane summoned Vance, telling him to pack an overnight bag and make whatever arrangements he would need to keep his personal business going for a couple of days. When Vance arrived at the War Office, Crane told him nothing until they were in his car and driving toward Stanmore. Indeed, he had little to tell. All he knew was that they were going to Scotland. He had no idea why. And that unaccountably worried him.

At Stanmore they were greeted by a Major Holland of the Royal Sussex Regiment and two military policemen, their escort. They boarded a passenger biplane, an old de Havilland Dominie, actually a DH.89 Dragon Rapide converted for military use. The five of them fitted comfortably into the passenger compartment with a couple of seats to spare. When they were airborne, Holland gave them a very sketchy briefing.

'You are going to Scotland to assist with interrogating a very important prisoner. I can't tell you where and I can't tell you who, because I don't know. That information is on a need to know basis and I don't need to know. This is a very tight operation. I have been instructed to ask if either of you speaks German. We have an interpreter standing by but if any of you are proficient in the language that is one less person who will need to know.'

Crane spoke a little German but expressed doubt that it would adequate for interrogating a prisoner. Holland sighed and said he would have the interpreter standing by to be called in if necessary. The man seemed distracted. Crane suspected Holland knew rather more than he was letting on. Oh well, he thought. He who asks shall be given.

'Why us, Major? We're specialists in several areas but interrogation isn't one of them. Why would Churchill want us to do this?'

Holland was clearly uncomfortable at being confronted on the matter. But he wasn't going to tell them anything. He merely shrugged, set his jaw and opened his *Daily Mirror* to the cartoon page, starting his reading as almost every serviceman did, with the risqué adventures of *Jane*. Crane idly wondered how much clothing Miss Gay would be losing by the end of the strip, then closed his eyes and dozed off.

Crane knew the man immediately. So did Vance, though he

didn't know the man's name. It was the same beetle-browed, anxious face he had seen in that vision on that disturbing evening at the Confabulists Club.

The prisoner sat on one side of a table. Two empty chairs had been placed on the opposite side. Crane gestured for his friend to be seated.

'*Guten abend, Herr Reichsleiter,*' said Crane, with a forced cordiality that could not disguise either his fascination or the repulsion he felt. The man sitting opposite him was the second-highest ranking Nazi, Hitler's deputy. As far as Crane was concerned the Nazi leadership were evil incarnate. He turned to Vance. 'May I present the Deputy *Führer* of the Third Reich, Rudolf Hess.'

Hess peered at each of them in turn then spoke in a mixture of reasonably good English and German Crane could barely understand. 'And who are you? I was not informed of your coming. Is this to be another useless inquisition by people who have no understanding of evil? Must I have more stupid questions about troop movements and tanks?'

The *Reichsleiter* appeared both bored and agitated. His face was expressionless but his eyes jittered, focusing on everything and nothing. Why, Crane thought, he's bloody terrified. And not of us – or anything else that's human, if I'm any judge. He regarded Hess carefully. Out of the corner of his eye he saw Vance reach out and tentatively touch Hess' hand.

'No,' Vance quietly told the German. 'You'll get no stupid questions from us. Tell us what you've seen. We'll believe you.'

'Our expertise is not military,' Crane added. 'We're not

part of the intelligence services, either. We deal in more – er, *unusual* matters. Tell us.'

Hess thought about it for a moment then evidently decided that he had nothing to lose by talking. He sighed and asked if he could have a cigarette. Bartley handed him a Lucky Strike and gave him a light.

'You will hear much nonsense about my presence here,' Hess began. 'I have not come to offer surrender or to sue for peace. But I have come to attempt to make an alliance between our nations. Yes, it is well-known that I am a friend to Great Britain and deeply regret that we are at war. But the most important thing I came here to tell you is that you have more to fear than Germany and our allies; at least, *most* of our allies.'

Crane knew at once that he was going to learn something fearful, something that the War Office and the military would be unable to comprehend. This was going to be wholly Yellow Room territory. 'Go on,' he told Hess.

'It began on the last day of April, the eve of May – *Walpurgisnacht*, when witches and evil spirits are traditionally said to be abroad. I was having a private meeting with the *Führer* – a light meal, a discussion of strategy, our political philosophy. It was a convivial meeting, as always. The *Führer* was confident of further victories in the field, and of swaying some hitherto neutral nations into joining us. But then he started talking about the Jews and something – something – happened to him. It was as if he suddenly inflated, became taller and more muscular. His eyes seemed to glow. There was a strange smell in the room, like bad eggs and bleach. It was disturbing, horrible.'

Hess leaned forward. Crane noticed that the man's

hands were shaking, and the worried eyes seemed to wobble alarmingly.

'I am no lover of the Jews. I am a proud German and proud to be a National Socialist. I believe in our cause. Believe me when I tell you that our goal has always been the removal of Jews from the Fatherland. It is unfortunate that there have been many incidents in which many Jews have died. But situations can easily go out of control when there are young, hot-headed men involved, men who do not understand that rhetoric is not always to be taken literally. I do not dispute it. But massacre was not officially sanctioned or intended. But that night the *Führer* began to talk not merely of removal but *extermination*. I am not a coward but I became frightened. When the *Führer* spoke it was as if he was possessed by something terrible. Then I thought I caught of an entity that appeared to be surrounding him – it seemed to be superimposed upon him. It was a being made of fire and sparks and consuming hunger. And it was not alone. There was something inside him, something worse. Then the *Führer* started to talk about the Soviet Union. It was imperative that we attack Russia sooner rather than later, he said. If we waited, Stalin would attack Germany. The Third Reich must not only be prepared for Russian aggression, he said – we must make a pre-emptive strike. I demurred, insisting that it was not prudent. But he was adamant. When I tried to convince him that it be an act of utmost folly, he grew angry with me. I pretended to be swayed by his argument and he – or rather the thing within him – calmed down.'

Crane was impassive. 'What are you suggesting – that Hitler is possessed by a demon? We operate in the realm of what many people would call supernatural but my belief has always been that so-called supernatural phenomena are merely natural occurrences that science has not yet named or explored.'

'Only a few weeks ago I might have agreed with you. I do not believe in magic or the old Aryan gods, like Himmler and his circle. But if had seen him – if you had heard what he said, if you had *smelled* him...'

Crane and Vance glanced at each other as Hess lapsed into silence and stared helplessly at the table-top. Vance somehow knew that this would be a delicate drawing-out of information. They had to reel Hess in gradually.

'Why did you call yourself Alfred Horn?' Vance was curious as to Hess' reasons for naming himself after the author of one of the stories he had read out at the Confabulists Club.

Hess shrugged. 'I don't know. It just seemed to pop into my head the next day, as I was discussing the *Führer* with my friend Karl Haushofer. That was when I decided to come to Scotland. The Duke of Hamilton was once a friend and I know he has influence. I was hoping he could help me persuade your government to end hostilities so we could join forces to do something about the *Führer*. You may think National Socialism is evil – I disagree, though I will admit that the Party has elements I would prefer not to be there, and who have committed acts of violence and depravity in the Party's name. We want peace and stability in a Europe that is strong against the Bolshevik threat. But if the *Führer* – this new Hitler I do not recognise – has his way then the Party's name, my country's name, will be reviled forever. And I believe that if the Bolsheviks prevail, what Stalin will do may make you wish for our return.'

'What do you think we can do?' Crane was disquieted by the *Reichsleiter*'s story. He caught Vance's eye and raised an eyebrow. Vance nodded solemnly. Hess' story was completely potty but if Vance thought the Nazi was telling the truth that was good enough for Crane.

Hess looked up from the table at last and held Crane's gaze. 'I want to see two very special men. They can give me what I need to defeat or at least neutralise the creature inside the *Führer*. When that is done I can take more conventional measures. When these men have given me the means to do so, you must return me to Germany so I can eliminate Hitler.'

'Tell me it wasn't us,' said Vance, the level, quiet voice not masking his inner turmoil. He and Crane had left Hess and retreated to a private room that had been set aside for them. 'Tell me it wasn't that bloody ritual we conducted at the Confabulists Club.'

'Sorry, old man.' Crane's eyes were haunted and old-looking. He lit a cigarette, with a great deal of difficulty because his hands were shaking so badly. He stared out of the window, visibly struggling to retain his composure. 'Haushofer was the target – he and Hess have been close friends for some time. As you know, Hess is an Anglophile and never wanted a war between our countries. The idea was to influence Haushofer to plant a seed in Hess' mind, one that would lead him to overthrow Hitler. Hess is one of the few men in Germany powerful enough to do it and get away with it. He's neurotic enough to be turned relatively easily, given a persuasive enough argument. Yes, it must have been our doing. The phenomena Hess describes are much as we would have expected; and the timing is exact. Instead of using an elemental to nudge a minor player, we somehow contrived to insert what sounds horribly like a demonic entity into a man who may already have been one of the most dangerous and powerful lunatics on the planet. We ended up removing from the scene one of our best hopes of getting rid of Adolf. All that and what happened to Liverpool. I didn't even think demons really existed. It's quite a cock-up, eh? Oh God, this is bloody dreadful. Is there any chance you could be wrong?'

'No, I'm sure Hess was telling the truth – at least, it was the truth as he saw it. Whether it was real is another matter. Personally I can't imagine anything that would make Hitler worse than he already was. I suppose it could be a delusion that only seems to relate to our ritual; though there comes a point where one can no longer invoke coincidence. What are you going to do about his request?'

'I'll have a word with Churchill but I have a bad feeling about it, Vance. In the first place, hardly anyone in the military or the government is going to listen to our opinion. Secondly, the War Office, SIS and the Cabinet are not going to allow Hess to return to Germany. He's too big a prize to let go, even if they were willing to trust him to get rid of Hitler.'

'I can understand Hess asking for Crowley but I don't know anything about this Austin Osman Spare fellow. Who is he?'

'Spare is a painter, an exceptionally talented but rather strange man. I know him, as it happens. My father was an amateur artist, actually travelled to Paris to meet the

Surrealists, and he thought Spare was the greatest draughtsman this country has ever produced. I saw quite a bit of Spare when I was a child – he was always talking about magic and gave me a few practical demonstrations of what he could do, which is why I became interested in psychical phenomena in the first place. When my father died in '36 he left instructions that I was to make sure Spare was looked after by their other chums. I drop in on him from time to time. He used to be a pleasant fellow but I hear he's become decidedly odd. You'll understand what I mean when you meet him. He lives at the Elephant and Castle. I'll get the War Office to bring him up here.'

'Another magician – that could be useful. Why haven't you brought him in as a consultant, or even as an operative?'

'As I said, Spare's an odd sort of chap, highly unpredictable. The last time I saw him was early in '39, when I went to an exhibition he was holding in the White Bear in Kennington Park Road. He was living in squalor, surrounded by stray cats, and didn't seem particularly interested in human company. He predicted the war, though. And he loathed the Nazis. I remember he said that by the time we came to our senses and realised what Hitler was, it would be too late and that millions would die. He told me that as I worked in the Ministry of War I would be ideally placed to help fight the Nazis in a way that might be instrumental in putting a stop to them, but that I had to be strong and stand up for my beliefs. I remembered that when the war began. It's what inspired me to set up the Yellow Room. Spare's magic works through what he calls sigils, signs that represent what the magician wishes to take place. His theory is that people cannot consciously perform magic. According to Spare the process takes place at an unconscious level and our consciousness only gets in the way. It's almost diametrically opposed to Crowley's magick, which requires intense focus of the will. Yet it's also similar in that it requires alterations in one's state of consciousness. That's why I've been trying various methods of distilling the two approaches to strengthen the innate talents of yourself and the others, inducing hypnotic trance to allow your individual magical abilities to manifest while directing the process from outside. It's worked so far.'

'Are Spare and Crowley acquainted?'

'Oh yes,' Crane grinned. 'And that's another problem. There's some sort of bad blood between them. As I understand it Crowley was once quite enamoured of Spare. Unfortunately for Crowley, Spare is exclusively one for the ladies. The Great Beast was not pleased when Spare rebuffed his advances. Anyway, I'd better get Winston on the blower and tell him what's what.'

'No, you bloody well can't.' Churchill was firm but not remotely polite. He spoke loudly and aggressively. Crane deduced that Winston had been drinking. 'I simply won't have it. Crowley can't be trusted to keep his mouth shut. And I know all about Spare – I paint myself, remember. As it happens no one knows where Spare is anyway. His home was destroyed by an incendiary bomb a couple of days ago. You know he was living above Woolworths at the Elephant and Castle? Well, that isn't there anymore. It's just a pile of ash and rubble now. He has been seen since the air raid, so there's no need to worry about him, but he's gone to ground somewhere. But all that's by the by – the important thing is that we have Reichsleiter Rudolf Hess in our custody. That's a massive propaganda coup, Crane. And he must surely have vital intelligence that we can use. There's no way on this earth that I'm letting him go back to Germany. As far as I'm concerned he's just another mad Nazi who cannot be trusted. SIS and the War Office agree. Hess stays here until the war is over. That is my final decision. You are not to repeat a word of this to anyone. Have I made myself clear?'

Crane swore coarsely as he replaced the receiver. He understood Churchill's stance but his gut told him it was the wrong choice. For one wild moment he considered disobeying the Prime Minister and calling for Crowley. But he knew that would be futile. SIS would have Hess locked up in a hermetically sealed room before Crowley was halfway to Scotland. Somehow he would have to limit the damage himself – the Yellow Room would have to step up to the mark and try to undo what they had done.

Hess didn't even look up when Crane and Vance re-entered the interrogation room. He seemed to guess that his request had been refused. He gave a short, weary laugh. 'I understand,' he sighed. 'Churchill is a very stubborn man. And my story is – well, shall we say it is unusual? I cannot blame Churchill for wanting to keep me as a prize rather than taking a risk. In his position I would probably do the same.'

'I'm sorry,' said Crane, galled to find himself apologising to the second most important man in the Nazi hierarchy. 'I don't think the Prime Minister fully comprehends the situation.'

Hess shook his head and laughed again. 'I do not think Winston Churchill is the kind of man who would easily change his mind. It is a pity, but then I did not come here to bandy words with that drunken buffoon. I was expecting to be allowed to talk with better, more pragmatic men. My aim was to prevent an enormous crime that history will be unable to forgive. I admit that in so doing I hoped to forge an alliance between our countries against the Soviet threat. Hitler will act impetuously and the consequences will be disastrous. It will not be long before Berlin declares war on Moscow; and then the Jewish question will be uppermost in Hitler's mind. Whatever you may think – and whatever Churchill may think – Hitler will use the expectation of Jewish resistance and the conspiratorial ties he believes exist between the different branches of European Jewry as an excuse to resolve the Jewish question once and for all. I see you are sceptical. You think Germany would not be so foolish as to fight a war on two fronts against two formidable foes. But as William Shakespeare wrote in *A Midsummer Night's Dream*: Lord, what fools these mortals be! You two seem to be less foolish than most, so I will tell you one word that will prove the truth of what I am saying: Barbarossa. That word will ruin Germany and bring Eastern Europe under the yoke of communism. And it may not stop there. Very well, it seems I am to spend the duration of the war as a prisoner. It is up to you to do something about it, Herr – I'm sorry, I do not know your name.'

'Laurel,' Crane extemporised, 'and this is my colleague, Mr Hardy.'

'Laurel and – ah, I see. It is a little joke. Most amusing. Of course you will not tell me your real names. That is of no consequence. But I do not think you are SIS. I always find the Fatherland's intelligence services rather unimaginative and I suspect that in that regard the SIS is no better than the Gestapo. No, you two are something else, something less ordinary than mere spies. Well, whatever you are, you must do what is within your power. I have told you all I can.'

In the corridor Vance eyed Crane with tired amusement. 'That's another fine mess you got me into.'

'You think Hess was lying?'

The Great Beast was reclining on a couch, smoking hashish from a meerschaum pipe. 'Of course he was lying. According to my informants in Berlin, Hess was tipped off that Hitler was planning to have him killed. Adolf seems to have decided that Hess was aiming for a quick promotion. I would suggest that Hess came here with his cock and bull story prepared in advance. The idea, I would wager, was to be thought insane so that he wouldn't be interrogated too intensively. Meanwhile, he could sit out the war and keep his fingers crossed that we and our allies would prevail. I daresay he's convinced himself that the lies are all true. The Nazis are good at that.'

'But what makes you so sure?' Vance asked. 'The timing, his description of what happened to Hitler – surely that can't be a coincidence?'

Crowley laughed good-naturedly. The hashish was cheering him up where the heroin had made him only morose. 'My dear chap, the whole point of coincidences is that they always seem so very improbable. If they weren't we would never remark upon them, would we? Believe me,

Vance – Hitler needs no demonic possession to make him wholly unpleasant. In any case, the elemental I summoned, powerful though he is, has no power to possess a human being. Very few entities have that ability. Why, I myself have only ever seen it happen once.'

'When was that?'

Suddenly Crowley seemed uncomfortable. 'Oh, no matter,' he replied in an unconvincingly airy tone. 'You'll just have to take my word for it. All I will say is that it would be a damned sight more spectacular than what Hess described. In fact, I very much doubt that Hess would have lived to tell the tale, in his present form at any rate.'

That was all Crowley would say on the subject. Vance left the magician contentedly sinking deeper into his hashish visions and went off to his job at the Confabulists Club.

Matthew Sanders was in a dreadful huff. Only one story had been submitted for that night's event and it was, he pronounced, completely naff. 'I'm tearing my ends out,' he complained. 'I've charpered high and low for a bijou story we could sling in but there's nanti in the cupboard. That dizzy tart Maggie Decker threw all the old ones in the bin. She might as well have flushed me down the bloody khazi after them. We've got a full house and only one story. They'll go mad! I'd rather plate Hitler than face this lot. I've got a good mind to scarper back to my lattie and hide.'

'Go and have a drinkette, old thing,' Vance said soothingly. 'I'll sort something out.'

Sod it, Vance thought as he mounted the podium several drinks later. *I don't have any stories to read but I can entertain this bloody mob. I'm an actor, for God's sake, and I have the greatest writer in history at my disposal.* He had a large sip of gin and tonic, took a deep breath, and offered a silent prayer to anything that might be listening. Then he launched into a selection of speeches from Shakespeare, beginning with Oberon's final utterance from *A Midsummer Night's Dream*, which he hoped would bring a smile to the face of the delightful Matthew Sanders. He was confident that Matthew would take the hint.

Now, until the break of day,
Through this house each fairy stray.
To the best bride-bed will we,
Which by us shall blessed be;
And the issue there create
Ever shall be fortunate.
So shall all the couples three
Ever true in loving be;
And the blots of Nature's hand
Shall not in their issue stand;
Never mole, hare lip, nor scar,
Nor mark prodigious, such as are
Despised in nativity,
Shall upon their children be.
With this field-dew consecrate,
Every fairy take his gait;
And each several chamber bless,
Through this palace, with sweet peace;
And the owner of it blest
Ever shall in safety rest.
Trip away; make no stay;
Meet me all by break of day.

The midsummer night's dream turned out to be a

nightmare. On the twenty-second of June Germany began Operation Barbarossa – a massive invasion of the Soviet Union. The *Wehrmacht* and its allied forces comprised nearly four million troops, over half a million motor vehicles, including more than three thousand tanks, and three-quarters of a million horses. Three days later Finland joined the fray, taking advantage of the Axis incursion to launch a separate assault on the Soviet Union.

On the last day of June, Crane was ordered to attend a meeting in Downing Street. To his surprise, when he arrived he discovered that his Yellow Room colleague Charles Bartley was already present. Bartley at least had the good grace to be embarrassed but Churchill didn't seem to care one way or the other. Indeed, he was positively ebullient. Crane observed that the Prime Minister was already making inroads into a large brandy, and it was only eleven in the morning.

'Excellent report on that Scottish affair, Crane,' Churchill enthused. 'Now we know what Barbarossa was all about, eh? It's the best news I've had all year. I've just been talking to Bartley here about increasing munitions production. His factories are going to need to produce much more in the coming months – we'll be providing support to the Soviets as well as increasing our own stockpiles. Hitler will never win a war against both us and the Soviet Union, especially one fought on two fronts. And when the Americans enter the war on our side the Nazis' goose will be well and truly cooked. Brandy?'

'No thank you, Prime Minister,' said Crane politely, wondering why Churchill had called him in. The interrogation of Hess had resulted only in their knowing that some sort of disaster was looming. Since that day, nothing more had been heard about the *Reichsleiter*'s bewildering appearance in Scotland. There had been no announcements in Parliament, nothing on the radio or cinema newsreels, and the press were apparently ignorant. Crane wondered why Churchill was sitting on his propaganda coup. He wondered why propaganda was even necessary. Surely being in the right was enough? Was there any need to use the Nazis' own tactics when the Nazi ideology was supposed to be the very thing they did not want to take root in Great Britain?

'I was thinking about what our German guest wanted from us,' said Churchill, rummaging in a desk drawer and producing a large cigar, which he unwrapped, cut and dunked in the remains of his brandy. 'Is there any way we could use Crowley and Spare to do what our guest wanted without involving the guest?'

Not bloody likely, thought Crane, uneasily. *Not after that fiasco with the elemental. I don't want any more cities on my conscience.* 'I don't think so, Prime Minister,' he replied. 'The technique is unreliable at best. Personally, I doubt that it would work. Besides, Crowley is a hopeless drug addict and Spare's incommunicado.'

'Yes,' said Bartley. 'That last attempt was a bad show.' He clammed up when Crane kicked his foot, which was fortunately shielded from Churchill by the large mahogany desk.

Churchill tutted and puffed on the cigar. 'That's a shame. It would be nice to have Adolf out of the picture when things start to warm up. But I suppose it's for the best. Crowley is a disgraceful man and Spare is an enigma.

We shall have to use what we've got – a stiff upper lip and the bulldog spirit. Well, thank you, gentlemen. Good day to you.'

Bartley stood but Crane remained firmly seated. Churchill squinted at him through a cloud of cigar smoke. 'Yes? Was there something else?'

'What about the Jews, Prime Minister? Our "guest" said that this would kick off an extermination programme. We're going to arm the Soviet Union, and God knows Stalin is almost as unpleasant as Hitler, and he too is no lover of Jews. What are we going to do to help the Jews?'

Churchill regarded him silently for a minute. 'Why,' he said at last, 'we shall do the best thing we can do to help them. We shall win this war.'

On the twenty-third of July, Crane abruptly decided that the mood of the Yellow Room had become intolerable. He and Vance were haunted by the prospect not only of war on a hitherto-unimagined scale but also Hitler's supposed determination to extirpate Europe's Jews. Bartley was exhausted by the new demands being made on his factories, and was constantly worrying over supplies of raw materials and labour. Ethel Bingham, who had recently taken up with a tank-driver assigned to the 7th Armoured Division, was fretting because her young man had just been sent out to a secret destination, which her cards indicated was North Africa. Mrs Pugh was upset because her pub had been badly damaged by the Luftwaffe a week earlier. Calum Archibald was still mourning his recently-departed mother. William Simmons was sad because Miss Bingham was romantically involved with a young man who was not William Simmons.

A Yellow Room

The Yellow Room was in desperate need of a morale-booster.

'Right, everyone,' he announced. 'We need cheering up. Vance here is doing one of his turns at the Confabulists Club tonight. I think it would be a jolly good idea if we all went along. Not only will I pay for you all to get in but I will stand you a fish supper, if we can find anywhere that has any fish. And the first round of drinks is on me. Mrs Pugh, you bring your old man – there's no point in him spending the night standing guard over broken bottles and empty barrels, is there? I'll phone the wife and see if she wants to join us. It's a bloody miserable world out there, and our sitting around and brooding will not help anyone.'

In the event neither Mrs Crane nor Mr Pugh wished to join them. They found a fish restaurant that still had a few sorry-looking pieces of cod in batter and some chips that had probably looked fine in a former life, and livened up the poor fare with salt and vinegar. Vance ate quickly and went on ahead of the others. He had stories to read, or so he hoped.

The stories went down well with the crowd. Vance interspersed the stories with Shakespearean monologues and a selection of poems from Wordsworth, Keats, Byron and Shelley, making sure his whistle was well wetted. Indeed, the drunker he became, the better he got. He had a pleasant, resonant voice and a commanding stage presence. Crane reflected that if it hadn't been for the missing leg, Vance could have been a star.

As Vance concluded *La Belle Dame Sans Merci* and left the podium to a chorus of semi-inebriated cheers, Crane became aware of a man standing next to him at the bar ordering a pint of Imperial Russian Stout. The man was in his fifties, with a small moustache and a thatch of wild, greying hair, dressed in a grubby reefer jacket and a seaman's sweater, with a grey woollen scarf tied round his neck. His eyes were on Crane but they may as well have been looking at the moon. There was something otherworldly about those eyes.

'Spare?'

The man nodded but did not smile. 'Austin Osman Spare at your service, I don't think. It's been a while, Tony.' The voice was pure Cockney. The clothing was indubitably second-hand or a charity hand-out. The lined face was that of a ruined god. The grin, when he caught sight of Ethel Bingham sitting at a nearby table, was that of an aroused satyr. Then everything changed and Crane found himself looking at a man old before his time. He noticed that Spare seemed to be having difficulty handling his pint glass.

'Are you alright?'

Spare shrugged. 'I've been bombed out and lost everything. My arms hurt and I'm dossing in a bleeding spike. Apart from that everything's bloody hunky-dory. Who's that bird with your mates? She looks a right dirty cow.'

'They're my friends, Spare. That's all you need to know.'

'Oh,' Spare chuckled. 'So that's the Yellow Room mob, is it? They don't look like a top-secret unit. That one's got lovely tits, though. And that old tart's got a nice fat arse on her.'

'I'd thank you not speak that way about my people. And how the bloody hell do you know about the Yellow

Room?'

'There's not much I don't know if I want to know it. I've got these.' Spare produced a cardboard packet containing what looked like a deck of playing cards. 'I once showed you what they could do, remember? Some of them can do things like cause thunderstorms, or make a woman want you. Others can make you see visions of what's happening a long way off. Take this one, for instance.' He selected a card and handed it to Crane, face-down. 'Go on, take a look.'

Crane turned the card. The design was strange. It was somewhere between a tarot card and a Surrealist painting. He looked at it more closely – then he was somewhere else.

'Oh, bugger,' said Crane as the scene unfolded somewhere in his mind. Then it had gone.

'Are you going to tell her?' Spare was regarding him with unexpected sympathy. Crane shook his head. If what he had seen was in any way real, Ethel Bingham would find out soon enough that her soldier boy was dead, torpedoed and drowned before he even caught sight of the Afrika Korps.

'How did you do that?'

'It's magic,' Spare unhelpfully explained. 'Real magic. It works by getting into the bits of your mind that you don't know about. This design is meant to tell you the truth about something you've been worrying about. I can see it with you because it was me that made the card. After I was bombed I used one of the other cards to see if anyone was looking for me, and that's when I learned about the Yellow Room. Thanks to these cards I know a lot of other things as well.'

'Such as?'

'Oh, I know about Hess going to Scotland and about what he wanted you to do. It's a good job you didn't ask Crowley. That bloke is completely gone, you know that. He would only have buggered it up again. Did you think he'd really conjured up an elemental? No, mate – that was the drugs. But he could still make you see what he thought he was seeing, and he's still got enough lead in his pencil to make Hess see it as well. Oh yes, Hess believes what he told you but he's wrong. What he saw was what Crowley saw. Hitler is about as possessed by a demon as that chair is. The thing is that Hess has cracked up under the strain of running Germany and because of the war. He was never strong enough for leadership. That hallucination Crowley sent pushed him over the edge.'

'So there's nothing we can do about Hitler? What about your cards? Couldn't you use them to try to get to him somehow?'

Spare laughed mirthlessly. 'He's not one man, Crane. Hitler's part of a group of people that are all connected, including me. I hate the bloody Nazis. Hitler wanted me to paint his portrait but I told him to fuck off. He's had it in for me ever since – unconsciously, of course. Consciously he's forgotten I even exist. But the grudge is in his unconscious and it will try to work itself out. Think about it. On the same night I get bombed, almost to the very minute, Rudolf Hess lands in Scotland. And he wants to see me. What are the odds, Crane? Christ, my bloody arm's giving me some gyp. Any chance of a pint? I'm giving you free information and I haven't got a pot to piss in. the least you could do is stand me a beer.'

Crane bought Spare another pint of Imperial Russian Stout and decided to try one for himself. It wasn't bad.

'You're right to be worried about the Jews,' Spare continued. 'Right this minute the Nazis are making plans to do away with all the Jews in Europe and Russia. They want a solution to what they think is the Jewish problem, Crane. It's going to get very, very bad. But it won't just be the Jews. It'll be everyone they don't like or think is a threat – prisoners of war, the mad, cripples, Gypsies – anyone they think will pollute the Aryan race. That includes queers like your pal over there.' He gestured at Vance, who was knocking back a gin and tonic prior to reading the evening's winning story. 'The Nazis are beasts led by madmen. They hate anyone who isn't one of them. What they will do will stain the human race, Crane. History will never forgive them. Before this war is ended, evil will reign unchecked. The horror and cruelty will be unbelievable, and it will be on a scale that will make you want to tear your own eyes out when you see it. And you will see it, Crane – you will see it at first hand. You've already seen a small part of it. One day you will see it all.'

Whether it was from relief that the Yellow Room's ritual had not been responsible for placing a demon inside Hitler, or the horror of the future Spare had just described, Crane began to feel faint and dizzy. His legs began to buckle. Black spots swam in his vision as he grasped the bar and strove to remain upright. When he had recovered, Spare had gone.

'I'll make you a cup of coffee and some toast. Well, it would be coffee if it had any coffee in it. Chicory, roasted acorns and dog-shit, at least that's what it tastes of. No butter either, I'm afraid. Will dripping do? It's bloody naff but it's all there is.'

Matthew Sanders rose from the bed. Vance sighed and turned onto his left side. He had a hangover – a well-earned one, in his estimation – but was happy. He was in love. He closed his eyes and dozed lightly while Matthew made him breakfast in bed. There was something to be said for being a one-legged queer – the man always made the breakfast.

He lit a cigarette when the toast and ersatz coffee arrived. Matthew ate his while sitting on the side of the bed.

'That was a bona meeting last night,' said Vance. The fake coffee wasn't half as bad as he'd feared.

'Yes, it was,' Matthew smiled. 'But I think I prefer what happened after. Don't you?'

Vance agreed that he did. 'I'm so glad I met you,' he said.

'Me too. It's bona to have a bit of love with all this going on. I know a lot of people would disagree, what with us being a couple of old queens with nanti prospects, but I feel really lucky. We're not involved in the fighting – well, apart from dodging bombs and whatever else Jerry has up his sleeve – and we've got a bit of work, and now we've got each other. I hate this bloody war, Edward. But I don't hate the Germans. Most of them are just ordinary people, doing ordinary things. They're not all Hitlers and Görings and Himmlers, are they? Why, I bet there are omis just like us in Berlin right this minute, as happy as we are. What do you think?'

Edward Vance remembered what an appalled Anthony Crane had told him about Spare's visions. *It won't just be the*

Jews. It'll be everyone they don't like or think is a threat – prisoners of war, the mad, cripples, Gypsies – anyone they think will pollute the Aryan race. That includes queers like your pal over there.

Yes, there were almost certainly men just like them in Berlin. But if they were happy now, they probably wouldn't be for very much longer.

The Wild Man of Bournemouth

The DO NOT DISTURB *card still hung from the door-handle. Alice shook her head in annoyance and concern. Room 3327 hadn't been cleaned for two days now, and in her book that was quite long enough. The elderly European gentleman who lived there – a strange, reserved man but disarmingly courteous in an old-fashioned way – had told the New Yorker Hotel staff that there would be times when he would be working hard and shouldn't be interrupted. That was all very well, but Alice didn't like the thought of the poor old guy sleeping in dirty sheets, maybe even dying in them. She didn't know how old the guy was but he must have been seventy at least. Taking a deep breath, she inserted her pass key and opened the door.*

The room was dark and stuffy, and smelled faintly sour: ammonia and stale sweat, a ripe, old man odour. Alice stopped just inside the door and stood still, listening carefully. The room was still and silent, the only sounds those filtering faintly through the windows and walls from outside. Nothing in there was moving. No one but her was even breathing. Alice's heart sank as she realised what she was going to find.

A Yellow Room

Billy Chambers was a most peculiar man. Sixty-three years old, he lived alone in a big, crumbling house by the sea on the western edge of Bournemouth, not far from Hengistbury Head. It had been his parents' home too, until they died. He'd lived there all his life, except for those four years he wanted to forget, the best years of his life though they had been. Most people knew him only as the Wild Man. To most people characters like him never really had names, only titles, like decayed royalty. But he knew who he was. He didn't really care, but he knew.

Billy's hair was grey and long, falling almost to his shoulders in unruly tangles that seemed to have a life of their own. His beard was just as grey and equally unkempt. His bushy eyebrows matched the facial ensemble. At night he wandered the streets for hours on end, sometimes frightening unwary old ladies and arousing suspicion in patrolling constables, his mouth moving silently as he communicated with himself, and only himself. Billy never shouted, not like the drunks who raised their voices to compensate for incoherence or the soldiers who were about to go to war and made a lot of noise to prove to themselves that they weren't really afraid of what was to come. He didn't smell bad like the tramps that appeared mysteriously, like unwanted and unsightly blooms, in the summer. He never swore or did anything that would offend. He rarely spoke to anyone but himself, and usually only in those unheard, inwardly-directed words. Most of the time he simply listened.

When he wasn't roaming the streets on his obscure nocturnal missions, Billy made only brief daylight forays to the shops. Otherwise he stayed at home. That old house, although kept scrupulously clean, was a labyrinth of baled newspapers and magazines that he refused to throw away, stacks of books with loose, wormy covers, broken furniture that belonged nowhere else, and his collection of second-hand packaging – boxes, paper wrappers and tins, all shapes, sizes and colours – and empty jars and bottles. The bottles had once contained soft drinks: Tizer, Corona and Lucozade. Billy Chambers never drank alcohol. He was happy to eat just about anything but especially liked fish and chips, sausage and bacon sandwiches, bananas and oranges, and ice-cream. Rationing had been a serious blow to his morale, though he had soon adapted to poorer fare. He smoked, favouring toothpick-thin roll-ups of Old Holborn in blue RizLas, of which he got through around forty a day. He had a mild smoker's cough, nicotine-stains on his fingers and beard, and had once set his greatcoat alight due to a misunderstanding with a Swan Vesta. Otherwise he was completely harmless. Children liked him, sensing his innate good nature, but he avoided them. A kindly man, Billy kept himself to himself because people always got the wrong idea when lonely men associated with children and he didn't want any trouble. Billy was an unsettling but model citizen.

And Billy had a secret.

Crane received the call at thirteen minutes past eight on the very first morning of 1943. His wife, herself feeling somewhat the worse for wear on the morning after a night before, had answered the telephone, immediately rousing her husband from his slumbers when she realised the caller was from the War Office.

It had taken Crane several minutes to get the story

straight. A man had walked into a Bournemouth police station and announced that he had overheard a message in German, and that he knew what it meant. When questioned, the man, a well-known local character, told police he hadn't overheard it in a public place; nor had he heard it on the radio. The voice delivering the message had been inside his head.

Naturally, the police had been sceptical. Even in wartime there were enough mad or malicious people who were only too happy to waste police time. Yet they had done their duty by the book. The informant was detained and a report sent to the War Office. A routine check had established that the message reported from Bournemouth matched one that had been picked up during routine monitoring of the radio transmissions known as 'numbers stations' to members of the public who tuned in to them, either through curiosity or in the hope of being able to decode one of the mysterious messages.

SIS had been notified first, but on learning that the informant was an eccentric known as the Wild Man they assumed that he had merely overheard the transmission via his wireless and had made up the rest. Crane supposed the incident had been passed to the Yellow Room to investigate as a joke. A man who claimed to hear secret messages in his head was a candidate for either the alienist or the Yellow Room. Anthony Crane kept an open mind about such matters. Just because someone had a reputation for eccentric behaviour, it didn't automatically follow that the fellow was insane. And he knew from personal experience that a strange story wasn't necessarily an untrue one. Instinct and his own brand of common sense told him that this case deserved investigation as much as any other. And if it turned out to be hogwash? Well, it had to be looked into and even a negative result wouldn't be time wasted.

Besides, it would be an opportunity to blood the Yellow Room's latest recruit, the mysterious, beautiful – and frankly unnerving – Miss Dorothy Harlow. He knew what she could do. Her demonstration had scared the living daylights out of him, and he had readily acquiesced to her request to say nothing of her to his superiors. Crane didn't trust the people running the war – as far as he could see, all they wanted was to find new and better ways to kill enemies and win battles. He didn't even trust Churchill, who he liked and respected. Winston was a pragmatist who weighed up losses and gains like an assayer. He may have wanted to save lives but Crane believed he was much too ready to take them. The War Office and SIS would surely sway Churchill to turn Miss Harlow into the kind of soldier the Nazis had tried to create – a creation the Yellow Room had foiled.

So Miss Harlow was officially the Yellow Room's clerical worker, a filer and indexer. She would accompany him to Bournemouth to take notes of the interview in the shorthand she couldn't write.

In 1895, when he was only fourteen years old, Billy Chambers had impetuously left home, stowed away on a ship, and found himself in the United States of America. That wasn't where he wanted to be – he'd boarded the vessel thinking it was bound for Hong Kong – but it was good enough, because Billy craved adventure. In New York he had affected the local accent, claimed to be an orphan from the Bronx, and found work with one of the local criminal gangs. Billy was all for relieving the wealthy of surplus riches but his romantic vision of the felonious life was shattered one night when what was supposed to be the routine burglary of a Manhattan mansion went terribly wrong. The owners were supposed to have been away in Paris, according to information supplied to the gang's leader by a maid who was sweet on him. And indeed, that much was true. Unfortunately the boss, a twenty-two year old whose looks and forceful personality far outstripped his intellect, led his boys to the wrong address. There was a scuffle, the boss produced a knife, and within minutes the home-owner and his wife lay dead. Billy didn't take that well. Horrified, he fled the city and took to the roads and railways, hopping freight trains when he could and walking when he had to. Three months later, he wound up in Colorado Springs, where he found honest work in a saloon. Three months after that, a mysterious stranger appeared in the town, a tall, elegantly-dressed man with a moustache and an exotic accent. Local gossip had it that the newcomer was something to do with that new-fangled invention that was the talk of the East Coast: electricity. Billy saw his chance. This was something more interesting than tending bar, sweeping floors and helping drunks onto their horses. This was something that had a future.

The stranger's name was Nikola Tesla. Billy found that out when he went up the hill to the astonishing laboratory under construction there, and asked if there was any work going. Tesla himself had interviewed him, those deep-set, blue-grey eyes studying him closely as Billy lied about his name, his background and his qualifications. When Billy had finished, Tesla gave a small, knowing smile and told him to begin again, and this time to tell the truth. Embarrassed into honesty, Billy spilled the beans while Tesla continued to stare.

Billy never knew why Tesla decided to employ him as an assistant. Perhaps it was his imagination, a commodity Tesla valued highly. Or maybe Tesla assessed Billy's intelligence during the interview and was of the opinion that it matched his enthusiasm. Perhaps it was the fact that Billy's detailed description of his imaginary life was so vivid that the scientist was impressed by his ability to seemingly live two lives at once without getting them confused in any way. Whatever it was, Billy began his new job immediately, working closely with Tesla and the others, learning as he went along. He learned a lot, and he never forgot anything.

Tesla confided in the boy, explaining ideas and theories in depth, and allowing him sight of notes and plans shown to no one else. Tesla's memory was as prodigious as his linguistic and scientific skills; but Billy's was better. Billy didn't precisely understand what he learned of Tesla's private researches but he was an invaluable assistant nonetheless. As Tesla's interests branched further away from mere electricity, so he involved Billy in ever more arcane experiments and research. One of his experiments was an attempt to refute telepathy. Billy, Tesla thought, would make an ideal test subject, and the boy, who had come to hero-worship Tesla, readily agreed to the proposed procedure. The experiment took place one night in the late autumn of 1899.

One week later, Billy Chambers was on a ship bound for Southampton, with a first-class ticket and a thousand dollars in his pocket. When he arrived on his family's doorstep in Bournemouth, his parents wept with joy to see him safe and well. Later, when they found out what had been done to him, they wept with grief.

'Blips and bleeps, hisses and clicks and crackles, voices and music and madness.'

He served them tea in mismatched but clean and gleaming bone china cups, with saucers from an entirely different set of crockery. The spoons all matched, though – shining, polished silver. He brought sugar in an Ovaltine tin and milk in a blue enamel mug.

Miss Harlow continued to scan their host, all her senses fully engaged. When Billy returned to his kitchen for biscuits she nudged Crane. 'He's not like your Yellow Room people,' she told him. 'He's just a normal man, no psychic talent whatsoever. I don't understand this at all.'

'Well, if he's not psychic, what is he? And what was all that talk about blips and bleeps and all the rest?'

Billy returned with a tin filled with what looked like home-baked biscuits. He seemed to be listening to something. He whistled a snatch of music, a couple of bars from 'Greensleeves'. Then he laughed.

'One, seven, eighteen, one, eight. Sixteen, twenty-one, eleven, three, three. Eight, three, one, nineteen, ten. Where do they all come from?'

'What can you hear, Billy?' Crane asked, opening his pack of Lucky Strikes and offering one to the wild-haired man, who shook his head and produced a thin hand-rolled cigarette from an Old Holborn tin.

'It was just noises at first – isn't that what you wanted to ask me about, what I can hear in my head? First it was hisses and clicks and crackles, some regular as clockwork, some random. There were great swooshing sounds, like waves against the sea wall. Then, a couple of years later, the others started – blip, blip, blip. That's how it began. Then there were more blips and bleeps, so many you couldn't tell them apart. After that there was music and voices and I thought I was going completely mad. Then a few years ago it was the numbers. I talk to them sometimes but they never answer, at least not so I can understand. I don't mind, but they get in the way. It's hard to talk to folk when all you can hear is noises. It's much worse lately, especially the numbers.'

Dementia praecox? Crane wondered if Billy was, after all, just another of the poor benighted souls who spent their whole lives arguing with the voices of their own insanity and striving desperately to ignore the internal commands to hurt and kill. But no, that was surely not the case. Billy seemed politely distant and distracted, but there was no aggression, agitation or fear. Besides, Miss Harlow seemed unconcerned – but Crane was beginning to suspect that it would take an awful lot to ruffle the young woman's composure.

'Are the numbers always the same, Billy?' he asked.

'Oh no,' Billy replied. 'They're always different, every one of them, every time. Most are numbers spoken in groups of five, with a pause. Some are more than five, a few are less. Some begin with a piece of music. It's not always easy to distinguish one from all the others but I usually can.'

'What about that message you gave to the police?' Miss Harlow enquired, smiling sweetly at Billy. Crane felt a flutter inside him but tried to focus on Billy Chambers.

'The one in German? Oh, that was unusual, very loud and clear. I knew it was all numbers because I learned German and a bit of Italian and Serbo-Croat in America. I repeated it exactly as I heard it. I was a bit surprised when the police locked me up. I've known Sergeant Peters since he was a nipper. Never dreamed I'd end up having breakfast in one of his cells just for trying to be helpful.'

'When did you first hear these sounds?'

'Well, the first one that made any sense was the three blips. That was in 1901. That came a few times, then there were more blips and bleeps over the following months, then it all went potty, like I said.'

'Blips and bleeps? Do you mean dots and dashes, like Morse code?'

That caught Crane's attention. He was a radio enthusiast – he'd built a crystal set to supplement the family radio, and another for his young nephew – and he knew his history. 1901 was the year Marconi had transmitted a short message in Morse code from Cornwall to Scotland: three dots, which in Morse represented the letter S. Crane knew that early experiments with radio had puzzled those working on it, who were baffled by the strange sounds that they now knew emanated from distant stars, the sun and meteorological phenomena. Was Billy somehow picking up radio signals? Billy's story suddenly made a great deal of sense, though that didn't make it any easier to explain.

Miss Harlow was still charming Billy into rational conversation. 'What was different about this one, Billy? What was it that made you tell the police?'

'I went to the police station because I recognised it, miss. I remembered it from when I was a young lad in America.'

'But what was it?'

Billy became evasive. 'I'm not sure all I should tell you – you or anyone else. He wouldn't have wanted me to, you see. Oh, he's told everyone it exists and that he'll give it to the world one day, but he won't. He couldn't bring himself to do it then and I know he won't now. He's a kind man, a gentle man – he knows what governments and generals would do with it if they had it. Can you imagine what Hitler would do if he had something like that?'

Crane was becoming exasperated. 'Something like what, Billy?'

The older man was silent for a few moments. 'I'd better start from the beginning,' he said eventually.

Tesla brought in a surgeon from New York to carry out the procedure. Billy was given a dose of laudanum and his scalp was anaesthetised with cocaine. Then the surgeon set to work, complaining occasionally when the smoke from Billy's cigarettes stung his eyes. Tesla had tried to talk him out of smoking during surgery but Billy had been adamant. 'If you're not going to knock me out, then I'm going to smoke. I'm not going to sit there without a gasper while that man carves me up.'

The operation took a long time, a second dose of laudanum and several more injections of cocaine to keep Billy's skull numb. It involved removing a portion of cranial bone close to the left ear, screwing the device securely into place, and attaching it to Billy's eardrum with fine gold wire. The device was a miniaturised version of a machine Tesla had devised to detect Herz waves. The Serb had started out with a large model then refined it over a two-month period, making each successive version smaller than the last. While the operation was underway he was putting the finishing touches to his Herz generator.

'Telepathy is a superstitious fancy,' he had told Billy three months earlier. 'I have an idea for building a machine — actually two machines, one to transmit and the other to receive, that could precisely mimic the effects these foolish psychical researches claim for telepathy.'

'Why don't you build them?' Billy had asked him.

'Because I would need a human subject,' Tesla replied, 'and I do not think anyone would care to participate as my laboratory animal.'

'I would,' Billy instantly responded.

The transmitter Tesla devised was based partly on the machines he was developing for wireless transmission of electricity and partly on the phonograph. It would render human speech as electrical impulses, but instead of transferring these onto a wax cylinder it would send them directly into the ether. The receiving mechanism reversed the process. Tesla had demonstrated the principle to Billy using two tin cans and a length of twine. 'Vibrations,' he had insisted. 'Resonance is the key to everything, young man.'

Now Tesla fiddled with his transmitter while the surgeon stitched Billy's head back together. Billy could hear thunder outside the building and sparks occasionally arced between metal objects inside the laboratory. Tesla's electrostatic experiments always kicked up a mighty storm. It was typical of him to be working on two simultaneously. Three if you counted the other one.

Tesla allowed Billy a couple of hours for the laudanum and cocaine to wear off. Billy occupied the time by retiring to the bunkhouse where he now lived, to smoke a few cigarettes and read a battered, crudely-printed pornographic pamphlet recently given to him by one of Colorado Springs' most notoriously unreliable drunks, who claimed to have acquired it during a visit to a brothel in Mexico. He'd been looking forward to reading it – though it would have been more accurate to say that it was the pictures that really interested him. But the illustrations were poor, the paper was cheap and the ink had bled across the pages. After struggling to make out anything beyond a vague suggestion of the female form, a disappointed Billy gave up and dozed off.

He was woken at midnight. Tesla gave him one of two matching watches. 'These watches have been synchronised. Walk to the far end of the building. At precisely thirty minutes past twelve I shall transmit a message. When you hear it you will return and tell me what that message was.'

Billy dutifully did as he was told. It was a clear night but not too cold, and the stars were out in all their glory. He was happy to look at them while the minutes ticked away, wondering if somewhere, on some world orbiting one of those stars, someone was looking back at him. At twenty-nine minutes past twelve he closed his eyes to focus on receiving Tesla's words.

Inside the laboratory, Tesla pulled the switch that powered his transmitter. At exactly half past twelve he uttered what should have been a historic message.

Then there was thunder and lightning and everything stopped.

'What happened?' Crane was on the edge of his seat. Miss Harlow was outwardly composed but her eyes suggested she was equally expectant. Billy merely shrugged.

'I don't really know,' he confessed, with a sheepish smile. 'One moment I was standing there with my eyes shut, waiting for Tesla's message to come through, then there was a brilliant white flash and an enormous clap of thunder. Then I was on a ship to Southampton. Couldn't remember a damned thing about what had happened in between. I just sort of woke up one day and I was halfway across the Atlantic.'

'And what about those numbers? What do they have to do with Tesla?'

'First you need to understand that Tesla hated war. He thought it was stupid and wasteful. He had this idea for a weapon that would be so terrible that everyone would be afraid to use it. If everyone had it then no nation would attack another because retaliation would ensure their mutual destruction. It was a brilliant idea, I thought. Anyway, Tesla was working on several projects at once, as usual. There was the electrostatic research, which was his official work; but there was also the telepathy machine and his teleforce weapon, what everyone called a death-ray. He used to tell me things, very complicated ideas that he probably thought I wouldn't understand or that I'd forget straight away. But Tesla didn't know I have a very good memory, especially for numbers. Read me a list of numbers and I'll remember them all in the correct sequence, no matter how big the numbers or how long the list.'

'A photographic memory?' Crane was fascinated. 'I've heard of such a thing but never once seen it demonstrated.'

Billy shook his head emphatically. 'No, it's not really photographic. I can't remember faces or conversation or anything else any better than other people. It only works that way with ideas and numbers. Tesla wasn't a modest man. He liked to show off a bit. Every now and then he would read me extracts from his research papers. One morning we had started work as usual when he suddenly said to me "Billy? Would you like to learn the secret of my teleforce weapon?" I said of course I did. Then he took a sheet of paper from his pocket, a piece of foolscap covered in numbers, and he read them out to me. "What do you make of that?" he said. I told him I didn't make anything of it, it was only a list of numbers and I couldn't see any pattern or connection with anything else. Then he laughed and said I hadn't read the right book, and we resumed work. He never mentioned it again.'

'And you remembered. All those years ago but you still remember the numbers. Did he give any indication what the book might be?'

'No. He had quite a few books, hundreds. It could

have been any one of them, or maybe one that he didn't own. I still don't know what he meant by that.'

'So what the hell happened to Billy, Tony?' Miss Harlow was a smart cookie, as they said in her native land, but she wasn't a scientist.

'What I think happened was that Tesla's electrostatic experiment reached its climax just he began transmitting the radio signal. It somehow increased the power of his Herz waves to a much greater degree than he'd anticipated, or perhaps even thought possible. And it did something to the device in Billy's head, overloaded it to such an extent that it was changed in some way. I'd guess that it was supposed to have been powered by a tiny dynamo that used his bodily movements to charge a capacitor. Perhaps the electrostatic discharge also permanently fused the device to his skull. But I'm only guessing. The only person who knows how the device worked and might know what happened is Tesla.'

'What about the numbers? And the book?'

'It's a cipher,' Crane explained. 'The numbers are in pairs. The first refers to a page number, the second to the corresponding word on that page. So the fifteenth word on page five might be "the", for instance. It's simple and virtually unbreakable if you don't know what the book, the key text, is. Billy has the numbers. If we knew what the book was we could decode the numbers and learn the secret of Tesla's death-ray. It would win us the war, save thousands of lives.'

Miss Harlow stared intently at him. 'You don't believe that for a second, do you?'

'No, I don't.' Crane seemed crestfallen. 'I believe that

yes, it would help beat Hitler; but after that Britain and America would turn it against Japan, then the Soviet Union. And if Stalin or Hitler got hold of it – why, I dread to think what might happen.'

'I agree, Tony. So the problem is this. We have a series of numbers that could help build the most terrifying and destructive weapon the world has ever seen. We don't trust the Allied governments to use it wisely or judiciously; and we really don't want Adolf and Joe to get their hands on it. The only way to decode the numbers is to use the same book Tesla used. And Tesla's the only person who knows what that book is. So we have to get to Tesla before anyone else does.'

'What do we do with Tesla?'

Miss Harlow looked down at the pavement. 'I won't kill anyone, Tony,' she said quietly. 'Not unless it's in the immediate defence of an innocent. I won't be an assassin.'

'And I wouldn't want you to be one, Dorothy. I'd never ask that of you. But Tesla is a genius and if he says he's invented a death ray, then I for one believe it. If the Germans have the secret of Tesla's weapon, even if it's in a code they can't yet break, then we must do something. There's no point telling SIS – you know how they look down their noses at us and never take us seriously. And Churchill's instructions are that the Americans mustn't know about us, though after the Worthington fiasco I believe they have some idea of what we are. No, we need to warn Tesla that the Nazis are after his invention and perhaps work with him to find a way to keep the information out of their hands.'

'And out of everyone else's hands,' Miss Harlow

suggested.

Crane did not disagree. 'Perhaps there's something else we can do. Dorothy, have you ever been to New York?'

'Sure, it's my home town. You want me to go?'

'Not yet. We can't delay too long, but we need to work out a plan. I think we can safely assume that if we accurately report what Billy told us then it won't be long before he has operatives from SIS, OSS and all the other Allied intelligence services queuing at his front door. And what they know the NKVD will know, so you can add them to the potential guest list. The Gestapo already know about the teleforce weapon, it seems, so if we breathe a word about this to anyone poor old Billy is in danger of becoming the most popular man in Bournemouth. That means we mustn't tell anyone else in the Yellow Room. It goes against the grain, but the less any of them know about this, the safer they'll be. Back to London first. God, what a way to spend New Year's Day.'

Miss Harlow grinned wickedly. 'Yeah, I meant to ask. How's the hangover?'

'Not much better, thanks for asking. That's the last time I have you lot over for a party. Where did you get all that whisky? Even Charles couldn't get hold of that much and he makes Croesus look like a pauper.'

'Oh, I have my sources,' she replied, eyes wide and innocent.

Billy was wearing his full Wild Man costume, as he did whenever he went out on one of his nocturnal strolls, whatever the weather. The threadbare army greatcoat, a souvenir of his time in the trenches – even his strangeness hadn't prevented his conscription; in those days only cowards went mad – was tied tightly against the cold with an old dressing-gown cord. His hobnailed boots were badly scuffed and would probably have fallen apart without their twine bindings. His ancient trousers were patched with squares snipped from even older trousers. A scarf made of sections of other scarves was wound round his neck and trailed down his chest and back like parti-coloured tentacles. Billy never threw anything away if it could be reused, salvaged or cannibalised to keep something else going. Like Mr Tesla, he hated waste.

The chill wind ruffled his beard and sculpted his hair into constantly-shifting Medusa poses in the moonlight, blew tiny embers from the roll-up protruding from the corner of his mouth. Billy squinted myopically into the darkness. The streets were empty this far from the centre of town, on such a cold night. Certain that it would rain, he'd stuffed a battered sou'wester into one of his coat pockets before setting out. If he had to wear that it would further restrict his vision. Suddenly feeling vulnerable, he wondered if perhaps he should return to the warmth of his fireplace. The business with the police had rattled him and the visit from Mr Crane and Miss Harlow had completed the job of unnerving him. His visitors had been pleasant and polite enough but Billy didn't like intrusions from officialdom. It always meant trouble. And if they were so interested in him, who else might be?

Somewhere off to his left, two cats began to yowl loudly, that eerie sound they make when disputing territory, as if they are trying to articulate human speech in bodies not designed for it. It is the sound of haunted houses and malign imps. No wonder the creatures have always been associated with witches, the darkness and the Devil. That bloodcurdling racket was enough for Billy. He carefully pinched the roll-up out and stowed the dog-end in a pocket. It was time he went home. A nice cup of tea would soothe his nerves.

Five minutes later it began to rain so Billy fished out the sou'wester and jammed it onto his head, taking care to tuck his hair into the oilskin. As predicted, it meant he couldn't see much apart from the pavement directly ahead as he walked. It also meant he didn't see the two trenchcoated, trilby-hatted men who were following him at a discreet distance. He didn't see them until they rushed at him as he was opening his front door, and by then it was too late.

'You look exhausted, Tony. Shall I drive?'

Crane didn't need asking twice. He chivalrously opened the driver's door for his colleague, closed it when she had clambered into the vehicle, and settled himself into the passenger seat. He was dog-tired and desperately needed to sleep but was determined not to be so rude as to do so while Miss Harlow was being so kind as to drive on the return leg of their journey. His eyes, however, had a different idea and began to close almost as soon as his rump made contact with the leather upholstery. He forced them open, unwilling to burden Miss Harlow with a long, silent drive back to London. As if of their own accord, those rebellious orbs stole a glance in her direction.

Dorothy Harlow was a lovely woman. That much was unarguable. The lustrous black hair tied in a French plait, those big, brown eyes and generous lips, not to mention the luscious figure that even on occasion managed to tempt young William Simmons' gaze from the equally delightful form of Ethel Bingham. Miss Harlow appeared to be around twenty-five years of age but seemed older. Always stylishly-dressed, outwardly good-humoured and friendly, her confidence and wisecracks didn't disguise a hint of something dark and tragic beneath the veneer. He knew next to nothing about here. God only knew where she was from – her accent veered between several varieties of American, plus Home Counties and Cockney. He didn't know what she did for money or where she lived. The official records were, he knew, an excellent fabrication. He didn't even know what she was – only that she was considerably faster and stronger than she looked, could read people's characters and intentions with apparent ease, and was able to eavesdrop and enter buildings without being detected. He wasn't even sure that she was human.

'Mr Crane? My name is Dorothy Harlow. I believe I can be of assistance to the Yellow Room.'

That alone was enough to worry him – a stranger, in a public place, who knew who he was and the name of his supposedly top secret team – but the way she had suddenly appeared, stepping from a shady corner of the Wagon and Horses, a corner he could have sworn was empty of all but dust only a split-second before, had been positively terrifying. He was still recovering his composure when he found himself offering to buy her a drink. At the time he'd pretended to himself that it was because he was intrigued and wanted to find out a bit about her before he decided what to do about what must surely have been a breach of security. But the truth was much simpler than that – as simple as one look at her face.

Nevertheless, he feigned puzzlement. 'I'm sorry, Miss – Harlow, was it? I don't have the first idea what you are you talking about.'

She laughed. 'Playing the wise guy doesn't suit you, Mr Crane. I know all about you and what you do. I know all about the Yellow Room – Bartley, Simmons, Archibald, Miss Bingham and Mrs Pugh... Need I go on?'

'Please do,' he replied, keeping his features expressionless. 'It may help me understand what you want from me. Perhaps a drink will help you collect your thoughts.'

The woman took a seat at his table. 'I'll have a half of bitter, if you don't mind.'

When Crane returned with her beer she was smoking. A pack of Lucky Strikes and a box of Bryant and May matches were stacked neatly on the table. 'I hope you don't mind,' she said. 'Not at all,' he replied, and lit one of his own, a Black Cat.

'The Yellow Room was established in late 1939 by you, with the support of Hore-Belisha,' she told him. 'You're a bit of a joke with SIS, but you enjoy Churchill's confidence, though he's a bit half-hearted about it. You use unconventional techniques against the Nazis – psychics, fortune tellers, clairvoyants and so on. Sometimes you're successful, sometimes not. You've had a problem with one of your top consultants, a man who likes to call himself the Great Beast.' A knowing smile curved her lips and she laughed sourly. 'Not the man he used to be, so I hear.'

'A fascinating story, Miss Harlow, but utter fiction, obviously. Anyway, even if it were true, what could you possibly offer such an organisation?'

She smiled briefly then lowered her eyes. When she raised them again he knew exactly what she had to offer, to him at least. But that wasn't good enough. He had a duty to the people of Great Britain –

even the King and the War Office – and another, no less profound, to his wife and son. He was dimly aware that something about her had changed – she was listening and watching intently, inhaling his smell, rapidly processing the information. She seemed first surprised then disappointed, but quickly recovered her poise.

'Tell you what,' she said, the smile reappearing, 'how about a little practical demonstration?' She rummaged in the canvas bag he hadn't noticed because his attention had been focused on her face, and withdrew a manila folder. It bore a label in Crane's own neat handwriting.

'Here,' she said. 'This is what you consider your greatest failure: the Worthington case. I've heard you talk about it, though you didn't even know I was there.'

'Dear God,' Crane exclaimed when he had regained the power of speech. 'How on earth did you get hold of that? And how the hell did you hear me talking about it?'

'Ask me no questions and I'll tell you no lies, Mr Crane. All I will say is that for me it was a piece of cake. This is what I have to offer – and much more besides.'

She smiled again and that made the decision for him.

He jolted awake at the shock of being drenched with ice-cold water. Panicking, he attempted to stand only to discover that he was unable to do anything more than shuffle the chair he was tied to. The two men regarded him dispassionately. One had removed his coat. The other, who was standing so close to Billy's hearth that he must surely be in danger of catching fire, hadn't so much as taken off his hat. They were tall, lean men with eyes as cold as the water running down Billy's face and chest.

'Leave me alone,' Billy whined through chattering

teeth. 'Why are you doing this? I haven't done anything to you. Do you want money? I've a couple of pounds in the kitchen cupboard but all the rest is in the bank. I don't have anything else worth taking, honestly.'

The coatless man pulled a chair close to Billy and sat. 'We don't want money. There's only one thing you have that interests us and that's information. Tell us what we need to know and you might just get out of this alive.'

'What do you want to know?' Billy asked, though he knew full well what they must be after. There was only one kind of information he had that would be worth anything to people like these men. Their eyes told him they would go to extreme lengths to tease it out of him. He'd met people like them on his travels in America, people for whom the pain of others meant only pleasure or a means to an end. Billy was determined that they would not learn the little he knew about Tesla's weapon. Nobody would. Because Tesla was wrong – he'd believed that no nation would deploy the teleforce weapon because the destruction and consequent retribution would be so terrible that no one would dare. But Tesla was an idealist who lived in a world of ideas and had no real experience of men like these; bad men whose masters were even greater monsters.

Billy knew that the man was lying, that he would not be alive at the end of this ordeal, which would be a long one. They would be careful to keep him alive for as long as possible – if he did not talk. And he had made up his mind that no matter what they did to him, he would not utter a single word.

'You know the numbers,' said the man without a coat. 'We know they are a secret that can only be unlocked with the right book. Tell us what that book is.'

Billy almost laughed. As he'd told Mr Crane and Miss Harlow, he didn't know what the book was. But these two would never believe him.

He braced himself for pain. It began soon after.

The Yellow Room was empty except for Anthony Crane. Bartley was away on business – financial and national – and Crane had told the others to take the day off. He needed to think, something he did best in solitude. Inevitably, the team had divined that he was troubled. You couldn't really run a team of psychics and seers without them getting wind of emotional turbulence. No doubt some of them would be discussing his state of mind at corner tables in quiet pubs. That couldn't be helped. But he refused to involve them in this. He and Miss Harlow were about to embark on a course of action that would endanger them both – and which might even threaten the Yellow Room's existence as a semi-autonomous branch of the Ministry of War. Crane would hate to see his people end up as part of SIS, which by all accounts squandered its operatives' lives as casually and recklessly as any Great War general ordering his men over the top for yet another futile sortie, and routinely pushed them to breaking point and beyond. No, he did not want that; but he had to risk it or sit back and do nothing until all that was left was to watch the world being torn apart by Tesla's weapon, no matter whose hands it was in.

Miss Harlow had told him she was a native of New York and a means of making contact with people there. She would arrange for someone to warn Tesla and keep an eye on him. They would also, Crane realised, need to make sure

Billy Chambers was kept safe. In the meantime he had to think.

Evidently, the Nazis had somehow got hold of the numbers that encoded Tesla's secret weapon. Billy had recognised that and had tried to alert the authorities. Fortunately for Billy, he had been dismissed as a crackpot by SIS and the Ministry of War. That meant he was safe from them, but Crane had to assume that sooner or later the Nazis would find out about Bournemouth's so-called Wild Man. The official Yellow Room record and his report to Churchill would say that Billy had merely overheard the numbers on his radio, that he was delusional, and that he knew nothing of any consequence or value to national security or the war effort. The Gestapo, more ruthlessly efficient than SIS in Crane's view, would surely have someone in a position to discover Billy's involvement. They would leave nothing to chance. First thing in the morning, Crane would discreetly arrange for the Bournemouth police to mount regular patrols by Billy's house. It wasn't much but it was the best he could do for now.

Then there was Tesla. Only he knew which book could be used to crack his code. Miss Harlow's contacts might be able to warn him of possible danger. They might even be able to protect him. Yet that wasn't really good enough. Tesla's very existence exposed humanity to a danger greater than anything it had faced before. Something had to be done about that.

To his horror, Crane realised that he was beginning to believe that the best thing would be for Tesla to be killed, and that he might have to arrange it. It was only the second time in his life that he had seriously considered killing another human being – the only other was Jack Worthington, the homicidal madman Crane had come to regard as his personal nemesis. At least with Worthington he had been prepared to kill the man himself, in anger and horror at what the man had done. But to sit comfortably in an office an ocean away while someone else carried out his orders – no, he couldn't do that. It would put him on a level with the generals and bureaucrats he despised, and with Worthington. Whatever else Crane thought he might be, he wasn't that.

Perhaps there was some way the Yellow Room team could neutralise Tesla? Could they find a way to make the Serb forget the name of the book used to encode the secret of the teleforce weapon? No, that wouldn't do, either. For one thing, Crane didn't have the first idea how they might go about it; for another, that would mean telling his colleagues something they were better off not knowing.

He sighed and rubbed at his eyes. 1943 wasn't quite two days old and he was already exhausted and depressed. There was also the small matter of Miss Harlow to consider. There was no denying that he was falling for the enigmatic woman, and that she seemed to be attracted to him. That was going to be very tricky indeed. Anthony Crane was devoted to his family and refused to believe he would ever betray his wife – for whom, he was surprised to find, his feelings remained resolutely unchanged. He had always believed that if a man committed to one woman fell for another his feelings for the first would change. Maybe that would explain how some men he knew were able to have wives and keep mistresses and have genuine affection for both. Indeed, one or two of his friends cheerfully led what to all intents and purposes double lives. But that wasn't for him. Family and the Yellow Room made his life complicated enough already, thank you very much. He would just have to resist his feelings for Miss Harlow. The awful thing was that he didn't want to.

Billy Chambers was in considerable pain. The evidence was visible in the bruises on his bare chest and arms, the blood leaking from his nose and mouth, the left eye that was swollen shut and surrounded by puffy reddening skin, and the cigarette burns on the soles of his feet. The crotch of his trousers formed the epicentre of a spreading urine stain. He'd pissed himself several times – as soon as one lot dried he did it again. He didn't have much choice.

They were giving him water but not food. He was still tied to the chair, though they had untied his ankles to afford them easier access to his mistreated soles. He had lost track of time and had no idea how long he'd been restrained, how long he'd been tortured, how long they'd asked the same questions, over and over again. 'Which book did Tesla use? What do you know about the weapon?'

In response to the questioning he'd told them the truth. 'I don't know what book you're talking about. I know nothing about any weapon.' Yes, he'd been truthful, up to a point. He hadn't let on that he knew what weapon they meant or why they wanted to know about the book. Eventually he realised that they weren't sure if he knew anything at all. They were just making certain that every avenue was being explored. That was good. While they were giving him a bad time they wouldn't be hurting anyone else. And the longer he kept them there, the greater the chance that Mr Crane and Miss Harlow might come back and catch these sadistic thugs in the act.

Both men were coatless and hatless now, their shirtsleeves rolled up. They'd kept the fire going too, so at least Billy wasn't cold, for which he was grateful. He hated being cold, unless fresh air and a good long walk went with it. The men had been taking it in turns to sleep, only a couple of hours each at a stretch. They looked as though they needed more than that. They were unshaven and red-eyed from interrupted sleep and too much cigarette smoke, their shirts stained with sweat at the armpits and along their spines. Billy didn't remember seeing either of them eat anything, though they'd used plenty of his tea. Actually, their constant smoking was the worst torture of all. Billy was desperate for a cigarette.

Suddenly he heard a series of crackles and whistles in his left ear, followed by a man's voice speaking German. Despite his discomfort Billy began to laugh wheezily.

'What's so damned funny?' one of the men angrily demanded. Billy didn't know which of them had spoken – he could no longer tell them apart.

'I have a message for you,' Billy chuckled. '*Sieben, dreissig, zwölf, drei...*'

He was still laughing when they started breaking the toes of his right foot.

She'd done her research. When Daphne Bow knocked on the door of room 3327 she was prepared for the frail, elderly man who opened it. Most extant photographs showed Tesla in his thirties or forties. At eighty-six years old he was still recognisable from those pictures and still handsome, though now grey-haired and with a face lined to a degree appropriate for a man of his age. Tesla still possessed that old European charm and politeness. He showed her to a chair by the window and offered tea, which she accepted.

'I am not at all surprised by this,' he replied when she had delivered the warning and explained what had happened. 'I was occasionally indiscreet when associating with my assistants. Like all scientists, I like to talk about what I do, and naturally I kept notes. My design for the teleforce weapon is kept inside my head; but the basic principles were recorded in a notebook, one of several that went missing when I was forced to leave Colorado Springs. At the time I had several young German-born assistants, a couple of whom hated Jews and blamed them for all the world's ills. I have no doubt they would have become ardent supporters of Hitler. I can only speculate that one of them made off with my notebook and has only recently realised that my weapon could decide the war in Europe.'

'Why did you create such a weapon? You have a reputation as a humanitarian.'

Tesla shook his head and smiled sadly. 'When I was younger I wished for the world to be run on rational, scientific principles. Now that I am older I see the folly of that youthful idealism, which mistook efficiency for righteousness. I believed in eugenics, rigid control of society – and look where such beliefs have taken us, Miss Bow; to the Nazis and the Soviet Union, and war between ideologies. Yet I believed absolutely in such things. And in those days I truly believed that my teleforce weapon would be a boon to humanity, the weapon so terrifying that it makes war obsolete. But that was long ago, before the madness of the Great War – before Hitler and Stalin. Now I agree with you – I know you have not said it but I can see it in your eyes, Miss Bow – that it should never be used, that it should be forgotten.'

He nodded when Daphne Bow asked if she could smoke. There was already an ashtray on the table, though it was empty and clean.

'I have heard rumours, Miss Bow. People tell me, very discreetly of course, that the United States has a secret project to harness the power of atomic fission as a weapon. I have made my own calculations and believe it is impossible to construct such a weapon. It is a wasted effort, a pipe dream. My teleforce weapon, on the other hand, is a reality. It is possible that only one such weapon, if used, could lay waste to huge areas and kill countless thousands of people, perhaps millions. It would not be a military weapon, designed for one soldier to use against another. It would, by its very nature, be a weapon against humanity, barely controllable and with horrific after-effects. It might even destroy the planet on whose skin we live. My conscience does not permit me to allow my device to be used. You have my word that I will never reveal the secret or how to discover it.'

Miss Bow sighed. 'Mr Tesla, I hope you realise that you risk being targeted by unscrupulous, ruthless people who will stop at nothing to obtain such a weapon. I do not refer solely to the Nazis and their allies. I believe you understand that the people we consider to be on our side will be just as bad as those we think of as our enemies.'

Tesla gave a short laugh. 'Believe me, Miss Bow, I am

fully cognisant of the perfidy of governments, no matter what flag they like to fly. I am also well aware that the military mind covets advantage on the battlefield. The nature of military glory has changed since the Great War. Valour is no longer relevant and honour is a relative term. Victory is the only outcome considered worthy of respect. And I have seen what this war is doing to us. We are only free insofar as our freedom facilitates victory. It is an interesting paradox. Our freedom is curtailed to protect our freedom. It is, I understand, even worse in Great Britain, where you have spent some time, if my ears are any judge of your accent. I know full well that I will be in danger from all sides.'

'Is there anywhere you can go to hide out until this is all over?' Miss Bow was referring to the war but even as she uttered the words she knew in her heart that it would never be over as long as Tesla remained alive. He seemed to know what she was thinking.

'No, there is nowhere I can go. It does not matter, Miss Bow. I am an old man and I shall not be getting very much older. My heart is the same age as me. It will soon stop beating. It has done its work and must soon rest. So my doctor tells me, and I have no reason to disbelieve him.' Tesla paused as if struck by a sudden thought. His features softened. 'Tell me, Miss Bow – how is Billy Chambers? He must be what, sixty by now. Is he well?'

'Yes. I – I am told he was quite well only a few days ago. But he has suffered, Mr Tesla. He never quite recovered from his time with you in Colorado Springs.'

Tesla bowed his head. 'Poor Billy. I truly regret what happened to him. He was a good boy, intelligent and a quick learner, pleasant and friendly, and so loyal and dedicated. I hoped for great things for him. If I had known what my experiment would do to him...'

'Billy doesn't regret it, Mr Tesla,' said Miss Bow softly. 'Billy is proud to have been your assistant. It was obvious from the way he spoke about you.'

'You've seen him?'

'That's what my informant said.'

'That is good. I am glad he is well and that he does not hate me for that.'

'Tell me, Mr Tesla – do you know how long you've got left?'

Tesla shrugged, a sad smile twitching his grey moustache. 'How long is a road? It is as long as it is. I do not know. It might be weeks – it could be minutes.'

'Then we will have to take steps to protect you, Mr Tesla. We must watch over you until the end. The teleforce weapon must never be built.'

'Ah.' Tesla arched an eyebrow and grinned, just a little sheepishly. 'I think you may be too late for that, Miss Bow,' he told her.

'He did *what?*' Crane was aghast. For a moment Miss Harlow was afraid he might burst a blood vessel.

'Tesla built a working model of the teleforce weapon, back in 1916. He was going to give it to both sides but then he found out what was happening in the trenches and figured it might not be a good idea. He actually showed it to my contact. It looks like a chrome-plated clarinet, only much heavier, and it has a kind of bowl at the business end. According to Tesla it has a component missing. The device won't work without it but he reckons any competent theoretical physicist or electrical engineer should be able to work out what the missing part does, and how to make a replacement.'

'For God's sake, are you telling me he keeps it in his hotel room?'

'Not only does he keep it in his room, he keeps it in a wooden box with *TELEFORCE PROJECTOR* painted on it in big red letters. He even tried to explain how it works but my contact isn't too bright when it comes to physics. Something about using vibrations to strip particles from a block of aluminium and then fire them along a radio beam. Hell, don't ask me what any of that means. I'm not entirely sure he wasn't speaking Serbo-Croat.'

'Couldn't your friend have just taken the blasted thing from him?'

'No,' replied Miss Harlow firmly. 'My friend may be faster and stronger than Tesla, and sure, it would have been easy to bully him into letting her take it. But threatening old men isn't what we're about, is it? It would be against everything you believe in, Tony. Would you really have wanted that?'

Crane was ashamed of his outburst. Not for the first time he wondered if he was really up to the job of leading the Yellow Room. Since Worthington had escaped justice, leaving him feeling helpless and ineffectual, those doubts had surfaced on a daily basis. Sometimes he felt that his brain was about to implode under the strain.

'No,' he mumbled, rubbing at his brow, behind which a fearsome migraine was brewing, 'of course not. But what can we do? Are your New York contacts able to keep a close watch on Tesla and be ready to remove that weapon when the time comes? I don't like the idea of waiting for Tesla to die – it's positively ghoulish. Yet I can't see any other course of action.'

Other than to break all my principles and beliefs to keep our God-forsaken species safe from annihilation, he thought gloomily. *I know enough good men who have sold their souls to fight what they believe to be evil, and some have unquestioningly done terrible things. And if I consider myself a better man, a more* humane *man, than those who unblinkingly give the orders for men to die, and those who unthinkingly carry out those orders, then what would be the point of perpetuating humanity?*

'It's OK, Tony,' Miss Harlow said gently, once again seeming to know exactly what was going on in his mind. 'I know you won't do that. We'll think of something. Look, I think we should check up on Billy down in Bournemouth. I have a real bad feeling about him.'

But Crane wasn't listening. His vision was scored by bright, jagged forks and the pain on the left side of his skull was crippling. Light and sound were unbearable; speaking would have been sheer agony. He sat heavily in one of the Yellow Room's big, comfortable armchairs and closed his eyes. Miss Harlow knew of his migraine attacks and knew what to do. She drew the blackout curtains and covered him with a blanket; then made sure he had a glass of water and a couple of aspirins to hand. Then, satisfied that she had done all she could for him, she went to Bournemouth.

When he awoke, all he could feel was pain, in almost every part of his body. There was something stuck to his thigh. It looked like a tooth, the blood on the root still wet. Running his tongue round the inside of his mouth, Billy counted several possible sources. His feet hurt the most, with every toe broken and his soles seemingly scorched to a crisp. They'd made a start on his hands but so far only broken the little finger on each. He was still alive, though. They'd made sure he had enough left in him to suffer for as long as they wanted him to, until he'd told them what they wanted to hear or they were satisfied he had nothing to offer after all.

One of the men was asleep in one of his old armchairs, snoring loudly. The other was in the kitchen, rustling up a meal by the sound of it. Billy's belly growled at the thought. It must be a couple of days since he'd last eaten. If he did live through this, he hoped the bastards hadn't eaten all his eggs and bacon.

Outside, Miss Harlow hesitated before knocking on Billy's front door. There was something wrong. The sounds weren't what she was expecting – the place sounded too crowded for one lonely old man – and she could smell blood. Miss Harlow stood on the doorstep, straining her senses until she was pretty sure she understood what she was dealing with. Then she took a deep breath and went inside.

Billy looked up in surprise when she appeared in the doorway. The woman put her finger to her lips and smiled reassuringly, though she was dismayed by what had been done to the old man. Billy radiated distress and it arrowed into her heart. She quietly crept over to him, knelt and began to untie him. As she was working at the cords a loud voice came from behind her.

'Who the bloody hell are you? How did you get in here? What do you think you're doing? Come on, get away from him!'

Miss Harlow glanced over her shoulder and saw that the speaker was carrying a gun, a brand-new Parabellum by the look of it, and the other man was waking up, roused by his colleague's voice. She smiled sweetly at the old man.

'Close your eyes tight, Billy,' she said softly. Billy took one look into hers and did as he was told.

Churchill was in a dreadful mood. He dropped two Alka-Seltzer tablets into a tumbler of water, thought for a second, and added a third. He used the effervescing liquid to wash down three aspirin. Crane surmised that Winston was suffering from a severe hangover, probably brought about by an attempt to drink his dreaded 'black dog' into submission. The war left Churchill little time in which to paint, his favoured method of overcoming depression.

'Right then, Crane,' the Prime Minister barked. 'I know you well enough to see through this report you sent me on that chap in Bournemouth. It's utter balderdash. A child could see through it. Furthermore, I have a strong suspicion that this flimsy subterfuge is in some way related to an incident that took place yesterday evening involving that very same man. According to the Bournemouth police, they were called to the address of a Mr William Albert Chambers, a local character known as Billy, by a neighbour who heard screams and shooting. In addition to your secretary, a Miss Dorothy Harlow, the police found two young men, tied hand and foot, and Mr Chambers, who had clearly been badly used by those fellows. Miss Harlow told the officers in attendance that she had come to see Mr Chambers and found him tied to a chair and the other men in a state of disarray. She said that because of the way they were shouting and raving she thought they were drunk. She claimed no shots were fired in her presence.'

'Yes,' said Crane. 'That's exactly what Miss Harlow told me.'

Churchill fixed him with a beady and sceptical glare. Crane clammed up.

'The police found that the men's identity papers were forged. Both were in possession of Luger pistols. And both proved to be fluently bilingual in English and German. When the police arrived one of them was shouting "*Lieber Gott, lass es nicht mich.*" The other was crying and calling for his *liebe Mutter*. Mr Chambers was badly injured – he'd been tortured and starved for several days – and claimed he didn't know what happened. One minute, he said, he was being beaten; the next he was free and a pretty young lady was asking if he was alright. In short, Mr Chambers and Miss Harlow both claim to know nothing. I don't suppose you have any idea what happened, Crane?'

Crane shrugged and did his best to look innocent. In truth, there wasn't much he could to Churchill's summary. After all, it was precisely what Miss Harlow had told him. Churchill continued to skewer him with that gimlet eye.

'So this has nothing to do with Mr Chambers going to the police and being detained; nor with your trip down to Bournemouth a few days ago to find out what he knew about the OWVLS?'

'Owls? I'm sorry, Prime Minister, but I really don't see what owls have to do with this.'

'OWVLS!' barked Churchill. 'One Way Voice Links, known by some people as "numbers stations". Get a grip,

Crane!'

'Oh, those transmissions. Well, as you'll see from my report...'

'...which is complete and utter bloody nonsense, and you damned well know it! Look here, Crane – I know you don't trust the intelligence services or the Ministry of War. I don't entirely blame you for that. Between you and me, I don't trust the buggers, either. But you can trust me.'

No, I can't, thought Crane. *I'd love to be able to and I desperately want to, but I know what you are. You're a politician and a patriot, and you'd do the wrong thing for the right reason. People like you must not have access to Tesla's weapon.*

'I'm sorry, sir. My report is an accurate record of what transpired when Miss Harlow and I visited Mr Chambers. I myself wasn't present in Bournemouth yesterday, as you know. I was incapacitated by a migraine. I'm afraid I can't help you.'

Churchill continued to glare, that famous lower lip jutting like a battering ram. He seemed disappointed and furious in equal measure. He downed the remainder of his Alka-Seltzer. It didn't help his mood.

'Get out of my sight,' he growled. 'But mark my words, Crane – if I ever find out you've lied to me, I'll have your bollocks for Christmas tree decorations. Go on, get out!'

'Hello, dear,' said Mrs Pugh as she hung her coat on the rack just inside the door. The rack was pine painted yellow and the hooks were polished brass. 'How's your headache today?'

'Much better, Mrs Pugh,' Crane replied brightly 'Thank

you for asking. And how is your Bert's back? Still playing him up?'

'Well, he's grumbling a lot so that means he's on the mend. The silly old so-and-so – fancy trying to move beer barrels around at his age. He should have left it to Jimmy the cellarman. He's a big, strapping lad only half Bert's age. Is anyone else coming in today?'

'I'm expecting the full team today, Mrs P. Miss Harlow left a message to say she'll be a bit late, probably about half past nine, but the others should all be here soon.'

'Oh, I had a dream about Dorothy this morning. I dreamed she was talking to this old gent, a tall man with a moustache. A foreigner, I think. Very handsome he must have been when he was younger. He was showing her a funny-looking instrument, a bit like a clarinet it was.'

That gave Crane a start. Mrs Pugh, whose talent for dreaming of things as they took place was, in his mind, absolutely genuine, could only have been talking about Tesla and his teleforce weapon. But it couldn't have been Miss Harlow in Mrs Pugh's dream vision. She had left the Yellow Room shortly before midnight and there was no way that she could be in New York with Tesla and return to London by half past nine. Even in peace time that would have been impossible. No, Mrs Pugh had obviously tuned in to Tesla, probably picking up on Crane's own concerns, but that had somehow become mixed up with a genuine dream.

'Sorry, Gladys – I think that one really was just a dream.'

But he wondered.

A Yellow Room

At that early hour there was no one to see her arrival. The door had a sign dangling from the handle: DO NOT DISTURB. She'd been in the room before so it was easy to get in. Nikola Tesla was in bed, looking grey in the face and sunken-eyed, clearly very unwell. His breath came in irregular, shallow gasps. She pulled a chair close to the bed and sat down.

'It's OK, honey,' she said, gently taking his hand. 'I'm here. You're not alone.'

His eyes conveyed gratitude. Daphne Bow was glad to have arrived when she did. The poor old guy was clearly afraid, and with good reason – he was coming to the end of the road. It wasn't right that anyone – least of all this guy, possibly one of the greatest scientists the world had ever seen, certainly up there with Newton and Einstein – should die alone and all but forgotten except by hoodlums and spooks. The least she could do was to hold his hand as his body ground to a halt and his spirit slipped away. She didn't know if Tesla believed in any god, except perhaps electricity, or what his views were with regard to post-mortem survival of the human spirit. In fairness, she didn't really know what she believed either, only that she did. Death wasn't the end. What came after was a matter of conjecture, but she knew there was no final blackout and silence.

At first Tesla weakly squeezed her hand. He was too tired and weak to speak but she could sense his gratitude and was touched by it. She sat there as the old man's grip grew weaker until she was holding only a limp hand, and as his breaths became shallower and the spaces between each became longer and longer. Eventually one breath was followed by an interval that continued until it was obvious that it wasn't an interval but a cessation. Tesla was gone and the secret of the teleforce weapon had gone with him.

Miss Bow bent and kissed the dead man's forehead, a gesture of respect rather than affection. Then she went into the suite's second bedroom and took the long wooden box from the wardrobe in which Tesla had concealed it. The teleforce weapon was just as she had last seen it. She removed it from the box and, with an impish grin, replaced it with a few items from Tesla's workbench – an ammeter, a dynamo and a couple of wireless valves. She knew what to do with the device – there was a place she remembered where it could be buried deep and would never be found.

'That should keep the Feds guessing,' she chuckled as she left.

Two hours later, Alice Monaghan came to clean the room.

He smiled at the pretty young nurse when she brought him a cup of tea. It had been a very strange and terrifying fortnight and he was glad to see friendly faces that wanted nothing more than to help him and make him well again. His feet were still too sore and various toes and fingers were taped and splinted, but the pain was diminishing daily and his bruises were fading. He was safe, warm and comfortable and had discovered that he didn't miss his home at all. That had been a surprise; but then, he now accepted that his old life was over.

Miss Harlow had come by to visit him the previous afternoon, and told him she had arranged a new identity for him, if he wanted it. It would mean a change of town, name and appearance. He hadn't taken long to make up his mind. Billy had no wish to be imprisoned and tortured again. Guardedly, he thanked Miss Harlow for her kindness and agreed to her plan. As soon as he was discharged from hospital he would dress in his best clothes, take his savings, valuables and a few items of sentimental worth, and have his hair and beard trimmed and combed. Miss Harlow had given him a rail ticket for a town a long way from Bournemouth. It was not a return. She had also given him a fair sum of cash, a thick wad of five-pound notes that he hadn't bothered to count.

Billy wasn't wholly grateful, though. To tell the truth, he had accepted her offer because he was afraid not to. Admittedly, he believed that she was acting out of kindness and concern for his well-being, but he wasn't a man to tempt fate. And the last thing he wanted to do was risk making Miss Harlow angry.

When she had come to his house that day, he had closed his eyes tightly, as she asked. But he had opened them out of sheer terror when the shooting began. He had seen what happened to those two men and understood why they had pissed themselves with fright. He too had wet himself and quickly closed his eyes again, wishing to see no more. He didn't know what Miss Harlow really was, but the lovely young woman she appeared to be was only a part of it. He knew he would never forget what he had seen but he could at least try not to think about it. He wouldn't tell anyone about her, not even if he found someone mad or drunk enough to believe him. Because she might find out and that was the last thing he wanted.

Billy Chambers had another secret.

The Actress and the Bishop

Conspiracies were traditionally spawned in the darkest hours of night, by men in dimly-lit, smoke-filled rooms; and this was no exception to the unwritten rule. Cigars dominated the reek, save for a solitary cigarette, a Black Cat. The Freudian ambience was not lost on the man with the cigarette, who was well-read and understood how powerful men were inclined to exaggerate penis size through symbolism. True to psychoanalytical expectation, the most powerful man in the room had the biggest cigar. That man, a stocky, balding man in his late middle years, gestured aggressively with his choice of smoke.

'We need more, something that will be so persuasive that the enemy will accept the information we are feeding him as genuine. We need something – dramatic.' The thrusting cigar illustrated his point.

A bespectacled man raised his own, somewhat smaller cigar to get their attention. 'I have an idea, though I doubt any of you will like it much.' With his free hand he rubbed absently at his head. The wound he'd received in Spain, nearly eight years before, was itching again. 'But we must all make sacrifices in wartime, don't you agree?' Quickly, the man outlined his plan. 'And we must keep it absolutely tight,' he concluded. 'Only a handful of people must know, including us. Secrecy must be absolute.' The last sentence was more heartfelt than the others knew. This was a man with his own secret, a man for whom duplicity and lies were second nature.

Only one of the conspirators, a soldier, objected. While deception was now his trade, the plan was not at all to his liking. The bespectacled man had swayed their fellows. The soldier had no choice but to play their game.

The cigarette-smoking man leaned forward. 'We need to make it as realistic as possible. The piece we play will need to be seen to be eliminated.'

'Yes, and we must keep it secret even from our own people. Just one word of shop-talk might ruin everything.'

'In that case, we must make it real,' said the balding man. 'I don't like it but if that's what needs to be done..' He gestured helplessly, a man with too much resting on his shoulders and too many lives on his conscience.

'This isn't something we can assign to our usual people,' said the bespectacled man.

'Then who do we use?' The bald man was more anxious than he'd been in a long time, since before their cousins had taken their side at last.

'I know just the man for the job,' said the man with the cigarette.

Anthony Crane was in an unusually dark mood. His foul temper was partly due to a ferocious hangover incurred during what had started out as a 'quiet drink' at the Coach and Horses in Soho to celebrate his birthday – an intended low-key outing that had spilled over into several other hostelries he could only vaguely recall and ended with a War Office driver pouring him through his front door at two in the morning, much to the disgust of Mrs Crane and the amusement of their young boy. Some of his spleen arose from the torment of his suppressed feelings for a member of his team. The rest was the fault of the man who had just exited the Yellow Room, a fellow he could not abide and who he regarded as an egotistical idiot, but who had somehow attained a position of authority. And there was the buff folder on his desk, of course. That bloody folder marked with his name and the legend FOR YOUR EYES ONLY.

It contained a single sheet of foolscap but that was enough. As if his team didn't have enough work to be getting on with, now they were expected to do SIS' dirty jobs. Not content with getting the Yellow Room to track troop movements, predict air raids and attempt to psychically persuade high-ranking Nazis to make bad decisions, now SIS had tasked him with locating and eliminating a German spy. When he'd protested that the Yellow Room personnel were all civilians – they were women, elderly or disabled – and couldn't possibly be expected to undertake combat missions, Fleming had just laughed at him.

'We're all combatants now, my good fellow. The first time Hitler dropped a bomb on a residential street he turned every patriotic Briton into a soldier.'

'But we don't have combat or espionage training,' he'd countered. 'You really can't expect an old lady or a chap with one leg to take on the cream of the bloody Gestapo! What about your own operatives in Naval Intelligence? Or SIS?'

'We're spread pretty thinly at the moment,' Fleming

had replied, sucking on that ridiculous cigarette-holder. 'Our boys and girls are preparing for something. Very hush-hush, I don't need to tell you that. But it's a critical point in the game and this piece must be taken off the board before we make our next move.'

Typical bloody Fleming – everything was a game to him, an adventure story like the ones he claimed to be planning to write when 'the show' was over. Crane detested him more with every day that passed. Given the degree of loathing he'd had from the moment he met the man, it was quite an achievement. 'And what,' said Crane sarcastically, 'do you expect my people to do? Beat him to death with a tin of bully beef or take a false leg to him? Choke him with an antimacassar? Throttle him with a hairnet?'

Fleming waved away Crane's remarks. 'Some of you have had firearms training, including yourself. But it needn't come to physical confrontation. Surely one of your team can get into his head somehow – make him jump under a train or shoot himself? Frankly, I don't give a damn what you do so long as you do it and do it bloody quickly. This man – assuming it is a man – has been a thorn in our side for the last two years. Whoever he is, he's operating here in Whitehall and he simply cannot be allowed to jeopardise forthcoming operations. If we're to have any chance at all, we must beat the Bishop!'

And that was where it had ended, with Fleming striding arrogantly to the door, leaving the folder lying on Crane's desk – the folder that contained everything the so-called intelligence services had on the Nazi super-agent codenamed the Bishop. When Crane opened the folder and examined that single sheet of paper, he saw that they didn't really know very much at all.

'And that's it?' Charles Bartley was incredulous. 'This Bishop has access to Whitehall, possibly the War Office, perhaps the Home Office, maybe even the Treasury or Foreign Office. Might be a man, could be a woman. He – or she – is possibly German-born, possibly a British traitor. This document consists of three paragraphs and the word that occurs most often is "possibly", closely followed by "perhaps". They don't even know what secrets the Bishop might have passed to the Nazis! In fact, the nearest thing to solid information here is the statement that *der Bischof* was named by a German spy – under interrogation, and we all know what *that* means – as the Nazis' key agent in Whitehall. Tony, are you sure Fleming's not playing you for a fool, sending us on a bloody wild goose-chase to make us look stupid? It wouldn't be the first time, after all.'

Crane glumly shook his head. 'Don't think I haven't thought of that, Charles. The first thing I did was sound out Wheatley – had to be rather circumspect but it turns out he's heard rumours of this Bishop character. Nothing of substance, unfortunately, but he said the Bishop is rarely mentioned and then only between people who've known each other for years. He was actually whispering on the other end of the line, said he couldn't risk being overheard in case it was by you-know-who. Of course, it was possible he was in cahoots with Fleming, so I took what he said with a pinch of salt. But then I had a phone call from Churchill himself, impressing upon me the importance of doing away with the Bishop. I'm sorry, but it isn't a joke. Winnie isn't one for pulling legs where the Nazis are concerned.'

'Blimey,' said Gladys Pugh. 'I don't think I could *kill* anyone, Mr Crane. My Bert would have a blue fit if I did anything like that. And I am getting on a bit, you know.'

'Don't fret about it, Mrs P,' said Bartley, with a straight face. 'Of course you won't have to kill anyone. But we might have to parachute you behind enemy lines to act as an advance look-out.'

Mrs Pugh began to protest then stopped abruptly, not quite sure if Bartley was being serious. Then he burst out laughing and she joined in. 'But I'll do it if no-one else is willing,' Bartley continued grimly. 'I've been itching for a personal confrontation with Jerry since the war started. I did try to join up when they invaded Poland but the medics turned me down. Flat feet indeed! I don't even know what flat feet are!'

'Never mind, old man,' said Crane consolingly. 'You've made a terrific contribution to the war effort through your factories and the money you gave to the Government, not to mention what you do here.'

'I'll do it,' put in the careworn young woman in black sitting to one side of Crane's desk. 'Those cowardly bastards torpedoed my Frankie. I'd kill every last one of them if I could.'

Crane didn't doubt it. There were many bereaved young women in London who said much the same thing. None of them had asked for a war with Germany. None had asked to be bombed or for their loved ones to be slaughtered and maimed. All they wanted was a kind of justice; or bloody revenge. They didn't care which. He supposed there were women in Germany who felt the same way about the British.

'You haven't had the training, Ethel,' he told her. 'The Bishop would do for you before you even knew who it was. And that's the crux of the matter: we don't know who it is. Any ideas as to how we could find out?'

'I know a few runic spells for discovering thieves,' said Calum Archibald, rubbing at his craggy chin. 'There's a really good one from medieval Iceland. Don't know if it work on spies, mind. Actually, I don't know if it works at all but there's no harm trying.'

'What does it involve?'

'Well, you write the runes and a symbol on a piece of wood, and then you recite some Latin verse. When you've done that you leave the wood where the thief is likely to find it. It afflicts them with paralysis and makes them easy to get hold of.'

'Right,' said Crane. 'The only problem with that is that we have no suspects and no known location or regular haunts. Do you have anything a little less hands-on?'

Archibald made a pained face. 'Not really, But if you do find him I'd be happy to stick the fascist swine with my *sgian-dubh*.'

'Yes – unfortunately the finding is going to be the tricky part.'

Bartley suddenly snapped his fingers. 'How about trying what we did for the Heligoland Affair?'

'It's unlikely to come off. For the Heligoland operation we had a rough location, a known target and the assistance of a dead airman. This time we have bugger-all – if you'll pardon my language, ladies. But I suppose we could give it a try.'

'It seems to be going well so far.'

'Yes, he's taken the bait and done exactly what I expected him to do. Now all we have to do is wait.'

'Does our main asset know the truth?'

'I didn't bring him in. Quite honestly, I don't trust him an inch. A man who plays a double game might easily be playing a third, and I'm not taking that chance. As far as he's concerned our piece is one of theirs. Contact was made using known enemy protocols and his report makes it clear that he believes she's the real thing.'

'I don't know if we're doing the right thing. Not after Coventry. I still have sleepless nights about that. I believe I always will, even though worse would surely have happened if the enemy knew we had broken their codes. Must we really take it so far?'

'It won't be the first time and it won't be the last. It's what happens in war. Every life lost is a sacrifice to victory.'

'So now we just wait?'

'Yes. We'll need to string our wild card along. Give him whatever he asks for but only if he persists, as he surely will. We don't want him to think it's too easy. In fact, the more difficult we make it, the harder he will try. He's a man of unusual integrity. We can always give him a nudge in the right direction if necessary. But for now we wait.'

'Nothing. Four bloody hours and not a thing.'

The Yellow Room was littered with bodies – nearly the full complement of operatives lying seemingly asleep on cushions or slumped in armchairs, wired up to odd-looking electrical devices built by Bartley's technical staff to Crane's specifications. Some of these machines measured heart-rate, blood-pressure and body temperature; others monitored electrical fields and electromagnetism. Crane was gathering evidence to support his theory that his people's abilities were bio-electrical in nature. His goal was to develop mechanisms that would enable them to capture the energies they emitted and somehow feed them back, amplifying and enhancing their talents. At least, that was the theory. If it didn't work, at least he'd be able to keep an eye on their physical health.

The best results they'd had so far was when Mrs Pugh was wired up to an electroencephalograph. That had shown remarkable parallels to the readings obtained by Gibbs, Davis and Lennox in 1935 – although she'd been tested by several doctors and found to be as healthy as a young dray-horse, when she demonstrated her talent Gladys' brain-waves showed clear similarities to clinical absence seizures. In other words, the evidence indicated that Gladys Pugh was an epileptic while she was dreaming, but not when she was awake or in ordinary sleep. Crane couldn't wait to replicate the tests using the other Yellow Room staff as subjects, and was particularly keen to see what the readings showed when they were all in trance together and psychically linked, as they were at the moment. But Bartley's tame boffins were still constructing the individual EEGs he'd need, and were working on ways to get a combined reading.

The only absentee was the mysterious Miss Dorothy Harlow, who although nominally employed as Crane's clerical assistant had never been known to take minutes or file so much as a single sheet of paper. She had taken a leave of absence a week earlier to attend to some unspecified business. She hadn't said when she would return. Crane suspected that she was spending some time with a lover. The thought was depressing. He was sufficiently honest to admit to himself that he had strong feelings for Miss Harlow; and responsible enough to refuse to allow his emotions to influence his behaviour. He had a wife and child, and would do nothing to jeopardise their happiness. Furthermore, he did not love his wife any less than he had before Miss Harlow had entered his life. It was a conundrum without a solution, so all he could do was carry on as usual and hope for the best. However, the cause wasn't helped by his conviction that Dorothy felt the same way about him.

Crane muttered an obscenity and decided to rouse the Yellow Room operatives from their collective slumber. Now he had another insoluble problem to add to his collection.

As he began disconnecting the machinery prior to waking the sleepers, Dorothy Harlow suddenly appeared, seeming to step out of a shadow in the corner by his desk. She was dressed as if for a night at the theatre, smart and sleek in a black dress with red piping and a scarlet beret-like hat with a veil. She'd changed her hair again – the plait had gone and it was much shorter, almost a bob. She was smoking a cigarette in a holder.

'I really do wish you wouldn't do that, Dorothy,' Crane complained, though he was smiling broadly as he always did when she made one of her unorthodox entrances.

'Sorry, Tony,' she grinned mischievously. 'It's faster than taking the stairs. Say, what's going on here? Was your daily briefing even more boring than usual? I'm not at all surprised. These civil service meetings get me the same way every time.'

'Oh well, I might as well let these sleeping beauties get another ten minutes in the Land of Nod while I tell you what's happened.'

He quickly told her about the Bishop and Fleming's unreasonable demand that they find and eliminate the spy. Miss Harlow became wary.

'I'll help find this Bishop but I've told you before – I won't kill anyone in cold blood. If we find this guy we take him alive and hand him over to SIS. Let them do their own dirty work, *capisce*? Anyway, it's hypothetical. Before we find him we'll need someone to look for and somewhere to look. As far as I can make out, we ain't got either of those things, and there's no way of getting them. If SIS don't have anything then nor do we. We may as well hold a goddamned séance.'

The woman was clearly an unwilling visitor. She ostentatiously refused to speak to Crane, offered only a tight smile to Mrs Pugh, and roundly ignored everyone else except Miss Harlow, who she took pains to avoid either touching or looking at. Crane wasn't at all surprised that she cut him dead. He had, after all, been instrumental in sending her to prison only weeks before. He regretted that; but she would have regretted it more if Crane hadn't intervened.

'It's bloody ridiculous,' Churchill had complained. 'I see no purpose in wasting resources on this woman, especially in wartime. We'll be a laughing stock.'

'It's got to be done,' Crane countered. 'Helen Duncan is the genuine article. She knew about the *Barham* sinking even when it was successfully kept from most of the

Admiralty. Alright, she embellished whatever she was told by whatever told her, but I've questioned her myself and my people have assessed her. Whatever a medium is, she's one. The problem is that she can't keep her mouth shut, and at this stage of the war whatever she discovers through her talent could cause serious problems. She's already served one prison sentence for fakery, though I'm not entirely sure Harry Price himself wasn't responsible for some of that.'

'I don't like it, Crane,' Churchill huffed. 'The Witchcraft Act indeed! And using such obsolete tomfoolery to put an innocent woman in gaol would be morally reprehensible.'

'It has to be done,' Crane stubbornly replied. 'Security is paramount.' *And so is the life of that innocent woman*, he thought. *SIS will kill her to keep her quiet, and I'd rather she lost her freedom than that.*

And so Helen Duncan had gone to prison. And now here she was in the Yellow Room – a chubby, unhealthy-looking woman with wary eyes and a bitter countenance, accompanied by two police constables and a pinch-faced woman prison officer. Getting her out of Holloway for the evening hadn't been easy. Reportedly, there had been a stand-up row between Churchill and Herbert Morrison, the Home Secretary. But the Prime Minister had prevailed. Mrs Duncan was allowed out, albeit under guard and in manacles, which the prison officer had only reluctantly removed when Crane instructed her to do so.

Eventually Crane ordered Mrs Duncan's escort out of the room. Miss Harlow had requisitioned a large dining table from somewhere, and an assortment of chairs encircled it. Crane told everyone to be seated.

'Do you know why you're here?' he asked the medium.

She looked at him for the first time. 'Aye – you want me to do what you tried to prove I couldn't do, even though you know I could. Don't worry – I know why you did it, and I forgive you for it. But don't expect me to be grateful for nine months in Holloway, laddie.'

Crane's face burned with shame. Mrs Duncan looked around the table, now openly curious about the company she was in. 'All of you have got something like I have – all but you two.' She nodded at Crane and pointed at Miss Harlow. 'You're ordinary, Mr Crane; no talents at all. As for you, lassie – I don't know what you are but I do know you're not like anyone else I've ever met. There's a fog around you and the spirits won't even admit you're there. You two should leave the table and sit over at the desk, in the candle-light. Shall we make a start?'

Crane and Miss Harlow did as Mrs Duncan asked, sitting so that they faced the medium. Then Crane addressed her. 'Mrs Duncan, we need information about a person we know only as "Bishop". This person is a Nazi spy and is attached to Whitehall in some way. Whatever the spirits can tell us about the Bishop may be helpful. Please, continue in your own time.'

'Light the candle and turn out the lights, please. Now everyone join hands. Please be silent, do not break the circle, and do not disturb me while I'm in trance as it could be dangerous to me. I ask the spirits if there are any among them who know of the German spy Mr Crane speaks of.'

Miss Harlow put a match to the candle and Crane switched the electric lights off. The room was silent but for the sound of Mrs Duncan's hoarse, rhythmic breathing. The flickering shadows settled and deepened. The silence stretched on. Crane's attention was focused on the portly Scotswoman.

After what seemed an eternity, he realised that the room was less dark. Helen Duncan's face appeared to be glowing softly. He leaned forward expectantly. Mrs Duncan had been examined thoroughly by a prison doctor and searched before leaving Holloway, and she'd had no contact with anyone except her escort until arriving in the Yellow Room. Whatever spirit or psychic phenomena took place now would not be fakery.

The glow intensified. Crane saw something like semi-solid smoke seeping from the medium's mouth and nose, an emission glowing with the same light as her face. It slowly formed wreaths around her head, coils that shifted sluggishly in the draught from under the door and the breath of the sitters. Shapes like vague, half-formed faces appeared and dissolved. He shivered as the temperature dropped rapidly. The smoke settled around Mrs Duncan's face and she became someone else.

'Dear God!' The voice was deep and masculine and anguished. The Scottish accent was gone, replaced by a cockney one. 'Everything's burning! The bloody ship's going down! Jimmy, look out!'

There was silence, broken only by a low sob from Ethel Bingham. Then the voice issued again, calmer this time, from Helen Duncan's lips. 'Ethel? Don't fret, love. It's over now. It's peaceful here and they're looking after me. You live your life and be happy, girl. Be strong for me. And no more wearing black, you hear me? It doesn't suit you. I'll see you later.'

In the candlelight Crane saw tears flowing down Ethel's cheeks. To her credit, she didn't say a word and did not break the circle. Crane realised his hair was standing on end and the room was getting cold. Mrs Duncan's chin sank back onto her chest and the rhythmic breathing resumed. Then she spoke again. Or rather, something spoke through her.

The voice had changed. Now it was a grating, buzzing sound like nothing he'd ever heard before. It wasn't the kind of voice that could come from human vocal chords. It reminded him a bit of Mr Punch from the seaside shows of his childhood, only this was flat and emotionless, and sounded like it was made by a swozzle in the mouth of a mechanical demon. If the voice had been human it might have been urbane and cultured. Crane's skin was crawling with what seemed to be static electricity. He hoped the boffins in the next room were getting readings.

'So this is the famous Yellow Room. I was expecting something a bit grander than this. You over at the desk – you must be Anthony Crane. It is too early for you to be the son. It is a pleasure to meet you at last. I have heard so much about you. Most of it good, though I suppose it depends on your point of view. At this time you may ask me three questions. I suggest you choose your words carefully.'

The business at hand takes priority, thought Crane. *No matter how fascinating this is, no matter how much I might be able to expand my own knowledge and understanding of this phenomenon, I must focus on what needs to be done.*

'How do we identify and find the Nazi spy known as the Bishop?'

'You must do three things, in this order. First, examine the source of the little information you have. Then follow that to wherever it leads. Finally, you must sacrifice a queen. I will say no more on this matter.'

Crane didn't understand but he let it pass. If nothing more was going to be said then it was pointless wasting his remaining questions. 'A couple of years ago I met someone who called himself Jack Worthington, though I don't know if that was his real name. Will I ever encounter him again?'

'You will. You must. But it will be too late.'

The reply sent a shiver along Crane's spine, a tremor that had little to do with the plunging temperature. Jack Worthington was the last person he ever wanted to see again; but there was unfinished business between them, and Crane was certain that its conclusion was his personal imperative. He knew he had to kill Worthington, or die in the attempt. But why would it be too late? He found he didn't really want to know. That information might dissuade him from his intention to put the man down like the rabid dog he was.

'Who are you?'

Mrs Duncan emitted a pulsing screech that sounded like sheet metal scraping along a telephone wire. Appalled, Crane understood that it was a species of laughter. 'We do not have names, Mr Crane. We have identities, codes that describe us, but not those labels you transients so casually adopt as synecdoches. The overwhelming majority of us have no interest in you. But some of us work in your interests, others against. I am one of the former. If you must call me something, call me Tom. That is how I am most often known to your kind. And that's all you need to know because it's all you can understand. I must leave now – this physical vessel cannot contain me for very long. But before I return to my realm, I have a message for one of you: Delilah must keep watch over her sleeping Samson, and when the time is right she must betray him.'

Crane realised he was shaking like a leaf and his teeth were chattering. Beside him, Dorothy Harlow gasped, the exhalation visible as a plume of condensation. Mrs Duncan's head fell forward and she began to snore loudly. The séance was over.

At first, SIS had refused to hand over the documents relating to the interrogation in which the Bishop had been named. 'Top secret, old chap,' Fleming had said, condescendingly. 'It's need to know only, and you lot don't need to know.' A quick telephone call to the Prime Minister, followed by a rather longer and much louder one from Churchill to Major-General Sir Stewart Menzies, the head of SIS, had changed that. Within the hour, two sullen SIS agents appeared at the Yellow Room door with another cardboard folder, somewhat bulkier than the one Fleming had brought. Crane took delivery of the file and, when they looked as though they wanted to hang around while he read it, told them in no uncertain terms to bugger off.

The file made for grim reading. It detailed the interrogation of a minor War Office civil servant named Alfred Walter Fairbrother, whose older brother Arthur was a one-time Labour councillor in one the East End boroughs, ex-member of Mosley's Blackshirts, latterly a Conservative activist unceremoniously ejected from the party in 1942 when his connections with the Right Club were exposed. The file contained cuttings of pro-Nazi letters Arthur had written to local and national newspapers; photographs of him with known Nazi appeasers and sympathisers, including Archibald Ramsay and the Duke of Westminster; and transcripts of correspondence between Arthur Fairbrother and Tyler Kent, the US Embassy clerk whose arrest for spying had delivered the Right Club's so-called Red Book, which contained its membership list, into the hands of the authorities. Arthur was at present residing in one of His Majesty's prisons.

Because of his job, Alfred Fairbrother had been investigated extensively but nothing incriminating was unearthed and SIS had concluded that he did not share his brother's political views. If anything, his ideals tended toward communism. Although that in itself was cause enough for suspicion, any interest in Alfred cooled when Germany attacked the Soviet Union, which became Britain's ally by default. At the time of his arrest Fairbrother was in possession of top secret documents pertaining to an Allied military force referred to only as 'FUSAG' – the relevant documents in the dossier had been severely redacted and were unreadable – and appeared to have been on the brink of passing them to another Nazi agent. While Fairbrother's guilt was self-evident, SIS had been eager to extract from him the identity of the other agent. But Fairbrother had refused to speak and so the interrogation became increasingly brutal. He had been kept naked and cold, deprived of food and sleep, given electric shocks, beaten, drugged and repeatedly subjected to an ordeal which involved covering his head with a thick towel and pouring water upon it. This procedure did not break him, however. All he would say were two words: *der Bischof*. It was obvious to Crane that Fairbrother was actually more afraid of the Bishop than he was of prolongation of his interrogation. After two weeks of extreme mistreatment, Fairbrother died. Officially, the cause of death was heart failure. Of course it was. It had to be, because unlike the despicable Gestapo, our boys were gentlemen who would never stoop to torture or summary execution.

Fleming, naturally, had been less than honest with him. The transcripts and commentaries made it quite clear that SIS had known of the Bishop for some time. The name had been extracted – invariably under duress – from at least three other German agents. It was true that nothing was known except for the code name, but the Nazi's cat's-paws had worked at the War Office, the Admiralty, and even SIS itself. It was no wonder they were so intent on catching the Bishop. He – or she – wasn't only dangerous but was also potentially highly embarrassing.

The file made Crane feel sick but he had to read it all because somewhere in there was the clue that would eventually lead him to the Bishop. *Follow it to wherever it leads*. What did that mean, exactly? Then it came to him. The file gave Fairbrother's address. It was the only solid information in the sheaf of documents so logically it was where he should start his search.

'There's not much left.' Edward Vance adjusted his stance to ease the chafing, wondering for the umpteenth time why his tin leg's harness always seemed to rub more painfully when it was raining. Someone had once told him it was the leather strapping swelling as it absorbed atmospheric moisture but he wasn't convinced.

'Fairbrother lived in the next street but one,' said Crane. 'I understand it escaped the worst of the bombing. They say the Devil looks after his own, don't they? Well, he does until the SIS goons get hold of them.'

Vance puffed irritably on his Lucky Strike. 'I'm surprised you took that séance seriously. That message for Ethel sounded genuine enough but most of it was gibberish. I mean, what was all that nonsense about Samson and Delilah?'

'No idea, old man. Come on – let's see what Alfred Fairbrother's home can tell us.'

Fairbrother's widow was as hostile as Crane expected. He waved aside her protests with a search warrant and told her to remain seated in the parlour while he and Vance had a look round. Vance's talent was for psychometry, the ability to obtain information from handling objects. Now he limped round the house, his hands trailing across surfaces and objects. Crane was reminded of a bloodhound casting around for a scent.

'Crane, come over here. This cabinet – I think I've got something.'

They were in the parlour, where Mrs Fairbrother sat regarding them balefully. She was short, fat and wide-mouthed. Vance thought she looked like a venomous toad. 'They've already searched in there. You won't find anything.'

The woman was referring to either the police or SIS – perhaps both. Crane didn't have a high opinion of the police, and he ranked SIS operatives several places below the police in the intelligence stakes.

At first glance, the contents of the cabinet were disappointing. 'Alfred collected theatre programmes,' said the man's widow. 'Nothing illegal about that.' She folded her arms and thrust out her chin, daring them to contradict her.

'Indeed,' Crane replied, leafing through the programmes. There must have been nearly a hundred of them. 'Keen theatre-goer, was he?'

'Yes. He went to at least one play a week. If it was a good production he'd see it several times, usually a week or so apart so he could see where they'd made changes to improve the performance. Always bought a programme – that's why there are so many duplicates. They're all dated, as you can see.'

Crane did see. He saw that Alfred Fairbrother had been to see *Blithe Spirit* at the St James's Theatre no less than eight times in the three months leading up to his arrest. One of those dates coincided with Crane taking his wife to see it as a birthday treat. His wife loved it but he hadn't thought much of the play as a whole – Coward was a bit frivolous for his taste. He was, however, willing to concede that Margaret Rutherford's performance as Madame Arcati had been splendid. He knew Vance had seen the play too; indeed, it was he who had suggested to Crane that Mrs Crane might enjoy it.

Outside the Fairbrother house he passed the *Blithe Spirit* programmes to Vance and was gratified to see his colleague's eyes widen with interest.

'This is it,' he said. 'It's something to do with this play. To be precise, I'm getting a mental picture of Kay Hammond, who plays Elvira Condomine. But surely *she* can't be the Bishop? Her father's Sir Guy Standing. He fought Jerry in the Great War and – and – he was in *Lives of a Bengal Lancer*, for God's sake!'

Crane smiled at his Vance's consternation. 'I agree she seems a little too well-known to be a Nazi agent, and obviously the daughter of a man who was in one of your favourite films could never be a spy. However, I would point out that half our aristocrats and politicians are Nazi sympathisers, some more openly than others, but your opinion of the Standing clan is good enough for me. Honestly, Edward – it probably means nothing more than that Fairbrother took a fancy to her. Nevertheless, it is clear to me that the St James's Theatre is our next port of call. It may not be Miss Hammond but something drew Fairbrother there and we need to find out what that was. First I need to make a call.'

'They're all telling the truth,' said the little Armenian. 'Each and every one of them is exactly as he or she seems, with the exception of Coward, who plays so many roles at once that he has become trapped like a man in a labyrinth of mirrors. But whatever he may be, one thing he is not is a Nazi agent. Edward knows why.'

Vance coughed to hide his embarrassment. 'I presume you mean that Mr Coward is of the same – er – *persuasion* as myself and thus not sympathetic to a regime that would like to exterminate people like us. And you too, if I am not very much mistaken, Mr Dakessian.'

Mikaiel Dakessian smiled and inclined his head. 'Yes, I too am a friend of Mrs King, as they say. I will not deny it here. Besides, I have often seen Coward and his set at the

Pink Sink. Do you go there, Edward?'

'My pocket doesn't stretch to it, I'm afraid. I usually go the Willie or the Vauxhall Tavern, or one of the Soho bungeries if my leg's playing up and I can't walk too far.'

'But that's ridiculous,' Crane snapped. He was aware of his friends' persuasions and didn't care one jot about either that or their favoured watering holes. 'We've interviewed the cast, the understudies, the director, the stagehands and theatre staff – everyone from Noël Coward to the bloody cleaners. Surely one of them must have rung the alarm bells?'

Dakessian shrugged. 'Tony, you know I am never wrong. Edward shook their hands, all of them, so he will have come to the same conclusion. I know he was a little in awe of Coward but his talent does not lie. We both are quite certain: they are all clean.'

'What about Miss Hammond? Not even a tingle, Edward? No hint at all of anything untoward, Mikaiel?'

Vance's shrug and outspread hands were mirrored by Dakessian. 'Nothing,' said the Armenian. 'She is patriotic, and numbers many Jews and people of *our type* among her friends. I have no doubt as to her loyalties.'

'But this is absurd,' Crane groaned. 'How am I supposed to follow this wherever it leads if it doesn't bloody lead anywhere?'

'That entity which spoke to you through Mrs Duncan – why do you believe it was trustworthy?' Dakessian asked.

'I believe it because the medium was Helen Duncan. I haven't told any of you this before, but she was imprisoned because of me. I'm not proud of that but I had good reason. Those fools at SIS were convinced she was a Nazi spy but they had no proof except for an accusation by that ghost-hunter chap, Harry Price. You know what a great self-publicist he is? Well, SIS believed his version of events – that she was an intermediary of some sort, passing secret information to the enemy and also using it for personal gain. Personally, I've always found Price's methods as questionable as those of the fraudulent mediums he claims to have exposed. I was tipped off that they were going to do away with her – their reasoning was that Jerry was going to do it sooner or later anyway, so they might as well plug the supposed leak permanently before the Nazis got anything else out of her. The whole thing was utter codswallop but you know what SIS are like. They honestly believe they're licensed to kill. So I had a drink with my father's old chum Herbert Morrison, and we cooked up the prosecution, made sure there was a big public hoo-ha, and saw to it that she was put in Holloway, hopefully out of harm's way. As you heard last night, Edward, she knew what I'd done.'

'Yes,' Dakessian persisted, 'but why do you believe Helen Duncan is a genuine medium? I know for a fact that you don't really believe in the supernatural. You believe all these phenomena can be explained in scientific terms.'

'Well, I don't believe in gods or ghosts, that much is true. But I do think there are forces, presences that we sometimes come into contact with that seem like magical or divine entities but in reality are perfectly natural. I am confident that one day we will understand them and the laws that govern them – perhaps we may even replicate their apparent powers. I think some people have even made a start – Swedenborg would have made a top-notch scientist if he hadn't been so completely immersed in a religious worldview; and today we have people like Heisenberg, Dirac and Bohr working in areas that could hold the key to these mysteries. There are people, like the Yellow Room operatives, who are able to access these phenomena; and there are others who seem to be conduits to the inhabitants of worlds we cannot even see. I doubt that Mrs Duncan or anyone else is able to commune with the dead. But something out there may be sending us messages using the voices and faces of our departed loved ones as a kind of disguise. That is why I believe Mrs Duncan is genuine – that and the fact that when I attended one of her séances a few years ago she had a message from my late father, a message that contained information only he could have known. And before you say anything, even if she was reading my mind, would that not be equally remarkable?'

'Genuine or not, she's sent us on a wild goose chase this time,' said Vance impatiently. 'There's nothing here for us.'

As the three of them skirted Parliament Square, Crane stopped dead. 'I say, I've just had a thought. All the people we interviewed today – what if one of them was an intermediary between Fairbrother and the Bishop but didn't know it? Would that have been enough to mask their involvement from you two?'

Dakessian conceded that he would have been unable to distinguish between ignorance and innocence. Vance was unequivocal. 'If there was a connection – any connection – between Fairbrother and any one of them, I would have sensed it. And I didn't, which means there isn't one. Yet

I'm wholly certain that production of *Blithe Spirit* is what connects him to the Bishop. I can't explain it, Tony.'

'Of course!' Dakessian slapped his forehead in exasperation. 'How long has it been since Fairbrother was arrested? Two months? Three? Yet we didn't ask if any of the cast or staff had left in that time! Elementary police work – and we missed it!'

'Right,' said Crane decisively. 'Mikaiel, we'll go back to the theatre. Edward, get back to the Yellow Room and get the gang together, just in case. Include Miss Harlow in that. Tell them we need to be ready for anything.'

'Ah, yes,' said Dakessian, 'the mysterious Miss Harlow. I was wondering when I would get to meet her. I was beginning to think she was avoiding me.'

'Well, she's usually around somewhere, but she does have a habit of sort of appearing and disappearing at inconvenient moments.'

Dakessian and Crane strode back the way they had come, toward the St James's Theatre. Vance continued up Whitehall, whistling 'Mad about the Boy' as he limped along.

It turned out that three people had left the St James's Theatre since Alfred Fairbrother's arrest. Two were stagehands who left because they had received their call-up papers and were presently in the final stages of military training; the third, a man of sixty formerly employed as a costume designer, had been dismissed for turning up for work once too often in a state of advanced inebriation. That in itself probably wouldn't have sufficed to earn him the sack – it was the theatre, after all – but drunkenly insulting the cast proved too much even for such a liberal profession. Working on the assumption that the new soldiers probably wouldn't be going anywhere for a while, Crane decided that he and Dakessian would pay the ex-costumier a visit.

Edmund George lived in a seedy two-room flat above a tobacconist's shop in Old Compton Street. The dwelling consisted of a tiny lounge and an even smaller bedroom, decorated with cheap, blue rose-patterned wallpaper that looked like it was a veteran of the Boer War, frayed and worn rugs and the ubiquitous black-out curtains. A standard lamp without a shade loomed over a grubby brown settee, a rickety wooden chair and a battered drop-leaf table that had no room to spread its wooden wings. The floorboards were black with trodden-in grease and dirt from the streets, and the flat stank of stale cabbage, cigarette smoke, and the contents of a chamber pot in dire need of emptying. One corner of the lounge was occupied by an untidy heap of old beer and rum bottles; while another was taken up by a precariously-leaning stack of yellowing newspapers.

Crane and Dakessian hovered uncertainly in the middle of the room, hardly daring to breathe and unwilling to sit on either the filthy settee or the fragile chair. George matched his surroundings perfectly. He was short and thin enough to be relatively comfortable in such a restrictive space, and his clothes were sufficiently grimy and threadbare to enable him to blend in with his surroundings. Even his body odour merged seemingly with the ambient stench. George was unshaven and his grey hair was in need of a trim. Red-rimmed eyes and trembling fingers told a parallel story, one of alcoholic despair.

'Alfred Fairbrother? Never heard of him,' he rasped.

Dakessian smiled and shook his head. 'Please don't lie to us, Mr George,' he said. 'You have not only heard of him – you knew him well. It may be your habit to lie to the police, and that habit may even be both necessary and successful. But do not lie to us. We are not the police. We are – ah – something else entirely, something more powerful and far more dangerous. Besides, we do not care that you are a queer. I myself prefer boys to girls. We're not here to take you in for indiscretions with soldiers in Hyde Park or acts of gross indecency with brewery hands in public toilets. Yes, I know exactly what you did in the early hours of this morning, so please do not insult me by denying it.'

The older man's eyes darted wildly from the door to the window, as if he was weighing up which exit afforded him the best chance of escape. Crane saw that George clearly didn't believe that he was not about to be arrested for the crime of expressing his sexuality with consenting partners. 'We're not here to arrest you for being a homosexual,' Crane put in. 'That's true enough. But we are here about an even more serious matter and it would be better for you to co-operate with us. Now tell us about Fairbrother.'

George licked his lips nervously. 'I met Alf a few months ago, I don't remember exactly when. It was in the Willie. I don't know what he was doing there – it was obvious he wasn't one of us. I was sitting having a pint and a gasper when he came over. I had a programme for *Blithe Spirit*; it was just after opening night. He said he was interested in the theatre, so we talked about that. He knew quite a lot about Shakespeare and theatre history. He had me worked out right from the start. He knew I was queer and that I liked a drink. He also seemed to know that I was short of money and offered me a bit of business. No, not *that* sort of business – not with Alf. He liked the ladies. I saw him with several different women at performances, and none of them looked like the sort of girl you'd marry, if you get my meaning.'

'What sort of business was it?'

'He said it was black market goods – American cigarettes, nylons, meat, medicines, what have you. Alf said he was being watched by the police so he had to be careful and do all his business through intermediaries. The arrangement was that he would attend a performance once a week and leave a package in the cloakroom. During the performance I would collect it and replace it with another identical one.'

'What then?'

'After the show I'd deliver the package to an address in Bermondsey – Knight Street, just off Jamaica Road. The man I delivered it to would give me another in exchange, and pay me five pounds – good money and worth taking a risk. The new package would be exchanged for another of Alf's next time.'

It was a convincing ruse, Crane thought. There was plenty of money to be made on the black market, so five pounds was a tempting and entirely reasonable carrot to dangle before a man with financial woes. 'What about the man you delivered to? Do you have a name? Can you describe him?'

'He was small, not much over five feet, slim build, dark hair, clean shaven. I'd say he was aged between twenty and thirty. Always wore a double-breasted dark grey suit – well-tailored, expensive. English, posh accent, soft voice – not the sort you'd expect to hear in a Bermondsey slum. He wouldn't let me in the house, just stood in the doorway in the dark so I never got a really good look at him. He told me to call him Mr Mitre. Seemed to think it was rather funny.'

'What do you think?'

'George told us everything he knows,' Dakessian replied. Soho Square was empty for the time of day and for once it had been easy to find an unoccupied bench. 'He held nothing back and didn't lie. Well, it looks like we've located our quarry. "Mr Mitre" must be the Bishop.'

Crane laughed. 'Oh, I don't think so, Mikaiel. It's clever, arrogant word-play. Yes, the word "mitre" can mean a bishop's headgear – but in carpentry it's also a kind of join between two pieces of wood. I'd say we have another intermediary. Still, it shows we're on the right track.'

'So what's our next move?'

'We keep Mitre's address under observation. If the Bishop is the Moriarty figure SIS believes him to be, then Alfred Fairbrother won't have been his only source of information. We'll watch him for a week and pass whatever we find out to SIS. With any luck we'll be able to deliver not only the Bishop but a whole Nazi spy ring. That ought to keep Fleming off our backs for a while.'

'In that case you'll have to manage without me. I'm off to Paris in a couple of days. We lost a whole network in March, thanks to that incompetent fool in Baker Street ignoring Juggler's warning. Vera's putting on a brave face but it doesn't take my powers of perception to know she's heartbroken and tormented by guilt at the loss of so many of her boys, and especially the girls. But we have to set up a new network very quickly. The briefing begins in a couple of hours. I don't know what's brewing but SOE operations across France are being stepped up and it looks as though I'll be eating baguettes and camembert for some time. It's such a shame. I really was looking forward to meeting Miss Harlow. I wanted to see if she felt the same way about you.'

Crane froze. He'd expected the uncannily perceptive Dakessian to see through his studied indifference to Dorothy sooner rather than later, but this was a shock nevertheless. 'Mikaiel, what are you on about? Why should she feel anything for me?' The protest was a matter of form rather than a genuine attempt to dissemble.

'Tony, we've known each other for several years. And you know that I see deeper than other people. Even if I didn't know you so well, I would still be able to see that you have strong feelings for her – just as I can see that your loyalty to your wife and son is unbreakable. That secret will remain between the two of us. But the path you have chosen will not be an easy one, my friend. I want you to know that I am here if you feel the need to unburden yourself. At least, I shall be when I return from Paris – if all goes well, of course.'

'You're quite fond of Paris, aren't you?'

The Armenian smiled nostalgically. 'I'm as fond of Paris as you are of Miss Harlow, Tony. It's where I first met Crowley, Duchamp and Breton, Cocteau and Dalí. I lost my virginity there, to an American painter *manqué* named Butch, believe it or not. He was a dreadful painter but a magnificent lover. My second favourite city is Berlin. I once got terribly drunk in the Kit-Kat with Isherwood and an appalling Russian fellow who thought vomiting over my trousers was hilarious. I'll spare your blushes by not saying what he had been doing down there.'

'You've led quite a life, Mikaiel,' Crane laughed.

'And will continue to do so for a very long time, I hope. I have an idea this Paris mission will be rather dangerous so I've taken the precaution of updating my will. I'm leaving you my first edition of Burton's translation of *The Perfumed Garden of the Shayk Nefzawi* and a set of deliciously outrageous Beardsley prints. I'd keep them out of the wife's way, if I were you.'

'I'm sure it won't come to that.'

'No? It's already come to that for so many men and women, and children, in this damned war. So many lives cut short and ruined because of a handful of madmen and a multitude of fools. It's a supreme irony that Owen, Brooke and Thomas died in the Great War yet the likes of Hitler, Göring and Stalin survived to ferment this bloody tragedy. The poets are dead while the maniacs live on to continue the slaughter where they left off in 1918. Tony, this war has become an article of faith for too many fanatical nationalists. Every world leader now has a vested interest in keeping the world at war, because treason is the only way to depose them. I fear it will only end when someone invents a bomb so big and powerful it can blow entire cities to kingdom come. And when military men have weapons that give them an advantage they use them, no matter how appalling the carnage. The surviving leader will be lord of all he surveys; but all he will see is an ocean of ash and corpses, and a few broken survivors rooting for food among the ruins. He'll be like Ralph Richardson's character in *Things to Come*, a big pig in a little sty. Perhaps one day it will turn out like the film, that humanity's only hope for peace and civilised sanity will lie in Iraq, where civilisation began. Perhaps that will be where our hope lies, where we can start all over again and begin to build a better future as we look to the stars instead of squabbling over money or patches of earth or antique grudges. "All the universe – or nothingness? Which shall it be?"'

They sat in silence for a few minutes. Then Crane asked Dakessian to explain how he knew about George's early-morning liaisons.

'I deduced those from the smell of fresh hops and yeast, and unwashed urinals; and the aroma of Blanco, gun oil and rhododendron. Also, Mr George had traces of two distinct – um – *emissions* on his shirt, and both soil and carbolic acid on the knees of his trousers. Hyde Park was a lucky guess.'

'You're like Sherlock Holmes,' said Crane admiringly. 'How do you do it? Did you have special training – yoga or Tibetan mysticism or something?'

Dakessian shrugged. 'No, I have only nature's gifts. I was born with exceptional senses and a reasonable degree of intelligence. Those senses present me with more information than is available to other people, and that's all there is to it. But I don't know of another soul who has such sharp senses.'

But Crane did, and the thought made him sad.

Women thought Fleming handsome but Crane couldn't see

it. To him the man's face spoke of arrogance and superiority, even cruelty. The eyes were unreadable, little mirrors that reflected only the fears and insecurities of those who gazed into them. The mouth was by turns petulant, sneering and disapproving. The only exceptions were the smiles it bore when something bad was about to happen to someone Fleming didn't like. Crane didn't like the man at all, trusted him no further than a child could throw an elephant, and refused to meet him anywhere but the Yellow Room, which Fleming loathed. It was just a shame the room didn't make Fleming physically ill, the way it affected Wheatley.

'I do wish you'd redecorate this bloody place.' Fleming's mouth was a moue of distaste. 'It practically turns my damned stomach.'

'I rather like it,' Crane responded cheerfully. 'It wasn't all yellow when we moved in but Mrs Pugh said the colour brought out her psychic abilities so I thought we might as well go the whole hog. It's a nice, happy colour, don't you think?'

Fleming's scowl was a Shakespearean soliloquy of disagreement. 'I didn't come here to talk about interior decorating,' he snapped. 'I want to know if your gang of frauds has made any progress in identifying and eliminating the Bishop.'

The insult didn't bother Crane. As much as Fleming disparaged the Yellow Room and its operatives, he knew they got results. He was, despite his sneers, a believer in ghosts, magic and psychic phenomena. The question was, how much should Crane tell him?

'We've had a chap under observation in Bermondsey

for about a week now,' he said eventually. 'He acted as a go-between, passing packages from the Bishop to Fairbrother and back again. There was another intermediary – but he was a dupe who knows nothing. The man we've been watching is Andrew Dugdale, also known as "Mr Mitre" – I'm sure you see the pun. So far, Dugdale hasn't made any suspicious moves. But we think it's only a matter of time. Fairbrother can't have been the Bishop's only informant, and we think the Bishop must use as few intermediaries as possible, to reduce the risk of discovery.'

Fleming lit yet another cigarette. 'Perhaps we should bring Dugdale in and interrogate him. It would be quicker than just watching and waiting. What do you know about him?'

'The local gossip is that he's a racketeer, though no one has ever seen him hawking illicit goods. He doesn't drink in the local pubs. He buys newspapers from a corner shop but nothing else – that's where we found out his name, if that is indeed his real name. He has no known friends or associates in the area. All we have is a description – small, aged around twenty-five, dark brown hair, ordinary, polite but reserved, quietly-spoken. The thing is, we haven't been able to find any official records concerning Mr Dugdale. No identity papers or ration books have been issued to a person of that name in that street. We've checked with Somerset House but there's no birth certificate for an Andrew Dugdale who would fit the bill. None of my people have seen him leave or enter the house. The fellow's a cipher.'

'So what do you think – someone Jerry dropped in?'

Crane shrugged. 'Perhaps – though I have a funny

feeling that there's more to Mr Dugdale than meets the eye.'

The sneer was inevitable. 'I seem to remember you telling me that you're not psychic, Crane. Maybe you've been associating with those fey, sensitive souls for too long.'

'Maybe I haven't been associating with them for long enough. You'd do well to remember that they are all civilian volunteers who lead ordinary lives when they're not working here. They may not bear arms but they're soldiers in their own way. I'd thank you to respect their intent, even if you can't bring yourself to accept that they are genuinely gifted.'

Fleming held up his hands. 'No offence meant, old boy. What I believe is neither here nor there. I was merely wondering if some of what they have has rubbed off on you.'

I know what you meant, and that wasn't it. Fleming's smirk and tone of voice were enough to give the lie to the words and the placatory gesture. But Crane wasn't in the mood for an argument. He just wanted Fleming out of the room and out of his sight. 'I'm sure we won't have to wait too much longer,' he said. 'Mitre has got to show his face sooner or later. When he does he will lead us to the Bishop.'

'Let's hope so for all our sakes,' muttered Fleming. 'This is a critical time and we need to be sure our plans are not compromised. Don't let us down, man.'

'It's progressing well. He's trying everything, as you know. I almost admire his tenacity. And now he's getting very close indeed.'

'He's good at what he does, even though some of it's completely mad. I don't know why you've always been so set against him.'

'The man is politically unsound – he's practically a socialist. And he's squeamish. Remember that business with the American? He came close to sabotaging our relationship with our cousins, all because he thought a few tarts were more important than the war effort. I trust him to do a good job, but I don't trust what he might do in the long term.'

'Do you think he'll carry out his instructions to the letter?'

'I'm quite sure he won't. That's why we need to bring in another piece.'

'Do you have someone in mind?'

'Yes, and this fellow is a patriot who won't let sentimentality get in the way of his duty to king and country. If push comes to shove, he will even eliminate our wild card. I'd like you to invite him to your home-from-home so we can discuss the matter. He's already got top security clearance so we can depend on him to keep his mouth shut. He's a close friend of our wild card so I've been holding him back – we don't want to give him too much time to think about it in case he changes his mind.'

'I can see him this afternoon.'

'Good – it won't be long now, so this is the right time to bring him in.'

It was William Simmons' turn to keep watch over the house in Knight Street. Tonight there was a full moon, so he could see the darkened windows and front door without too much trouble, and hidden in the shadows of the shop doorway opposite he was confident no one in the house could see him. He was dying for a cigarette but he knew that as soon as he struck a match a warden would materialise from thin air and berate him for making such a small spark of light in the blackout. That was his sort of luck, the kind that meant he'd fall for Ethel Bingham, a woman who barely acknowledged his existence. Yes, his luck was rotten. And, just to prove it, the rain began to fall. It really had been a miserable August.

He stepped further back into the doorway, almost falling over a bundle of unsold newspapers awaiting collection. Because of that he nearly missed the short man who scurried along the street and turned abruptly into the front garden of the house he was keeping under surveillance. Simmons frowned. There was something wrong with the way the man was walking, hobbling slightly as if he wasn't used to his shoes. The man was humming to himself, that song by Vera Lynn that Simmons couldn't stand, the one about the white cliffs of Dover. That wasn't right either. And the fellow's posture was, well, *odd*.

Simmons' talent was for making connections, solving riddles that no one knew were even there; and this time he excelled himself. He smiled as he realised what he was seeing, and the smile quickly became a broad grin. This was something Crane needed to know straight away. There was a telephone box in the next street. With any luck the local spivs wouldn't have rifled the coin box or vandalised the receiver. And for once his luck held – not only was the telephone working but he found some pennies in his trouser pocket.

When Crane's car pulled up Simmons was surprised to see that he was accompanied by Charles Bartley, Edward Vance and Dorothy Harlow. He'd expected Crane to come alone and assess the situation fully before deciding upon further action. Really, though, he should probably have expected Miss Harlow to be there – his talent had long ago told him that something was going on between her and Crane, a conclusion drawn from the coded language each used to let the other know how they felt without actually letting them know. Love was a complicated business, as Simmons knew all too well, especially love that was either unrequited or forbidden. He wasn't shocked that the respectably-married Tony Crane had fallen for the admittedly beautiful and charismatic Dorothy Harlow, who always dressed like a Hollywood starlet, as she was tonight; though as far as Simmons was concerned she wasn't a patch on the lovely, heartbroken Ethel Bingham. Nor was it remarkable that Miss Harlow felt just as strongly about Crane, who was not only handsome but a thoroughly decent and good man. No, the only shock was that as far as he could tell they hadn't yet done anything about it. That knowledge had increased both his respect for Crane and his sense of kinship with the man. Love's fools were all brothers and sisters under the skin.

'Are you sure?' It was a redundant question, as Crane trusted Simmons' talent as unreservedly as he trusted those of the other Yellow Room specialists, but he was duty-bound to ask it.

'I'm sure,' Simmons replied. 'The way he walked, as if he wasn't used to wearing those shoes; the way he hummed that song; the posture, stooped as though there was something about his physique that he didn't want anyone to notice. It added up to one thing.'

'Well, I'll be damned. So Mr Mitre is a woman pretending to be a man. That's why she would never let Edmund George see her clearly. Has anyone else gone in there? Is she alone?'

'Well, I had to go round the corner to the phone box, but no one else has been there while I've been here.'

As if at a pre-arranged signal, all five of them turned to gaze at the house. Crane was uncertain as to what they should do next. Now they had 'Mr' Mitre in their sights, would it be better to snatch her and hand her over to SIS for interrogation – or should they bide their time and follow her to her true lair, in the hope that she would lead them to the Bishop?

'I just had a thought,' said Bartley. 'If Mr Mitre isn't what we thought he was, perhaps she's really the Bishop. If we took her out of the game now we might be saving ourselves a great deal of time and effort.'

'She might well be,' Crane agreed. 'And if she's not we might alert the real Bishop that we're on to him. No, we'll wait until she leaves that house and follow her back to wherever she came from. Dorothy, I believe that is a job for you. Charles, you wait here with William and Dorothy. If anyone makes a delivery to Mitre tonight, you tail them and find out where they live and who they are. Don't confront them and don't inform SIS – it's liable to be another mug like Edmund George and we don't want SIS to torture some poor man or woman who thinks they're delivering a box of stolen nylons. As soon as we have an address we can take it from there. I'll be in the car with Edward and we'll be waiting if you need us.'

It was nearly midnight when an elderly man carrying a small parcel knocked on the front door. Mitre opened it, keeping well back so her face was shadowed. The three watching from the shop doorway across the street couldn't make out what was said, but they saw the old man exchange packages with Mitre then accept a piece of white paper which he folded and put in an inside pocket. A five-pound note, no doubt. When the door closed and the man left, Bartley moved out from the doorway and followed him at a discreet distance.

Thirty minutes later, the house door opened again and Mitre emerged, clutching the package the old man had given her. Dorothy Harlow waited until Mitre was almost out into Jamaica Road, then slid out of the shop doorway and along Knight Street as silent and lithe as a hunting cat, at a speed William Simmons would have sworn was impossible in those heels.

James Pilkington was not so much co-operative as effusive. Crane knew the type – an old man with no surviving friends, relatives who had all but forgotten his existence, little money and nothing to occupy the long, lonely hours of his remaining years. The myopic seventy year-old eagerly admitted them to his run-down but clean and well-maintained house, insisted on making tea, and seemed quite happy at the prospect of serving time for aiding and abetting black market activities. The old boy was probably looking forward to a bit of company. But he wouldn't end up in prison.

'Mr Mitre? Oh, that young fellow. I met him a couple of months ago while I was in Kennington Park walking Rover.' He pointed to a Jack Russell terrier sleeping in a wicker basket. At the sound of his name Rover opened one eye and sleepily wagged his tail. 'I sat on a bench to get my breath and Mitre sat down beside me. We talked about the weather, the war, the usual things strangers talk about to be civil. He asked me how I was managing with rationing and everything, so I told him times were a bit hard. My Civil Service pension doesn't go very far, you know, and my savings are long gone. So he asked me if I'd like to earn a bit of money by collecting and delivering packages once a week, a fiver a time. Well, that sounded a bit too good to be true so I asked him what was in the packages. He told me it was goods smuggled in by American servicemen, things that he bought cheap and sold for a profit. Obviously he was a black marketeer, though he didn't dress like a spiv. I asked him why he wasn't in uniform. He laughed and said he had a physical condition that made him unsuitable for front line military service. Well, I suppose you've seen how he stoops, and that unusual gait. I'd guess at a spinal problem. And between you and me, I think he might also be, you know, a ginger beer.'

Pilkington's story thereafter ran parallel to Edmund George's account, except that the old man collected his parcels and delivered the returns to a café in Marylebone. He told them all he knew and much more besides. When Pilkington launched into a labyrinthine anecdote about his dog and a postman, Crane politely bade him goodbye and left with Vance close on his heels.

Marylebone was obviously their next port of call. The café, on the south side of Melcombe Street, was owned by a middle-aged Canadian widow named Olivia Greenspan. Like Pilkington, her first thought was that she was about to be arrested for dabbling in the black market. Unlike Pilkington, she was not at all disappointed when Crane made it clear that they weren't from the police.

'Yes, I do give packages to Mr Pilkington,' she

admitted with evident relief. 'Once a week on a Wednesday afternoon. He comes in with one, I give him another and he goes away again.'

'And where do you get the packages you give to Mr Pilkington?' Vance enquired.

Mrs Greenspan was reluctant to answer until Crane suggested that, although he wasn't going to arrest her, the police would most certainly be interested in anything he told them about her illicit activities. 'Look,' she said, 'I don't want to get anyone into trouble.'

'It's them or you,' Crane replied. 'It's your choice.'

'It's no choice at all, then. Oh well, I suppose it was too good to last. The packages are delivered by a woman. She also collects the ones Mr Pilkington brings me. She pays me five pounds a week as a sort of retainer.'

'Do you know the woman's name?'

'She calls herself Ginnie Raine. I think she's French or something, though you wouldn't tell from her accent. She lives not far from here, in Siddons Lane, or so she said. She comes in now and then for a cup of tea like any other customer, acts like we never met, though she always gives me a wink.'

Crane frowned. This wasn't quite making sense. The French were allies. Only Vichy collaborators had anything to do with the Nazis, and they tended not to be in London. And there was something about this location that made him uncomfortable. As for the café's proprietor, that too was wrong, unless the Bishop was playing a very cruel joke indeed.

'Greenspan – is that by any chance a Jewish name?'

The woman nodded, smiling though her eyes were

now wary. 'Yes. We came over from Toronto soon after we married in 1925. My husband fought in the Great War, visited London when it was over. He wanted to live here, so he saved to buy this place. I'm also a Jew. My maiden name was Cohen. My son Bernie is in the Eighth Army, in Italy now, I think. He's twenty-four. He fought with Monty at Alamein,' she said proudly.

'Then I wish him well, Mrs Greenspan,' said Crane. 'I wish them all well.'

'Well, that ties in with what I found out.' Dorothy Harlow was as fresh as a daisy, despite having been up all night watching and waiting for the woman known as Mr Mitre to make any sort of move. 'Virginia Raine, 79A Siddons Lane. She went in and didn't come out again. In the morning I knocked at the apartment below and asked the woman who lives there if she knew the lady upstairs. The old harpy was only too glad to gossip about her neighbour – you know, one of those dried-up old witches who hate any woman younger and prettier than themselves. According to her, Miss Raine keeps strange hours and only has one visitor, a young guy with a funny walk and a stoop. Does that sound familiar? Anyway, old lemon-face thinks Miss Raine is a whore. We know different, huh?'

'It's got to be her,' said Bartley excitedly. 'Virginia Raine must be the Bishop. We should take her out of the game as soon as possible.'

'We'll apprehend her right enough – but we'll deliver her to SIS and wash our hands of her. I won't have any one of us killing in cold blood. Are we all clear on that? Good. Dorothy, Charles and Edward, you'll come in my car.

Charles, do you have your revolver? Excellent, though I hope you won't need to use it. William and Mrs Pugh, you hold the fort here until the others arrive. If you don't hear from us in two hours, contact SIS and tell them what we've found out. Right, let's go.'

Ethel Bingham arrived at the Yellow Room soon after Crane and his party departed. She was eager to learn the latest developments but was shocked when they told her the name of the woman they believed to be the Bishop.

'Virginia Raine? But I know her! She's an actress, usually only small parts in stage productions but she's been in a few films as an extra. She was in that strange film by Powell and Pressburger, *A Canterbury Tale* – and she's had small parts in public information films. Ginnie's a really nice girl and I know for a fact that she hates the Nazis. For one thing, she's French; and for another her fiancé died at Dunkirk, so I know just how much she hates them. She'd never be a Nazi agent, not in a thousand years. This isn't right, William. I don't know what's going on – but it isn't *right*.'

She sat at Crane's desk and produced a pack of tarot cards from her handbag, quickly shuffled and cut the deck, and selected three cards at random: the Queen of Swords, reversed; the High Priestess; and Death. She chose another card and turned it over – the Magician.

Ethel looked up at Mrs Pugh and William in wide-eyed horror. 'It's a trick. They're walking into a trap. And someone is going to die.'

The woman who opened the door to them was young, no older than twenty-five. She had fair hair cut in an Eton crop, and was handsome rather than pretty. Crane discreetly glanced at her breasts, which were large. It was no wonder she walked with a stoop when she dressed as a man – an upright stance would have given the game away immediately.

'Miss Raine? Virginia Raine?' He held out his warrant card, issued at Churchill's insistence, which gave him the same authority and powers as any police officer. It was the first time he'd ever used it.

'Yes. Is there something wrong?'

'It's a rather delicate matter. May we come in?'

Only Crane and Miss Harlow were at the front door. Bartley and Vance stood on the other side of the road, ready to join their colleagues.

'I suppose so,' said Virginia Raine, smiling uncertainly. 'I must say, this is a bit of a relief. I've been expecting you, of course. But it's been a bit of a strain wondering when you'd find me.'

Crane and Dorothy exchanged puzzled glances. As Miss Raine went back inside, leaving the door open for them, Dorothy held Crane back. 'Tony, don't go in there. Something real bad's gonna happen and you don't want to be part of it.'

'Look, I trust your intuition. You're never wrong. But I don't exactly have a choice in the matter. Besides, we're here now and I can't back out.'

'OK, but I'll wait out here if it's all the same to you. And Tony – when you get in there don't trust *anyone*, you hear?'

'I'll be careful, Dorothy,' said Crane, holding her gaze. She was clearly anxious. No, it was more than that; she was afraid. Crane had never seen Dorothy Harlow anything but relaxed and confident. He nodded and beckoned Bartley and Vance over, and the three men entered the building and made their way upstairs to Virginia Raine's flat.

She had already put on her coat and was fussing around with a jug, watering plants. She began tidying away newspapers and books. 'I suppose the dishes can wait until I get back,' she said. Crane noticed the trace of an accent. Although her English was excellent, she did sound French. An alarm bell sounded distantly in the back of his mind. The woman finished making her flat look presentable and looked at each of the three men in turn, smiling mischievously. 'Right, we'd better make this look good for anyone who might be watching. As soon as we get outside I'll start struggling and you chaps will have to be firm with me. But don't get too rough. Vera Watkins will go barmy if you hurt me. I wouldn't want to be in your shoes if that happens. She can be rather fierce.'

The mental warning grew louder, more insistent. 'Miss Raine, what on earth are you talking about?'

She grinned. 'Fortitude, Mr Crane. We must have fortitude.' She laughed. 'Garbo will need a convincing story to tell Jerry so we have to make this look good. That way the Hun will believe all those FUSAG documents we've been passing them.'

Crane's jaw dropped. Either the woman was mad, or –

He didn't have a chance to develop the thought. Charles Bartley strode rapidly across the room, pressed his Webley against the woman's forehead, and pulled the trigger.

'What have you done? Charles, what have you fucking *done*?' Crane was almost in tears.

'My duty,' said Bartley, dully staring down at the young woman whose life he had so swiftly and unexpectedly extinguished. She lay untidily on an imitation Persian rug, the varnished floorboards behind her liberally spattered with blood, brain matter and fragments of her skull. 'I was doing my patriotic duty.'

'But you heard her – she was one of ours, for Christ's sake! She was SOE!'

'No. As far as the Nazis are concerned she was one of *theirs*, one of Garbo's network of German spies here in London. And she had to die while resisting arrest so they would be assured that she didn't talk under interrogation. Her death was always part of the plan. That way they'd be more inclined to believe the information she helped pass to them. I had to protect the integrity of the operation. Thousands of Allied lives depend on it. The outcome of the war depends on it.'

Crane seized Bartley by arm and found himself looking down the barrel of the revolver. He raised his eyes but Bartley refused to meet them. 'Me too, Charles? You'd kill me too?'

'I'd kill all of you if it meant taking us one step closer to beating Hitler. But I hope it won't come to that.'

'What are you? SIS?'

Bartley shook his head. 'No, but I've been working with them. This little scheme was cooked up by Churchill, Philby at SIS, and Fleming representing Naval Intelligence, with the assistance of Gubbins at SOE. I was brought in to ensure that it would all go to plan, that they would believe the Bishop was a real spy feeding them crucial information. They knew you wouldn't have the stomach for it.'

'Churchill was party to this abomination?'

Bartley pocketed his weapon and turned away. 'It was his idea to sacrifice Miss Raine, to make it look more real.'

Vance, who had been standing motionless, transfixed by horror, broke in. 'Did she know, Charles? Did she know she was going to die?'

'Of course she didn't know. She wanted to help liberate the land of her birth. She thought that when this operation was over she'd be parachuted into France. We have quite a few SOE girls working over there. We lost some recently, as you know. What difference does one more make? Anyway, it was quicker and cleaner than anything the SD would have done to her. War's a brutal business, especially for a woman.'

The weird voice from the séance echoed in Crane's mind. *Finally, you must sacrifice a queen.* Virginia Raine, a brave young French woman who thought she was about to go into action conducting secret operations against the Nazis, slaughtered in cold blood to conceal an even greater secret. The French word for a queen was *reine*. And the bloody evidence of the sacrifice lay at his feet.

'It makes all the difference, you bastard,' Crane called, now weeping openly. 'It makes us no different from them. You're no longer welcome in the Yellow Room, Charles. You're no longer welcome in my home.'

Bartley paused at the door to the landing. He didn't look back. 'I know,' he said wearily.

'An excellent result, said Philby, *pushing back his spectacles back up*

his nose with his left index finger. 'If that doesn't convince the Hun, nothing will.'

Gubbins glared at him. 'Yes, and because of it one of my agents is dead and will go down in history as a Nazi spy, her name tainted forever.'

'Officially, she'll have been killed in action, which is true enough,' Philby replied. 'We can rely on Crane's discretion. He's as patriotic as anyone in this room.'

'Gentlemen, please.' Fleming lit a cigarette and smiled. 'The deed is done, so there's no point arguing over it now. Garbo reports that his other masters in Berlin are cock-a-hoop at getting confirmation that the Fourth US Army Group is real and will invade at Calais, and they are already diverting forces there from the true locations of our attack. The Bishop's death was the final piece we needed to make our move. It was a magnificent subterfuge and we should congratulate ourselves on a job well done. You, Colin, should be grateful. Your agent's death has redeemed SOE after that mess in the Netherlands earlier this year.'

Churchill forced a glum smile, raised a glass of brandy. 'Yes, but it was a bloody dirty job and we must put it behind us. At least we had the tools to do it. We are in your debt, Charles. A knight has taken a queen and enabled us to begin the endgame.'

'A knight?' Bartley seemed uncomfortable in this company, even though they were the kind of people he mixed with almost every day.

'At the very least,' Churchill assured him. 'Perhaps even a baronetcy. It will officially be for services to industry or some such nonsense. You know how it is. Gentlemen, I propose a toast – to Operation Fortitude, victory, and an end to this blasted war.'

Bartley raised his glass with the rest of them and drank to victory. But the words had a hollow ring and the brandy tasted as bitter as tears.

The Beautiful Beast

Hamelin, 13th December 1945
The solemn man called her name. She left the tiny room and stood to attention in the corridor as he fastened her arms to her sides. He said something but she didn't understand. Another man, a soldier, repeated the order in her own tongue. Folgen Sie mir. *She was led into a much larger room lined with people, some of whom she recognized. To her surprise, there was the Englishman who had questioned her in the prison at Celle, only a few months ago, though it seemed liked decades had passed. She smiled briefly at him but he didn't smile back. He looked sad and somehow afraid. The man who collected her from the cell guided her up some wooden steps and pointed at a cross marked in chalk on a square set into the platform. She knew what was expected of her so she took her place on the mark. A white hood was put over her head, and the rope was placed around her neck, the noose tightened.*

Schnell, *she said breathlessly.*

The trapdoor opened and she fell into a welcoming night. It was twenty-six minutes to ten on a cold and gloomy morning.

The First Day
Many of the men and women were naked, sprawling or squatting on the muddy ground, uncaring of onlookers and far too weak or sick to care about anything else. Stick-thin, lethargic and blank-eyed, they seemed to be awaiting instructions from voices only they could hear. Those with the strength to move, those whose skeletons still bore fat and meat, the men and women still clad in the remnants of clothing, the ones who hadn't been there long enough to merge with the living dead – they were as fearful as they had been before, still not able to bring themselves to believe they were free.

But they were not free, not yet; and thousands would never taste freedom. There were too many for their liberators to deal with – a multitude of the sick and dying, men and women and children starved and driven insane by constant terror and monotonous brutality. They were ravaged by disease, crawling with lice. They spoke many languages, held many different beliefs. There were too few doctors and nurses, insufficient interpreters, and not enough Allied troops to maintain order. There was not enough food and no running water. The maze of brick barracks, wooden huts and canvas tents promised only madness and death. And the stench of excrement, disease and decay was indescribable.

'How many have you got here?' He whispered, though those around them probably couldn't understand him and wouldn't have given a damn if they did. For the first time since he'd boarded the Mosquito at Biggin Hill, he wasn't cursing the itch and chafing of the unfamiliar battledress. He lit another Lucky Strike, more to try to mask the smell than anything else.

'We don't know yet,' the lieutenant replied. 'Maybe fifty thousand, probably more. Kramer, the former *Kommandant*, is being helpful, in an unhelpful sort of way.'

'How many dead, do you reckon?'

'We've only been able to make a rough estimate,' the lieutenant replied, rubbing his eyes tiredly. 'We think at least ten thousand, maybe as many as twenty thousand. Who knows? We're finding more bodies all the time. Typhoid, tuberculosis, dysentery and typhus are rife – probably more diseases we don't know about yet. And just look at them – even the healthier ones are nearly all starved, just walking bags of bones, covered in sores and crawling with lice. Some of the SS guards are in almost as bad shape. And we can't even feed the poor wretches with what we do have. Basic rations are too much for their digestive systems. If we feed them more than they've been getting, we risk killing even more of them. They'll die anyway if they don't get food. It's a vicious circle and we don't have what it takes to get out of it.'

Crane closed his eyes. His head throbbed badly. In a little over six hours at Bergen-Belsen he'd seen enough horror to last him several lifetimes and it was threatening to give him a migraine. 'Look, this isn't my area of expertise at all. What am I doing here? I was dragged out of bed before dawn this morning, given this bloody uniform and put on a plane without a single word of explanation, just a message that Churchill had a little job that was right up my street. Perhaps one of you gentlemen could enlighten me?'

The others exchanged guarded looks. Eventually the man from the BBC spoke. 'We've been documenting everything we can – radio commentary and photographs so far, with film crews coming. This isn't something the Germans should ever be allowed to forget. Nor the rest of the world, come to think of it. But anyway, I was with a couple of soldiers, poking our noses around the women's camp, when we found something. We immediately contacted the lieutenant here and he had the thing sealed off. Then he called London and here you are.'

'It was just outside the camp perimeter, to be exact,' the lieutenant said. 'It looked fairly new. Not more than a few months old, I'd say.'

'Gave me the creeps,' the BBC man added. 'The men I was with took one look and got the hell out of there. I could feel it several yards away – like walking under a cold shower, only it wasn't water coming down on us.'

'I saw it later,' said the lieutenant, 'But I know what he means. It was evil, pure evil. The Devil's work.'

Crane gazed irritably at each of his companions in turn. 'For God's sake, can't one of you just tell me what you bloody found?'

'Best you see for yourself,' said the man from the BBC. 'But that can wait until the morning. It's not somewhere you'd want to be at night, believe me.'

Lüneburg, 17th November 1945

She didn't look at all attractive when she frowned, and here she frowned all the time, every day. The only exceptions were when she glared with unalloyed hostility at the witnesses and prosecution lawyers. She had given her testimony, said her piece – but she knew it was all for nothing. Everyone did.

A placard on her chest bore the number 9. For some reason, the number sent a chill down his spine. He could hardly bear to look at her with that hanging round her neck. Why had he come here? He knew what was going to happen. It had all been pre-arranged, of that he was certain. He'd pulled all the strings he could and tried to blackmail SIS into helping him coerce the psychiatrists into finding her insane and unfit to stand trial. It hadn't worked.

He still didn't know if she was innocent of the charges or as guilty as the blackest sin, but he pitied her. What chance had she had, with a disapproving father, a mother who had committed suicide and left a thirteen year-old girl rudderless and bereft? Perhaps, in a different time and place, it might have been different. Perhaps, without the relentless Nazi indoctrination and crazed pseudoscience she had been exposed to, she could have grown into a gentler, better person who would never have done those brutal things. Perhaps she would have been the nurse she aspired to be, or the film star they said she craved to become.

Now she sat there in a different kind of spotlight – Number Nine, one among many that had been called to account for their crimes.

Eventually, the sentence was pronounced. Soon, it would end. He wished with all his heart that he believed in her guilt.

The Second Day

The hut was different from the other buildings – a cube, twenty feet to a side, with a flat roof. There were no windows and the door was a mere hatch, two and a half feet square, just big enough for a decent-sized adult to crawl through. It was in the women's section, set in a patch of bare earth, tight against the camp's perimeter. He guessed the walls were aligned to the cardinal points, the door at the north.

'You say there was a woman in here? Was anyone with her?'

The lieutenant shook his head. 'No, she was alone. At first the lads who found her thought she was a prisoner in solitary confinement, a recent one who still had a bit of flesh on her bones. But if that was the case, what was she doing outside the camp? And what she was doing when they found her – well, it made them think she'd gone completely off her rocker.'

Crane walked around the hut. His scalp itched and he wondered if he might have acquired a few of the lice that infested the camp. Then he realised his hair was actually standing on end, his arms goose-pimpled and tingling. He felt vaguely afraid. The lieutenant smiled tiredly. 'Yes, that's what experienced. And this is what we found later, when we took a closer look.' He scuffed at the ground with his boot, revealing a curved length of rusted iron. 'It's a circle, completely surrounds the hut.' He squatted, picked up a handful of soil and showed Crane the soft white crystals that made up about a third of its mass. 'Rock salt, covering the iron circle. Go on, take a look inside.'

Crane crawled through the little door and found himself in a nightmare world. Every surface was painted white, but someone had painted a large red pentagon inside a black circle. The east and west walls bore black swastikas, with inverted pentagrams to the north and south. In the corners lay complicated lattices of human bone, each surmounted with a skull. The features seemed delicate. Crane surmised that he was looking at the neatly-arranged remains of girls, probably in their early teens. The lieutenant joined him just as he recognized the object resting in the centre of the pentagon.

'Is that what I think it is?'

The lieutenant nodded, his features betraying fascinated distaste. 'Yes, it is exactly what it looks like. She was – er – making use of it when the boys found her, stark bollock naked, chanting some gibberish and apparently in the midst of a, um, climax. We think it's made from a human femur.'

'Christ, it's bloody enormous. And that looks like blood splattered all over the bones and around the circle. Jesus Christ, no wonder you sent for us. As I was coming through that door I noticed that the walls are alternating layers of wooden boards and sheets of copper. It's like a battery of some sort. Look at this.' He raised his arms and brought his hands slowly together. Just before they touched, there was a sharp retort and an arc of blue light flashed between them. 'The hut's crackling with electricity. No wonder our skin's crawling.'

'Yes,' the lieutenant agreed, 'but does that explain why anyone who comes in here feels so bloody rotten if they spend more than a few seconds in here? Can't you feel it?'

Crane did indeed feel it. His stomach was beginning to churn and he felt nauseous. Then he felt bile rising in his oesophagus and hurried outside to vomit copiously on the brown earth.

'The lieutenant tells me it was you two who found the woman in the hut.'

The soldiers exchanged uneasy glances. 'We didn't do nothing improper, sir,' said the corporal, a Londoner named Gallagher. 'If she told you different, she's a bloody liar, begging your pardon.'

'It's alright, Gallagher. I'm not accusing your or Private Smith of anything. I just want you to tell me, in your own words, what happened.'

'Well, sir – it was like this. Me and Smithy here were assigned to check that part of the women's section for bodies. There are so many deaths here every day that we can't keep up with burying them. We make a note of where they are and a team goes round and collects them, then we bury them in a bloody great pit. Anyway, like I said, me and Smithy went to take a look at that hut just outside the fence, the one on it's own with the tiny little door.'

'And that's when we heard it,' Smith broke in. 'All this grunting and moaning, like someone was going at it in there. You know what I mean. And words, like a prayer or something.'

'It was Latin,' Gallagher clarified. 'I'm a Catholic, so I'm used to hearing it spoken. But I don't understand it.'

Smith broke in again. 'So then we opened the door and had a gander. And there she was in that circle with her legs spread, not a stitch on, ramming that what's-its-name up herself. It was…'

'I know what you're thinking, sir,' said Gallagher. 'Me and Smithy are normal blokes and she was a gorgeous little piece. And I daresay normally the sight of her doing that would have given us both the horn. But it was…' He groped for words that wouldn't come.

'It was dirty,' Smith said in a hushed tone. 'I don't mean dirty like French postcards or blue jokes – I mean disgusting, *unclean*. It was – I dunno – it was wrong, sir. It was just plain wrong.'

Gallagher nodded. 'Smithy's right, sir. I tell you what, normally, seeing a tart doing something like that, I'd have gone in there and helped her out, know what I mean? But the truth is that I don't think I could've even got it up. I didn't even want to. I wouldn't have touched her with Smithy's, sir.'

'And not with that…' Gallagher kicked Smith in the shin and the private fell silent.

'Please continue,' Crane prompted.

The two soldiers exchanged glances once more. 'You wouldn't believe us,' said Gallagher. 'You'd think we've gone barmy.'

'Try me.'

Gallagher coughed. 'Permission to smoke, sir.'

'You don't have to ask, man. And please stop calling me "sir". I'm not an officer. I'm a civilian. Here, have one of mine.' He offered his pack of Lucky Strikes and they all lit up.

'That thing she was using on herself,' said Gallagher reluctantly. 'It was like it was a part of something bigger.'

'Like it was part of some big bloke we couldn't see,' Smith chimed in. 'The grunting noise we could hear – that was him, sir. That was him.'

Lüneburg, 17th September 1945

Today it would begin. She knew all the names they were calling her. The Hyena of Auschwitz. The outcome of the trial was, she was sure, predetermined. The Beast of Belsen. There would be days, weeks, perhaps even months of boredom leavened only by the acid barbs of calumny and defamation; then she would learn the fate that she already knew. The Blonde Angel of Auschwitz. Then there would be more waiting, more time wasted on pointless breathing and sleeping and eating and shitting. The Beautiful Beast.

At least they thought her beautiful. That was something. And she had once tried to be an angel and come so close, oh so close, to becoming one. And once she had almost borne an angel of her own. Perhaps if she had been less strong she would have gone through with that. Even the barbaric British would not hang a pregnant woman. Weakness of will might have saved her. But she had been strong and now she was going to die. The weak had prevailed and the strong would perish. It was the exact opposite of what she had been taught.

The world was turned upside down.

The Third Day

'Are you sure this is the woman Gallagher and Smith saw in that hut?'

The lieutenant shrugged. 'No, we're not a hundred per cent certain. The men didn't pay a great deal of attention to her face, as you can imagine. All they could say with any confidence was that the woman they saw was blonde and attractively-built. The woman we have in custody was captured with some SS men a couple of days later. But a couple of the women inmates have accused her of using extreme violence against them, and murder. One woman has told us the prisoner engaged in sexual perversions. Mind you, I have serious doubts as to the sanity of that particular witness. To be candid, there are few people here whose testimony I would trust without question. Who could remain sane after weeks and months in a place like this? Frankly, I wouldn't place too much credence in what Gallagher and Smith told you, either. This place has us all spooked and the men wind each other up so stories grow with the telling. Tiny things get magnified out of all proportion.'

'I'd like to talk to her.'

'Of course.'

She was sullen, pouting and clearly exhausted. When he gave her a cigarette she smiled briefly and instantly became what she should have been, an attractively plump young woman with blonde hair and shining blue eyes, the epitome of Aryan maidenhood. Then she was grim-faced and dull again. It took more than one small act of kindness to make her forget that her war had ended very badly.

'How old are you Irma?'

'I shall be twenty-two on the twenty-third of October.' The voice was soft and lazy, almost seductive.

'And what did you do at Bergen-Belsen?'

She shrugged, the sulky resignation flaring monetarily into anger. 'I am a Work Service Manager. I wanted to be a nurse but I was assigned to camps as an *Aufseherin*. I became *Oberaufseherin* at my previous posting but one. Then I was sent to Ravensbrück. Eventually I ended up here.'

'Where was it that you were promoted to *Oberaufseherin*?'

'It was in Poland, at Birkenau, which was part of a larger camp, Auschwitz. There was a doctor there, everyone said he was a great man. He was studying the inmates so that he could use his findings to eliminate weakness, disease and deformity.'

'Was Auschwitz as bad as Bergen-Belsen?'

The young woman bowed her head. 'Some very bad things happened at Auschwitz, I will not deny it. I'm told Bergen-Belsen was a good place once. But we had so many to look after and supplies were scarce. Then more and more came and the diseases began to spread until we could no longer cope. So few doctors and nurses, and so many sick people – it has been dreadful.'

'Why didn't you let at least some of them go?'

'How could we? They are criminals, many with highly contagious diseases. And there are so many Russian prisoners. Do you know what Russian soldiers do to German women? How could we set them free?'

'But there are other inmates, not prisoners of war or criminals.'

'Well, there are the political prisoners, and the perverts, the men who go to bed with other men. Do you not imprison such people in England?'

Yes, we do, thought Crane, *and it is to our shame*. 'What about the Jews, the Gypsies?'

'We are told they are not really people, that they are the enemies of the Aryan race. We do not all believe that.'

Crane gave her another cigarette. He wished he had thought to bring water, or a flask of Dimbleby's whisky. The all-pervading stench was making his aching head spin. After a few more minutes of silence he gave in and asked the interpreter, a young German Jewish woman in rather better condition than the majority of Bergen-Belsen's inmates, largely because she had been there only a matter of weeks before it was liberated by British and Canadian troops, to fetch some water.

'I have already answered these questions,' said Irma when the interview resumed. 'What more can I tell you?'

Crane glanced down at the preliminary report on allegations made against Irma Grese. The rumour was that

Churchill wanted as many Nazis as possible charged with war crimes and brought to trial, strung up if at all possible. If only a fraction of the accusations made against her were true, the woman was destined to end her days on the gallows. And this was only early testimony taken from a small number of Bergen-Belsen's inmates. God alone knew what would emerge from her time at Auschwitz.

'You can tell me about the doctor at Auschwitz. What exactly did he do?'

'He was engaged in important research. It was about heredity – he studied identical twins and subjects with congenital deformities. I don't know the technical details. I'm not a scientist.'

'Why was he so interested in the twins?'

'If one died through disease he could compare the sick twin with the healthy one.'

'How did he do that?'

'He dissected them.'

The implication was obvious. The healthy twin too would die so that the doctor could make the comparison. *That's enough. I do not want to know any more about this. What I'm about to ask is going to be bad enough.*

'Thank you, Irma. You've been very co-operative. There's just one more thing I'd like to ask you about. What were you doing when you were captured?'

When she laughed, the woman wasn't merely pretty in a plump sort of way. She was almost beautiful, sexually magnetic. The laugh relaxed into a complicit smile. 'I was running away from the British soldiers. Wouldn't you, if you were a woman?'

Lüneburg, 15th November 1945

They hadn't believed her, none of them. When she told them how she was not allowed to carry firearms except for that one short period, that she never had a dog at Auschwitz, she knew her words were falling on deaf ears. Her little whip of plaited cellophane, designed only to sting, had been magnified into a riding crop, a horse-whip, a scourge. The regulation-issue high boots she wore, so much more practical for the camps' mud and filth than the smart shoes she preferred, had been transformed into weapons for the most brutal of assaults. So the truth, as established by a court of law, was that she had shot, beaten and trampled people to death, and set her invisible dog on them.

She was, they said, a fanatical Nazi. Her membership of the Bund Deutscher Mädel *was evidence of that, even though no German girl had a choice in the matter. Nor had she any choice in her employment. She had not chosen to work in the camps. No one listened when she tried to explain that in the Reich all unmarried women were forced to work wherever and however the state ordered. Nor did they pay any heed when she tried to tell them how she was only nineteen when she was posted to Auschwitz as an* Aufseherin, *or how being promoted to the position of* Oberaufseherin *when she had only just turned twenty was not an indication of either her devotion to the Nazi cause or her effectiveness as a guard, but simply the result of the attritional nature of the job. And no one cared when she told them that she was effectively a conscript and had never applied to join the SS.*

The Fourth Day

The woman still wouldn't answer his questions. She would talk about music, films, anything but what Crane wanted to discuss. Her mood continued to fluctuate between sulkiness and pleasure, though not to extremes of either. She ascribed her equanimity to medication.

'What is it?' he asked her during the second interview. 'What are you taking?'

She showed him a small brown bottle of white tablets. 'A doctor prescribed these in Auschwitz. I was – upset for a time.' She leaned forward, whispering; the interpreter bent closer to hear what she was saying. 'It was his, you know. But I didn't want it. A film star should be unencumbered, don't you think? I would have been in a lot of trouble if anyone had found out. It was forbidden.'

Crane didn't understand what she was going on about. He wished he had some of his Yellow Room people with him – the psychometrist Vance would have been useful in this situation, or Dorothy Harlow, whose powers of perception were rivalled only by those of Crane's friend Mikaiel Dakessian. But Dakessian was in Paris mopping up Nazi agents and collaborators and the Yellow Room had, with the war in Europe clearly about to end, been given indefinite leave. No, he would have to manage on his own.

'It's called MDMA,' she said unexpectedly. 'Would you like to try it? I have enough to last for a few months.'

At first Crane demurred. Then he changed his mind. It might help him establish a greater rapport with the prisoner. 'Alright, Irma – I'll try it.'

She carefully shook two small tablets onto his outstretched palm. 'It'll take a short time before it has any effect. Here, I'll take one too, keep you company.'

The verbal dance went on. Crane suddenly recognised that he was enjoying her subtle evasions and circumlocutions, relaxing in her presence for the first time. She was, he thought, quite likeable when she wasn't talking about the war or the camps. Maybe that was because of the subject. Perhaps she thought the same of him.

'Do you remember when the British troops found you in that hut? They say you were undressed and doing something rather – er – unladylike with an artificial phallus. Is that true?'

She regarded him calmly. 'It is a lie,' she said. 'I was never in that hut. As I told you, I fled as the British approached. When I was captured I was with other camp guards. There had been fighting in the camp, an uprising by recent arrivals from the camps further east, and many *Kapos* were killed. The guards feared summary execution. I feared that – and worse.'

'We found occult symbols and paraphernalia there. Who was responsible for that?'

She shrugged indifferently. 'I don't know and I don't care. I think I have my own problems without helping you solve yours.'

'Did you know about the hut?'

'Well, I knew it was there, naturally. You seem to think that because I was *Oberaufseherin* I know everything that went on at Bergen-Belsen. Let me tell you that I was one of two *Oberaufseherinnen* and, despite Himmler's fine words about us being equal to the men, Elisabeth and I were quite a way down the pecking order. There were some things we were not allowed to know. Even *Hauptsturmführer* Kramer did not know everything that went on in this place. Besides, I've only been here a few weeks. The hut was there when I arrived.'

'So you've no idea who built it or why?'

She shook her head. 'There were others who came

here sometimes, men and women, some in SS uniforms, others in civilian clothing. I have no idea who they were. There were rumours.'

'Rumours of what?'

Irma bit her lip. 'People talk such nonsense when they don't understand something. And sometimes people say things you don't want to believe are true. I'm not what you'd call an educated woman, Herr Crane. I'm a farmer's daughter. I left school when I was fourteen and the only education I've had since then was when I was trained for menial jobs and being an *Aufseherin*. But I'm not ignorant and I'm not stupid. There are things best not spoken aloud. Sometimes that's because a stray word can get you killed – and sometimes it's because it can make people think you're not quite right in the head.'

'Can you not tell me anything?'

She frowned, and abruptly ceased to be pretty. 'I'll think about it. But not today.'

Lüneburg, 16ᵗʰ November 1945

She sang softly to herself, an old song she remembered from when she was a child. She wasn't much more than a child now, and tomorrow she would die, a noose around her neck, dangling below an open trapdoor. She'd met the hangman, a sombre Englishman who'd introduced himself as Albert Pierrepoint. He was polite and gentle, and it seemed to her that hanging her by the neck until she was dead was the last thing he wanted to do. She'd liked him and was obscurely glad that she would meet her end at the hands of such a nice, considerate man.

She hadn't expected anyone to believe her but still she was disappointed by the verdict. And that was all she felt, sadness that her life was all but over, disappointment that her words had been wasted, regret that she'd ever been born into this place and this time. There was no anger or bitterness. After all, someone had to die to balance the scales, so why not her? Really, it could have been anyone. She believed herself to harbour less guilt than many of those who had been sentenced only to serve time in prison, and she knew for a fact that worse things had been done by some of those that had been acquitted.

Without warning, she began to cry. Twenty-two years of toil, hardship and pain, the last few spent being forced to deny and submerge her true nature so that she could survive in those cruel, soul-destroying camps, a small girl doing as she was told because it was too dangerous to do otherwise, carrying weapons because she felt too little and weak to control her charges without them, brutalising herself as she brutalised others.

Why did you leave me, *Mutti*? Why did you leave me to face this alone?

Only one night left. She would be with her mother soon enough.

The Fifth Day

The evidence against Irma Grese was mounting up. All of it was accusation and hearsay, most of it was the kind of thing that would ordinarily be unacceptable for a civilised legal process. The sheer number of accusers was being substituted for hard evidence. Crane was reminded of a medieval witch hunt. He wouldn't have been at all surprised to learn that Irma Grese had been accused of curdling milk, making cattle barren and casting spells to cause miscarriages.

'I don't know why you're bothering to read all this,' said the lieutenant. 'There's nothing in those documents about that damned hut.'

'I just want to know what kind of person I'm talking to,' Crane replied. 'Though to be honest, these witness statements suggest she's Lucrezia Borgia, Messalina and Elizabeth Báthory all rolled into one. Are you really taking this material seriously?'

'It's not for me to have an opinion one way or the other,' the lieutenant shrugged. 'I'm just helping to run this bloody camp, not organise a prosecution. We still don't have enough food or water or medical supplies, and I don't have enough men. You know we've had to use some of the SS guards to help us keep order? That leaves a bad taste in my mouth, believe you me. But the worst thing is that we're spending most of our time burying people. Dozens, hundreds more die every day, Crane. And it shows no sign of slowing. Are you going to talk to her again today?'

'I have my orders, just as you have yours. If I'm going to find out about that hut, Irma's my best shot. I spoke to Kramer yesterday evening – the man's an idiot and seems to know bugger-all about his own camp.'

The lieutenant grinned. 'So it's Irma now, is it? You're not getting sweet on her, are you? I admit she's a pretty little thing when she's not sulking, but I should warn you that I won't have that sort of thing on my watch.'

'I just prefer to be on first-name terms. I think she'll respond to the friendly approach.'

'Well, don't get too friendly. I have a feeling Fräulein Grese is destined for a sticky end.'

Was that it? Did he doubt her guilt precisely because she was so pretty? Experience had taught him that a person's looks had little correlation with their inner nature, but like most people Crane found it hard to accept that the beautiful could be evil. But even if that was true for him too, it didn't explain the niggling voice that told him Irma Grese's story was not a straightforward tale of good *versus* evil. Life was always more than a simple choice between black or white. No, it was because she was so small and afraid and young, and looked so vulnerable. How was someone like that supposed to survive, surrounded by armed men and forced despite her inexperience into responsibility for thousands of people who were hostile and would have hated her solely because of the position she occupied?

Any way she could, replied a voice inside his head. *And anyone else would have done exactly the same.*

'Good morning, Irma. I have a present for you.' He placed two Hershey bars on the table between them, then stood and gave two more to the interpreter, who gazed at them uncomprehendingly for a second before snatching them from his hand and secreting them in a pocket crudely stitched onto the side of her dress, nodding a curt thanks as she did so.

Irma slowly reached out and took one of the bars, tore the wrapper just as unhurriedly and bit off a small piece. She closed her eyes and let the chocolate dissolve on her tongue. 'It's been so long since I had this,' she whispered. 'Thank you, Herr Crane. I do not understand why you are being so kind to me. You know of what I am accused.'

Because it's what I am. It's because that's what makes me different from the men who dreamed up these hellish camps and imposed their twisted idea of order upon them; the men who made you what you are, no matter how deep your guilt runs, regardless of your own complicity. He smiled wryly, wondering how it had come to this, how he now felt the need to justify every action he took, every thought he had. The horrors of Bergen-Belsen were forcing him to examine his own motives as closely as he scrutinised those of the camp guards and their Nazi paymasters. He needed to know he could never be like that.

'Would you like another of my pills, Herr Crane?'

'Thank you, Irma. They do seem to make me feel a lot better, and God knows I could do with a tonic. Now then, are you ready to tell me what you know about those rumours you mentioned yesterday?'

'As I said, it is only rumour. The people who told me have gone now, dead or escaped, I don't know. But the strange thing is that I was able to relate it to things of which I was told in Auschwitz. Do you know of the *Ahnenerbe*?'

'The Ancestral Heritage people? Yes, I know of them. They mounted expeditions all over the world, searching for evidence of Aryan prehistory. I know of some of the work they did before the war – crackpot stuff, for the most part.'

'Good – that means you may be able to make sense of the fragments I have been told. As well as searching for the lost heritage of the Aryan race, the *Ahnenerbe* commissioned medical experiments in Dachau and tried to do the same in other camps. The doctor I told you about – he was approached by them but refused because he thought their ideas were stupid. He did not say so in so many words, of course. He was not so foolish as to antagonise Himmler. But the doctor told me that they tried very hard to impress him, telling him that with Himmler's blessing they were working with other groups to accelerate evolution – to bring about the *Übermensch*, the next stage of the Aryan people's evolution.'

Crane smiled. The German high command was nothing if not predictable. But then he remembered how close they had come to success on Heligoland five years earlier and the smile vanished.

'The doctor said the *Ahnenerbe* had been working with the Thule Society and similar mystical groups in other countries, including America, England and Russia. But these organisations were only puppets, the public faces of something older and more powerful that was itself known only by a name that was both a rumour and a lie. The *Ahnenerbe* men he spoke to called it the Vril Society.'

'Wait a minute. You're saying that there's a secret group controlling these others? That sounds a bit far-fetched to me.'

Irma shrugged and took a cigarette from Crane's pack. 'I am only telling you what I was told, and I am doing so at your request. I don't know if there's a word of truth to any of it.'

'I'm sorry. Please continue.'

'As well as the known expeditions mounted by the *Ahnenerbe*, there was a secret one, to the Siberian wilderness, directed by the Vril Society. There they found ancient artefacts, guarded by a strange cult. They brought the artefacts and some of the cult members to Berlin. According to the doctor, the cult knew how to create an *Übermensch* by harnessing what they called *vril*, a force of nature that is not normally accessible. The doctor said it is also called *odil* and *orgone*. I did not understand the technical details. The doctor thought they were ridiculous, superstitious rubbish.'

'He told you a good deal, that doctor.'

'We were close, but not as close as some believe.'

'It's a fascinating story, but I don't see what it has to do with that hut.'

She sighed impatiently. 'I was coming to that. The expedition took three years altogether. They returned to Germany in December last year.'

'Good God, they were in Russia all that time while the war was raging on the Eastern Front? How were they not discovered?'

'Siberia is a big, empty place, Herr Crane. Even I know that. The doctor said they travelled to Shanghai on ships from neutral countries, then flew to the Gobi Desert in Japanese planes. After that, they journeyed overland, on horseback and riding camels. It sounds so romantic, don't you think? Anyway, the return journey was also overland, by way of Bactria, Iran and Turkey. From Istanbul they flew to Berlin. I am telling you these details as the doctor told me, so you will understand how important they believed their finds to be.'

'What happened after Berlin?'

'That is where the rumour begins. Some of the SS men whispered that the hut had been built according to the specifications of a man named Haushofer, who came here in January with eight others, including a beautiful Russian woman. I don't know why it was built here. The others left soon after the hut was completed but they say the woman stayed.'

'Do you have any idea who she might be?'

'No. They say she looked very young but was much older. She hated the Bolsheviks and all who stood with them. I do not know her name but the soldiers called her *das Ekel*.'

'I'm sorry, I don't know what that means.' He turned to the interpreter and raised his eyebrows questioningly.

'It means one who is disgusting, nauseating, revolting,' the interpreter told him. 'In English you would say "the Beast" – but the closest word I can think of is from Romanian. Before the war I was a lecturer in linguistics at Heidelberg, specialising in the Romance and Germanic languages. When I saw the film as a young woman the title intrigued me so I researched its etymology. The Romanian word *nesuferitu* means a horrid, unbearable person. It is thought to derive from the Greek dialect word *nousophoros*, which means disease-bearing, infectious. The Romanian word I speak of is related to others meaning unclean and insufferable.'

'What word? What film?'

'The word and the film are one and the same: *Nosferatu*. And that is the word I heard spoken in whispers by Roma in the camp when so many people began to waste away and die.'

Celle, 19th May 1945

'I wanted to become a nurse but was made to join the SS as a supervisor at concentration camps. This was in July 1942. I first went to Ravensbrück where I was made an Aufseherin *and placed in charge of female working parties consisting of about twenty prisoners. In March 1943 I was sent to Birkenau near Auschwitz, where I remained up to January 1945. I then went to Ravensbrück for four weeks and arrived at Belsen in March 1945.*

I know from the prisoners that there were gas chambers at Auschwitz and that prisoners were gassed there. Dr Mengele came in the camp at Birkenau and sorted out the people unfit for work for these transports. I knew what was happening and have hidden mothers and children away in order that they should not be chosen. I was once denounced by the Jews for having done this and was put under arrest for two days in my room. Jews were used as spies in this camp and had certain privileges. I never took part in choosing people and was only on parade for roll call and seeing that no one escaped.

I have never beaten or kicked any prisoners. It is true that I made people stand on Appell *for long periods but never until they dropped. I was once told by Drechsel that if it was necessary I could hit prisoners but I never did this.*

Conditions in the concentration camps were bad for everyone including the SS. The only time I was allowed home was for five days after I had finished my training at Ravensbrück. I then told my father about the concentration camp and he gave me a beating and told me never to come home again. Himmler is responsible for all that has happened but I suppose I have as much guilt as all the others above me. Conditions were very bad at Belsen but there was little I could do although I did all I could do to help.'

The Sixth Day

The lieutenant shook his head and laughed in disbelief. 'I saw that film in Berlin not long after I graduated from Oxford. Some of my friends had been waxing lyrical about what the German film-makers were doing so I popped over to see what all the fuss was about. *Nosferatu* was one of the first pictures I saw there. It was a bit of a sensation, and I'll admit it gave me a few shocks. But it was based on Bram Stoker's book, *Dracula,* spiced up a bit so that the vampire was also a plague-carrier. He even looked a bit like a giant rat. It's fiction. Honestly, Crane – are you seriously suggesting we have a ruddy vampire on the loose?'

'Not at all.' Crane wondered for the umpteenth time why he could never remember the officer's name. 'But that hut is proof that there's something odd going on here and I believe there may be a grain of truth in the story. I need to speak to a few of your men and some of the inmates here to see if they've heard anything or noticed anything out of the ordinary.'

'Crane, in case you hadn't noticed, in this bloody place *everything* is out of the ordinary.' The lieutenant sighed and looked down at his smouldering cigarette. 'Look, I know a chap who might be able to help you. He's been supervising a group of SS guards, making sure they don't get up to their old tricks while we make use of them. And he's had a fair bit of contact with the inmates. He may have heard something.'

'You won't get much out of the inmates. Most of them won't talk until they're ordered to, and then the best you'll get is one-word answers. It's understandable, I suppose. They see a man in uniform and expect only what the SS bastards gave them. The fact that we're using the SS as guards doesn't exactly give them cause to trust us. Poor wretches.'

Sergeant Hadding was no more than five feet and six inches tall, but he seemed much larger. In spite of his small stature and low rank he had an undeniable air of authority, the confidence of one who was used to command. Crane couldn't place his accent, which sounded to his ears to be well-educated English but with something of the lilt of Swedish and the vowels of rural Kent.

'Where are you from, Sergeant?'

'A little island not far from Faversham. You won't have heard of it. My family's been there for a long time, along with the other local families. There's a whole squad of us and we usually stick together. It was one of the conditions of our joining up.'

Crane was mystified. He hadn't been aware that conscription could be conditional. But then he wasn't a military man and had only a hazy idea of how these things worked. 'Tell me, Sergeant – have you heard anything unusual while you've been watching the watchdogs?'

Hadding's gaze was shrewd. 'I take it you mean unusual comparatively speaking. Well, I've seen a few things and the SS men gossip. They think I can't understand what they're saying but I studied German at school and I've got an ear for languages. I also know a bit of Romany, from the travellers in Kent, and I've even picked up a bit of Russian and Yiddish while I've been here. I've been hearing stories about something they call *die schöne Blutegel* – the lovely leech. She's a sort of camp bogeyman, visits the dying and sucks their last breath, touches the healthy and they start to waste away.'

'They imagine this creature to be a woman?'

'Yes, and a beautiful one. She's a sort of combined vampire and Typhoid Mary. The SS also blame her for the cannibalism.'

'Cannibalism?'

'We've seen a few bodies that look as though they've been butchered for meat. Given the level of starvation here and the lack of supervision after the diseases spiralled out of control, it's hardly surprising.'

'Just how bad is the disease? The lieutenant has stopped even talking about it. When I ask him he just shakes his head and reaches for a smoke.'

'That's what we all do,' Hadding laughed grimly. 'None of us like to even think about it now. We chain-smoke to steady our nerves and treat our noses to something other than this bloody dreadful stench. It's very bad, Mr Crane. Thousands have died since we supposedly liberated the camp and thousands more are dying. When we came we found thirteen thousand unburied bodies. Even with so many dead the camp was seriously overcrowded. Out of approximately sixty thousand survivors, nearly all were dying of either sickness or starvation. The typhus is spread by lice, and the place is crawling with them. The typhoid is caused by contaminated food and water, poor sanitation and hygiene. The TB is airborne and becomes epidemic with overcrowding. The dysentery goes with the typhoid and typhus, and increases the spread of those diseases. Bergen-Belsen didn't need a lovely leech to spread disease and kill all these people, Mr Crane. The SS saw to it themselves.'

Celle, 14th June 1945

'I have said in a previous statement that I have never beaten or ill-treated prisoners. I have thought it over and I now wish to confess that I have done so and to tell the truth.

'My duties at Belsen included taking Appell *or roll-call twice a week. My rank was* Kommandoführerin. *I was employed as* Aufseherin. *In this capacity it was my duty to supervise tidiness and*

general cleanliness in the camp. My duties were in the women's camp only. I never struck prisoners during the three and a half weeks I was at Belsen. While at Auschwitz I struck female prisoners on the face with my hand for using dixies as latrine buckets. I myself did not strike prisoners often but quite frequently when they did something I didn't like.

'*On the whole I consider that I treated prisoners well. I did not think that any of them were hostile to me when I was working in the camp. I now find that they all appear to be hostile to me. I think that is because they were hostile to all SS because they cannot forget the number of people among them who were gassed at Auschwitz. I myself think they are perfectly right to feel hostile towards us.*

'*I have again reflected and I wish to add that I have in fact beaten prisoners other than with my hand as already described. This was at Auschwitz when for at least a week several of us SS women had short whips made in the camp workshops with one of which I several times struck prisoners before these whips were taken away from us as unauthorised arms were never carried or possessed by any SS women. I also now admit that I punished prisoners by making them kneel on the grounds for periods of a quarter of an hour at a time. I did not at the same time make them hold their hands above their heads but I saw this being done when I have made my report to another part of the camp at Auschwitz.*

'*I remember saying in the first statement I made to an English officer that 'Himmler is responsible for all that has happened, but I suppose I have as much guilt as all the others above me.' I meant by this that simply by being in the SS and seeing the crimes committed on orders from those in authority and doing nothing to protest or stop them being committed makes anybody in the SS as guilty as anybody else. The crimes I refer to are the gassing of persons at Auschwitz and the killing of thousands at Belsen by starvation and disease. I consider the crime to be murder.'*

The Seventh Day

Conditions in the camp had improved gradually as inmates were moved from the concentration camp to the adjoining barracks, now designated a camp for Displaced Persons. The site still reeked of death and horror, and people were still dying in their hundreds, but the lieutenant had confided to Crane that he could now see a glimmer of light at the end of a very long and dark tunnel.

Crane had moved to the small city of tents well outside the camp, where most of the Allied soldiers were billeted. The soldiers had dug latrines a good distance from their tents, and they were well-maintained and sanitised. The air was slightly cleaner. But the stink from the concentration camp hung over everything like the shadow of death.

He was sitting with Sergeant Hadding, smoking and talking quietly in the unreal spring sunshine, when the SIS messenger finally located him. The man had a sealed letter. When Crane opened it, he saw it was an order from Churchill relayed via none other than Menzies, the head of SIS. Clearly this was something too important to entrust to even his most valued staff.

'Bad news?' Hadding enquired. Crane's face was expressionless but he had paled considerably and his eyes betrayed consternation.

Crane knew he wasn't supposed to share the contents of the letter with anyone else but he'd seen too much at Bergen-Belsen to care anymore. 'Churchill's read my reports and notified Eisenhower and Tedder. They're interested in what Irma Grese told me about the Vril Society, and they want that hut removed intact and transported to a military research station in England, along with the iron circle and soil samples.'

'Won't that be a good thing?' asked Hadding cautiously. 'If it does have military applications, surely it's better for the Allies to have it?'

'This war's nearly over. Whatever this thing may be, who would we use it against? I can't see Britain or America sharing it with the Soviet Union, can you? The West and the Soviets are already manoeuvring for dominance in the post-war Europe. And if Japan is beaten, China will certainly join the Soviet Union's political orbit. The Americans won't let communism spread any further than that. Weapons have increased in power and effectiveness since 1939. We now have jet planes, radar and missiles. I daresay we'll plunder what we can from the Nazis' secret laboratories. And I hear rumours of something terrible being created in America. Can you imagine a Third World War fought with weapons far greater than those we already have?' Crane recalled Tesla's teleforce projector and hoped Dorothy Harlow had disposed of that as completely as she had promised. And what of Dorothy herself? Was she not also a potential weapon to be kept out of hawkish hands?

His train of thought was interrupted by another visitor. The newcomer was dressed in civilian clothing, though he had a pistol holstered at his hip and a Sten gun slung over his shoulder, where it jostled for space with a bulging rucksack. 'Anthony Crane?'

Crane groaned. 'Does the whole bloody world know I'm here? I'm supposed to be on a secret mission, for crying out loud.'

The man grinned, held out his hand. 'Fred Alliss, SOE. I've come from Paris to deliver a message. Had to hitch-hike half the way. I did have a jeep but I got strafed by a Stuka just outside Mainz and that was that. Took me a while to track you down. I was told you were at Bergen-Belsen but I had no idea how big this damned place is. It's taken me all morning to find you.'

Crane scowled crossly but shook the proffered hand out of habitual courtesy. 'Tell Churchill he can piss off. If it's from anyone in SIS you can tell them something worse.'

The visitor continued to grin. 'No, this is from a mutual friend. Mikaiel Dakessian sends you his regards, and a message from the Yellow Room.'

'Alright then, let's see it,' Crane sighed.

'It wasn't written down. But it's quite short so it was easy to memorise. "Ethel says the Beast awaits you; Dorothy says she can't see through the fog, so there is danger; and Mrs Pugh says salt and fire." And if any of that means anything to you, then you're either a genius or in charge of a lunatic asylum.'

'What do you know about the Yellow Room, Alliss?'

'Only what Dakessian has told me, and that's precious little. Some hush-hush outfit using psychic abilities to confound the enemy, I understand.' Alliss neither laughed nor looked scornful.

Crane looked him up and down appraisingly. 'And you don't think that's a bit, well – peculiar?'

Alliss shook his head slowly. 'I experienced some strange things in Paris. Before that I would have thought you were barmy, but now...' He shrugged. 'And after what I just witnessed back in that camp, I'm not sure the world's a sane place anymore. Anyway, if Dakessian works with your lot, then you must be pretty special. If you're here that means there's something uncanny going on.'

'You don't know the half of it.' Crane told him about the mysterious hut, *das Ekel*, the Vril Society and *Nosferatu*. Then he explained why he was reluctant to comply with Churchill's latest orders.

'This Irma Grese. Do you believe her story?'

'I don't know what to believe. She's a Nazi and she's facing a war crimes trial. I suppose anyone in her position would spout any old nonsense to save their skins, but... Look here, Alliss, Irma's basically a peasant girl with a minimal education. I'm fairly sure she was telling me what she'd heard, even if she didn't really understand it. I already knew something of what she told me and I strongly doubt that a young German farm girl would have heard of Edward Bulwer-Lytton, Wilhelm Reich or Karl Haushofer through her own reading. And, of course, there's that abominable hut.'

'May I take a look at it?'

'It'll be dark soon. It'll still be there in the morning.'

Celle, 14th June 1945

'On further reflection I wish to say that in three respects the statements I made in my previous deposition were not accurate. First of all I previously stated that I never carried arms. In fact Aufseherinnen *at Auschwitz did carry pistols, I among them. My pistol, however, was*

never loaded and I did not know how to use it nor did I ever do so. Second, when I stated that the only time I had used a weapon to beat prisoners was when I had a whip for a week, this was untrue. I did in fact always have a whip which I used consistently whenever necessary. Third, I admit that there was also a walking stick which we kept in the Lagerältester*'s room and which, although it was unauthorised, we frequently used to beat prisoners. I usually used to beat them on the shoulders, but there were times when, because of the numbers involved, they were beaten on any part of the body that happened to be easiest. All the beatings to which I refer were immediate and I have never taken part in deliberately organised punishments.'*

The Eighth Day

He awoke not long after midnight, sweating and uneasy. His heart was beating fast and it was a struggle to breathe, as if all the air had been sucked from the tent. And he'd had bad dreams, nightmares of being chased along endless labyrinths by formless creatures made of blood-lust and sickness. He coughed and flicked away droplets of perspiration from his wet brow. Perhaps he'd been smoking too much. He hoped that was the case. He had no desire to fall victim to any one of the diseases that continued to ravage the concentration camp.

He rose shakily and somehow managed to insert himself into the khaki trousers, then padded barefoot and bare-chested into the night, pausing only to retrieve his canteen, Lucky Strikes and Zippo lighter from under the bedroll.

Outside, the night was quiet and cool. The moon was ominously full and the grass beneath his feet moist with an early dew. For once the wind blew toward the camp and the blessedly fresh air was a huge relief. He sat on a jerry can and inhaled deeply, then took a long drink of tepid water, keeping his fingers crossed that it came from an uncontaminated source. When he felt a little better, he lit a cigarette. The light from the Zippo was almost blinding and for a few seconds his vision was obscured by multicoloured after-images. When he could see properly again, he was no longer alone.

She sat on the ground, cross-legged like a child, careless of the damp, blonde hair hanging down straight to her slender shoulders, clad in a long, loose black dress. At first glance she looked enough like Irma Grese for the mistake to be understandable – but a closer look gave the lie to any similarity. Her face was long and pale, her eyes were unnaturally blue, her lips as scarlet as if she had been drinking blood. She was incredibly beautiful, though he would have been unable to tell anyone how old she was.

She made him feel sick to his stomach, and so very afraid.

Neither of them spoke. He watched her with trepidation and mounting nausea; she regarded him coolly and with evident contempt and a trace of amusement. At last she stood and spoke, holding his gaze all the while. He didn't understand the Russian words but their meaning seared into his brain. The Beast had quoted Coleridge:

Her lips were red, her looks were free,
Her locks were yellow as gold:
Her skin was as white as leprosy,
The Night-mare LIFE-IN-DEATH was she,
Who thicks man's blood with cold.

Then she laughed, the sound like a lover's moan of

passion, and vanished. Crane awoke, still perched on the jerry can, when the cigarette burned down to his fingers.

'How many people do you have left to move to the Displacement Camp?'

'Not many now,' said Hadding. 'We should be done by this afternoon. Why are we out here, Mr Crane?'

The hut squatted by the wire fence like a sick toad. Even from ten yards away, the four men could feel their gorges rising, their bowels churning. Crane motioned the lieutenant, Hadding and Alliss to move back until they could no longer feel the influence.

Crane's face was impassive. 'Sergeant Hadding, do you have any incendiary charges, thermite grenades or something similar?'

'Yes, we have thermite bombs. We use them to decommission enemy artillery.'

'And they sent several Churchill Crocodiles and some chaps with flame-throwers yesterday to help with cremating the bodies now we can't keep up with the burials,' added the lieutenant. 'Why, what are you planning to do?'

'Gentlemen, we all agree that there is something unwholesome about this building. It's connected with Nazi experiments in human evolution, a folklore vampire, and the rapid spread of disease in Bergen-Belsen. Yes, it sounds far-fetched and I haven't a bloody clue how it all adds up. But it's clear to me that the hut is a kind of battery or capacitor, storing some sort of electrical energy. I think the charge is built up through a slow release of human life-force, sexual activity and geo-magnetism. It's an unholy hybrid of science with the sort of magic Crowley preaches. I believe that is why the Nazis began transferring so many camp inmates to this God-forsaken place. They're fuel. Something here both preys upon them and feeds this structure. I suspect that something is a person hiding in the camp, a woman. But she can't hide among the inmates any longer – she looks so healthy that she'd stick out like a sore thumb. Now, she'll be forced to conceal herself within the fabric of the women's camp. Are there priests nearby, perhaps a rabbi?'

'Yes,' said Sergeant Hadding. 'We have chaplains, and there is a Roman Catholic church nearby. Obviously, there are one or two rabbis in the Displacement Camp.'

'Good. Do you have access to salt? Rock salt would be best.'

'There are a lot of salt mines in this part of the world. There's bound to be quite a bit in the nearest towns.'

'Excellent. Send a few trucks out to get some. We'll need rather a lot. Then round up a priest and a rabbi, and get those Crocodiles over here. And Sergeant, get me a few gallons of petrol and a dozen thermite bombs.'

Alliss was perplexed. 'Priests? Rabbis? Thermite? Crane, what are you planning to do?'

'I can't allow that thing,' – he pointed toward the cuboid hut – 'to be investigated and turned into a weapon or used in any other way. You can feel it, Alliss – it's tainted beyond redemption, a thing of evil spawned in a place of suffering created by the damned. Churchill can go to hell. Tomorrow morning, I'm going to get the whole place blessed by a priest and a rabbi, then we'll pressgang a few SS guards into sowing the whole loathsome place with salt. When that's done, I'm going home.'

He turned haunted eyes on his companions. 'But first we're going to burn the hut and the camp to the fucking ground.'

Lüneburg, 16th November 1945

The whole thing was a tragic farce in a hall of mirrors, a depressing iniquity endlessly repeated with only minor variations. The interpreters were unable to adequately follow the prosecution lawyers' questions; they mistranslated the defendants' responses. The complexities of camp rank, hierarchy and responsibility were impenetrable. The lawyers themselves, defence and prosecutors alike, were all serving British and Polish military officers who had neither practised nor read law for years. They frequently confused the procedures of civilian criminal law with those of the new regulations for military trials of alleged war criminals. They framed their questions in ways that made them seem like statements of fact that could only be either endorsed by the accused or countered with a lie. None of the court officials, from the President and Judges down to the clerks and stenographers, could keep track of the multiple accusations, the accused or even their accusers. At times it seemed none present had the faintest idea of what they were supposed to be doing. It wasn't even sufficiently competent to be a show trial.

But the sorry display of understandable confusion and bumbling ineptitude was a mere sideshow, of course. The main attractions sat in rows with numbers hung around their necks like entries in a livestock competition. The winners would be garlanded with rosettes that proclaimed them to be not guilty. The luckiest of the losers would return to the prison they'd been setting out from each morning. The less fortunate would follow the Pied Piper to Hamelin and an appointment with Pierrepoint's noose. It was doubtful that anyone really cared which of them would hang, just as long as enough of them took that final drop to satisfy honour and slake the thirst for retribution.

The young woman he had spoken to in Celle prison had looked even younger than her twenty-one years. Now she looked much older, tired and drawn, dull-eyed and downcast, bags under her eyes and haggard with exhaustion and stress. Over the summer she had twice amended her initial deposition, each time allowing that she had been a little more brutal than she had first claimed. In court, the questions had been asked and she had given answers. And yet even now, after fifty-four days of tortuous legal process, the inquisitorial back-and-forth, all the witnesses and exhibits – even now he still had no idea if she was innocent or guilty of the most serious charges. The court had made up its mind and established the facts as it saw them to its own satisfaction. But he simply did not know.

He sat in the gallery and watched the play unfold and progress toward its inevitable conclusion.

The Ninth Day

'You look terrible, Herr Crane. What has happened to you? Are you ill? Is that why you haven't been to see me for a couple of days?'

'Just a spot of dysentery, Irma,' he lied. 'I'm feeling much better now. It seems to have burned itself out.'

She smiled tiredly. The prettiness was fading along with her hope for a future. 'Did you discover anything more about *das Ekel*?'

'That's all sorted out now, I think. I – I think I met her, though it might have been only a dream.' *A nightmare.* 'But I believe she is gone now.'

'Was she as beautiful as they say?'

'She was, but in a terrible way. Do you know we burned the concentration camp? It has been completely destroyed.'

'No one here tells me anything.' She smiled sadly and looked down at the table. 'Here, it is I who am *das Ekel*.'

'No, you're just an ordinary girl who got caught up in bad circumstances that got out of control. You're not a bit like that woman.'

'Thank you, Herr Crane. It is nice of you to say so, though I doubt anyone will believe you. What would you like to ask me about today?'

'No more questions, Irma. I just came to say goodbye and to thank you for being so helpful. I'm going home in a few hours.'

'Oh. That will be nice for you. Where do you live?'

'I live in Surrey, just south of London. I'm looking forward to seeing my family and friends again.'

'Do you have children?'

'One, a little boy. His name's Joel. And there's another baby on the way. I'm hoping for a daughter this time.'

'That is good. I wish…'

'What? What do you wish?'

'I wish for very little but it is far more than I will ever have,' she said wistfully. 'Goodbye, Herr Crane. Perhaps one day we will meet again.'

'Perhaps. Who knows what the future might bring? I hope you find justice, Irma. I hope you find peace.'

'I think justice will find me before I find it. As for peace – that is something I have never known.'

Lüneburg, 17th November 1945

He sat upright as Major-General Berney-Ficklin impassively read out the sentences. Her name was one of the earliest. 'Number Six, Bormann; Number Seven, Volkenrath; Number Nine, Grese. The sentences of this Court on each of you whom I have just named is that you suffer death by being hanged.'

And that was it. Had it really taken fifty-four days of ritual and rhetorical inquisition to tell her what she already knew she was going to hear? He watched numbly as she was led out of the court with the other accused, her head bowed. Berney-Ficklin was praising the defence lawyers for carrying out their duties conscientiously in such difficult circumstances. One part of the Major-General's speech remained with Crane for a very long time.

'There is no need for me to remind you that it is the basis of all discipline that an officer not only accepts orders unquestionably, but carries them out to the very best of his ability.'

The irony, he was sure, would be lost on posterity.

The Rocket Man

February 1946

The newcomer was making a big impression. He was popular with the ladies, though reportedly never taking advantage of their attentions, even the usually irresistible Betty; and was someone quite a few of the men appeared to look up to. Ron in particular held the man in high esteem – though not as high as himself, naturally, even though the signs were that Betty was ready to move on from him, as she had from their host not so long ago. The light stubble on his chin gave Jack Marshall a roguish air that went well with the boyish good looks and that knowing grin. But the smile never reached those hard eyes. For all his bonhomie, wisecracks and attentiveness he wasn't an especially likeable man. The charm and Groucho-quick gags were calculated and came so readily they just had to have been rehearsed. Jack Parsons didn't trust him an inch. There was always room for another Jack in the Parsonage, but not one like this.

At that moment Marshall was talking to Candy. Unlike

Betty – indeed, unlike all the other female residents, guests and passers-through – she was openly cool toward the latest arrival. While Parsons made no claims of ownership or exclusivity on any woman, somehow the thought that Candy might find Marshall sexually attractive made him feel sick. As he watched she caught his eye. Ron said something that drew Marshall's attention from Candy. She flashed Parsons a quick grin and rolled her eyes. Parsons was glad Marshall hadn't seen that. He thought it wouldn't go down at all well.

Marshall wasn't a member of the OTO or any other occult order Parsons knew of. He told Parsons that he was seeking additional knowledge and ideas to help his quest for spiritual enlightenment. Parsons had expounded his version of Crowley's Thelemite philosophy, but Marshall had practically sneered at him. 'Yeah,' he'd said, 'but what *you* mean by "do what thou wilt shall be the whole of the law" seems a bit watery to me. All this talk of *agape* and love tells me that you still compromise your will by implicitly negotiating with others. It's still a dialogue, isn't it? You're not expressing your true, pure will. You're expressing only a part of your nature within your relationship with other people, specifically women.'

'So what would you suggest?' Parsons had been curious to know what kind of Thelema the other man envisaged.

Marshall had shaken his head and laughed. 'Well, for one thing you should get away from the notion of magical workings with another person as a focus. That compromises your true will straightaway, because you have to accommodate the other person. And all that crap about

Babalon and the Scarlet Woman – it's a kind of marriage, isn't it? This is someone you *relate* to, and I bet you express tenderness and even love while you're doing the work. Believe me, my friend – there's no true will being expressed in those circumstances. To do that you need to reject all such feeling and treat the other person as a tool or an object. Divest them of identity and personality. Make them the things they should be to the man you wish to be. Speaking hypothetically, of course.'

Parsons wasn't at all comfortable with that. After all, the underpinning principle of Thelema was 'love is the law, love under will' – as far as he was concerned love was the essence of what Thelema should be. Marshall's philosophy troubled him. The way the man looked at women troubled him even more.

Now Marshall had moved on from the distinctly underwhelmed Marjorie and was selling some idea to Ron, about the way religion should be marketed like any other commodity. 'The more people invest in it, the more they'll be prepared to believe it. You do that by alternating hard sell and soft sell. First you tell them that they want what you're selling; and when they've bought into it you tell them that you're going to give them the secrets to happiness and success that you've promised. But then you make it known there are greater secrets that can be theirs for a small further investment. Hell, it's the way the Freemasons work, isn't it? Even if people become disenchanted most won't say anything. No one wants to admit they've paid good money for garbage. And the true believers will keep the doubters in line, if you invest a little authority in them, give them a bigger stake.'

'Yes,' Ron eagerly agreed, running with the idea as if it was his own, which it probably soon would be. 'And you can wrap it all up in bullshit jargon that doesn't actually mean anything – though you tell them it does, only they won't find out what until they pay to receive teachings that will take them to the next level. And you can repeat that as often as you want. Hey, you could make it even more efficient by setting up franchises in different towns, get other suckers to do all the work while you sit back and count the bucks.'

And so it went on. Ron was just the kind of guy to buy Marshall's cynical crap. Parsons knew damned well that Ron lied about pretty much everything. All those war stories – he knew bullshit when he heard it and Ron was full of it. He'd be glad when Ron and Betty finally worked up the courage to get out of the Parsonage, out of Pasadena, and out of his life. But he'd have to keep a close eye on his money, even if that business proposition they'd made was damned tempting.

If Ron was becoming an annoyance, Marshall was clearly dangerous. Some of Parsons' own magickal working was out on a very shaky limb. He was impatient with the protracted ritual and detail of the OTO, and Crowley could be a bit obsessive about that kind of thing. Parsons preferred his rituals a little more adventurous and liked to take magickal risks. But Marshall was right in one respect – Parsons' brand of Thelema was all about love and he would never be able to treat anyone as a mere object or tool to be used. They were people, for God's sake. And they were people he liked. In Candy's case, it was simply love – maybe not as Mr Average American might understand it, but love nonetheless. What Marshall proposed was the antithesis of what Parsons believed magick was for and what Thelema was all about.

Marshall had candidly admitted that his own occult activities revolved around the image of Sammael, the Angel of Death in Jewish tradition, who had eventually merged with Ahriman, the Zoroastrian principle of evil, to become the Satan of Christian belief. Parsons had no problem with that. Satan was just another potent idea in a pantheon of such concepts of higher power, albeit a crude one. Oddly, Marshall professed atheism and claimed Sammael was really just a metaphor for the essence of his own nature. Parsons had the uncomfortable feeling that looking into Marshall's innermost being would be a deeply unpleasant experience. He wasn't keen on the people who sometimes accompanied Marshall – the older one called Mack, a man in his late twenties, was distant and bored; but it was the kid, a brooding, sixteen year-old boy they called Dave, touchy and prone to angry outbursts, who really gave Parsons the creeps. He looked at the women as if they were pieces of meat and he a starving man. Sometimes that same hunger was in Marshall's eyes. It was the look of a wolf, and they were the eyes of a shark.

May 1946

London was gradually returning to normal. Anthony Crane often went for long walks in the evenings just to enjoy the electric lights shining from windows, the street lamps and shop signs. After years of darkness those ordinary urban illuminations made him feel as though they were strolling through fairyland. Sometimes he took the whole family on his outings but most often he walked alone, occasionally roaming more or less aimlessly until dawn broke, trading one kind of light for another. He did so for the same reason there was always a lamp burning in the Crane household at night. Anthony Crane craved the light because he had gazed into the deepest darkness.

He still had nightmares about the concentration camp. Every night he dreamed he was back in Bergen-Belsen, or watching that seemingly interminable trial which he believed had shown British justice to be nothing more than a whore servicing public opinion. Sometimes he was in the prison at Hamelin, watching the bodies drop through the trapdoor, the women singly, the men in pairs. Often he saw Irma Grese's doomed face. Once or twice he'd seen that creature he thought he'd encountered there, and that was the most terrifying thing of all. Invariably, he awoke distressed and afraid, though he did his best to conceal the fact from his family. They should never know of such things, especially the children.

The Yellow Room was still in existence, though not at anything like its former strength. Charles Bartley – now Sir Charles – continued to be *persona non gratis*. The older members had announced their retirement from active duty on VJ Day, all but the recently-widowed Mrs Pugh, who said she had nothing else to do, and poor old Tompkins, still languishing in the clinic in Buckinghamshire. Ethel Bingham had unexpectedly married William Simmons, and the pair had unveiled plans to emigrate to Australia to start a new life and a family. Dorothy Harlow had appeared in her usual way one night as he struggled to type a report, stepping out of a shadow in the corner of the Yellow

Room, dressed in her usual film-star way. She hadn't spoken, simply kissed him tenderly on the cheek, smiled enigmatically and evaporated as if she'd never been there. When she'd gone he noticed she'd left a lemon-yellow envelope on the desk, though it blended in so well with the décor that it could well have been there for days.

Tony, go get him.

The too-brief note told him that his work was not yet done. The kiss told him she was saying goodbye. Both messages troubled him greatly.

For now, the Yellow Room consisted of Crane, Mrs Pugh and Edward Vance. They had official status but little support. After Belsen Churchill had been furious. Crane had even found himself sacked and locked up in the Tower of London, of all places, for a few nights following his return from Belsen; but eventually Winston had calmed down and reinstated him. After all, there were enemies still to fight. Germany was defeated but the Japanese were refusing to lie down.

Then, Hiroshima and Nagasaki. The atomic bomb confirmed Crane's worst fears and proved beyond all doubt that his mistrust of politicians and generals was well-founded. People like that would do anything for victory, right or wrong. Churchill had gone by the time two Japanese cities were incinerated and many thousands of people killed in a combined time of only a few seconds. It seemed that most of the dead were civilians. In Crane's book it was a war crime, an atrocity to match anything the Nazis did. The new Prime Minister seemed a decent enough man on paper – but if Attlee had agreed to the bombings with any degree of knowledge of the likely outcome, then he too had innocent blood on his hands.

When he returned to Germany for the Belsen trial and consequent executions, Crane was appalled by the amateurish way the trial was conducted. The current Nuremburg trials were more reassuring but a bad taste lingered from the Belsen shambles. The Allied leadership had done as bad, if not worse, than the Nazis, as those mushroom clouds amply demonstrated. He doubted Churchill, Stalin or Harry S. Truman would ever stand before a military court like the SS had in Lüneburg, but as far as he was concerned they deserved it just as much.

And now the corridors of power were buzzing with rumours of further conflict. The new bogeyman was the Soviet Union, just as he'd feared. The peace was as vulnerable and fragile as any neonate. Hawks were still hovering hungrily and the doves were too timid to spread their wings and fly. Any thoughts Crane might have had about resigning were banished. The watchmen needed watching now more than ever.

At first he thought visiting Crowley was a bad mistake. The magician's Hastings flat was depressingly squalid, cluttered with rubbish, foul-smelling and in dire need of cleaning. But the biggest shock was Crowley's physical deterioration. The last time Crane had seen him, the self-styled Great Beast had still been fairly well-built and, although ageing, still in command of his faculties. The haggard scarecrow that now lay propped up in the noisome bed was almost recognisable as the man the supposedly Wickedest Man in the World had once been. The straggling goatee was stained with nicotine and dribbled food; the voice was reedy and querulous, the resonance and assertiveness long departed. The rheumy eyes and tremulous hands were surely those of a much older man. But, Crane realised with a start, Crowley must be in his early seventies and he had never exactly deprived himself of the pleasures of the flesh. And the needles on the sideboard told him the man was still in thrall to heroin.

Crowley ranted in his unsettlingly thin voice, waving a letter he'd received only that morning. 'The damned fool's trying to walk before he can run. Says he's successfully completed the Babalon working and has his Scarlet Woman. And now he's got the bloody temerity to say he's going to create a Moonchild. The idiot will destroy himself, just as I nearly did!'

'Steady on, Crowley,' said Crane. 'I haven't the foggiest idea of what you're talking about.'

Crowley glared at him with too-bright eyes. He was dying, Crane realised, and not very slowly by the look of it. The Great Beast held his gaze, and eventually the ferocious expression softened. 'It's my American protegé,' he grumbled. 'Jack Parsons is the most naturally gifted magician living today. In many ways, he's what I used to be, Crane. He's the head of the OTO in the United States but is also a recognised expert in explosives and rocket science, a brilliant fellow. He's done exactly what I did and opened his home to creative and spiritual free-thinkers. And he employs the same methods I once used.'

'If he's so much like you, why are you angry?'

'Because he doesn't understand the dangers involved,' Crowley said, closing his eyes and running a fragile hand over his face. 'It's not just the hangers-on and opportunistic charlatans that attach themselves to every such man – they are merely human and can be ignored, dealt with and forgotten. No, the dangers I speak of are those of the soul; and of nature perverted. I once…' He fell silent.

'What's a Moonchild?'

'Ah, that's the crux of the matter,' Crowley replied. 'In 1917 I published a novel of the same name. It was the story of a magician's attempt to create a magickal child. The protagonist kept a woman in seclusion for a time, made lengthy and elaborate ritual preparations, then impregnated her with the intention of making a living, physical vessel that would be fit to contain an Aethyric being – a Moonchild.'

'And in plain English that would be – what, exactly?'

'A terrible mistake, Crane. All the complex magick I described in that book is completely unnecessary for the initiated. It always is, and that's simply to discourage the wrong sort of person from undertaking such procedures. I came to understand that early in my career. The true exponent of magick has already prepared himself to cause change in conformity with his will. It's an apprenticeship, if you like. When the apprentice has become a master of his trade, only the simplest rituals are needed. Everything else is already in place in his mind and spirit. An act of will is then all that is required, if the circumstances are right.'

'I understand that. But what is an Aethyric being? Is it an angel or a demon, or an elemental creature, something like that?'

'The Aethyrs are other worlds that exist alongside and outside this one, Crane. I have seen them in visions induced by meditation and certain drugs. The beings that dwell there sometimes have strange forms – indeed, some have no form at all but are simply a kind of essence, a sort of raw consciousness without shape or personality. I once…' He hesitated, began to fiddle with a meerschaum pipe and a pouch of tobacco. 'No, I will not speak of that,' he continued quietly. 'All I wish to add is that in my experience those Aethyric entities are dangerous toys. I have thought long and hard about them since… Well, what happened does not concern you. But it is my opinion that in their natural state they do not have personality or identity as we understand them. The nature of their manifestation in this world is dictated by how they are brought into it, and by the intention of whoever does the bringing. I further believe that on occasion they spontaneously intersect with this world, and they have a particular attraction to women. I'm not sure why that should be.'

'I can see how that might be disturbing for the individual concerned,' Crane shrugged. 'But I don't understand why it's dangerous.'

'Because the damned things can *change* you,' Crowley snapped. 'I've… I've *seen* it, and it isn't pretty. Parsons must be warned that what he's doing could bring about something worse than the concentration camps, the Black Death, the atom bomb and all the wars in history rolled into one. And these idiots he's gathered around him, the fawning sycophants, the thrill-seekers and the schemers – they encourage him and tell him how wonderful he is, but they don't realise that all they're doing is egging Parsons on to bring about their own destruction. That's why I've suggested he resigns his OTO position. If he sees I'm deadly serious it might bring the damned fool to his senses.'

'Crowley, you must tell me. What can these Aethyric

beings actually do to someone? How can they change people?'

The magician met Crane's eyes, that disconcertingly impassive yet dominating stare into infinity that had lost none of its power even as Crowley's health declined and his life ebbed away. Now, though, there was something else. Crowley was afraid. When he spoke again, his voice was hoarse and low.

'*Nosferatu*,' he whispered. 'A symphony of horror. More than that – a disease of body and soul that would turn all humanity to a horde of rapacious, sadistic beasts that would prey upon one another when the last fully human man and woman and child have been consumed for their pleasure. And Crane – I believe *I* was responsible for bringing it into existence.'

June 1946

'This is the man all tattered and torn that kissed the maiden all forlorn…' He chanted to himself as he made an adjustment to the latest ornament. '…that lay in the house that Jack built.'

The man chuckled. It wasn't exactly a house, just a well-appointed cave in the San Bernadino Mountains, not far in from where the range abutted the Mojave Desert. Nor was he what you'd call tattered and torn – the white linen suit had cost him a dollar or two more than most guys could afford, and he had taken pains to avoid getting it dirtied as he worked. But the maiden was certainly all forlorn, as were her twelve sisters in death, whose heads adorned the stakes arranged in a circle deep inside the cave. This new lady was on the one in the centre. The rest of her was buried out in the desert with the discarded remains of the others. And like the others, she was no maiden when she died. If she had been when he started work, she surely wasn't by the time he'd finished with her. He planted a big wet smacker on her dead lips for old time's sake then carefully pressed the ruined neck onto the sharp wooden point, releasing the head only when he was sure it was held fast.

He stepped back to admire his handiwork, swatting away the flies that hummed around the decaying heads. The flickering torchlight caused their shadowed features to seemingly shift and move in a grotesque imitation of the life they'd lost, the life he had taken from them. It was quite artistic, he thought. Those simpering simpletons in Pasadena would approve – before they passed out with shock and horror. Never let it be said that men of action couldn't be creative too.

And the setting was perfect. He'd discovered the cave by chance one day while scouting for a suitable playground. The ancient petroglyphs told him straight away that this was his place: the huge horned, bat-winged being with a blunt head and enormous cock dominated the rock walls, which were otherwise decorated with the outlines of hands and feet, wavy lines and zig-zags, and numerous tiny pictures of women, their sex obvious from breasts and exaggerated vulvas, kneeling submissively or with their legs spread, some lying dead and dismembered at the demon's taloned feet. The pictures radiated power and purpose. Whatever else it may have been, this place was emphatically not the ancient Indian equivalent of a Tijuana bible.

The other figures were less propitious – on the wall to the left just inside the cave entrance some long-ago hand had pecked out what looked like a giant wolf or coyote and a similarly-sized bobcat flanking what seemed to be a pair of Siamese twins with sunburst heads; while to the right of the entrance were images of a woman with wings and a man in what looked weirdly like medieval armour, each with an intricate spiral instead of a face. They'd probably been made by some Anasazi medicine man out of his mind on peyote or jimson weed. Something about them unnerved him but he couldn't say what it was.

It didn't really matter, though. Not with everything else pointing to this being the spot on which a new world order would be born. He surveyed the cave once more and was pleased.

The Timex watch on his wrist said it was nearly one in the afternoon, time to get back to LA and call the boys. Time to start the next phase. It was going to be quite a party.

The ceiling fan was big but lacked the speed that would have made a difference. It whirled lazily above the bed, not even taking the edge off the dry heat. At least the Coca-Cola was cold. He pressed the dewed bottle against his forehead. The relief he craved did not come. Perhaps he was going down with the 'flu.

No, that wasn't it. The shivers were the product of fear, as was the tidal ebb and flow in his stomach. It had been happening on and off ever since Belsen. He was afraid, that was all; very afraid. And it was too damned hot.

He supposed sooner or later he would get used to the unfamiliar climate. After all, he wasn't the only Briton here, and most appeared to be thriving. The day before he'd seen David Niven in a Hollywood restaurant, cool as a cucumber, chatting with Errol Flynn over drinks. He'd seen a lot of film stars in the two days he'd been in Los Angeles. In the flesh and at normal human size they seemed surprisingly ordinary; and he supposed that without the make-up and lights and magnification that's what they really were, men and women just like him and the other people he knew. The silver screen made gods and goddesses and devils out of mere mortals. But it wasn't the only thing that could do that. He'd learned that much from Crowley and Belsen.

Now he had to bite the bullet and force himself to visit the place they called the Parsonage, the artistic and Bohemian enclave where someone might unwittingly be creating a monster to rival anything Hollywood had ever shown on celluloid. And he had to do it alone. Vance was holding the fort in the Yellow Room, on the off-chance that the Soviet Union had managed to cobble together an army of psychic assassins or Marxist black magicians. Mrs Pugh simply wasn't cut out for what this mission, strictly off the Yellow Room's books, might entail. He had no one else, nothing else.

Officially, he was on holiday. But the trashy, hastily-purchased souvenirs and the postcards written quickly in his hotel room the night before were only camouflage. It might have been paranoia but he was increasingly sure he was being watched. He didn't know who might be keeping him under surveillance, or why they would be doing it. There were, after all, many possible reasons. If it was SIS or another British intelligence service, it would probably be because he was an employee, if only on paper, of the Ministry of War abroad in what was still, in spite of any supposed special relationship, a foreign country. The Americans, of course, would know about his run-in with the psychopathic killer Jack Worthington back in 1941. It would be no surprise at all to find that the FBI or the new Central Intelligence Group were tracking his movements; or even the NKGB, not that he had the faintest idea if the Soviets knew anything at all of the Yellow Room's existence. While those organisations might watch, he doubted they would do anything more. If it was anything else, someone who operated without rules and laws, he could be in trouble. If, that is, he was being watched at all. It might be nothing more than his overwrought imagination. Fear bred fearfulness.

In the end, he could do nothing but what he'd come to Los Angeles to do. Reluctantly, he rose from the bed and dressed, smoked what he fervently hoped would not be his last cigarette, and left the hotel. In the street, he hailed a taxi and told the driver to take him to 1003 Orange Grove Avenue, Pasadena. It was still damnably hot. But, he had to admit, the sunshine was bloody glorious.

'How many more do we need?'

'Another seven,' said the leader, sipping a Coors. He nodded to himself, appreciating both the cold beer and the mood of his companions. The kid was keen and would be an excellent operator, though he had yet to learn the value of patience and prudence. The other guy was so crazy for action it made him want to laugh aloud with the nearest thing he had to joy. 'It won't be a problem.'

And it wouldn't be a problem. More arrived in Los Angeles every day, each thinking her name was already written in lights above movie theatres the world over. Their wide, shiny eyes and scrubbed, innocent faces marked them for what they were: prey for the dope peddlers and pimps, prey for men like them. There was a filtration system. Most would find themselves on their knees or their backs for the fleeting pleasure of jaded old men with too much money and no scruples. Those who refused or failed their humiliating audition on the casting couch would become waitresses or shop girls. Many would become whores. The really unlucky ones would meet him and his pals. After that, they'd be beyond caring.

He knew the look, that bewildered desperation that marked the ones stranded in LA with no money to get back to their shitty little home towns, the ones who had defied mommy and daddy and burned their bridges to a cinder when they left home with their little suitcases and fragile ambitions. All he had to do was walk up to them in that expensive suit and fedora and say the words they wanted to hear. 'Hey, gorgeous — I can make you a star.' It was so damned easy, like plucking low-hanging berries from a bush.

'*Where are you keeping the others?*'

'*I got them chained up at a ranch in the desert, Dave,*' *he told the kid. This operation had been carefully planned, and knowledge was compartmentalised, a trick he'd learned during the war. The fewer people who knew all the details, the less chance there was of being discovered.* '*It's owned by an old movie star but he's out of the picture, sick and dying so I hear. When we've got the full set we'll go out there and load them into a truck, take them out to the cave. If George doesn't get here in time, well, that'll be too bad.*'

'*What's it like, this cave?*' *the other guy asked.*

The leader grinned hugely. '*Mack, it's fucking beautiful,*' *he said.*

No surname necessary — typically relaxed American attitudes, instant informality, quick-setting acceptance. The price of admission to this odd circle? One short sentence: 'I'm a friend of Aleister Crowley.' Not that the circle was anything to shout about. The mansion Crane had heard so much about had been abandoned, sold, demolished. Parsons and his Scarlet Woman were living in a coach house in the grounds, with only occasional guests. It was oddly disappointing.

If Jack Parsons was, by anyone's standards, a handsome man, his companion, a slender woman with a shock of red hair and a wide, cartoon grin, was startling — a vaguely androgynous, awkward-looking creature who seemed to emanate a raw, sexual heat that made a mockery of her lack of conventional beauty. Crane wouldn't even have called her pretty, yet he could understand why Parsons so obviously found her irresistible.

'So what brings you to the US, Tony?' Parsons sipped a martini, heedless of the early hour. 'Not just to bring felicitations from Frater Perdurabo, that's for sure. You here on business?'

Crane swallowed a mouthful of the lemonade he'd accepted in lieu of the alcoholic alternatives on offer. 'I suppose you could say I am. Tell me, has Crowley told you anything of what he did during the war?'

'Not a peep. I guessed he was up to his usual tricks. I know he used to work as a British secret agent of some sort but I thought he'd have been a bit old for the cloak and dagger stuff. I figured he'd been working behind the scenes in his own way – rituals to assure victory, putting the whammy on the Nazis.'

'Actually, he did some work with my outfit, as a consultant.' Crane was now contravening the Official Secrets Act; not that he gave two hoots about that any longer. 'We were formed at the end of 1939 to combat the Nazis by employing – er – unorthodox methods.'

'What, you mean witchcraft? It's OK, I know all about that. Perdurabo said that Firth woman and some others were doing that. He thought it was hilarious. Are you one of them?'

'No, though we did have dealings with them now and then. My team consisted of diviners and psychometrists, mostly. We were mainly tasked with locating enemy agents and influencing Nazi decisions. My idea was to use scientific methods to study and perhaps enhance the team's natural abilities.'

'Interesting. Did it work?'

'We had some success – not much, but enough to encourage us to further research. In operational terms, however, we were highly effective. In the course of the war I experienced a few very interesting things. And some that were frankly terrifying.'

Parsons laughed. 'You want terrifying? Since we began the Babalon working this place has been the focus of all kinds of weird phenomena. We've had poltergeist activity, strange mechanical-sounding voices coming out of nowhere, you name it.'

'Ah yes, the Babalon working. That was to acquire what you call a Scarlet Woman, wasn't it?'

'Yeah, and it worked,' Parsons gestured toward the red-head, who was talking quietly with another woman. 'And there she is, my Wormwood Star.' He paused and it was as if shutters had come down over his eyes. 'I've got her for maybe seven years, no more than that,' he said very quietly, as if talking to himself. He shrugged, gave a small, self-conscious grin and his eyes were twinkling again. 'And even then it won't be all the time. But it will have been worth it.'

'What is a Scarlet Woman, exactly?'

'A magickal partner, the woman who represents female sexuality and freedom, fertility and the imagination; and earthly incarnation of love, lust and desire; an archetype, the embodiment of the female principle. Babalon is the magician's complement, his other half, simultaneously a lover, a confederate and an object of veneration. Together we make one greater soul and have no limits.'

If you're in love with her, just say so, Crane thought. What was it about occultists that made them use such extravagant language to describe the most ordinary things? 'Tell me about the Moonchild,' he said.

'Crowley's been talking, it seems,' Parsons chuckled. 'I've already had one letter – a very *long* letter – from Crowley warning me not to do it. And it appears I've been fired from running the Agape Lodge. Technically, I quit – but it amounts to the same thing, I guess. Tell you the truth, I'm not sure how seriously I should take it. Are you sure he didn't send you just to light a fire under me?'

'No, but I share his concerns. Something very worrying happened to me last year and I've been trying to understand it. If you'd care to take a walk in the garden, I'll tell you all about it.'

Whining, complaining bitches, all of them. The nine women were shackled to a steel bar set in concrete in the stable, a neat line of them. They had mattresses and blankets, a couple of buckets to piss and shit in, a metal trough filled with water they could use to drink and keep themselves clean. He fed them once a day, burgers and French fries, courtesy of J. Wellington Wimpy. They even had cigarettes, their cosmetics, brushes for their hair.

Everything had been carefully planned. On the big day he would unchain them, one at a time, and take them at gunpoint into the ranch-house for a bath and a change of clothing. He wanted them clean and looking their best. Whatever else he might be, he was a stickler for personal hygiene and presentation. Presentation was important. When they were all fixed up – washed, perfumed and presentable – he would handcuff them to another steel bar, this one welded into place inside the truck, where more latrine buckets would be placed if they needed to use them. Then they would be driven into the desert, to the foothills of the San Bernadino Mountains, to his secret cave. The other guys would be with him in the cab, all of them dressed as labourers. Well, it wouldn't do to get stains on his fancy suit, would it?

Outside the stable he could hear the newcomer sobbing, the low voices of the other girls as they offered empty comfort. They knew what was coming. Well, they thought *they did. So would the dumb broads he had yet to collect. He hoped they all liked surprises. Not that he gave a shit one way or the other.*

Joshua trees didn't provide much in the way of shade and they weren't what you'd call pretty, but they had character. And that was important for survival in this place, where you could be boiled alive in your own skin in daylight and damned near freeze to death at night, where food and water were always in short supply. Parsons sat under this particular specimen of *Yucca brevifolia* smoking and drinking at irregular intervals from a bottle of sun-warm water. The hat gave him some protection against the sun's glare but he was sweating out fluid nearly as fast as he could add to his body's shallow reservoir.

Overhead, two electricity lines hummed and fizzed with energy where one passed over the other. A couple of hundred yards away, a patch of ephedra moved and a grey-brown head emerged, the nose raised high and twitching. A coyote, sniffing for dinner. There were probably rabbits or chipmunks nearby, though coyotes would eat just about anything that flew, walked or crawled – and anything at all that was no longer able to do those things. Like the Joshua tree, the coyote was a survivor; clever, adaptable and hardy.

A scorpion scuttled out from beneath a rock by a barrel cactus a yard to his left. Another survivor. He watched it without fear. The creature wouldn't harm him if he left it alone. It turned on the spot, ninety degrees anticlockwise, ran back to the space under the rock. Scorpio, the dark sign of the zodiac, emblem of treachery, betrayal and violence. The animal didn't bother him but the symbolism did.

The spot wasn't far from where he alone, then he and Ron – and latterly Candy – had performed a few of the Babalon rituals, which were now directed to the creation of a Moonchild through the union of magick and biology. That would have to end. Crane's words had seen to that. The Moonchild was supposed to be the embodiment of a higher being from one of the Aethyrs, a focus for peace, love and liberation from the moral and intellectual shackles of the Judaeo-Christian theology that had held humanity back for nearly two millennia. It was not meant to be a maleficent thing of the kind Crane said Crowley claimed to have called into existence; or whatever it was Crane had encountered that night in Bergen-Belsen shortly after the camp was liberated, and which he had taken steps to eradicate with fire and salt and prayer.

It was getting dark, clouds on the western skyline slashed with orange and purple among the grey. Night fell quickly in the desert and it would soon be cold. Parsons had a sweater and a blanket in his bag, more water, a couple of sandwiches. He settled himself more comfortably against the tree. He loved the Mojave, a place he had always felt safe and wanted – by what he couldn't exactly say, but the sand and rocks and vegetation called to him as a mother mountain lion calls to her cubs, as a lost wolf is called by the pack. Nothing out here would hurt him, at least nothing that walked on more than two legs or crawled on less than one.

The darkness grew and the night wore on. Parsons thought about the Moonchild he and Candy had been trying to bring into existence. He meditated upon the nature of those beings that dwell in the Aethyrs. He thought again of what Crane had told him. In the end he looked up at the stars, the constellations spinning so slowly around the Pole Star, the heavenly bodies he wanted so badly to reach with his rockets. Well, that was out of the question now. The Jet Propulsion Laboratory was no longer his, and he was unwanted in the field of rocket science. Uncle Sam no longer trusted him – Jack Parsons was a Satanist, a moral degenerate, a man with a socialist past. Ron had run off with Betty, his wife's younger sister – the woman who had claimed to be more of a wife to Parsons than his actual wife was – and taken most of Parsons' money. And Helen, his wife, had left him for Wilfred Smith, his predecessor as head of the local OTO. Love only went so far it seemed – and the more free it was, the higher the price. Freedom was a two-edged sword.

For most men, the betrayal, theft and deceit would have been bitter blows; and losing both his business and his trade would have finished some. But Parsons didn't care about any of that. He had a talent that could be turned into cash – he'd already had an offer of a job with North American Aviation and another to join one of the movie studios as a pyrotechnician – and, above all, he had Candy.

It wouldn't be for long. As soon as she arrived at the Parsonage he'd known a prophecy would be fulfilled. There was always that price to be paid and the meaning of that ancient text – the personal meaning, as it applied to him and him alone – was now clear to him. The final seven years of his life would be counted down in seven trumpets that were also seven thunders. And the countdown had already begun, on the 6th of August the previous year, when a little boy fell out of the sky and obliterated a Japanese city and getting on for a hundred thousand people. The first echo was heard three days later, another city and forty thousand more souls turned to ash by a plummeting fat man.

The seven trumpeting angels of *Revelation* were interpreted by Christians as sounding the death-knell for an age and heralding the birth of its successor. The sky would open and the world would be afflicted with a hail of fiery rocks and scorching heat. What the fires did not destroy would be poisoned. Life would be extinguished and the world made dark. Then, in the smoking ruins, pestilence and war. What else could it mean but the atom bomb? It was the harbinger of Armageddon. Biblical prophecy was coming true in our own time!

Well, it sure sounded good. But Christians saw the Bible variously as literal truth, code or allegory as it suited them. If they couldn't understand scripture one way, they'd try another and another until made sense to them. Their belief had to be stretched to fit the facts, and *vice versa*. Parsons had no such intellectual restrictions. He knew everything was metaphor, that nothing existed except in terms of something else. Early on in the Babalon working, he'd taken a dose of a new drug called *Lysergsäure-diethylamid-25* that the detestable Jack Marshall said came from Sandoz Pharmaceuticals in Switzerland. The drug, in tandem with ritual and focused meditation on the imagery of *Revelation*, had shown him the historical truth – that not only did John of Patmos write the text while under the influence of a similar drug, but it wasn't a prophecy at all. It was a kind of memory, drawn from that timeless astral realm where all things are recorded, of something that happened thousands of years ago when the world was showered with fragments of a passing comet. The two biggest pieces struck land, to devastating effect. From the ground the smaller pieces would have looked like burning hailstones dropping to the accompaniment of a sound like thunder and clouds of smoke, steam and noxious gas. Many thousands of people died and the survivors endured a winter that lasted for years. The event was commemorated in myths and legends handed down from one generation to the next, a tale that became a blueprint for heroism – how the bright warrior god with the thunderbolt or spear of lightning defeated the great dragon whose stinking, fiery breath polluted the waters and turned paradise into a cold, sterile wasteland. And once you started looking at the ancient myths with clear sight, the evidence was plain to see.

But the vision he'd experienced that night – on this very spot in the Mojave – took Parsons deeper into the old story than John of Patmos had been able to see. He knew the lines by heart.

I saw a star fall from heaven unto the earth: and to him was given the key of the bottomless pit. And he opened the bottomless pit; and there arose a smoke out of the pit, as the smoke of a great furnace;

and the sun and the air were darkened by reason of the smoke of the pit. And there came out of the smoke locusts upon the earth: and unto them was given power, as the scorpions of the earth have power... And they had a king over them, which is the angel of the bottomless pit, whose name in the Hebrew tongue is Abaddon, but in the Greek tongue hath his name Apollyon.

Abaddon and Apollyon both meant the same thing: *destroyer*. The personification of death and ruin. In the vision Parsons had seen how the falling star had inspired fear, sparked violence as the survivors fought over food and shelter, and caused widespread sickness as humanity was ravaged by cholera and overcome by toxins in the atmosphere. He believed that the subsequent mythologisation of the event was at least partly due to the cometary impact somehow intersecting with an Aethyric being, a spiritual entity that became trapped in the comet's substance and imprisoned somewhere deep in the ground. Lucifer had fallen.

Now, after his talk with Anthony Crane, Parsons understood something else – that the nature of an Aethyric entity when it was manifested in the physical world was influenced by whoever called upon it, how it was done and the reasons for the summoning. The Devil was in the detail, and in this case the detail comprised mass panic, aggression and pestilence. The destroyer. Jack Marshall called it Sammael.

He took the blanket from the bag and covered himself, falling asleep almost as soon as he closed his eyes. When he awoke, the eastern horizon a mirror image of the one he'd seen at sunset, he knew three more things. The first was that if he and Candy were one day to have a child it would be conceived the old-fashioned way. The only preparatory rituals would be the time-honoured ones of foreplay and tender words. A Moonchild was out of the question. Too much could go wrong – and besides, he didn't really trust his own motives.

The second thing he knew was that whatever Crane might think, he wasn't here solely to deliver a warning. No, the Englishman was in Pasadena for another, even more compelling reason, of which he was not consciously aware. And Parsons believed there was no choice but to help him.

Last of all, he was aware that to the west and slightly to the south, barely concealed by the planet's curvature, something dark and powerful and thunderous was stirring. It was the first day of July and the second trumpet was about to be sounded.

July 1946

Eleven frightened faces did their best to avoid his gaze. It was quite a collection. He'd got hold of a few really good-looking broads. The worst of them was merely pretty. Their figures ranged from voluptuous to slender, but build wasn't a consideration. They just had to look good – all the better for the horror they would inspire later.

At a whim, he'd rearranged them – blonde, brunette, red-head, then the same again. He had one blonde too many and was short of a red-head to make the pattern work but that was easily fixed. A bar, a diner, a bus station – there were many places in LA to acquire raw materials. He looked slowly along the row from left to right and back again, and by the time his gaze returned to the blonde with big tits on his left-hand side, his pants seemed far too small to contain what he had in store for them; well, they had more than that coming, but that could wait. In other circumstances he would have ordered the bitch to get on her knees and open her mouth, but he had to save his juices for the big night. Then, and only then, he would unload in style. They all would.

He thought back to the last time he'd spoken to Sam – the other Sam – on the telephone. It had been strange, hearing that he was going to be a father. When was it, four months from now? He'd been apprehensive at first, wondering if biological reproduction might change him in some way, bring out some hitherto unsuspected nurturing, caring instinct. He needn't have worried – that night he'd gone out on the town, picked up a drunken floozie in a bar and done what he did best. The cops would never find the body, and if someone did discover any of the several different places he'd buried it, no one would ever put two and two together. Not with so many pieces still missing. That had been the last time before he gathered his team and began to implement the plan he'd conceived while gleefully shooting Japs out of the sky over Midway and strafing them mercilessly on sea and land at Guadalcanal.

A couple of the bitches were crying, but at least they weren't making any noise about it. One of his criteria – which though exacting had enabled him to complete the decoration of his magic cave, only without the preliminary fun – was that their bodies shouldn't be marked in any way before the festivities commenced. That made it difficult to punish them for such infractions as shouting for help, trying to escape, giving him lip or otherwise being an annoyance. He got round that by pushing hatpins under the fingernails. Sure, they yelped like whipped mutts at first but they soon got the idea.

He smiled mock-benevolently at his silent slaves. It didn't fool them for a second, not with the Smith and Wesson held lazily in his right hand. Still, not long to wait now.

One of the girls noisily sniffed back tears. Just as he was reaching for the educational hatpin, an idea struck him. 'Any of you ladies know about Plato's Cave?' Inevitably, the only response was silence. They'd learned the hard way that sound would not be tolerated. 'It's a story told by Plato. He said that if you chained a bunch of people up in a cave so that they spent all their lives staring at a blank wall, they would believe that the shadows cast on that wall by people walking past a fire burning behind them were the only reality. Plato says a philosopher is a prisoner released from a cave just like that and is now awake to the knowledge that what he thought was real isn't real at all, that there is a greater reality, and others beyond even that.'

Their fearful faces were as blank as the wall in the philosopher's allegorical cave. People like that would never understand men like him, the awakened ones. The dumb bitches had probably never even heard of fucking Plato. He grinned to himself and told them about the cave of Polyphemus instead. They'd come to understand that one, eventually. Only they wouldn't have an Odysseus to save their pretty asses.

'They tested an H-bomb a few days ago, a place called Bikini Atoll in the Marshall Islands, wherever the hell they are.' Parsons drew hard on his cigarette, sipped a margarita. 'Another girl has gone missing, according to a newspaper guy I know. And I've told Candy to go away for a few days, visit her folks.'

'I'm sorry, is there a connection between those three events?' Crane was puzzled and not a little alarmed. Nearly all Parsons' guests and visitors openly took drugs – marijuana, cocaine, Benzedrine and something called peyote, which Crane gathered was some sort of cactus that made you see things – and Parsons indulged with enthusiasm, often mixing herbs and chemicals with alcohol, including what appeared to be home-made absinthe. Now he was wondering if Parsons was becoming unhinged by his intake – not that it was easy to identify incipient insanity in someone who existed in a world where magic reigned unchallenged.

'Maybe,' Parsons shrugged. 'Listen, Tony. I know a guy who reckons he spent some time in London just before we joined in the war. He was a pilot with the US Navy, claims to have been an advisor of some sort, had some dealings with the intelligence services. I don't suppose you ever ran into anyone like that?'

Crane froze with a margarita poised at his lips. He gazed into Parsons' eyes and wasn't surprised to see his own fear reflected there. 'Would this man happen to be called Jack Lloyd Marshall Worthington?' he asked, rather more calmly than he would have thought possible.

Parsons nodded. 'Close enough. He's calling himself Jack Marshall these days. He's been an occasional visitor here since he was discharged from the navy late last fall. He's very – disturbing. He knows a lot about the occult and magick but isn't a believer as such. I think he follows a pretty dark path.'

'How did you know I'd met him?'

'It was something he said once, when he was talking about his time in London. He said something like, "I know plenty of Limeys and I met some good ones, my kind of people. But believe me, some of them are just plain *yellow*." Then he laughed. It was the emphasis he placed on the last word that stuck in my mind. When you told me about the Yellow Room it seemed to add up.' *And it added up with what happened in the* Marshall *Islands the other day*, Parsons thought but did not say.

'Do you know where he is now?'

'I haven't seen him around since just before you showed up. The last thing he told me was that he's staying at a ranch near Chatsworth, on Santa Susana Pass Road. That's west of LA. I think maybe I know the place, used to belong to a movie star.'

Crane toyed with his cigarette carton. Marlboro, an American brand with the usual pathological US misspelling. They weren't too bad. 'The Jack Worthington I knew murdered several women,' he said. 'He worked with a few other men, ritual sex followed by sadism and slaughter – very messy slaughter. One of his friends was found guilty of murdering other women and hanged in 1942. I recognised his photograph in the newspapers.'

'Shit,' Parsons frowned. 'That's just what I didn't want to hear. I kind of expected it but even so I didn't want to believe it.'

'I tried to kill him,' Crane continued, 'but I was stopped by British intelligence people. Apparently killing Worthington would not have gone down well in the White House. I think Worthington has influential friends. He certainly has money.'

'Yeah, that's the impression I got – well-heeled and well-connected. You know about Sammael, right?'

Crane nodded. 'Yes. I know he doesn't believe in supernatural forces, but he seems to have faith in Sammael as an ideal or essence of some sort.'

'An Aethyric being,' Parsons asserted. 'A force or creature that comes from another plane of existence.' He wasn't going to tell Crane about his vision of that ancient comet strike and its aftermath. That should stay forever buried. 'I think he's going to try to manifest Sammael here in our world – I think he's going to try what I was going to do. A Moonchild or something similar, only to a different end. *The* different end.'

'The Russian woman I encountered in Belsen – who I *think* I encountered in that waking dream or vision or whatever it was – was possibly part of a group that did something similar. Worthington told me he had like-minded contacts in Germany and here in the US. Why not the Soviet Union? He said their aim was to stir up the war so they could operate freely amid the chaos. Well, at that point the war against Hitler was practically over. Nazism was effectively dead. That would leave only conflict between the two remaining major ideologies – Communism and Capitalism, East against West. Imagine someone as powerful and twisted as that woman in each hemisphere.'

'You said the woman made you feel afraid and unwell, that she was somehow tied in with the death, cruelty and disease in Belsen. That fits in with what I think such a being could do – the cause and a symptom at the same time. Time works differently in the Aethyrs and its inhabitants might have the ability to affect us retroactively when they manifest among us.'

'They called her *nosferatu*. It means "the unbearable one". People couldn't abide her presence. I don't know if she was like the vampire in Murnau's film, but I didn't take the chance. She's why I ordered the concentration camp to be burned. She was hiding in there somewhere so I burned everything,' He laughed, a short, embarrassed bark. 'I also had the ashes sown with rock salt and blessed by a Catholic priest and a rabbi. I'm not a religious man, Jack; and I'm not at all superstitious. But at the time I was operating on a level that was…' He spread his hands, struggling for the right word.

Parsons smiled. 'Magical? Irrational? Intuitive? That kind of thinking is the only way to comprehend situations that fall outside everyday experience. You did the right thing, Tony. Symbolism can be as real as action. Obviously, these beings can change the human organism and alter the way we think and act. They're all about infiltration and corruption – and our behaviour determines how they do it and what they become when they manifest. They're an essence, like thought itself, and we can fight them on that level. That doesn't rule out good old firepower, though. When they inhabit a physical form incineration would be the best option, perhaps the only way to eliminate them – good, hot flame.'

Or something like Tesla's teleforce projector, Crane thought wistfully. As he had so many times, he wondered what Dorothy Harlow had done with the weapon.

Dorothy, he had begun to suspect, was in some respects not dissimilar to the Belsen *nosferatu*. She was much faster and quite a bit stronger than any man he knew of, and a whole menagerie would be required to provide metaphors for the acuity of her senses. She could, to a degree, foresee the future. And as for that astonishing ability to move unseen and instantly from one shadow to another – well, if that wasn't supernatural, what on earth was? And yet Dorothy was good-natured, kind and compassionate, reluctant to harm any living creature. He didn't know how she became what she was. Indeed, he knew nothing at all of her past. If she had been born that way, it was a miracle, plain and simple. But if her extraordinary gifts were the product of a process like the creation of a Moonchild, as described by Crowley and Parsons, then she had been fortunate. It could so easily have gone wrong. One misplaced word, a lapse in concentration, a single selfish thought…

How many Dorothy Harlows walked the earth? And how many *nosferatu*?

Perhaps it was time to walk away. Parsons wandered through the wreckage of the mansion on Orange Grove Avenue, remembering the rituals, the orgies, the talking and drug-taking, the parties and booze that now all seemed to blur together, years of excess and extremes concentrated into a single timeless moment of ideas, sensation and emotion. His mind, body and spirit condensed into a kaleidoscopic droplet of time.

In three months he'd be thirty-two years old. Most men were grown up at that age. Why not Jack Parsons? He still believed in Thelema but he now saw that the Babalon working had never been about what he once saw as its true aim, dissolution of space and time, but about fulfilment of his own buried yearning. It was his own blood and seed that brought Candy to him – the abstraction of love given flesh – and that was when it should have ended. Ron had used him badly, first influencing him to misdirect the Babalon project, then seducing Betty, and finally making off with most of his money. Along the way Ron had subtly sown dissent and set Jack's friends against one another. He was a persuasive bastard, you had to give him that. He really would make a great salesman. And that was the crux of the matter. Where Parsons' brand of individualism was rooted in socialism, Ron's was pure capitalism. Ultimately, what Ron wanted was wealth, power and adulation. For him Thelema was liberation for Ron and serfdom for everyone else. He wouldn't keep the name, of course. He'd give his perverted version of Thelema some fancy pseudo-scientific name and charge big bucks for the privilege of consuming his bullshit. Well, fuck him.

Jack gazed around him, suddenly hating the Parsonage and everything that had taken place within its boundaries. He was tired and dispirited. All he wanted now was peace and quiet and an ordinary life with Candy, not that living with her could ever be mundane. Helen, Betty, all the others, they were only markers along the road that led to Candy. He resolved then and there that their future would be great, while it lasted. He would make his rockets and help pave the way for what he hoped would be interplanetary flight, not the perversion of the science that Werner von Braun and his cohorts had promulgated. He would continue to study and practise magick, but to a new purpose. Candy would paint and create wonderful art. And kids, kids might be nice – one day, but not yet, not while there was still so much groundwork to do. For one thing, to become the benign magus he aspired to be, Parsons would have to undertake a prolonged, dangerous ritual that would make the Babalon working seem like a cakewalk. For that, he needed something to return to, a home in both the physical and metaphysical senses. He would ask Candy to marry him as soon as his divorce came through. First they would move out of the coach house and out of Orange

Grove Avenue, out of this fucking derelict mausoleum. It was no longer his home.

Number thirteen, the new brunette, was a tough one, screaming and cussing and kicking like an angry mule no matter how many times he slid that pin under her nails. In the end he'd knocked her out with chloroform, tied her hands together and gagged the slut to keep her quiet. OK, so she might throw up and choke to death, but so what? He could always get another one. He stared down at her unconscious form. Some of the names she called him had been downright uncivil. When the time came he would live up to them. That bitch was going to suffer worse than any of the others, and they would suffer badly.

His comrades-in-arms were assembling in LA, all but Dave and Mack, who had moved into the ranch so they could help him move the women out. The rest had their instructions, the time and location. At eleven that night he would meet them at the cave, trusting them not to enter until he arrived in the truck with Mack and Dave and the cargo. They knew him well enough not to disobey. He didn't particularly enjoy killing me but he didn't exactly lose sleep when he did, and he'd done it quite a few times.

The one with the gag was beginning to come round from the chloroform. Elizabeth, that was her name. The surname was irrelevant and he had made no effort to find out. All he needed was the first name, so they would know which one was to follow which orders. Otherwise he wouldn't have bothered with that, either. Names were identity, a suggestion that something was living within the meat, thoughts and feelings moving and making the body more than a puppet. But try as he might, he could not conceive of any such thing. The walking, talking dolls were there for his pleasure and nothing more. Now she looked up at him with those dazed blue eyes, still not quite able to bring herself to believe that her life was probably approaching its end. 'Elizabeth... Oh, Elizabeth...' He spoke her name in a tone that made it clear he was mocking its existence, that for him it signified less than nothing.

There was only one Name that truly mattered, and it wasn't hers.

The Chevrolet Deluxe, rented because Parsons thought his Packard might be recognised, bounced over the uneven ground and came to a halt behind a stand of mixed scrub oak and sycamore trees. Crane disembarked and followed the tyre marks back to the road. Confident that the vehicle was adequately concealed from view, he strode back to the car and signalled to Parsons.

'This is the place,' said Parsons, stubbing out his cigarette on a low branch. 'At least, that's what my reporter friend says. We don't know for sure that it's Marshall staying there, though. I guess I should call him Worthington now, if that's his real name.'

'Did you remember the gun?'

By way of reply Parsons removed the semi-automatic from the waistband of his trousers and held it up. 'Colt Woodsman, Sport Model. Doesn't look like much but it packs a hell of a punch. Hemingway shoots horses with one of these. I like hunting jackrabbits, they making for good eating. But shooting horses after using the poor suckers as bait for bear? I always said Hemingway was an asshole.'

'Good,' said Crane, who'd never heard of Ernest Hemingway and was mystified by Parsons' scorn. 'Keep it cocked, or whatever you do with that sort of gun. Worthington's more dangerous than you can imagine.'

Parsons grinned uneasily. If there was one thing he had in abundance, it was imagination. He believed he had a pretty good idea of Worthington's capabilities.

They approached the ranch, keeping to the trees and scrub wherever possible. At last, after what seemed like hours of dodging furtively from one patch of overgrown vegetation to the next, they came to the ranch house and its surrounding buildings. About a hundred yards from the house they crouched behind a partially-collapsed wooden fence and peered between the loose boards. To Crane's dismay, two men he didn't recognise were standing on the porch with Thompson submachine guns at the ready.

Parsons tapped him on the shoulder. 'This is the place, alright,' he whispered. 'Those guys are Dave and Mack, Jack Worthington's pals. A pair of real creeps. There must be something going on. You don't need Tommy guns if you've got nothing to hide.'

'Whatever it is, they've got us outgunned. Perhaps we should call the police.'

'And tell them what? That a guy we don't like much is possibly conducting screwy magic rituals on his own land and has hired a couple of bums to guard the place? This is LA, Tony. No one cares a shit about anything but money and the movies. If Worthington was cutting up Shirley Temple, Betty Grable and Mae West in the middle of Mulholland Drive the cops might pay attention, but probably only to get autographs.'

'We need help, Jack. Surely you know one or two people who'd be good in a scrap?'

'This isn't the movies, pal. I can't whistle up Philip Marlowe and Sam Spade and ask them to help us out of a jam. I used to know a guy called Jake who'd be useful in a tight spot but he's lying low because of some trouble he had in Chinatown a few years back. Let's see – Ron's gone, and good fucking riddance; Ed's out of town on business; Bob's sick again… The Seventh Cavalry's in Japan and John Wayne's on set. Nope, that's it. Ixnay on the reinforcements, *amigo*. It's just you and me and Mr Colt here against two nuts with machine guns and whatever Worthington has up his sleeve.'

Parsons shoved the gun back into his waistband, replaced it with a handkerchief and wiped sweat from his brow. 'Why are we here, Tony? Did you really come here to kill Worthington? Because you don't strike me as a cold-blooded killer.'

'I made a promise to myself,' Crane replied quietly. 'In London, when I saw what he did to that woman, the people he'd gathered around him… Worthington's a monster and he has monstrous ideas. He must die, for humanity's sake.'

'Well, if you put it like that…' Parsons frowned. 'Actually, I agree. The guy has to go. But we can't get to him with Stan and Ollie and the Thompson Brothers watching over him. Now I don't know if you noticed but Dave and Mack are dressed as construction workers. They told everyone at the Parsonage they were in advertising, down from Little Rock to start a new business in LA. That's bullshit. Worthington's accent is pure Philly; and if Mack isn't an Arkie I'll eat my hat with salami and mayo on the side. Dave's a local boy and he's just a kid, no way he's in any business except playing hookey from school. Did you see the truck parked up by the stable? It's a Caltrans truck. They manage the state highways. Sherlock Parsons deduces that those guys are in disguise and the truck is camouflage. I further deduce that as they're in disguise now, they have something planned for tonight, the kind of work best carried out incognito and under cover of darkness – and if they need wheels, it isn't happening here.'

'Well, we can't just sit here and wait for them to make a move. We must do *something*!'

Parsons smiled enigmatically. 'Actually, we do sit and wait, but not here and not yet. And don't worry, Tony – I have a little surprise lined up for them. Let's go back to Orange Grove Avenue and get it.'

Relocating the women from the stable to the truck by way of the bath and a dressing table took an age and a half. Mack and Dave prowled the area, Tommy guns at ready to take care of any uninvited guests. When the women were dressed, scented and stowed in the back of the truck with their mouths taped shut, the three men clambered into the cab and they drove off into the night.

They drove east to pick up Route 101 at San Fernando, going north before heading east again on Route 6 and eventually, several hours later, leaving the road altogether and slowing as they negotiated the darkened desert and approached the foothills.

Ten men waited at the cave entrance. Worthington hopped down from the cab to greet them with an ironic salute and a sardonic grin. 'Good evening, gentlemen,' he drawled. 'Greetings in the Name of Our Lord Sammael. I'd be grateful if you fellows could help Frater Cimex and Frater Inscitus unload our offerings. I have to prepare the amenities and ensure the integrity of the circle.'

Some of them, educated men who understood Latin, laughed heartily. Worthington had given Mack and Dave their grandiose-sounding magical names knowing a few of the others, men of learning and influence, would find them amusing. It was true that Mack was an asshole and Dave was an ignorant greenhorn – but he had to admit they were efficient soldiers, and damned good at what they did best. Hell, they were all damned good. It was why they had been chosen, perfect disciples for Jack Worthington the prophet of Sammael, the angel of death. And tonight, he was the man who would bring Sammael bodily into this world and usher in a new age of conflict and mayhem.

Up ahead, the truck's rear lights were just about visible. The Chevrolet was about three hundred yards behind and matching Worthington's vehicle for pace, slowing or speeding as and when the distant lights appeared to get bigger or smaller. When the twin red glows suddenly winked out, Parsons drove past the place he estimated Worthington's vehicle had left the road, killed his own lights, performed a U-turn at what Crane thought terrifying speed, and drove back to follow their prey into the dark desert.

'How do you know they're going this way?'

Parsons shrugged. 'If it was me, I'd turn off at the nearest place on the road to where I'm going. And I'd make sure I knew the route, head out at right angles to the highway to conserve gas. The land's pretty flat until you get to the foothills. We'll follow as far as we can in the Chevy then strike out on foot. There's a couple of flashlights in the trunk, still shaded for the blackout.'

'You had a blackout here?'

'No, but we were ready if we needed one. After Pearl Harbour we were expecting the Japs to bomb San Francisco, LA and San Diego. That didn't happen but we've had balloons carrying incendiary bombs falling here and there.' Parsons sniffed disdainfully. 'They were crap, a boy scout could have done better. We also had an invasion scare in '42 when they shelled the Ellwood Oil Field near Santa Barbara; and they attacked Oregon a couple of times. Piss-poor stuff, really, all aimed at starting fires. I was making bigger explosions in the garage at home when I was a kid. Shit, I was in more danger from myself than I ever was from the Japanese.'

Crane stared out at the desert as they bumped along, wondering if the Chevrolet's suspension was up to the terrain – and if he was up to the task that lay ahead. Parsons was right in his assessment – Crane was no dispassionate, calculating killer. Even the mild and quiet Albert Pierrepoint, who Crane had met briefly in Hamelin the night before Irma Grese's execution, had more of the murderer about him, a trait he recognised from his meeting with Worthington's companions in London in 1941. They too had been superficially modest, unassuming men but they'd had the same look he'd seen in Pierrepoint's eyes. Yet for Pierrepoint it had been a job, and he seemed to genuinely care that hanging was carried out in an efficient, dignified and compassionate way. The men Crane was dealing with now killed as a vocation, and they specialised in rape, torture and humiliation. Their trade was the exercise of power by giving pain. Crane had no such well of cold sadism to draw from. He wasn't even sure that, without the anger and grief he'd felt at their previous meetings, he had sufficient courage to put down the rabid dog that was Jack Worthington.

The gloomy thoughts were interrupted when Parsons brought the Chevrolet to a sudden halt. 'Well, I'll be f...' Parsons sat, open-mouthed, and pointed through the windshield.

'What is it? Why have we stopped?' Crane couldn't see anything but the night and the desert.

'Right there, sitting straight ahead. Can't you see them?'

Crane strained to see what Parsons was seeing. 'All I can see is sand, plants and those spiky trees.'

'I can't believe you can't see them, Tony. They look so real... Hell, they *are* real, as solid as you and me.'

'Jack, just tell me. What can you see?' Crane was exasperated, and not a little alarmed. He was beginning to suspect that Parsons had taken a drug of some sort.

'OK, well – if you're sure you can't see them... It's a coyote and a bobcat, just sitting together, right in front of us, looking right at us. I think this is it, Tony. I think this is where we get out and walk.'

'What makes you so sure of that, Jack?'

'In Indian legend these are powerful spirits, representing life and death. Seeing them tonight that can mean only one thing. It's a showdown, *amigo*. Gunfight at the OK Corral. Either Worthington dies – or you do. It won't be me because it isn't my time. The universe has other plans for Jack Parsons. But it's going to be do or die for Tony Crane. Are you sure you want to go through with this?'

No, thought Crane, swallowing hard. *I don't want to do this. I want to go home and hug my children and cuddle up in bed with*

Irene and dream about Dorothy. He opened the car door and clambered out. 'Come on,' he said testily. 'Let's do this.'

Parsons joined him, carefully scanned the desert for sight of the phantom animals, shrugged and opened the trunk. When he rejoined Crane at the front of the car, he was wearing a large, backpack and had a four-foot metal cylinder hoisted on one shoulder and steadied by a deceptively delicate-looking hand. Crane suddenly appreciated how big and muscular his companion was, easily six inches taller and built like a circus strongman. In his free hand he carried another large backpack, which he gave to Crane, and a smaller one.

'What's in the packs? And that pipe?'

'Pesticide,' said Parsons, waggling his eyebrows like Groucho Marx and grinning like a good-natured Satan.

They started walking. Parsons seemed to know exactly where he was going – that or something was showing him the way.

The ceremony was proceeding exactly as he'd envisaged – better, in fact. The cave echoed with the women's screams of pain and fear. Over there, the Senatorial hopeful from Colorado and the New Jersey industrialist were going at one of the blondes, one at each end. The stupid, weeping bitch thought that if she didn't fight, if she just gave in and did as she was told, they might let her live. Two of the offerings were already dead and one wasn't far away from the end, not if what Mack was doing to her was any indication. Dave and the cop from New York were having fun with one of the brunettes; and the Hollywood guy, George – Jesus H. Christ, was he really eating *that? Looking around, it was difficult to see where he'd got it – all the bitches were torn and bleeding, some badly; others were screaming, dying. Everyone was dosed up on that new drug his pal had brought back from Switzerland, though he'd made sure the women had double what the men had received. It added dimensions previously only hinted at by madmen and mystics, quantum physicists and Surrealist painters. Maybe he'd just imagined the Hollywood doctor had chopped out a woman's heart and was chewing on it. But he didn't think so.*

Only one of the bitches had yet to be touched, the one called Elizabeth. That slut was to be his and his alone, the final offering, when both he and the ritual would climax. He laughed loudly to himself, hearing the sound repeated all around him, replayed and recycling as a glorious, endless hymn to death. Here he was, playing with the very best rapists and murderers America could provide, invoking a god he didn't believe in yet utterly certain he could make that god real.

Jack Worthington raised himself from the broken body beneath him, dropped the severed body part he was holding – he couldn't even remember which part of that slut he'd sliced off or cut away – and stood, erect in every sense of the word. He stared at the bitch Elizabeth, naked now but still tied and gagged in the centre of the circle, right next to the head on the stake, and grinned savagely. Shit, he was so fucking hard. He'd split that bitch in two as he attained apotheosis. Around him the cave quietened as the women died and the men finally expended themselves and assumed their positions. He moved into the circle and began to chant in the Enochian language, a summons for Sammael. The terrified Elizabeth wept and wriggled but was unable to break free.

It was time to introduce her to the Angel of Death.

In the end Worthington was easy to find. The noise of suffering and mayhem issuing from the cave mouth was indescribable. Crane started to run toward the entrance but Parsons grabbed him by the arm and held him back.

'Go carefully, Tony,' he said. 'And take this.' He thrust the Colt into Crane's hand. 'My friend, something truly terrible is taking place in there and I think we're too late to stop most of it. Maybe we should have called the cops when you said, I don't know. What I do know is that this is your moment. So go in there and do what you have to do. I'll be out here, preparing my little surprise. It won't take me long. Take these packs in with you and call me when you need me. I think you'll know when that'll be.'

Crane nodded dumbly and walked to the cave. At the entrance he turned. Parsons was doing something to the metal tube, arranging it on a metal frame and fussing over parts Crane couldn't quite make out. He looked like an overgrown child playing with a fascinating new toy. Despite the screams and sobs coming from the cave, the terror of their circumstances, Crane smiled. Jack Parsons really was a most remarkable fellow, and one of the most likeable men Crane had ever met – even if he was in many ways one of the most unsettling.

As he resumed his journey into the darkness – and although he could see flame flickering ahead of him he was sure that what he would see at the end of the rocky passage would be nothing but the deepest, most dense kind of darkness – the noises died down, only to be replaced by a sonorous, rhythmic, unintelligible chanting. Crane walked more quickly. He knew he didn't have long.

The scene that met his eyes when he emerged into the main cave was one of sheer horror. Naked bodies and parts of bodies were strewn across the bloodied ground, everywhere but within the circle of severed heads on stakes. The scarlet-spattered cave walls were carved with what appeared to be a picture of Satan, surrounded by suppliant women, with strange symbols scattered throughout the depictions. Twelve men knelt around the circle, one by each of the perimeter stakes. They seemed exhausted, entranced, their gazes fixed on the naked man and woman at their centre. Jack Worthington sliced through the young woman's bonds with a scalpel, threw her roughly to the ground and stood over her, continuing to chant in that strange language. Then he quickly knelt and brutally thrust himself into her.

Crane dropped the packs and raised the Colt. Without pausing to think he strode up to the edge of the circle and shot the nearest man in the head. Then he entered the circle, caught Worthington by the hair and unceremoniously pulled him off the sobbing girl. Worthington fell to his knees, moaning horribly as he reached orgasm. Appalled, Crane put the gun to the back of the man's head. This would end now.

To his surprise, he was unable to pull the trigger. For a moment he was unable to work out what was happening to him. Then he realised he felt physically sick and his bowels were threatening to erupt; and he was afraid, so very afraid – afraid of everything – that he was completely immobilised. Worthington laughed and stood, then turned to face Crane. His face was a ghastly parody of itself, luminous and white and elongated, like the creature Crane had met in Belsen. *Nosferatu* – the unbearable one, the bringer of sickness and fear and death, the pestilence on two legs. Involuntarily, Crane took one step back, then another.

'Well, well,' Worthington grinned, and his face was like a shark from a nightmare. 'Anthony Crane, as I live and breathe. I guess you've come to finish what you wanted to do to me in London, huh? I think you'll find it a little more difficult now, Crane. I'm not the man I was, as you can see.'

Crane couldn't speak. He wanted desperately to call Parsons but the words dried to dust in his throat.

Worthington's grin became even wider, a gaping maw bristling with teeth like a forest of straight razors. 'Fuck, but this feels real good. I can see so much, Crane. I *know* so much more than I would have thought possible. You really don't have a fucking clue how things really are, do you? You have no idea what the universe is or how it works, what there is beyond what you can see. But I do. I've been waiting for this moment, you sanctimonious, self-righteous prick. You should get down on your knees and worship me. What the fuck do you think you are to judge *me*?' He extended his arms, much longer and thinner than they should have been, and seemed to grow several inches in height. Crane took another backward step, his heart racing with terror.

Abruptly, Worthington cocked his head. Someone was speaking in a loud voice from the cave mouth. Parsons seemed to be reciting very bad poetry. Somehow, that struck Crane as hilariously funny. Worthington's bemusement and the crazy incongruity snapped him out of the blue funk. He chuckled and pulled the trigger, emptying the magazine into the creature standing before him. As Worthington fell to the ground, Crane stepped past him and pulled the weeping girl to her feet. 'There's a friend outside,' he told her. 'Get out of here now. He'll look after you.'

The woman didn't need telling twice. As she scampered unsteadily away, Crane noticed that several of Worthington's gang had also fled. Mack and Dave were nowhere to be seen. Those who remained still seemed paralysed, their eyes glued to Worthington's eerily phosphorescent body. Crane backed away. It was time to get out. But as soon as he turned to go, Worthington's voice sounded behind him. 'No you don't, asshole.'

Worthington was sitting up, clutching the bullet-riddled ruin of his chest, breathing heavily and grimacing. 'You can't kill this body, Crane – not for good. To do that you'll need to destroy it completely, with fire, just like you did in Belsen. Oh yes, I know all about that. We're all connected, you see. Me and the Russian woman and Paul – on the inside we're all the same thing. Sammael. That's what I was called to be. Fire is the only way, Crane. And by the time you get that fixed I'll be as good as new. Why, I'm healing even now. In a few minutes I'll be whole enough to tear you into very small pieces without even breaking sweat. After that, I'll do things that would give Adolf Hitler bad dreams.'

Acting on some impulse borne of folklore and Bram Stoker's famous novel, Crane uprooted the stake at the centre of the circle, shook off the rotting head that crowned it, and shoved it with all his strength through Worthington's heart and into the ground, pinning him there. To his dismay, Worthington merely laughed.

'I can keep this up all night, Crane. Even if you could kill me, which I doubt, it would be too late. Sam has many sons out there, sons who will be only too willing to continue their father's work. As soon as I saw this cave and those petroglyphs, I knew California was to be where my empire began. What I've done here tonight will reverberate, spreading outward like ripples on a pond. You can't stop it, nor can Tom, or Delilah, or even those others, the old ones that have always guarded this world. That's because this is the very oldest way, the one that dragged us out of the slime and into the oceans, out of the sea and onto land, into the trees and down again. The survival of the strongest and most savage, the most pure. You call it evil; I call it evolution.'

At a loss, Crane briefly considered trying to throttle Worthington with his bare hands. He became aware of a quiet, wordless murmur all around him. The remnants of Worthington's gang were *praying* to their leader, gazing at him with appalled, adoring eyes. Worthington grasped the stake and casually yanked it from his chest, casting it aside with ease. He gasped but continued to grin, visibly growing stronger by the second. Crane began to feel nauseous again, sure that this time he really would foul his underwear. This was a lost cause. He'd been insane to come here. But what else could he have done?

A strong but gentle hand took him by the arm. Parsons had come to help at last, though surely there was never anything he could have done. 'Tony, let's get out of here, pronto. This shit-hole is about to get lit up.' He dragged Crane out of the cave, pushed him to one side, where the surviving girl huddled, wrapped in a blanket, bent down to the where the metal tube rested on its supporting frame, and struck a match. Then he too dived to one side.

Flame and yellow smoke erupted from one end of the tube, and suddenly it hissed and roared and shot into the cave. A rocket – Parsons had brought a rocket along. Crane could have kicked himself. But before he had the chance to metaphorically apply a boot to his posterior, light blossomed within the cave, followed by a wave of pressure and heat, and a billowing ball of fire.

'What was that, Jack?' It was an hour later. Dawn was breaking in the east. They stood at the cave mouth, waiting to see what havoc Parsons' creations had wrought. They were relaxed and relieved. It was impossible to feel guilt or sympathy for the men they had killed.

Parsons exhaled smoke and sighed contentedly. 'One pack of home-made thermite; one pack of solid rocket fuel, my own recipe. Plus whatever propellant was left in the rocket and a pack of powdered magnesium tied to the nose. It's what I do for a living, my friend. Explosions and rockets. It's a hobby as well as a livelihood. And though I say so myself, there aren't many people as good at it as me. While we were in there I noticed one of those assholes had brought a can of gasoline to keep their torches and their fire burning. Every little helps. We were lucky Worthington had chosen a cave – explosives and incendiaries are much more effective in an enclosed space. I figure it burned pretty good in there. Should be cool enough to go in by now. Shall we take a look?'

The cave was filled with soot and shapeless fragments of metal, scattered pieces of carbonised bone that crumbled to the touch of Crane's booted toe. The rock walls had been partially melted smooth, the petroglyphs obliterated, save for the distinctive ones on either side of the entry passage. Crane found that strangely comforting. Those carvings were of a different order to the others. They made him feel somehow safe, hopeful that there really were benign entities that stood against creatures like Jack Worthington and whatever forces he had invoked to make himself that way.

Back in the early morning light, the air was fresh and clean beneath the reek of chemicals and fire. The girl, the only innocent survivor of Worthington's insane ritual, was sleeping, still bundled in Parsons' blanket. It wasn't a peaceful slumber but Parsons thought she would probably recall the night only as a bad nightmare. The drug Worthington had given her was, it seemed, astonishingly powerful and caused vivid hallucinations. 'She'll be fine when we get back to LA, I think. She can stay with me and Candy for a few days. We'll look after her and when she's better she can go home, if she has one. How about you? You going to hang around for a while? I'd love to show you our Gnostic Mass – it's not what you might think. It's the exact opposite of what Worthington was doing here. It's about love and true will – not hate and subservience to destructive powers.'

'No, I'm going to go home. There are people waiting for me. The wife, the children, the Yellow Room.' But not Dorothy. In his heart Crane knew he would never see her again. That would probably be for the best. Why was it that whatever was for the best was always so bloody painful?

Parsons nodded. 'It's always good to go home. You can tell Crowley to quit worrying about me. There will be no Moonchild. Actually, Perdurabo might approve of what we've done here. It might even get me back in his good books. Tell him I recited his *Hymn to Pan* while we slugged it out with the bad guys. He'll be tickled pink.'

No wonder the poetry had been so bloody awful. 'I've had many dealings with Crowley over the years,' Crane mused. 'He never struck me as an evil man. He's undoubtedly arrogant, conceited and self-centred; and he certainly plays to the gallery. He can be spiteful, even cruel, yet in so many ways he's as far removed from Worthington as you can get. I think that fundamentally all he wants to do is wake us up, to release us from self-imposed moral and intellectual slavery.'

'I dream of a movement dedicated to peace and love and self-discovery. I think it could take root here in California.' Parsons laughed. 'We have the weather for it and we have Hollywood, our very own land of make-believe. But it won't be this generation. People like Crowley, me, the science fiction guys – we'll just be the inspiration. It'll be the kids that build it, the ones born in the shadow of nuclear war. We only have to teach them the right way to live, to ignore the fear, to make love and not war. I want to set everyone free to love how and who they will, without phoney divine commands or financial exploitation. And that means being free from people like those bastards we just roasted.'

Crane lit a cigarette. 'It won't be easy for the youngsters. There are too many men out there who enjoy killing and hurting others, or causing it to happen. For every dove there will be a hawk. For every Jack Parsons there will be a Jack Worthington. He talked a lot of nonsense in that cave but was right in one respect – what he represented lives on. I wonder if it's hereditary, if perhaps there are whole lineages of viciousness and cold-heartedness.'

Parsons laughed again. 'Then we work at it. We keep on trying to do things the right way, Tony. Peace and love are the goal, and I believe they will eventually triumph over hate and violence. It'll be a rough ride, though – a real helter-skelter.'

'What about you, Jack? What's next for you?'

The tall man gestured expansively toward the horizon. 'The sky's the limit, Tony. I have another dream: rockets, travel to the planets, maybe even the stars. I have a few years left to keep dreaming. One thing's for sure, though. I'm going to go out with a bang.'

Author's Note

The Yellow Room stories are arranged chronologically around actual events during and just after the Second World War. I've used quite a few real historical figures as characters in these stories – people from the wartime intelligence services, politicians and military men from both sides of the conflict, scientists and occultists, artists and writers. Some are portrayed in a less flattering light than the history books usually allow – some more sympathetically.

The list includes a number of murderers of the time, the type nowadays popularly known as serial killers. 'The Enemy Within' has cameos from the UK's very own Gordon Cummins (the Blackout Ripper), George Haigh (the Acid Bath Murderer) and John Christie of 10 Rillington place notoriety. Their fictional magical names reflect their respective killing techniques. 'The Rocket Man' features the American serial murderers Mack Ray Edwards and David Joseph Carpenter (the Trailside Killer) – and references George Hill Hodel, a Hollywood doctor who was possibly the Black Dahlia killer of 1947, probably murdered his secretary, and has been suggested as the Zodiac killer.

John Marshall Lloyd 'Jack' Worthington was inspired by the two men named by Eleanor Louise Cowell as the father of her son, Theodore Robert Cowell, better known as the prolific serial killer, rapist and necrophile Ted Bundy. Eleanor Cowell was known throughout her life as Louise. Bundy's birth certificate names a former Air Force man named Lloyd Marshall as the father; but later Louise claimed to have been impregnated by a sailor called Jack Worthington. However, there is a strong possibility that Bundy's biological father was actually his grandfather, Samuel Cowell. Sam Cowell was a violent, sadistic, racist bully who was known to hold conversations with invisible entities. The young Ted Bundy was brought up to believe that his grandparents were really his parents and Louise his older sister, which may be partly true.

The life of John Whiteside 'Jack' Parsons as described in 'The Rocket Man' is more or less historically accurate, though the character's thoughts on the Biblical *Revelation* and other occult or metaphysical matters are fiction. 'Candy' was the nickname of Parson's real-life 'Scarlet Woman', Marjorie Cameron, who became a celebrated artist and an important counter-culture figure in the 1950s and '60s. Parsons died on 17th June 1952 following an explosion at his home laboratory while he was working on a rush order for special effects explosives for a film studio. Although there have been suggestions of murder or suicide, it should be noted that Parsons casually disregarded procedures for safely handling and storing explosive substances, and had a tendency to smoke while working.

The ranch where Worthington keeps his captives in 'The Rocket Man' is the same one that later became infamous as the Spahn Ranch, where Charles Manson and his Family stayed at the time they slaughtered the actress Sharon Tate and several other people in 1969.

Some readers may feel that I've dealt too sympathetically with Irma Grese, who was hanged as described for crimes committed at Auschwitz and Bergen-Belsen, the youngest woman to be executed for war crimes in the aftermath of the Second World War. However, it seems to me that justice was not served well at the first Belsen Trial. It was hastily convened and conducted according to rules that were patently confusing for the judges, prosecution and defence, as well as those on trial. The disposition of evidence and testimony were just as confusing for all concerned. Furthermore, the interpreters were evidently not up to the job of translating English legal arguments and lawyers' questions into German, or the defendants' responses adequately into English.

In 'The Beautiful Beast' I've tried to imagine how Irma Grese thought and felt during the process. The story includes several quotes from her testimony, edited to reduce repetition, and gives some background on the recruitment of camp staff and some other contextual information. Was she guilty as charged? Well, I've read the complete trial transcript and quite a bit of material written after the event and, to be honest, I still don't know.

Nor do I know if Nikola Tesla's teleforce projector actually worked. But I sincerely hope it didn't, just in case some lunatic out their has one in their possession...

About the Author

Alby Stone was born and grew up in Southend-on-Sea in Essex but has lived and worked in London for many years.

More fiction by Alby Stone

The Forgotten Stars
Secret Songs
The Hand of Fire
(The *Havensea* trilogy)

The Sorrows of Angels
The Shadow Woman
Disappearer
Intruder
(The *Wonderland Investigations* series)

Cherry Blood
Dummy
A Single Drop of Night
The Girl in the Tie-Dye Dress

Sparks and Ashes: Short Fiction

Further information and short fiction by Alby Stone and others:
http://www.vaingloriouslunacy.com
http://clerkenwellwritersasylum.wordpress.com

Printed in Great Britain
by Amazon